M000031585

You Call Me Angelo

The Godfather's Been Shot

George B. Longstreth, MD

© copyright George B. Longstreth, MD - 2018
All rights reserved. This book or any portion thereof may
not be reproduced or used in any manner without the
written permission of the author.

This book is a work of fiction. Any similarities to persons,
places, events, or other entities are purely coincidental.

Acknowledgements

This book would not have been possible without the help of many people.

Of special note are: Orthopedic surgeon David Johnson, MD; Brooke Scarpa Salsbury who painfully formatted my manuscript; Molly Longstreth Jacobs who was my proof-reader; Judy Zalesne, my faithful editor as well as my late-in-life English teacher; Al, once a Marine- always a Marine, Townsend; my friend and CIA confidant Dana Morton, may he rest in peace; and most importantly, my long-suffering and faithful wife Betsy who read and re-read my manuscript over and over, offering corrections, ideas, and inspiration.

On the abstract front, I need to acknowledge "the rumor mill" where so much fiction starts and inspires, but where there is no known author other than the DNA of one's imagination. In this case, I was inspired through the rumor mill which informed me that in the late 1960s there was an attempted assassination of Joe Colombo in Columbus Circle in New York. The rest is pure fiction.

Chapter 1 – Tonight's The Night

He had the area in front of him covered. Many years of a dangerous, murderous life had taught him that. His back side was covered by Tony, a trusted, intimidated, but confident goon, Tony. His front was covered by Willie, also a trusted, intimidated, confident goon. Lower in rank than Tony, but reliable. So it was a bit of a surprise when the shooting started.

It was Herbie, the waiter. Herbie was also reliable, so the Godfather thought. Herbie had been a part of Pasgucci's Italian for years. Pasgucci's Italian, with its fading red walls, and gaudy, gold-framed travel photos of the Vatican, the Leaning Tower, the Ponte Vecchio, and several scenes of Sicilian peasant life surrounding the Formica tables. Herbie was like an old friend to the family. But Herbie done it. That was Angelo's last thought.

Tiny Gambini had told Herbie, "Tonight's da night. You do it tonight, or dere's no tomorrow. Not for you. You got dat?"

Herbie got it all right. He owed the Gambinis twelve thou. *Fuckin' horse didn't win. Didn't win, hell, didn't even place or show. Fifth place. Can you believe that? Fifth place on a sure bet.*

But that was over a month ago. Five weeks to be exact. He had tried to double his money so he could pay off the loan. Six thou turned into twelve thou in less than three minutes. Now he had a job to pull. He remembered Tiny's words, "Do dis, an' yer inna clear, wid us. Got dat?"

Herbie wasn't the brightest bulb in the candelabra, but he wasn't stupid either. He planned for this. Careful. Planned good, so no slip ups. No suspicion. No warning. He had to get Angelo, the Godfather of the Ginnini family. Tonight. That was that. Bruno had got him the twenty-five millimeter, silencer screwed on, with the hollow point rounds. Seven of them. Loaded. Ready to go.

Lom had put the linguini carbonara up on the pass-through shelf, steaming. Herbie prepared the tray, as usual, the way he knew the Godfather liked it with the large, white, linen napkin draped over the small tray so the sides hung down. He centered the hot pasta, added another linen napkin, neatly folded, and the fork and tablespoon. The salt, pepper, and the grated parmesan in the shaker were already on the table. Just like usual. Everything normal.

But Herbie was scared. Sweating inside his white waiter's jacket with the washed old marinara stains. Heart pounding, fast, in his chest. *This is the worst thing I ever done. I done some bad stuff before, but nothin' compared to this. This is big time. Jeezis, this is the Godfather. I could get myself killed on this one. Tiny Gambini said there was back up. But I don't see none. What about Tony and Willie? Now or never. Shit!*

He set the tray down for a minute and went into the men's, into the left stall. The door swung shut behind him. He reached up behind the toilet tank high on the wall. It was a new model toilet they put in a couple of years ago. New plumbing, but made to look like one of them antique Victorian kind. Old fashioned like. Yah, there it was. Just like Bruno said, up behind the tank. Herbie carefully palmed the gun, and, turning, he put it in his baggy black waiters' pants pocket, and went out. He was beginning to tremble.

Still in the serving area, he was alone. Lom was bent over the stove, in the steam. Couldn't see nothing. Swinging doors to the dining room, closed. No one looking. No one. He reached in his pocket for the gun. It barely fit in his hand, the end of the silencer sticking out some. He had it all worked out. Practiced it with a dummy all last night. Gun in right hand, under tray. Not heavy. Balanced, like usual, on tips of his bridged fingers. Get to the table. Swing tray down for the Godfather to see and approve the carbonara. Gun hidden by the overhanging napkin. Left hand swoop the plate in place on the checkered tablecloth before the Godfather's ample belly. Left hand then take the tray, and bango. Shoot the Godfather.

Just that easy. Easy? Not easy. He was trembling. *Gotta control it. Stop the shakes. Can't stop. Maybe a shot of booze. No, too far away. Not usual. No good. Take a deep breath. Okay, let's go.* He wiped the sweat from his forehead with his jacket sleeve. *The pasta's gettin' cold. Don't matter. He ain't gonna taste it anyhow.*

2

He picked up the tray, gun in hand, kicked open the swinging doors to the dining room, and went out, with the best smile he could muster, straight for the right side of the Godfather's table. It was almost as if he were in a dream. Everything like he practiced it. Swooped the tray down. The Godfather nodded. Left hand arched the plate with a flourish up, around, and down, centered in front of the Godfather. The Godfather bent to sniff the aroma. Pleased, he sat back with a small smile. Herbie's left hand grabbed the tray. Gun in right hand, finger in the trigger guard came up low. Thup. Right in the middle of the big belly. Just above the belly button.

The Godfather jerked back with surprise. Eyes widened without understanding. Then he lurched forward, almost catching the gun and Herbie's right hand with his flailing arm. Herbie, pulled back, and almost instinctively, thup, he put a second shot across the Godfather's skull, just behind his right ear, like he was told. Both shots barely audible.

Holding tight to the gun, he sensed time slowing to a crawl, as it always does in these extreme situations. He wheeled around to see Willie put a shot into Tony's forehead, then heard the whiz of a second shot just over his left shoulder, before it smashed into the big, etched glass mirror behind the bar. Herbie's jaw dropped. Willie was running out the door, and he, Herbie, was still alive. The bar tender was nowhere to be seen. Dead quiet. No one moving. No one else there. Tony had fallen back across a table, slid off, and was motionless on the floor, as blood from his head pooled on the floor. Herbie turned. Looked at the Godfather. *Motionless also. Must be dead.*

Suddenly his senses caught up with him, and Herbie ran across the dining room, busted through the swinging doors, out the back door, into the dark alley. There it was. Like they said. The black sedan. Rear door opened. In he went. Speeding off into the night.

"Done?" More of a grunt than a question.

"Yah. Done." Herbie gasped. "Gimme a drink, will ya."

Chapter 2 – Dey Got'im

Dead quiet. A full minute must have passed before a sound broke the silence in Pasgucci's Italian. Lom peered out between the swinging doors, and the bartender got up off the floor and peeked over the bar.

"Holy shit!".

The bartender's eyes huge, mouth wide open. "Holy shit. Hoooo-ly sheee-it!" He turned, confused, flustered. *The phone? The cops? The boss? The Godfather? No, he's dead there. Dead. Jeezis! The boss!* He grabbed the phone. Punched in the speed dial. Rang once. Rang again, a third time. He looked back over his shoulder at the mess. "Jeezis."

Click. A sleepy "hellllooo?"

"Boss. Dey got de Godfather. Right here. Eatin' dinner, his usual table." he blurted.

"They what? Slow down. They what? What're you tellin' me?" the voice asked.

"Dey shot de Godfather. No. Not dey. It was Herbie. Herbie shot de Godfather. Shot him. Right here. At his own table, ya know. Right here. Right in front of me."

"What are you talking about? Someone shot? In my restaurant?"

"Yah. Like I said, Herbie shot de Godfather. Ya know, Angelo Ginnini."

"Arright, arright, arready. Someone got shot. Pipe down. Stay dere. Don't do nuthin'. Don't touch nuthin."

"I should call the cops?"

"No. Don't call no one. I'll be right dere. Just shut up and don't do nuthin'."

Meanwhile, Lom had squeezed out between the swinging doors. "Wha hoppin?" he asked. Chinese eyes squinting, he tiptoed, bent slightly at the waist, inching his way toward the inert Godfather, face down on the fresh carbonara, bleeding on his neck. Eyes wide, Lom stopped several yards away and ran back into the kitchen, to his nice, warm, familiar stove. "I don' see nuttin'. I don' know nuttin'. Nuttin', I don' know from nuttin'." He automatically put some water on to boil in a big pot, not knowing why, and stirred the water into a whirlpool. "Nuttin'. I don know nuttin'. I don' see nuttin'."

The sirens screamed in the night, getting louder for several minutes before the two cops barged in the door, guns held rigid in both hands, way out front. Frantically looking right and left. Back to back.

"Clear?"

"Clear here."

"Kitchen clear."

"Rest rooms and back hall clear."

They relaxed, holstered their weapons. One cop went over to the two guys leaning on the bar. One, he guessed was a bartender, by the look of him. The other guy, next to him, was dressed in a disheveled tee shirt and sweats. The second cop went to the big guy on the floor. No sign of life. He started over toward the bloody guy, face down in the spaghetti. He turned toward his partner, "Gonna need the M.E. fer the guy onna floor." He felt around for a carotid pulse.

"Jeesiz-h-kryz! This one here's alive. He got a pulse. Git over here. Call the ambulance."

The other cop rushed over, and together they pulled the hulking frame out of his dinner. The first cop tried to stop the bleeding by stuffing a napkin from the next table onto the wound at the base of the skull. The other wiped the sauce from the fleshy face, just as the victim hiccupped, then coughed, spraying a load of saliva and carbonara sauce.

"Hey buddy, you okay?" the cop asked. He could see the victim was still breathing as the guy's head lolled onto his chest. "You okay? Hey buddy! Buddy! You okay?" No reaction.

The new sirens stopped abruptly outside Pasgucci's Italian. EMTs rushed in. They all jerked to a stop. Looked at the carnage.

"Here. This guy's alive. At least he's breathing," the cop directed. The entrance crashed open again, followed by two more cops with guns drawn.

It took three men to carefully get the Godfather out of his chair and onto the stretcher that the third EMT brought in. It was then, as they were putting the O2 mask on his face, that they noted the small blood stain in the front of his shirt. The head EMT ripped the shirt up the front, popping buttons, tearing the silk. Big hairy belly with a single punctate wound half way between the sternum and the belly button. "Gotta be a gun shot," he said.

Suddenly, one of the EMTs shot upright, took a step back, the back of his hand to his mouth. "Hey, this guy's Mafia, I think. Ain't he that guy, Angelo what's-his-name? Yah, ain't he Angelo Ginnini? Looks like him. Ya-know, like from the Mafia." He bent forward, but not too close, looking harder. "Yah. Ain't he that Godfather guy? That Mafia boss. Ginnini. Yah, Angelo Ginnini?"

The second EMT stood up and looked down, carefully. The third was trying to put an oral airway into the Godfather's mouth to help his breathing.

"Billy move over. Can't really see him." Billy Turner finished with the oral airway and moved. "Shit yah. You're right, that sure looks like him. Hey Smitty, check this out." He motioned to one of the cops talking to the man in the sweats. "Come here. Check this out."

"Holy cow. You're right. Looks just like him. That Ginnini guy. You check his pockets fer ID?"

"That's your job, man. You find cash, we split it. Right? Except, I guess not if this guy's Mafia." More of a statement than a question. The EMTs continued their work, dressing both the abdominal bullet wound and the head wounds, rechecking vitals, which remained remarkably stable. They strapped the victim safely on the stretcher, pausing to let the lead cop check the pockets.

Eight hundred bucks in the Italian leather billfold in the inside breast pocket of the dark silk jacket. The lead cop left it all right there in the wallet. He also noted a driver's license, credit cards, a picture of some broad, and a condom.

Looking at the driver's license, he blurted out, "Shit. You're right. Angelo Ginnini. The man himself. Better tell 'em downtown."

"I'll call it in," said the third cop as he turned to go out.

"We gotta get him to the ER, now. While he's still breathing." They pushed the wheeled stretcher toward the door. "Don't want no Mafia boss dying on my watch. Not with my wife and kids in the same town. We're outta here." And with that, they disappeared out the door with the Godfather still breathing, but the bleeding was slowed.

"This here's a crime scene. I'm afraid you're gonna have to shut down a couple of days," the lead cop said to the bartender, then looked at the guy in sweats. "You the owner?" he said on a hunch.

"Yah. Amadeo Rossi, and, yah, that's Angelo Ginnini, the Godfather." The guy in sweats held out his right hand. It wasn't met.

"The crime boys'll be all over this place. Tonight. Yah, tonight, and for a couple of days. Then they'll probably leave you alone."

The guy in sweats nodded slowly in mute understanding, clearly not pleased. Not pleased by the incident. Not pleased by the whole damn evening. *Not only getting closed for a couple days, but the reputation of the place gonna be wrecked. Plus, I lost a real good customer. The Godfather come in here a lot. Big tipper.* Little did Amadeo know Pasgucci's Italian would become a tourist attraction, exactly because of what had just transpired this very night in his restaurant.

The owner in sweats stayed. The Crime Scene Investigation team, the CSI, did come. Shortly after, so did the press. And so began the new life for Pasgucci's Italian. Transformed from a quiet little hangout for the Mafia bigs, to a locally famous crime scene, now on the bucket list of many an inquisitive tourist.

Chapter 3 – Get'im Loaded

"Get'im loaded." said the lead EMT. The rear doors of the ambulance were still open, the halogen interior lights casting an eerie glow. "Watch the IV there."

Out of the surrounding darkness a large man with a thick head on almost no neck at all appeared, closely followed by two others, his clones. Black, full length trench coats, hands deep in pockets. Black wide-brimmed fedoras pulled down severely, blocking any view of a face. "Whachu doin' dere." Not a question. "Izzy breathin'? Means he's alive? Where you takin' him."

The EMTs, used to bystanders' interference and congestion, kept working the collapsible stretcher, ignored the intruders.

"I said where you takin' him." Still a command, not a question. "Where you goin' wid him." No response. The EMTs kept doing their job. "Dis guy's important to us. Where you takin' him." Then getting a little more aggressive, the massive figure grabbed William Turner's arm. "Where you goin' wid him."

"Get outta the way......Please, get out of our way. We've got a badly injured patient here. Move, please," said William in a rather routine voice, without turning to see the speaker.

The mass in black, tightening the vice-like grip into the arm, pulled a sharp tug. "Hey you. I'm talkin'-a-you."

William tried to shake his arm free, but the firm grip tightened, now digging into his biceps. Looking to face his nuisance, he was surprised by the dark form with the sneering thin lips and crooked teeth. "Stand back. This is an emerg....", staring at what he could see of the belligerent face. "Leggo. Let go my arm, I'm ...."

"Answer da question. You wanna see yer wife an' kids again, you answer da question." the hulk growled.

The young EMT froze, his heart hammering. Breaking out in a hard cold sweat, he stammered, "We're, we're, er takin' him to Emergency. To University Hospital...... He's, he's, he's, uh, badly injured. Now leggo my arm....... We gotta go here." He tried to shake free. "Please leggo my arm and back off. Out, out of the way. Please, sir, if you don't mind." He was sputtering, unable to react as he had been trained. He could only stare at the menacing face.

The dark creature released his grip, and William yanked his arm away. Because he was not helping with the loading, the two other EMTs paused and looked over. Neither EMT could really see the huge man clearly as he had retreated into the shadows. With his arm freed, William turned back to his duty, but he was trembling. No, actually shaking. *This guy was really threatening me. He could be dangerous.* He quickly thought about it. *If this vic is Angelo Ginnini, if he's the Godfather like they say, this guy here must be Mafia too. A henchman? A killer. Shit.* "Come-on guys, let's get outta here. This is no good here."

"Git over here and help us, and we will." said Lou, the boss EMT.

The huge, black coat moved in again, "Like I said, where ya takin' him?" This time a question. Then, perhaps lightening up a little, "We gotta know. So just tell me where, an' we leave ya alone.

William rubbed his arm and looked over at Lou. "Hey, Lou, wanna tell him. Tell him, so he leaves me alone."

Lou looked up and realized the situation for the first time. "What's he want?"

Both the black coat and the EMT answered at the same time, "Where ya takin' him?" and William added, "We're goin' to University, right?"

"Yah, we're goin' to University. University Medical Center. Emergency. And who are you? Who wants to know?"

"I'm me. I gotta know." the black coat answered roughly with a deep voice that sounded as if it had been dragged over five miles of gravel road.

"And who are you?" Lou asked.

"You don't mind who I am. You just do your job. You do it good, see. Real good. Mr. Ginnini dies wid you, and there's blood on your hands, you gonna pay for it. Gonna be very sorry. You give him the best. First class the whole way. You hear me on that. First class all the way. Or it's you payin' for it."

The EMTs, along with the Fire and Rescue Squads, were not new to threats and verbal abuses. Sometimes there were even gun shots when they were working in some of the tougher neighborhoods. But this threat was closer, meaner, and somehow more intense than the usual.

Lou looked hard at the big menace. *This was not your average street punk or gang member. This guy and them other two behind him gotta be Mafia or something like, and could be real trouble.*

Lou's first allegiance was to the patient. Next it was to his squad. He had to get them all out of there and back to the hospital. No confrontation, no other issues.

He took a deep breath and announced in his most authoritarian, voice, "Look pal. I dunno who you are, but stand back and let us do our job here." As they lifted the stretcher, he turned his head and said over his shoulder, "This patient is severely injured, and we need to get him to level one trauma care.........as quickly and as safely as we can. So please stand back and let us do our job."

The team gently slid the stretcher into the open ambulance. "Don't bother us, unless you want us to call the cops. They're right inside there in the restaurant." His hardest, toughest stare was met by the undecipherable shadow of the fedora brim over most of the face, and a smirking mouth, silent for the moment, then it spoke slowly.

"Like I said, first class all the way. First class, den dere's no trouble." With that the black mass stepped back into the shadows with the other black masses. They stood there, hands thrust into deep coat pockets, immobile until the rear doors were closed and locked. The two junior EMTs had climbed in alongside the stretcher, and Lou got behind the steering wheel, and with a lurch, tore off into the dark street, bright emergency lights flashing, quick siren wobblings at each street corner.

Like a dark, foreboding scene in an old Orson Wells movie, the black masses seemed to dissolve into the darkness.

Now that his ambulance was rolling, Lou was no longer scared, but he kept an eye on the rear-view side mirrors. After a couple of blocks, sure enough, there they were. Two big black sedans not far behind. Not rare in the city, but still threatening. He pressed the accelerator a little harder.

Chapter 4 – We Needa See Mr. Ginnini

Lou bumped the ambulance into:

Emergency - Ambulances Only

He swerved, hit the brake, popped it into reverse, stopped three feet from the automatic sliding glass door, and bailed out of the driver's seat. Two nurses, one male, one female, in pale blue, well-worn scrub suits, standing ready to receive, pulled open both doors. With practiced speed and grace, the two EMTs jumped out of the back, unlocking the stretcher, and hauled it out smoothly onto the cement ground. Angelo Ginnini was swiftly rolled inside, down the cluttered hall, and into Trauma Room 2. Three surgical residents and the two nurses leapt into action.

During the four-and-a-half minute ambulance ride, vital signs had been recorded every fifteen seconds. The IV, with the large bore catheter, which had been started back in the restaurant, was running Ringers Lactate wide open in response to the blood pressure of 90 over 50, pulse, 120, respirations 24. There was a fair amount of blood loss from the posterior scalp wound despite big compound dressings placed earlier. All the information during transit was electronically transmitted through the dedicated line to the hospital ER desk. Any needed advice was sent back to the EMTs.

The three surgical residents - first, third, and fifth year, plus the two trauma nurses, worked together as a well-practiced team. All were ATLS (Advanced Trauma Life Support) certified, and quickly got the resuscitative measures going. The on call Anesthesiologist had been notified, and the hospital based CRNA, (Certified Registered Nurse Anesthetist) was rushing down the hall toward Room 2. Both the general surgeon and the neurosurgeon on call had been notified and would be there within minutes. The team was ready for anything. Or so they thought. They didn't know that Angelo Ginnini, the Godfather, would add a whole new dimension to the process.

Arriving at the ER Ambulatory Entrance, at about the same

time, were several city police cruisers, and two black sedans, these last two parking in the handicapped section. Six men, dressed in long, black overcoats, black fedoras, and unfashionable shoes, moved like an avalanche into the ER, toward the front desk. They looked like characters in a b-grade gangster movie.

The Police Officers gave a familiar wave to the three women at the front desk, and proceeded through the second set of automatic, sliding glass doors, down the hall to Trauma Room 2 doorway, where they halted, peering inside to watch the team work their well practiced routine.

The six men dressed in black, stunned the three women at the Front Desk. All three were true professionals in the busiest ER in the city, but all three froze. One was a clerk, one a registered nurse named Brooke; one, a "Pink Lady" seasoned volunteer, with hundreds of hours of service to the hospital. The front desk was usually her favorite assignment.

It had been a quiet night so far, and they had been chatting. Abby, the clerk, a new grandmother, proudly showed pictures of the latest family addition. "Oohs" and "aahs", "so cute," "just adorable."

As the wave of black came up, any hint of adoring smiles vanished. Trying to be forceful, Abby spoke: "How may I help you gentlemen?" The nurse stood up, her response half conditioned, half fear. The Pink Lady sat rigid in her chair.

"Yah!" said the man in the lead, "We need ta see Mr. Ginnini. Mr. Angelo Ginnini. Dey brung him in here. We needa see him. Where dey take him." The voice was gruff, deep, and threatening.

"Can you tell me when he came in?" asked the nurse. To avoid eye contact, she bent over, looking at the intake list on the desk computer. She didn't like the looks of these guys. Under the desk top, the clerk inched her hand toward the security call button. The Pink Lady just stared, mouth half open.

"He just come in. Just now. We need ta see him." It appeared that the lead hulk was trying to appear calm and civil, but his tone was menacing. All three women were on high alert.

"Mr. Ginnini, Mr. Angelo Ginnini? Yes, here he is. He is in Trauma Room 2. They are working on him now, sir." Nurse

Brooke came erect, glaring at the lead man, and pointing at the computer screen. "I'm sorry sir, but no one is allowed in there. Not at this time. They are very busy right...."

"We gotta see Mr Ginnini. He gotta get first class care, First class doctor. Chief doctor. Now!" A second man in black had come up beside the lead man. He was even bigger, even thicker.

"I'm sorry sir, but no unauthorized people are allowed back there. If you would like to have a seat, we'll be glad to keep you informed.....", the nurse was interrupted, again.

"We gotta see Mr. Ginnini. Open da doors." the lead man growled.

"I'm sorry sir. That area's restricted. If you'll just have a seat, we'll..."

"Look lady, open de door, or do I gotta open it myself." barked the lead man. He took a step closer to the desk. The clerk's finger was on the security call button, ready to push it.

"Dats okay Billy." the bigger man said as he put a hand on Billy's shoulder. "You, Gonz, Phil, and Li'l Joey go back to Church Street. You got a few jobs need doin' tonight, anyhow. Me an' Leo'll wait here. Tell 'em we'll call when we know."

The lead man turned to the big guy, "Yah, but we got orders to secure the place, ya know."

"Got it covered. Go back to Church Street. Do what's onna schedule, like I said. I done dis before. Got it covered." the big guy mumbled into Billy's ear.

"Ya-but, dat's de Godfather in dere. We spose-a...."

"Go Billy. Now!" The big guy's voice now forceful. The clerk waited, her finger next to the security button. But Billy turned, nodded to three other men, who followed Billy through the lobby and out the automatic door. The big guy took his smaller colleague by the elbow and led him to the row of chairs facing the doors. They both sat. Mute. Hats on. Immobile, as though carved in stone, staring through the glass doors down the hall toward Trauma Room 2.

Nurse Brooke sat back down in her chair, and the clerk's finger came off the security call button. All three women let out a deep breath and swallowed, almost in unison. They tried not to stare at the two men sitting across from them. Dead silence. Unusual at 10:00 p.m. in the ER lobby.

Chapter 5 - Three Jobs Tonight

Billy, Gonz, Phil, and Li'l Joey checked in at the Church Street base, where Phil and Joey went down to the store room to get the supplies they needed. Then the four men left in the black sedan.

"Who's the first stop?" asked Phil.

"Jacobs's meat shop," Billy grunted. "I can't stand them rats. Get rid of them first."

Billy hated rats. Couldn't be around them. But it was Billy, who made the deals for the rats. From Dirty Eddie, who lived on the street. Eddie was never quite right after Viet-Nam. He used his food stamps to buy old meat and fish, to use as bait in traps he put down in the sewers. To catch the rats. He caught lots of rats. He was surprised by the size of the market for them, and it was growing even bigger. Not for the research labs. These were dirty, infested rats no lab wanted, but Dirty Eddie never told.

Jacobs' meat shop was a small butchery run by two brothers, Nat and Mart, struggling to make a go of it in a low rent neighborhood that ate mostly pasta. They continued to survive because the neighbors liked them. They were cheerful, always friendly, honest to a dime, and especially because their shop was spotlessly clean. An asset to the neighborhood.

Their only failing was they were behind in their protection payments. "We can't afford your price, now. Since the price of beef went up, we can't pay you so much. If we pay you what you demand, then our kids go hungry with me an' the wife. We just ain't got the dough."

Phil had told them, "Youse gotta week to make it up. A week or else you got no protection, an' youse knows dat can be dangerous for yer business."

Billy agreed, "That was three weeks ago. We give 'em enough time. Word gets out, everyone'll fall behind, an' there goes the business. No, they needs a little lesson."

A quiet entry through the back. Shut off all the power to the refrigerators and coolers, leaving the doors open. Throw some of the meat on the floor and counters. Then, last of all, after Billy has cleared out, let the rats out of the cage. Close the back door again, and on to the next job. It was Saturday night. The shop was closed Sundays.

Stop two: The White Goods Store. The ladies there sold household goods. Sheets, towels, dish towels, table cloths, and other domestic items. They were behind, too. In fact, they hadn't paid anything in six months. Miss Lindsay said that the priest had told her not to pay. That it was against the law, and not Christian. The priest had told her to remember Christ and the money lenders in the temple. So she stopped paying. Despite warnings. Her store was six blocks from the Jacobs, but she didn't know the Jacobs brothers or anything about them. Nor did they know her.

"Got the sprayer?" Billy turned to Gonz in the back seat.

"Yah, got it. Chameleon mineral juice. All set."

Their version of Chameleon mineral juice was potassium permanganate dissolved in water. It had a beautiful deep magenta-rose color that stained anything it touched. Water didn't wash it out. Other cleaning chemicals, reacting with the potassium permanganate, could be dangerous. Some were known to burst into flame. Billy and his boys loved potassium permanganate. It was cheap and readily available. Billy's mother even used to use it back in the old days on his scrapes and scratches as a good disinfectant when he was a kid.

In they went. Back door break in. Pulled neatly folded linens and other goods from the shelves, and sprayed them as well as across the walls, the counters, and the shelves. A haphazard mess. It might have been a pretty color if the lights had been on. But they weren't. They left as silently as they came.

Gonz preferred this kind of operation because he didn't have to hurt anyone, physically. No one died. Financial damage was part of the job. So far, he had never had to kill anyone. He hoped that didn't make him different.

The third job, Lonnie's Loan Land: quick and easy. Lonnie was a small-time loan shark. What Sal called a pip-squeak business; Lonnie really didn't make much of any competition for the family's loan business, the one run throughout the state and into the neighboring states by Marco. Marco Ginnini was the Godfather's cousin. Marco had done Lonnie a favor about six months ago. He let him launder some funds for the family, so it was untraceable by the Feds. Lonnie got paid for his efforts. Trouble was, Lonnie paid himself a little too much. He failed to remit the full amount, and to make his little mistake worse, he cooked the books. The family accountant found it immediately. Amateur job.

"You got it?" Billy asked Li'l Joey. "Is it clean? No prints, no labels?

"Clean, Billy. You know it's clean." The car stopped in front of Lonnie's Loan Land. The sign was the only part painted of the old wood frontage.

Li'l Joey got out, holding the canister gingerly. He pulled the ring off, counted to five, and threw the bomb through the plate glass window. It exploded. By the time Li'l Joey was back in the sedan, and the sedan was in full acceleration, the little office was engulfed in flames.

Chapter 6 —A Great Idea

Being an EMT was good, but it wasn't great. After just two months on the job, he knew that for sure. Medical school was what he really wanted, what he knew he really deserved. But the community college two-year certificate wasn't enough for medical school. No way could he ever go back to school for the college degree, not even a correspondence college. Even though he knew he would have been perfect for it. He knew the medical schools would want him.

So, okay, he settled for a correspondence nursing school. Pay the fee and you're accepted. He did pretty well— mostly 'B's. Easy to get a job, even at the mighty University Medical Center. They needed nurses. Not only that, but he got his pick: night shift on the Oncology Ward. Where the people with cancer go for what he considered hopeless treatment. They all died, and he loved death. Only a few didn't, and he figured he knew why.

He knew that he knew the answer. He could change history. His Mother always told him his ego was too big, but he knew he had the brains, and the talent. He knew he was different from others. He knew he could cure cancer. He just needed the opportunity.

His girlfriend and his mother, both told him he was crazy, but they just didn't understand. His Mother nagged at him, "You probably should have more training before you meddle too much in stuff you haven't studied." That proved she just didn't understand. No one did. She had always told him that he was an unusual boy, whatever that meant.

High school Science and Health were his favorites, a lot better than that other stuff because he'd always had a morbid curiosity about death and dying. As a child, he'd tried to pull just one wing off a fly to watch it struggle with death. In school, he'd had poor grades, because he always did his own thing. He had been kicked off teams, because he wasn't a team player.

In the military, he found a competitive niche, where he was pushed to the limits in basic training. On deployment he loved the death, destruction, and chaos. Shooting the enemy really turned him on. His best memory was an enemy head-shot, and watching the head explode. When he shot a senior officer who had given him an order he didn't like, he pleaded, "by mistake, sir". It was during a fire-fight in Afghanistan. He was dishonorably discharged.

Over the past few years, his friends — the few that he had — had drifted away, calling him "odd". With nobody on his wavelength, he took off on his own. Anyway, they all had become kinda weird, so he thought. His girlfriend finally told him she didn't like his whacky theories, or what he had become. So different. "Weirdo" is what she actually called him when she decided to split. But that was okay. He could concentrate on his ideas. His passions. His fame. He liked it by himself.

But the jerks at the Medical Center labs wouldn't listen, so he set up his own lab at home in his tiny basement apartment in that big old house on Clinton avenue. The house used to be some big industrialist's mansion, till after the war, when the heavy industries all moved South, where there were no labor unions. Hard times in the city.

But his basement apartment was perfect for him. No one paid him any mind. No one nosing around, asking any questions. The house was built thick, so the noise from the centrifuge and other equipment was never heard, and no one complained. And that's how he liked it. No one would notice him, till he published his results. Then those big-shot docs in their million dollar labs, in the multimillion dollar University Medical Center complex would know who he was. When he got his Nobel Prize, then they'd be sorry. Sorry that he wasn't working in their lab. Sorry that they snubbed him. Sorry they had told him his Nobel Prize idea was "ridiculous"; "crazy"; "didn't make sense"; "wouldn't work"; "there's a lot more to it than what you're talking about"; "would probably kill people." Those were the words they used. "Crazy" — that was the word they used most. But they were the crazy ones. Not him. He'd show them. Show them all for the phonies they all were.

His idea. His pearl. His pure genius of logic and common sense, of course it would work. He'd show them. In the meantime, he was accumulating data and results. Working slowly. And yah, a few people maybe died, but they were gonna anyways. And it was too early for the results to show in those he treated and had survived. Sacrifices always had to be made for ultimate good of mankind. And he knew that it was his job to select those that lived and those that had to be sacrificed. That was called research.

He had written out his mission statement and its methods on the first page of his lab log, his personal scientific record. They said all real scientists had one. He'd show it to the world someday. The principle was very simple: take the Tumor Necrosis Factor, popularly known in the business as TNF, from patients who had plenty of it and transfer it to those who needed it the most. The idea had come to him from that lecture a couple of months ago. This, when perfected, would save countless lives up on the Oncology Ward, where he worked. It would solve the cancer problem. He knew he could soon cure cancer.

Chapter 7 – CT Scan

"The head doesn't look too bad on the CT Scan. I think the bullet creased the posterior skull, but the meninges look intact, at least on these views. What do you think?"

"Yes. I think you're right there, Erv." Wally Huff, senior radiologist, was using a magnifying glass to study details of the CT scan images on the view-box before him. Erwin Anson, young neurosurgeon, new on the staff, but already making a solid name for himself, bent over Wally's right shoulder. John Pullman also examined the images looking over Wally's left shoulder. The three physicians had spent a quarter of an hour gleaning information from the radiological images just taken of Angelo Ginnini.

The patient, unconscious coming over from the ER, now had a slightly elevated blood pressure, and a slightly slow pulse, but otherwise stable vital signs. His APACHE II (Acute Physiology and Chronic Health Evaluation) score was low, and the Glasgow Coma Scale was 8, suggesting the patient wasn't in shock, but had a significant brain injury. All the requisite tubes had been inserted, either to add recorded amounts of prescribed fluids or drain other fluids out.

"I'm gonna need to explore the wound, but it looks to be mostly limited to the scalp and skull. I'll know better when I clean it up and get a closer look. It's my guess, John, that you've got the major problem there in the belly." Erv stated matter-of-factly, straightening up and folding his arms across his chest. "I think I can do my part without any anesthesia. He's completely non-reactive from a neuro point of view. The peripheral reflexes are okay, and so is the cervical spine. If I can't see it well enough, I can wait until you get done. I might put in a pressure monometer if there's any further signs of increased intracerebral pressure."

"No that's okay, Erv. You get your end squared away, then we can flip him and do his belly. That gastric-pancreatic-duodenal area is probably going to take some five or six hours. May even need a Whipple procedure from the looks of the scan. We won't really know till we get in there", said John Pullman as he also straightened up, rubbing his chin thoughtfully. Three residents, surgical, neurosurgical, and radiological, stood behind the attending physicians, jockeying to fully hear and see the discussion.

"Yeah, that whole pancreatic-duodenal area looks pretty messed up." Wally said as he scrolled the CT images down, getting back to the abdominal series. He stopped at several images showing the upper abdomen, pointing with a circular motion to an area of blurry tissues in the center. "We lose all tissue definition here just to the right of the bullet. Like I said, I think the bullet shredded itself on its way in, and it may have rebounded off the vertebral body. It's through and through the stomach, and has devastated the head of the pancreas, and probably some of the medial duodenum." Wally said as he pointed with his pencil. "I have no idea why it didn't hit the vena cava or the aorta. In that respect, he's one lucky dude. Like you said, his vital signs are stable, and I can't see that he hit any major vessels."

John Pullman leaned forward again, squinting slightly. "I think you're right, Wally. It looks like a lot of trouble in a tight, troublesome area. This is gonna take time to do properly." Straightening again, he looked at Erv, "You think the comatose state is probably concussive rather than intracerebral anatomical damage?"

"That's how I see it, currently, yeah."

"Well, I guess we better get to it. It's gonna be a long night." Turning to Wally Huff, John smiled warmly, "Wally, thanks so much for your expertise and confirmation, and thanks for coming in. Seeing as who this patient is, we better get this one right." The residents all nodded in agreement.

"No problem, John. My resident was not happy with either the pancreatic call, or the cranial call. And you're right, we sure don't need any trouble from this guy's family. That's for sure." Wally rotated his chair, got up, and the three men walked from the room with the residents following closely.

Walking back to the ER, John Pullman turned to Rick McIver, chief surgical resident. "Rick, my boy, this is going to be a long, tough case tonight, and I'm going to need some pretty strong help."

"Yessir", Rick replied, "David Allen is just finishing a small bowel obstruction. He's your partner. I'm pretty sure he could stick around and scrub with you, if you need him. As you said, considering who this patient is. In any case, I'd like to scrub in too."

"Rick, you're my Chief Resident, I can't think of anyone I'd rather have. Lets you and I tackle this one. Let David go home to bed. No sense both of us getting wiped out tonight. David and I have a full office facing us tomorrow."

"Yessir. Thank you, sir. Trip Hughes is around, to cover the ER and the house, if need be. He's got two fourth year med students to help him. Hopefully, it'll stay quiet the rest of the night.

Rick really wanted to scrub in with Dr. Pullman. The senior surgeon was his favorite in many ways: favorite teacher, favorite surgeon, and favorite mentor— a father figure. Ready with advice, if asked, which was usually profound.

Chapter 8 - Tumor Necrosis Factor

Maybe he wasn't supposed to be there, but his badge got him in. Everyone working at University Medical Center had an ID badge, the badge of honor. Besides his photograph and number, it announced to the world:

Steve Wojek, RN
University Medical Center

Its electronic strip allowed him privileged passage through closed doors into most of the medical center's restricted areas. He always wore his badge. That morning, the morning he would always remember, he wore it on the retractable lanyard clipped to the left lapel of his short white jacket, the same kind of jacket all the med students wore. In fact, this had once been a student's jacket, which he had permanently borrowed from a hook in the hall some months ago.

The green scrub suit, short white coat, and Medical Center badge was the uniform. Everyone wore it. Nobody noticed it or who was wearing it. Anonymity in the crowd was just what he wanted. Anonymously, he had walked into the Saturday morning lecture, as he had several times before. That particular morning's lecture had been on "Cytokines", a lot of which he understood, and some of which he remembered. That lecture had changed his life, had given his existence a whole new direction.

What he remembered was that the lecturer had said there were many types of cytokines. He vividly recalled that TNF was one of the cytokines. TNF, made by the human body and ready for release by the body's defense mechanisms, especially in response to major stress such as disease or trauma. Blah, blah, blah. That particular cytokine that caught his attention that memorable morning. Tumor Necrosis Factor, known as TNF, was a cytokine. It was a big, heavy molecule, a protein. It caused apoptosis, which, he learned, meant cell death, particularly in certain types of tumor cells. *Cell death of tumor cells. Apoptosis. I can't believe it. TNF caused cell death in tumor cells! Jeez-um crow, death in tumor* cells. *Hard to believe, yet so simple. Cell death in tumor cells.* He repeated this to himself over and over. *This was his answer. Had to be. Damn!*

He tried to force himself to try to concentrate on the lecture, taking some notes as fast as he could, but he kept thinking *TNF causes cell death in tumor cells.* He got some of what was being said, maybe, but missed some of it. Two kinds of TNF, alpha and beta. Alpha was a cytotoxin shown to cause tumor regression. That he heard loud and clear, tumor regression.

Just then his pencil point broke. He reached in his pocket and withdrew his trusty jack knife. *I always carry my knife in case someone quit breathing, and I have to do an emergency tracheostomy, because there's no one else around or something like that. Never seen one, but I'm sure I could do it.* He sharpened his pencil point, and resumed scribbling his notes. *Guess I missed something about other effects of TNF- alpha. Something about sepsis, shock or cachexia. Not sure. Got some of it. Forget it. Move on. Pay attention. Take notes.*

He tried to pay attention, but his thoughts wandered. *I get things backwards. Dyslexia they said. On the Ward, if I copy the orders into my little notebook from the computer, I have less of a chance of getting them backward.* He was ashamed of the problem, and kept it well hidden from others. *Listen to the lecture.*

The Saturday lecture had moved on to TNF-beta. He had to force himself to try to follow the lecture, to pay attention, to stop fretting about dyslexia. "TNF-beta is now called Lymphotoxin-alpha, also cytotoxic to tumors, causing cytolysis of tumor cells." Steve wasn't quite clear on all this mumbo-jumbo. "TNF is also a pyrogen causing fevers. It stimulates Interleukin-1, and activated T-cells." He was getting confused. *I might have missed something about TNF causing fatal complications. I'm not sure what all this other BS means, but TNF must be good if it kills tumor cells. TNF causes tumor cell death. A very simple concept.* He was so excited he couldn't concentrate on the rest of the bullshit. *How come no one else has picked up on this? TNF kills tumor cells. It's just as simple as that.*

Since TNF is a big, heavy protein molecule in the serum of the blood, it stands to reason that I can separate it out from the rest of the stuff in the blood. This he knew from his elementary chemistry course at Community. *And the way to separate parts of a fluid is to put it into a centrifuge. As it spins, the heavier substances are forced to the bottom of the test tube and the lighter stuff to the top. I can save the heavier stuff figuring that the TNF must be concentrated in the bottom. No way of testing this guess, but it made good common sense and probably must be true. It's a good enough idea to try it out.*

Working nights on the Oncology floor was perfect. He had easy access to plenty of sick and dying cancer patients, with plenty of tumors that needed to be killed. *Kill the tumor and the patient would get better. It makes perfect sense. Nature was really so simple and logical. I wonder why no one else has figured this out. It was as easy as one plus one equals two, or maybe even three.*

One question: *where could I get a good supply of TNF?* He thought about it for a minute. *Down on the trauma floor, of course. The lecture guy had stated that people with severe trauma mounted a big inflammatory response. That part I do remember, lots of cytokines, and plenty of TNF, and, probably a whole lot of the other stuff, too. I didn't get some of that other stuff in the lecture. Too complicated. Couldn't quite understand it. But the central principle, which had become his mantra: TNF kills tumor cells.*

During his 3 a.m. lunch break on his Oncology night shift, he started going down to Trauma. He found all the supplies he needed in the equipment room: fifty-cc syringes, 18 gauge needles, three-way stop-cocks, IV tubing, and empty, extra-large IV bags. The big white board in the hall listed all the cases by diagnosis in the different rooms, so when no one was around, he checked the charts for severely injured but young patients. Despite the much reduced staff at night, he was still careful to avoid any notice.

His first few runs were scary and worrisome, but he never encountered anyone. He knew which patients to tap. He'd just steal into the room, and if the patient was awake, he'd abort. But most patients, often drugged, were sleeping deeply. Harvest was easy. He'd connect the tubing, put the needle into the side-port of the patient's IV central line, suck out the patient's blood, ejecting it into his stolen blood bag. Fifteen such withdrawals equaled 750 ccs of fresh blood. Repeat, filling a second bag. He knew it was more than three times the amount they took at the blood bank, but he needed a lot to make enough TNF. Then he'd remove his set-up from the patient. Stuff the two big bags of blood and the rest of the mess in his tote-bag, and he'd sneak out of the room, down the stairs at the end of the hall, to his basement locker. The blood he put in his specially insulated back pack with the frozen freezer block. Lock the locker, grab a quick snack from the vending machine, and return to work on the Oncology floor right on time. *Piece of cake.*

In the morning, getting off shift, he carried his back-pack home, and while the TV dinner was heating in the nuker, he hung the IV bag full of blood and sucked out the liquid. By this time most of the blood cells had bound themselves up in a large clot, separate from the serum containing the TNF, which is what he wanted. He drew off the serum and threw the clot of cells away, guessing there was no TNF in that stuff. Then, he carefully squeezed out smaller portions of the remaining serum into the big, thick test tubes that fit in his new centrifuge — that big, shiny, new centrifuge had come faster than he expected, thanks to Amazon. Cheap too. And easy. Everything was easy.

He spun down eight big test tubes, full of the serum, for half an hour, and then poured the fluid on the top down the drain. Several cc's of the thick goo remained in the bottom of the test tubes which he sucked out into a single, large syringe, capped, labeled, and put into his refrigerator.

On his night shift, he carefully chose the sickest oncology patients; the ones he assumed had the biggest tumors of whatever kind. With latex-gloved hands, he wiped the TNF syringe brought from home with an alcohol swab, eliminating any prints. Then he uncapped the syringe, and twisted on a new 18-gauge needle. When the way was clear, he went into the chosen patient's room, and injected the full load of his precious TNF into the patient via the IV line, and flushed the IV line. Lastly, he neatly disposed of the syringe and needle in the sharps box, knowing that the container's contents would go straight to the incinerator.

It took a little over a month to treat his first six patients. He had collected eight loads of TNF. The first four patients each received one syringe full of TNF. One of these was able to be discharged to Hospice. The other three actually got worse. "Serum sickness due to blood-type mismatch", they called it, whatever that was. That was proof of how powerful the TNF was. The last two could get two syringes each, because he had drawn off twice as much from each donor down on the trauma floor. Both were very sick, and, unfortunately, they died later that morning. He figured he had treated them too late. *If I had been able to treat them earlier in the course of their disease, I'm guessing they would have done much better because the TNF had never had a chance to do its work. Too bad. Maybe I should choose patients earlier in their disease timetable. Probably a good idea. Yah. Definitely a good idea. Got to check trauma tonight to get some more TNF.* He loaded his back pack and headed off to the hospital.

Chapter 9 - John Pullman, MD, FACS

"John dis is Sal." The Underboss, Salvatore Ucciderita, called John Dominicci's cell phone late that night. John was the Family's enforcer, the hit man, who was also very capable on the computer.

"Yes, Sal, what can I do for you? And, yes, I heard about the Godfather. He's at University Medical center, right?"

"Yah, right. I wan'cha to look somethin' up fer me, ya know, do some what youse call re-search?"

"Sure, Sal. What do you want to know?"

"De doctor who's operatin' on de Godfather is s'posed to be a guy called John Pullman. Look him up an' see if he's any good. An' look up his family, ya know, just in case."

"Yes, sure Sal. Let me get to it. I'll get back to you."

An hour and twenty minutes later Sal's phone rang. "Yah John, what ya got?"

"You were correct," John answered. "The surgeon is a doctor named John Pullman. Here's what I found on him. His title is John Pullman, MD, FACS. The FACS means he's a Fellow of the American College of Surgeons, board certified in General Surgery. At University Medical Center, he is head of the sub-section of General Surgery and Trauma. It says some seventeen years ago, they asked him to chair the entire department, but he declined. He told them it was too much paper-work. Too much politics. This is from some guy's hand-written report on Pullman. It says that he told them he is a working surgeon, not a paper pusher, but agreed to head up the General Surgical sub-section, which he still does. He has a good reputation as a solid surgeon and is supposed to be what they call a compassionate humanitarian, which is why he is so well liked. For his family, it says that he's married to a woman, Ann Beard Pullman, who goes by the nickname of Annie B. They were married in 1996, and raised three kids, now grown and moved away. The oldest is a John Pullman, Jr., called Jake. Married. Financial Analyst in Wilmington, Delaware. The information says just Pullman and this Annie B live alone outside the city in a big, old house. I got the address if you want it."

"No. Save it." Sal replied. "You got it if we need it later."

"Yes, I plan to save the whole download. You want more?"

"Yah, gimme de whole deal."

"Let's see what we've got here that might come in handy if we need it." John sighed, then went on, "Pullman had first started in practice joining a Dr. Bob Stoehr, who retired five years later, as did a Marsha Myers, his longtime office manager. So those two are no longer in the picture. Annie B took over Marsha's role as office manager. Yada, yada...Let's see what else is pertinent. Okay, there's a Dr. David Alan, also a surgeon, who joined Pullman five years ago. The other doctor on the case is a neurosurgeon, who goes by Ervin Anson, MD, just out of training, but apparently one of those young hot shots. He's married to a Mary Anson, and aha, this might be helpful, with two little kids at home, also in the 'burbs. And that's about all I can see that's relevant to our current situation. I can look for more if we need it."

Angelo Ginnini had been wheeled from the ER to OR5, where the anesthesiologist and the CRNA were administering fluids and drugs to get the patient into optimal condition to withstand the anticipated surgeries, both the neuro and the abdominal. Rick McIver never left the patient's bedside, ready to call Dr. Pullman should any unanticipated problems arise.

Having scrubbed, Erv Anson gowned and gloved along with Sally Merrier. Sally, known as Sal, was the on-call neurosurgical resident, and both were concentrating on exploring the gunshot wound to Angelo's posterior head.

John Pullman strolled down the hall to OR5, and stuck his head in the door. "Is he stable? Any crises?" he asked.

"Stable as a rock from our end," the anesthesiologist looked up as he answered.

"Looks like no big problem here either," said Erv. Rick was still at the patient's bedside, vigilant and silent, as John knew he would be.

"I'll go get changed then," John said, as he slipped out of the door and walked to the Doctors' Lounge - Men's Locker Room.

It was quiet with no one else around at this hour, and, with the locker room lighting low, John wondered to himself, *What kind of a man is this Angelo Ginnini? What makes a Mafia Don different from others? He's a known killer, a mobster, a leader of the underworld. What are his associates like? What is his family like, presuming he has one? How will we relate to any of them? How different is his culture, his back ground? Will our different values clash? How will he behave post-op? If we have to do a Whipple operation, that'll carry a significant mortality in itself, especially in the trauma setting. What if he dies? Those henchmen in the ER didn't look any too friendly. Granted, I only got a look at them, and never really met them, but the ambulance boys didn't like them much, and those ambulance guys are a pretty tough bunch, don't scare easily. But if the Mob should come after me, they'll probably get Annie B too, and David Alan my partner, and Erv, new to the scene? What......"* John stopped, blinking, shaking his head. During this stream of consciousness he had changed into his scrub suit and cap, and dangled a paper surgical mask around his neck.

John had a reputation for self-confidence. But this case was worrisome, despite his confidence. *Jeez, what am I thinking about this crap for? This is not the time for daydreaming; we've got a big job to do.* He left the lounge.

David Alan was down the hall, operating on a small bowel obstruction as Angelo was being induced by the anesthesiologists. John stuck his head in the door of David's OR to check in and to tell him that he, John, would probably be up most of the night with a gunshot to the pancreas.

"You need help with that?" David asked, but John said that he had it covered.

John continued down the hall to OR5. Poking his head in the door a second time, John asked Erv, "What'd you find?"

Erv had just finished exploring the head wound of this new patient. He replied, "Looks like we were right. Scalp wound only, skull's intact. Gotta be a severe concussion which makes me done here, at least for tonight."

"Okay," John answered, "I'll scrub up."

Chapter 10 – The Surgery

Erv Anson watched as Sal Merrier finished wrapping the head dressing. Erv, stripping off his gown and gloves, looked at John Pullman, and announced, "As John Wayne used to say, 'It ain't much ma'am, just grazed me. Nuthin'to get excited about, ma'am'." His smile faded. "And, yes, I think he's concussed. Probably contra-coup, with brain bruises both posteriorly and in the opposite frontal lobe. He may be out for a day or two, maybe more, and he may be a little unsteady when he wakes up due to the cerebellar bruising. He may not have much of a sense of smell for a while from the frontal cortex injury. I'm guessing he'll wake up before your Whipple is ready for discharge."

"I'll hold you to that, Erv." John said with a smile.

"Anything else I can help you with tonight, John?" Erv asked, as he turned to go.

"Yes Erv, there is. There was a pair of fairly sinister looking characters out in the waiting area. Brooke, the nurse down in the ER said they were very interested in the patient and his condition. Considering who this patient is, and HIPPA notwithstanding, would you mind stopping by there and telling those guys what you've found, and your prognosis neurosurgically? Tell them we'll probably be another four to five hours before we're done with the abdominal problems, if they want to wait out there. I sure as hell don't want them charging in here, causing problems.

"Yeah, sure. Good point. Be glad to. Maybe I can find out a little more who or what they are. Let'cha know if anything of interest turns up." With that, Erv was out the door.

"Rick, come here a minute, if you will. You too, Rena and Emma." John Pullman was studying the abdominal bullet wound. "What can we tell about the gun shot from the wound?"

"It's likely the entrance wound. Small, round, punctate, not torn up like an exit wound." Rick was bent over examining the wound closely.

"Good observation. Anything else?"

Rick straightened up and stepped back a bit, "Uhh, not sure I can tell much more till we get in there."

"That's okay. I only recently learned this myself. From a forensic pathologist friend. Look at the wound. See those marks at the edges. That's called stippling. That means that the gun was fired at what's called an intermediate range. More than six inches but less than six feet away. With a second look you'll see there's no soot around the wound. The presence of soot would mean a close muzzle shot, less than six inches. A wound with no soot and no stippling would suggest that the gun was more than six feet away when fired. Just a little bit of trivia to tuck away until you bring it out on rounds some day and look like a genius."

"Wow", said Rena, stepping back to her instrument table. "I never knew that. Where do you learn all this stuff, Dr. Pullman. That is so cool."

Rick, the Chief Surgical Resident, was in his fifth and final year of training. John thought him a fine, up-and-coming young surgeon. He might even offer him a position in his office after his residency.

Rick had dried his surgically-scrubbed hands with the sterile towel Rena Catlin, the scrub nurse, had given him. Rena held out the sterile operating gown while Rick pushed his arms into the sleeves. He stood face to face with the tall, stately nurse, only inches apart and asked, "Nice to have you here tonight, but I didn't think you worked nights?"

John noted a special look between them. He'd seen it before. Something more than just professional collegiality. *Actually,* he thought, *they'd make a great couple. Both tall, dignified, and smart. Both athletic. He's the silent thinker, and she counters with the cheerful chit-chat. Yes, a nice match. Great kids.*

With a slightly saucy tilt of her head, Rena answered Rick, "One of the girls is out sick, so I said I'd fill in. I'm off for four days at 7:00. Think you'll be done by then?"

"Dunno. This promises to be a toughie. Doubt we'll be done by shift change." Rick was rarely chatty, and right now he felt distracted as he tried to concentrate on the daunting task before him, before them all.

Emma Buckley, a second year resident, and John Pullman — both scrubbed, gowned and gloved — joined Rick and Rena at the table. Rick made a long mid-line incision from the tip of the xiphoid, moving down, skirting the umbilicus, and half-way to the pubis. As was routine with trauma cases, especially with gunshot wounds, you never knew what you'd find inside. The abdominal exploration was thorough, although it only took a few minutes. Exploration of the pancreatic damage was much slower and meticulous.

"One thing about bullets," Rick said in his usual droll, understated tone, "you never know where they'll go or what they'll mess up. At least that's what I've come to learn."

"You're right on that, Rick," John agreed. Rick concentrated on his fingers deep in the abdomen, as he slowly nodded his head.

"Jeeziz, Dr. Pullman, it looks like he's destroyed most of his pancreas. Except for this area near the tail. Through and through the lower stomach, and a blast injury to the pancreas." Rick announced his findings as he explored the damage. "Surprisingly, the duodenum looks pretty good. So does the Porta-hepatis, the gall bladder, and the rest of the stomach."

John interrupted, always the teacher, "Emma, what is the porta-hepatis?"

Emma answered without hesitation, "It's the bile duct, and the blood vessels to and from the liver."

"I wouldn't have bet on it, but the spleen looks okay too." Rick continued as he turned to hand off a distorted bullet slug to Rena, "Probably a hollow point. Make sure this gets to pathology, along with anything else we take out. The police investigating the shooting will try to match it to a gun, if they find one."

The nurse glared at him. He noted her stare, swallowed, and with a subdued voice, begged, "Let me correct myself....... please...... make sure this gets to pathology?" She couldn't see his sheepish grin under his surgical mask, but she sensed it. She looked over at Dr. Pullman. His eyes were smiling too.

"So what do you think we ought to do, Rick?" John asked. Then, redirecting his gaze to Emma, "No. Your turn, Emma. What do you think we should do?"

Rick focusing on the bed of pancreatic destruction, started to answer, "We've gotta clean up this mess, and then...."

"No. I was asking Emma for her thoughts, Rick. I'm pretty sure you have the answer." The senior surgeon looked at the junior resident. "What's your plan, Emma?".

"Hmmmm." she murmured, thinking before speaking. "First, do no harm. Save what we can." She paused. John kept his gaze on the second year surgical resident, and waited patiently, while Rick used the suction to debride much of the shattered pancreatic tissues. "So I'm thinking a roux-en-y small bowel brought up to drain what we have left of that tail of the pancreas there. That's where the real danger is. Most of the head of the pancreas is gone." Pointing at the various structures she continued, "The duodenum looks a little chewed up. Don't know what it looks like inside it. The sphincter and all. Stomach needs repair, but the pylorus looks okay. What's it feel like, Rick?" Without waiting for an answer, she noted, "I know the risk if we leave the duodenum intact and hope it does okay. Or should we take the duodenum out and do a formal Whipple? Tough call." She straightened and turned to John, "If this were my case, I'd call for help on that one, sir." She looked over at Rick, smiled to herself, and added, "This is obviously a judgment call. I'd ask the Chief Resident what to do, Dr. Pullman. That's what I'd do."

John Pullman smiled too. *Clever lady,* he thought.

Working as a well rehearsed team, they dissected and removed all the pieces of non-viable pancreas they could find, including a careful dissection on the inner sweep of the duodenum, ligating what was left of the duct and blood vessels. A Doppler ultra-sound of the celiac axis and it branches showed good flow to their respective organs. The through and through wounds in the stomach were repaired. The small bowel roux-en-y was brought up and carefully sutured over the end of the pancreatic remnant. All the anastomoses looked tight and good. The pancreatic bed was thoroughly lavaged with many liters of saline, and several drains placed.

Rick straightened up and announced, "The biggest risk to the patient now, would be a pancreatic leak or infection, in addition, of course, to his head injury. How and when might he wake up?"

They were just finishing up at the 7:00 a.m. change of shift.

35

Both Rena, in her good natured way, and the circulating nurse, Pete Salls, graciously stayed a little overtime to help finish the case, rather than bring in a new scrub team.

"Thanks for staying", John Pullman said, looking each in the eye.

"Yeah, thanks for all your help", Rick said to both, but he only looked at Rena. "Let's do it again, sometime."

John caught the look Rick and Rena exchanged. Emma noticed it too.

Angelo Ginnini was clocked into the PACU (Post Anesthesia Care Unit) at 7:42 a.m., with his vital signs still stable, and all his multiple tubes and monitors functioning properly. Anesthesia had done a great job in a tough case. They were happy. Emma, Pete, Rena, and Rick were tired but happy. John Pullman was exhausted, but also pleased with the result. He stopped by himself, just outside the PACU, looked up, and very quietly said, "Thank you Lord." Never complacent, he knew that the patient still faced a tough, long, uphill battle. *Now to face the Mafia. What's this going to be like?*

Chapter 11 – The Family

She was a hefty woman. That was John Pullman's first impression, hefty. Not fat. Just a good, healthy, hefty woman. She was the predominant one in the room full of chattering, gesticulating Italians. *Probably Angelo's wife?* John Pullman was heading toward her when he was cut off by a big man in black pants with suspenders and a white polyester shirt — one of those same guys who had been down in the ER hallway some eight hours before.

"You da doctor? You da one workin' on da Godfather? On Mr. Angelo Ginnini? You da guy? Huh?" The mountain of human flesh pressed right up to John, right into his space. Glaring into the surgeon's face with his little pig eyes, full of distrust. John backed off a step, but the big man immediately closed the gap. "I said, you da doctor?"

"I'm looking for Mrs. Ginnini. Mrs. Angelo Ginnini." John said in as loud a voice as he could muster without trembling. He said it up into the ugliest face he'd seen in some time. Then he redirected and tried to speak over the monster's left shoulder, "Is Mrs. Ginnini here? Mrs. Ginnini?" The room suddenly quieted. All attention was on him.

"I'm Mrs. Ginnini. Whosa this?" The hefty woman slowly rose from her chair, clutching her oversized purse in her right hand, pushing off the chair arm with her left. "You the doctor for my Angelo? You him?" Her soprano voice almost trembling as she started across the floor. "Billy, let him in." The monster twisted toward her, still blocking John. "Billy move it. Let him in." she barked in a serious alto. He backed off, but not far, while two other black and white-clad replicas closed in behind him.

John's mouth dried as he tried for words. "Yes.... yes. I'm his doctor. I'm Dr. John Pullman." The crowd in the room rose up as one and jammed around John, whining, shouting, barking, crying all at once.

At that moment, Rick McIver came through the door. The two lesser hulks, peeled off from John and closed in on Rick, who, although he was taller, drew up sharply, raising his right hand to his chest in surprise. Instinct jolted him a half step back, his chin tucked in, and a worried frown.

The voice sounded like an AK-47 semi-automatic firing off. "Shaddup! Shaddup!" Billy roared. "Everybody shaddup! Shaddup and siddown! Now!" Immediate silence. The horde retreated to chairs, the wall, and the floor. In a gruff but quieter tone, Billy announced, "Mrs. Ginnini's tryin' ta talk ta yahs." He paused. Not a sound. John Pullman was stunned. Rick was stunned. Billy turned with a slight bow to the hefty woman, "Your turn Mrs. Ginnini." The hefty woman eyed John Pullman warily. She was starting to say something, when John put out his hand.

"Mrs. Ginnini, I'm glad to meet you. I'm Dr. John Pullman. I just operated on Angelo Ginnini. He's your husband, right?" Mrs. Ginnini clutched her little white, lace trimmed handkerchief in her left hand, and brought it up under her chin. Her moist eyes met his. She was nodding slowly. He looked squarely at Mrs. Ginnini, his expression sincere, yet trying to be friendly. "You are his wife, Mrs. Ginnini? Is that correct?"

"Yes, doctor, I'm the wife", her voice, husky, quiet, "How's my Angelo? He's not dead, is he? Please say he's not dead, doctor. Not dead." A tear rolled.

"No, Mrs. Ginnini, he's not dead. He has been shot, twice. He is in critical condition, but he is not dead."

Billy slid around behind Mrs. Ginnini, towering over her, a big, beefy hand laid gently on each of her shoulders. John guessed she was about his own age. Somewhere in her mid-fifties. With forehead wrinkled and wide wet eyes, she looked up at Billy, then back to John and said, "Yes, doctor. I'm married to Angelo." In whining pleas, she continued, "He's okay? He's sick? Got trouble? You say gun shots? He's okay, doctor? He's okay?", her soprano whined more a plea than a question.

"Mrs. Ginnini, he's in the recovery room. His condition is critical, but stable at this point." John looked around the room. "Come, let us sit down, and I will try to explain everything."

Billy bent to take Mrs. Ginnini's arm, and waved a gigantic hand at the nearest chairs. "Move it!" He growled. Immediately, three people jumped and scampered away. Billy led Mrs. Ginnini to the middle chair. John waited for her to be seated, then turned the chair next to her slightly in her direction. The person in the adjacent chair darted away.

"Angelo. May I call him Angelo?" John asked quietly, head bowed towards her, noticing her down-cast eyes.

"Yah. Dats his name." Billy stated as though it had been a stupid question. Mrs. Ginnini nodded her head as she quietly flattened out her small white lace handkerchief with both hands in her lap.

John focused on Mrs. Ginnini as though she was the only person in the room. "Angelo was shot twice. Once in the abdomen, and once in the back of his head," he explained quietly, with sympathy.

"Jesus, Mary, and Joseph! He was shot in the head? I didn't know. Is he dead? Oh, my god. Oh no.....no,no." Wringing her handkerchief, with both hands, she looked up at John, as another tear fell.

"No. He's not dead. He is alive, and has a good chance of recovering. He is not dead." John's reply was a little louder and more forceful. "He has some very serious problems, but it is our hope and intention that he will survive his injuries and recover."

Mrs. Ginnini, with Billy hovering again, seemed to straighten up and regain some composure. She tried a brief, hopeful smile. "Tell me doctor. Please tell me everything. Tell me the whole story. And tell me the truth, please, doctor. Tell me the truth, all of it."

So John told her all he knew. He told her that the posterior head wound had only fractured the skill and shaved a little bone, but the brain had not been entered. He told her that Angelo was comatose due to the concussive injury, but would likely regain consciousness within a few days, and that Dr. Erv Anson, a very capable neurosurgeon, had done that part of the operation. He told her Dr. Anson was optimistic that Angelo should recover, hopefully without much permanent damage, but it was too soon to tell. And that Dr. Anson and his team were monitoring this neurological part of his care very closely.

Billy signaled one of his men. "Make notes", he commanded, "Get da names."

John continued his explanation, "The abdominal wound is another and separate matter. Most of Angelo's pancreas has been destroyed by the bullet, and major internal repairs have been made to control the situation in there. Angelo's biggest risk would be a leak of the remaining pancreatic gland. This might cause internal problems, which could be very dangerous. I know this is all very technical, confusing, and scary for you."

"No, doctor. Please go on. Tell me everything. Tell Billy, here, too. I wanna know everything. Please, doctor. Please go on." Her hands were clasped under her chin.

John straightened a little, and continued speaking, focusing on Mrs. Ginnini. "A leak from the pancreas and infection might be possible. Hopefully they won't occur, but they might. If Angelo heals up without those problems, he should recover quite well. However, he might develop diabetes, because only a small segment of his pancreas is left.'

"Yes, doctor. I understand. There is diabetes in the family." She looked up at John. Her worry lines had diminished. "I can do diabetes for him. For my Angelo."

John thought she was taking it all in. *Am I bridging the cultural gap here? I've done it before, but this may be different. Who's Mafia, and who is a decent citizen?*

He could see the intelligence in her face. She was regaining control now. He decided to push on. *A tricky area?*

"Because he was shot by someone else, this is a criminal matter. He will be in a special intensive care room by himself. When he recovers some, he will be moved to a private room. There will be a police guard by his door twenty-four hours a day, around the clock."

John immediately wished he had not used the word 'criminal', but it was out, and no one seemed to have noticed. Mrs. Ginnini was intent on his every word, nodding her head, hopefully comprehending all John said. Normally, he might have taken her hand in his, but he really didn't know her. *This might be taken the wrong way, here,* he thought.

With a serious smile, he looked directly into her eyes and said, "I will be available anytime if you or any of your immediate family have any questions. Here is my card with my phone numbers. Feel free to call me anytime. We will be working very hard to give your husband the very best care." He looked up at Billy, "What you call first class care 24/7." John looked back at Mrs. Ginnini, "You probably know that University Medical Center has an outstanding reputation. He's in the right place, and we're doing the right things for him." John paused to let her absorb it all. He was exhausted, but he knew that gaining the family's trust and respect was very important, particularly with this family. He looked over at Billy and then back at Mrs. Ginnini, "Do you have any questions? Is there anything else I can help you with right now?

"No, doctor", she answered quietly. Then a noticeable silence. She looked around at a few who sat near-by, then up at Billy, and finally back at John. Shaking her head ever so slightly, she added, "No Doctor. No questions. I hope you do good for my Angelo. He's a good person. I hope you do good care. I pray God. He guide your hands, Doctor." At that moment, she looked so trusting, so sweet, so hopeful, that John worried that the future might bring disappointment, complications, bad news. He really didn't want to do that to her. Right now, she was a sweet old lady, begging for help, and he certainly wanted to help her. Little did John know, right then, that there would be trouble. Lots of it. But not from her. He stood to go, and held out his hand to shake hers. She looked up, smiled, and slowly shook his hand.

Just as he straightened to go, Billy grabbed the lapel of his white lab coat, tugged it, and growled, "First class. Treat him first class. All da way. You don't want no trouble here, den it's first class. We have our man watchin' too. Just like da cops. Any trouble, anyt'ing not first class, gonna be your ass!" John was startled.

Mrs. Ginnini, looked up at Billy, "Now Billy, you don't have to talk like that to this nice doctor. He's doing a good job. He saved Angelo's life, so far."

Billy glared at John. "Yah, Mrs. Ginnini, he better do a good job. He better do first class. Not if he don't want no trouble."

"Now Billy. No rough stuff. Not here, Billy." John didn't

know what to say, so he forced a smile. He turned and grabbed Rick McIver's arm, not only to get them out of there, but for support on slightly wobbly knees. They hurried out.

Chapter 12 – Trauma M & M

Trauma Morbidity and Mortality Conference was scheduled every Wednesday at 7:00 a.m., where major complications were discussed thoroughly, without prejudice at this intense teaching session. The conference was neither a witch hunt nor a bunch of finger pointing accusations, but an honest, scientific inquiry into the complications and deaths occurring on the Trauma Service each week. All the surgical residents and senior medical students were present unless called away by an emergent situation, and many of the surgical attending staff came regularly, especially those involved with most of the trauma care, and certainly if one of their cases was being reviewed.

"The next case is of a 24-year old white male who crashed his motorcycle into the end of a guardrail on Route 25 last Sunday afternoon. He had been traveling at a high rate of speed. According to the history, the patient said he vaguely remembers straddling and sliding along the metal guardrail cable, until the next wooden post sticking up a few inches above the cable. Sliding on the cable produced a sawing motion into his perineal area, but the post essentially emasculated him, amputating his genitals. The car he had just passed, stopped and called 911. The EMTs started IVs and applied compression dressings. On arrival in the ER the patient's vitals were BP 65 over 20, pulse 195, respirations 28, labored."

Tim Strang, third year surgical resident droned on in a sleep-deprived monotone, despite the rather unusual history. He stated the details of the patient's resuscitation "and prompt transfer to the OR. Both general and urological surgeons worked to control the hemorrhage and repair the damage as best they could. No complications there."

"The post-op recovery was stable in both PACU and on transfer to the trauma floor." Strang explained, "The problem came early the second morning. The patient was found unresponsive on the routine 4 a.m. bed-check by the nurse. A Code was called. Blood pressure palpable at 50 over zip, pulse weak and thready, patient unresponsive. Full resuscitative measures were instituted, including IV lines additional to the central line still in place...."

"Emma Buckley, what's your working diagnosis at this point?" Dr. Thornton Brooks, senior attending surgeon called across the auditorium to the cluster of sleepy surgical residents who bolted upright in their seats. Emma Buckley turned in her seat toward Dr. Brooks.

"It's obviously shock, Dr. Brooks, sir." Emma answered without hesitation, "The etiology is unclear at this point. It's too early for septic shock. He's young for cardiac shock. It might be hemorrhagic shock but there's no mention, so far, of any massive blood loss since PACU. I need more information, sir."

"Good, Emma. Go ahead Tim." Dr. Brooks said.

"The resuscitation was unsuccessful and was called after 45 minutes of a flat EKG, pupils dilated and fixed, and no improvement in vital signs or mentation. Of interest, his labs drawn at the start of the resuscitation came back with severe acidosis with a pH of 6.89 and hemoglobin of 1.5 which was a drop from a hemoglobin that morning of 9.6. Also his platelets were only 16 thousand, down from 62 earlier. The plan had been to transfuse the patient the next morning with two units of packed cells and a unit of platelets. A post mortem exam was....."

"Hold it Tim. Just a second." Dr. Amy Salis, surgical attending on the trauma team interrupted the presentation. "Ted Powers, what would you guess the autopsy might show?" Ted was a sharp first year surgical resident, with a keen, inquisitive mind. Before going to med school, he had spent six years in a very profitable business firm that he had started. According to his wife Sandy, "He's always trying to piece things together. Cause and effect, ya know?'

"I'm guessing," Ted said, "that he bled out from somewhere, Dr. Salis. Most probably, what with the thrombocytopenia and pelvic trauma, something let go in the belly. He might also have had an intracerebral bleed. But that wouldn't account for the drop in hemoglobin. Not that far. Most likely an intra-abdominal bleed. But that's just a guess, ma'am."

"I'd have to agree with that, Ted. Thanks." Dr. Salis said. "Go ahead Tim."

Tim Strang continued. "I should have mentioned that during the resuscitation there was no sign of clotting anywhere. The arterial puncture sites never stopped. The autopsy results only added to the mystery of this case. There was no evidence of massive bleeding from anywhere. No blood collection in the abdomen. The only abnormality was in the pelvis, which is what was expected from the injury and the surgical repairs. No bleeding in the head. The myocardium and coronaries were all normal. No sign of acute injury other than the immediate pre-morbid changes. Same with the rest of the organs. The case was signed out as death due to cardiac arrest, with severe anemia, cause unknown."

There erupted a loud squabble of everyone talking at once, attending surgeons and residents alike. After about two minutes of the non-productive noise, Dr. Erik Cromwell, surgical chair, called for order. He turned on the mike at his seat down in the front of the auditorium, and leaning into the mike, while turning half way toward the physicians behind him, he reminded the staff, "This is the sixth unexplained, unexpected, sudden death on trauma in the past five weeks. They all were sudden, with severe anemia. All the codes were called in the early morning. This, to me, is more than just a coincidence. Something else is going on here, folks. We need to look into this and get on top of it." Again the general hubbub arose.

The next two cases were straight forward homicide deaths of young black males killed by young black males. The last case involved an eighty-eight-year old diabetic woman with severe atherosclerotic vascular disease in an automobile accident on the thruway. Crushed chest with irreversible shock. Also straightforward. No complications. Nothing to discuss. The conference adjourned.

Dr. Amy Salis bumped lightly into David Alan. She had been looking over at John Pullman and Erik Cromwell on the other side of the auditorium.

"Oh, David, I'm sorry. I was......", she said.

"I'm not sorry.....at all. Don't know when I've been body-checked by a nicer creature." David's smile was inviting. "By the way, how'd you make out with that nasty gall bladder?", he asked, checking out her flawless complexion.

"It was nasty alright. Darn thing was gangrenous. Lots of early adhesions. Hadn't ruptured, thankfully. The patient's gotten a lot better since we got it out of there", she said.

"Yeah, gangrene is not good, no matter where it is."

"I was looking over at your partner, there." Amy said, glancing over at John again. David followed her gaze. "How does he manage to get himself into so many difficult situations?"

"Situations? What do you mean?"

"He seems to get the worst, most complicated patients. I mean complicated socially, not surgically. Socially. He's a darn good surgeon, one of the best. I'm not talking about that. I mean those patients he's ends up with often seem to get him into the worst scrapes. Life-threatening at times. Like this Mafioso Don-what's-his-name-Ginny."

"Ginnini. Angelo Ginnini. You're right, a Mafia Don. John was in the box that night, on call for the ER, and Ginnini came in, unassigned. In trauma. No choice. Neither chose the other. But yes, you're right, he does get himself into some tough situations. Through no fault of his own. Just the luck of the draw. He's just a regular guy, certainly not a saint, but he has a strong moral sense of obligation to anyone under his care, no matter what the circumstances. Always has, and always will, whether he likes the patient or not, and believe me, there are plenty of patients he doesn't like. Just like you and me."

"Yes, you're right about that, but he certainly has an ability to get into and out of a lot of troubles."

"One thing I know, don't ever underestimate him.....on any level."

On the other side of the room, Erik Cromwell had tapped John Pullman on the shoulder as he was about to leave, "John, can you spare a few minutes. I'd like your thoughts about these deaths with the severe anemia."

"Yes, sure, Erik", John answered. "I'm free till 11:00. Gotta make rounds at some point, but you want to meet now?"

"If that's good with you? My office then? In twenty minutes.?"

"That's good. Give me time to see a couple of patients. Your office at nine it is." The two men parted, heads bowed, each obviously in thought.

Chapter 13 - Unexplained Blood Loss

At 8:57 a.m., John Pullman strode into the Office of the Chief of Surgery. Wendy Williams, Erik's receptionist and administrative assistant, jumped to her feet. "Hi Dr. Pullman", she chimed her cheery sing-song greeting. John Pullman was one of her favorite surgeons. And likewise, Wendy was one of John's favorite admin people. Her cute, smiling, mid-thirties face reflected her joy. "Good to see you, sir." *She's like Annie B, pleasant, interested, and helpful,* John thought, *A diametric opposite of many of those phone Nazis these days, assigned to guard the doctors from their patients' interference.*

"Wendy, you make my day, every time. You look ravishing, as usual. And how is your wonderful Reid and little Reid, Jr.? Tearing up the place?"

"They're both fine, thank you, sir. Dr. Cromwell is expecting you. Please go right in."

"Right on time as usual. Grab a seat," Erik Cromwell said, looking at his watch. "So what do you make of this series of deaths on trauma?"

"I think you're right when you grouped these six particular fatalities. All very similar. And all in the last month or so. This is more than a coincidence," John declared.

"I wanna keep our suspicions confidential. At least for the time being." Erik frowned, head bowed, worried eyes. "I'm sure it will get out sooner or later, but I think there is someone or something going on that shouldn't be."

"You mean like intentional harm being done? You don't mean murder, do you?" John paused. "Lord, I hope not." He bent forward, elbows on knees, hands clasped out front.

"No. Probably not murder, per se. Hopefully not intentional murder, anyway. What would be a motive? Is it possible someone is doing something that causes these deaths? Let's consider these patients' situations. There are a lot of similarities. All young." Erik was pacing, thinking his way through the mystery. "All had had severe trauma a few days before, but all had stabilized...... All showed severe anemia on the post-mortems. None with any signs of bleeding or blood collection anywhere..... All with acceptably low, but stable hemoglobins recorded within 12 to 16 hours before death. All coding shortly after 3:00 a.m., mid-week. Each of the nursing staff, on that floor....... each one has been accounted for, doing something else......during that time frame........before the codes were called. Each patient was discovered and the code called by a different nurse or nurses' aide. No signs of a struggle, at any time, in any case." He stopped pacing, paused, and looked at John, "I'm at my wit's end on this thing. What are your thoughts John?"

"Erik, I follow you on each of those points and I totally agree. This is more than a coincidence. I've been suspecting that something unusual is going on that ties these deaths together, somehow. But it is a real mystery. What outside help do we have on this? Does Ollie know? George Emmely, head of security, does he know? How about Broune Malcolm, our hospital lawyer?"

'Yeah. I've been thinking about all those." Erik repeated, pacing again, hands clasped behind him. "Didn't think of Broune Malcolm, though. Good idea. I'll stop in to see Ollie Alberts today, if he's not tied up. Yeah, a good idea,"

"Think a private investigator might help turn something up?", John asked. "Remember when we had all that cocaine business going around here and Sam Motley got us that investigative guy. That retired detective. He uncovered a lot of stuff and helped a lot with the final solutions. Might think about hiring him again? And George Emmely did some sleuthing in the Navy. I think he served in NCIS at the start of his career, at least until he made Admiral. Good experience there."

"Good suggestions. You're right. We certainly need to get both Ollie and George in on this. Anything else you can think of right now?" Another thought struck Erik. "The sudden anemia, found on the posts. Why? How? Blood loss, but where did the blood go? Blood doesn't just disappear."

John stood. "That's gotta be the key. We find the blood, or where it went, we'll have the answers." Silence. Then John said, "You just said 'no sign of a blood collection'. You meant inside the body, but what about collecting blood outside the body, or rather, the patient? There was this thing, when I was in India. They busted this rogue blood bank group. As I recall, some guys were giving street people the equivalent of fentanyl, and when they passed out, the thieves drew out a couple of liters of blood, which they sold on the black market, fentanyl and all. Of course the street person, the victim, never woke up. Dumped into the paupers' grave, unmarked. No investigation. Not till one of the sanitation guys, or whatever they call them over there, this guy noted that there were a lot of these dead bodies in his section of the city. Abnormal. He reported it, and they started doing autopsies. They cracked the ring. Big news, Big scandal. Couple of docs got nailed."

"Yah, but our patients weren't street people." Erik stopped pacing and looked up. "But that doesn't matter. They were victims."

The phone on Erik's desk interrupted them. Both men jumped. Erik, charged around his desk in four large strides, and wrenched the receiver from its cradle, "Cromwell here", he barked, then listened intently, shook his head, and slammed the receiver down. "Supposedly another wrong number, been getting a lot of them." But he was looking at John, who was looking at Erik's stunned expression and slightly opened mouth.

"The blood. Where were we? The victims. Lost blood. Black market." Erik mumbled, his eyebrows raised.

"Black market blood." John's head craned forward, eyes wide. "Erik, were in over our heads here. This is not our area of expertise." He stood up, instinctively looked at his watch, then looked at Erik. "I gotta go, but this might very well be criminal, Erik. You want me to call George Emmely? Get him on board? And you talk to Ollie and see if he wants to get that detective back here."

Chapter 14 – Phone Calls

"Hello, this is Dr. Anson", Erv answered on the second ring. *Damn*, he thought. *Midnight. I'm not on call.*

"You betta be takin' da best care of da Godfather." The voice was guttural.

"Who is this, please. Who's calling at this hour?"

"Da Godfather dies an' you gonna hear from us, an' you ain't gonna like it. An' that family of yers ain't gonna like it none eidder."

"Who is this calling." Erv's heart raced in his throat. A cold sweat broke out. The hand holding the phone trembled. He knew who this was. Fear contorted his ashen face. "Tell me who this is. I'll try to help you."

"First class care. Youse better do more den try, buster. He dies, youse dies, all-a youse". The phone went dead.

"Hello?..... Hello?" Erv's thumping heart finally began to quiet. No one had ever threatened him like this before. Not directly. *This is a death threat — an actual death threat. What should I do? Oh my god! I've had never had a death threat before.* He tried to lie back in bed again. The clock downstairs sounded loud when it rang 1:00, 1:30, 2:00.

At 12:03 a.m., Dr. John Pullman's phone pierced the night. "Dr. Pullman speaking."

"Da Godfather dies an' yer wife dies. Only she die slow, real slow." A guttural voice —sinister, ominous. "You be sure da Godfather, he gets first class care. He dies, you got a problem, doc-tor. A big problem."

"Who is this? Who are you calling?" Pullman rasped, fear suddenly closing his throat. He had a long history of late night phone calls for help. Often difficult. But nothing like this. Nothing. He jerked upright. "Who is this!"

"Like I said, da Godfather dies, you got problems. Lots of 'em." Click.

Four minutes later, in a suburb outside Wilmington, Delaware, a phone started ringing. It rang, and rang, and rang. Finally, a very sleepy Jake Pullman picked up the phone. "Hellooo?" he gargled. *Who could be calling at this hour?*

"You make-a sure yer fadder treat da Godfadder first class. Or else we gonna pay youse a call. Youse an' det purdy li'l wifey of yours. We make yer life very painful fer youse and yer whole fucking family. You hear me good. First class care. If he dies, you die wid him. Tell yer fadder I called."

"Who is this! What are you talking about? Who is this? Who...." Click. Jake slowly lowered the receiver, staring at it as if it could answer. A cold sweat broke out under his cotton pajamas, and his mouth suddenly felt lined with cotton. He was wide awake now. "Jeeziz," he murmured to himself.

Three hours later, Erv thought he had just gotten back to some semblance of sleep, when the phone rang again. He answered cautiously, "Dr. Anson."

"Dat girl of yours? She be just right. What's she eight? Ten? Just the age I like'em." Erv stood paralyzed with the phone pressed to his ear. He couldn't put it down. He couldn't move. He couldn't speak. "You hear me doctor! You hear me real good. Cuz, doctor, dat's what gonna happen if da Godfadder dies." Click.

Erv stood there, immobilized, for what seemed like forever. Finally, in a sweat, he slowly moved the phone from his ear, and stared at it as if he might see the caller. His mouth hung open. Leaning against the night table to steady himself, he turned and looked at the bed. Somehow he got there and sat down in the dark. Then the tears of terror came.

His wife rolled over. Sleepily her whisper slurred, "Who's 'at, honey? Hospiddal? Everyfing all right?" She sort of heard his deep moan. Thought it was a yes. She rolled over back to sleep. She had no idea what she would be answering the next morning.

Mary Anson was born Mary Clapp of a New England Episcopalian family. She was tall and stood straight. She had just finished cleaning up the kitchen after putting her six-year-old daughter on the school bus. Young Steve had left on the earlier bus. Heading for the bedroom to change into her yoga pants and shirt, she stopped when the phone rang. *Who the hell is calling the land line mid morning like this.* She was slightly annoyed. She picked the receiver with a brisk, "Hello!"

"Da Godfather dies an' youse dies. Only you die slow, real slow." A guttural voice. "First we staple yer lips closed togedder. Den we squeeze yer nose." She went rigid with a spasm, and dropped the phone. She tried to head for the chair before everything went black.

A few minutes later, Annie B was about to get in her car, drive to town, and open her husband's surgical office, which was in the center of the bedroom town, serving the city next door. A typical suburban town: friendly people glad to greet each other as they shopped in neighborhood stores.

She always said she worked for John Pullman, and, now, also for his partner David Allen. But John said the opposite was true. That they worked for her. "What do you call the person who sends the bills, pays the bills, collects the money, pays you your salary, and makes your schedule, telling you what to do?" John said with a smile. "You call that person the boss, right?"

Affable and upbeat, Annie B knew everyone's' names. She was an office superstar. The patients wanted to come to the office just to see Annie B, sometimes even more than to see the doctors.

The house phone rang just as she passed it. *Probably just a robo-sales call,* she thought, but she picked it up anyway.

"You wanna see yer husban' again? You better tell him to go first class wid da Godfadder. Da Godfadder dies, we beat da doctor till he dies. Den we come getchu." The deep voice was demonic.

"Who is this! Who do you think you're speaking to. You must have the wrong number." Annie B was startled. She was a tough lady who had heard her fill of rude, nasty phone calls, but this one got her attention.

"Da Godfadder dies, yer husband dies. Long and slow. Lotsa pain. You don wan lotsa pain fer him. You tell him, first class fer da Godfadder. He fuck wid da Godfadder, den we fuck wid him,

den we fuck wid you. Botha youse. You got dat, lady! You better
got dat. You tell dat husband of yers." Click.

Annie B rocked back on her heels. Took a step backwards,
holding the phone receiver at arm's length. "Good god!" she said to
the wall. "That must be the same people John said called last
night. Damn, threatening, Mafia creeps." She took a deep breath,
put the receiver back in its cradle, then picked it up again, and
punched in the pre-dial for John's cell. Nervously tapping the toes
of her right foot, she waited for his answer.

Chapter 15 - The Threatened Four

John and Annie B agreed with Erv and Mary to keep secret the horrible threats made to each of them. They had been warned, "Youse tells de cops an' youse pays de big price." Telling would only spread the fear and make matters more complicated. John and Annie B's kids also agreed to keep mum.

Nevertheless, police cars were stationed in front of both couples' houses. How the police knew, none of the "Threatened Four", as they called themselves, understood. They guessed it must be protocol. Maybe this kind of thing has happened before to others involved with Mafia? Maybe doctors treating Mafia members automatically got police protection?

"It really is a different culture", John's worried frown spoke for all of them as they tried to understand how to handle their predicament. Maybe the police were fully aware the mob would threaten any "outsider" they had to deal with. Mob culture really was a different world, just as John had worried.

John and Erv continued to treat Angelo with the very best care, complete with consults where the expertise of others exceeded their own. Not necessarily because of the threats, but because that's the way they were trained. That's how they treated all their patients. Having pledged the Hippocratic Oath upon graduation from Medical School, they took that vow seriously. It was part of their core. If anything, the threats made them more tired, more on edge, not as sharp as usual, although they were not aware of any decline. "Stay the course", they told themselves. "It'll have to end at some point, sometime, somehow."

The police had told Annie B the cars out front were "routine procedure, Ma'am". She wondered, they all wondered, *Were the police getting paid off? Was the precinct "on the take?"*

John broke the silence. "Can we trust the police? Our own, local police-force? We know a couple of them. Good guys?"

The threatening phone calls continued nights and days. "Doctor, dat daughter of yers, lives in Philly? We make her a junkie-whore, do a gang bang on her." And, "Brain Doctor, dat little kid of yers. Da six year old? We get maybe fifty grand fer her. Sell her to da child porn guys. Dey pay big bucks." On one call, Mary Anson became hysterical and actually told the gruff voice, "Go fuck yourself!" and slammed down the phone. Later, when she went out to meet her daughter's school bus that afternoon, she discovered that the tires on her Volvo had been slashed, and "never hang up on us!" spray-painted on the car trunk. "Oh my god!" she told Erv, calling him immediately. "They can get that close. Even with that police car out front. Do they control them too?" When he got home, she bawled in his arms, shoulders shaking with hysteria. Erv was close to tears, himself. *This has to stop!* But he didn't say it out loud. Worse, he didn't know how to make it stop.

Midnight phone calls. Like clockwork. Every night. At least one during the day, every day. Deep, guttural, threatening. Different voices each call. Every night and every day for almost a week now. John was exhausted. Annie B was exhausted. Both were beyond frightened, numbed by the recurring messages with the outrageous threats and foul language.

Their children, young adults, with lives of their own, five hours away, were also exhausted and terrified from similar messages.

"Dad, hi. It's me."

"Jake? That you? Everything okay down there? Phone calls still coming?"

"Dad, it's worse. Ellie hung up on them yesterday. This morning we found a dead chicken hanging from the rear-view mirror in Ellie's car, in the garage, with a note saying "don't never hang up on us again." Ellie's a mess. She finally stopped sobbing."

Day and night. Erv and Mary were near panic. "Gotta tell the police." Their kids were too young to be directly involved, but they knew something was wrong with Mommy and Daddy. And for what? For this underworld crime boss, lying comatose in University Medical Center. And this was despite that both John and Erv, and indeed, the entire medical staff had been working tirelessly to see to it that Angelo Ginnini got the very best care that he, or any other human, for that matter, could get. UMC was a level one medical center. A great reputation to uphold with state-of-the-art care, twenty-four-seven.

After stoically trying to bear up under these verbal beatings and threats, never mind the foul language and revolting graphic images, the 'threatened four' decided to do something about it.

Chapter 16 - Help?

They all watched the phone ring. "Da godfodder better be getting' first class care. Any funny business an' he dies, you got problems. Big problems. Ya wanna know what we do wid guys like you? One guy we take an' dump him inna manhole, wid live steam. Dey say four-hunnerd degrees in dere. He's screamin' fer a few minutes er so. Real loud first. Den gets quieter. Gotta hurt bad. Slow death. Probably takes fifteen minutes to do him. Just like steamin' a lobster. You ever steam a lobster? Da lobster dies quicker. You fuck wid da Godfadder, you steam like a lobster. You got all dat?"

"Hey! Whoever this is, we're taking very good care of your Godfather. We're doing the very best we can. He's getting the best that medical science has to offer. What you call first class.... all the way. You know that, don't you. You know we're pulling out all the stops for him. To get him better." John turned slightly to face the agent working the machine. The agent who was waving him for more...... *Keep it going..... Almost got it.....* John continued, "We're, uh, we're working day an......"

The guttural voice interrupted, "Steamed lobster." Click.

"Did you get it?" Erv asked.

The agent was shaking his head. "Almost. Another ten, fifteen seconds." He turned off the recorder. " They're using paid-usage phones. Pay cash at CVS. Use 'em once and chuck 'em inna dumpster. Tough to trace. No ownership. No records. Sorry guys."

"We never should have told you", Mary said burying into her husband's arms.

That night, in bed, John and Annie B lay quietly in each other's arms, legs entwined, as they usually had for most of the nights of their twenty six years together. Quiet, at peace, sensual only in the feeling of deep togetherness that they shared. Lips and cheeks but a few inches apart, they consoled each other in soft voices barely above a whisper, talking of their problems together and separately. Old thoughts. New thoughts. An impenetrable bond, forged of love, usually ending with a thanks to God for His blessed gift of love, uniting them as one. Nothing could come between them. Nothing could destroy their confidence in the oneness of their souls.

Most nights, the problems were few and of small importance. This past week had made their time of peace and quiet all the more significant. Together, they could face anything. Even these threats from a deeply troubled culture, with evil and distorted minds.

John softly said, "I don't understand them. They profess to their Catholic faith, yet live by a code of fear, hate, and death. They ignore the safety and power of Christian love. At least the Christian love we have been taught to believe."

Annie B's gentle voice was so soothing, so calming, "Not just Christian love, my sweet. Love professed by all the religions of the world, past and present, all there for you and me, and for anyone who wants to take the time to recognize love, practice love, and believe in it."

"Yes, that's where our strength lies."

They lay there not saying a word for a few minutes, each feeling the warm, soft presence of the other, relishing the deep sense of attachment. As they lay there together, each could feel the stresses and tensions of the day leave their minds and bodies. Pulses slowed, muscles relaxed, as they settled toward sleep.

"Good night, my beautiful girl."

"Sleep well, my wonderful boy."

They rolled slightly apart, and let sleep - calm, peaceful sleep - overtake them, knowing that the other one was there, always there.

Chapter 17 - Post-op

Angelo did pretty darn well recovering in his own, private ICU. Because of the criminal nature of Angelo's injury, a police guard was stationed 24/7 outside his door. A mafia guard stood watch as well. Because he was considered a dangerous man, a special room, separate from the main ICU, had been hurriedly outfitted, with extra monitors, and supplies. Special, well-trained, private-duty nurses and LPNs were going to be hired, around the clock. Strangely, however, that large Mafia guy, who seemed to be their spokesman, had stated "I arreddy hired all de nurses we gonna need." These women, five of them were swiftly vetted by the hospital's nursing department as competent nurses and LPNs. Not on the State Register, but competent.

After about three hours sleep, John Pullman returned to the hospital, passed the door guards, and came into Angelo's special ICU. He looked like hell — deep circles under both eyes, skin pasty white. Will Lain, fourth year surgical resident had never seen him look like this. He put down the chart by Angelo's bedside.

"How's he doing?" asked the senior surgical attending, trying to have a normal tone of voice with a smile.

"He's doing well, sir. He has developed diabetes, just like we discussed. His blood sugars went sky-high. Even before the endocrinology guys answered the stat consult. Not surprising. Most of his insulin-producing cells are wasted."

Across Angelo's bed, Ruthanne Mariman, fourth year medical student, also smiled as Dr. Pullman arrived. "Good morning Dr. Pullman" she said, equally glad to see him. *Egad, he looks bad*, she thought to herself

"And a good morning to you Ruthanne," he replied with a quick check of her name badge. "Is Will right? Are his blood sugars high?"

"Yessir. 250 this morning at six."

"And why is that?" he asked Ruthanne. In his usual fashion, he was trying to get the medical students to show what they knew. Most students were eager to display their newly acquired knowledge.

"As Dr. Lain says, most of his pancreas was destroyed by the bullet wound, sir."

"And what does that mean to the patient? How does the pancreas control the blood sugar?" Pullman asked with an encouraging smile.

"The pancreas has insulin-producing beta cells located in clusters in the Islets of Langerhans, which make up about four to five percent of the body of the pancreas, but the beta cells make almost all of the pancreatic endocrine output. It would seem, sir, that so much of his functioning pancreas was damaged that his insulin output is not adequate to do the job. At least not at present, sir." Ruthanne smiled with an air of confidence, knowing just what she was talking about.

"Great answer. Well done. You know your stuff. Good job." John replied. "And how does the insulin work? Do you know?"

"Sir, I believe it is secreted directly into the blood stream from the Islet of Langerhans. From the beta cells, as I said. When a cell needs glucose, which is also circulating in the blood stream, the insulin drives the glucose into the cell to be biochemically metabolized into carbon dioxide, water, and energy for the cell's mitochondria, and then to be used in protein synthesis, for cell building and repair."

Will busied himself with the chart, pretending not to notice the discourse going on, but listening to every word the med student said. *Atta-girl,* he thought.

"Terrific." John said. "Don't ever forget your basic sciences. Good for you. So how are we handling the patient's blood glucose overload?"

"Right now, sir, we have an insulin drip running in one of his IVs. We're monitoring his blood sugars, and adjusting as needed. Ideally, we'd like to keep his blood sugars below 150."

"And what happens if we give him too much insulin?" Pullman was delighted by this bright, young student's knowledge — delighted despite his ragged exhaustion. But that's the way he was, that was John.

"His blood sugar might go too low, sir. He might develop hypoglycemia, with too much insulin, which can be quite dangerous. It can lead to dizziness, weakness, tremors, then convulsions, and coma. It is a medical emergency, and if untreated, can lead to death."

"Not a good thing." He said.

"No sir. Not a good thing."

Turning to Will Lain, John Pullman asked, "Cardio-pulmonary okay?" The patient was still on the respirator, still intubated with air being pumped through the endotracheal tube into the trachea and bronchi, the pulmonary airways. The EKG on the monitor showed regular sinus rhythm. "Fluid balance okay? Not third spacing? Anything coming out of the pancreatic drains?" John Pullman knew all was in order. The Intensivist, the physician hired by the hospital to handled the minutia of the inpatients' medical management, had been on top of things, and would continue to be so. John's questions were academic, he knew, but having the residents show their stuff, he considered part of their reward for hard work and dedication.

Will replied, "Sir, the cardio-pulmonary is stable, with stable vitals. We're watching for fluid overload. No third spacing, and 30ccs out the drain tubes, total. Considering what he's been through, he's remarkably stable. He's still comatose with no sedation, and no narcotics for pain. At least not needed yet, sir."

John pulled out his stethoscope and listened to the patient's breath sounds on each side, his heart sounds, and the silence of his abdomen. Active bowel sounds would not be heard for several more days, if everything went well. He was thankfully pleased so far. "Any family been in so far?" he asked Will.

"No sir. Not that we know of. There are two men standing some kind of guard outside the ICU door. One a city cop, and the other some sort of a tough guy. Looks like he's right out of the movies. A caricature. I've seen cops standing guard before in association with a crime or some-such, but a Mafia henchman? That's a new one on me. Not giving us any trouble though. He just keeps telling us to treat the Godfather first class. Mr. Ginnini is supposed to be some sort of a crime boss or something, I hear."

John noticed that the hired outside nurse was paying very close attention to the conversation.

"That's right, Will. He is the alleged boss of the Ginnini crime family here in the city. Apparently it's all over the media, so I'm told by the powers that be. The hospital admin has some special arrangement with the man or men standing guard opposite the police outside the patient's room. The hospital says they can stay there, as long as there's no trouble. No guns. No interference with patient care." John had been briefed by his old friend Olsen Alberts, the hospital CEO, on his way into the hospital that morning, after the few brief hours at home. His morning office hours had been cancelled by Annie B.

Chapter 18 - Private Room

Over the next week, Angelo's progress was quite remarkable, considering the extent of his injuries and the surgical repairs necessary. He was extubated of the endotracheal breathing tube on the third post-op day, so he could breathe on his own. That made it a little difficult for the respiratory therapists, because he was still comatose and unable to follow their instructions. Or anybody's instructions for that matter. The hired nurses routinely turned him, right-side, then supine, left-side, and back again every two hours. That, plus the random-inflating air-mattress and the corpulent shape of Angelo's body, kept any decubitus pressure points or bed sores from developing.

By post-op day four he was ready to be moved from his private ICU room to a private regular room on the Surgical Trauma floor. This decision required a rather unusual conference involving Olsen Alberts; Broune Malcolm, the hospital lawyer; Dr. Erik Cromwell, the chief of Surgery; Al Towns, the head nurse of the trauma floor; both Drs. John Pullman and Erv Anson, and three men in immaculate dark suits, demanded by the Family.

"Where's he goin'? Is da care first class? Good as 'tensive care?" asked one of the Family dark suits.

"We gonna get inta see him dere?" asked another.

"We gonna keep a man at da door!" demanded the third.

"Yes, first class care. Yes, a better environment for the patient. Yes, more rest. No twenty-four hour lights. Less infection threat. Yes, private duty nurses. Yes, that will cost extra. Yes, the doctors are going to stay on the case to the end. No, there is no increased risk in moving him to a better setting. In fact, his risk is lowered." In the end, the three from the Family seemed somewhat satisfied, but still very guarded and rather belligerent.

"You gotta know, any trouble wid da Godfadder, an' there be trouble..... fer all-a-youse", Billy, the largest of the men, and the apparent second in command, looked directly at John Pullman and then at Erv Anson. Back and forth. It was clear whom he meant to threaten. John recognized this guy from before, when he first met with Mrs. Ginnini.

The city police guard, in his pressed and clean uniform, maintained one side of the new doorway on the trauma floor. The soldier from the mob, in his tee shirt and suspenders, kept watch on the other side. Both guardians sported rather voluminous pot-bellies. The policeman was the only one armed. The thug's shoulder holster was empty. Much as they tried to ignore each other, the boredom led to rather friendly chit-chat, particularly at night, when things were quiet and no one else was around. One pair of these rotating guardians actually realized they had come from adjoining neighborhoods and very similar backgrounds. Similar, until junior high school, when their life-paths started to diverge. Now they both were involved in monitoring and manipulating human behavior, but with very different methods.

Chapter 19 – Progress

The Foley catheter draining the urine was left in the unconscious patient. On post-op day six, Angelo passed some flatus. Later that day he was incontinent of a small amount of stool, which his private duty evening nurse promptly cleaned up, with the help of one of the LPNs working in the room. There was another LPN on the other twelve-hour shift. Both LPNs were new to the hospital, as was this RN and the two other RNs working the other two eight-hour shifts. No one knew who they were, nor where they had come from, all five of them. They were quiet, but unusually possessive of the patient.

HR had instructed the Head of Nursing, Penny Field, that "these five are to work specifically and only with Mr. Ginnini." HR wouldn't say much about their hiring or placement. This was a little unusual, because the Surgical Trauma floor, run by Al Towns, already had its full compliment of trained staff, both RNs, LPNs, ward clerks, and janitorial, all shifts. The strangers didn't come from the temporary help company that the hospital usually used. No resumes. No one could or would state where they came from? All five were assigned by HR specifically to the Godfather's room, only. In addition, they were the only five nursing personnel allowed in the Godfather's room. Very unusual. HR never micro-managed nursing assignments. That was Penny's job. Hers alone. Strange? The Godfather's room was the last one on the right. The room across the hall and the room next to his were unaccountably vacant. Stranger still, because the hospital was so full. Beds were in demand.

By day eight, Angelo was regularly passing gas and semi-formed stools. He had active bowel sounds, and very little had come out of the two remaining tubes draining his pancreatic bed. He remained afebrile. His O2 sats (oxygen saturation in the blood) were normal. His lungs clear, bilaterally. Good heart sounds in normal sinus rhythm, with a normal blood pressure. No signs of phlebitis. Hemoglobin, white blood count, and differential were normal. These were all very good signs of his recovery — at least of his thoraco-abdominal area, i.e. his cardio-respiratory , GI, and kidney functions. The ileo-pancreatic anastomosis had most probably sealed, and was functioning as intended, as were the rest of the anastomoses and intestinal systems. Aside from the coma, the only abnormality remaining was the diabetes, which he did not, according to his special nurses, have prior to his shooting. But the diabetes was being well controlled by the IV insulin pump and monitored blood sugars.

Thank goodness! thought John Pullman as he made rounds that morning. The thug at the door still had glowered at him as if he were an arch enemy. But inside the patient's room, it was all good news. The nasogastric tube that had been passed through Angelo's nose, down his esophagus, into his stomach by the anesthesia team that first night in the OR (to empty the stomach's secretions and keep it empty), was taken off the intermittent suction, and small amounts of water were instilled. The tube was placed back on suction every few hours to check that fluid was not building up in the stomach. But nothing much was returned, indicating that Angelo's GI system was starting to function again and was handling the water doses adequately. Therefore, a slow drip of fluids was started, which he tolerated well, too. His diet was advanced to a commercially prepared liquid specifically for diabetics, and his IV fluids were slowed to a few drops a minute to keep the one line that remained. Normally, this advance to a GI-based nutrition would have been done sooner, but with the coma, the patient couldn't tell his physicians of any adverse symptoms, therefore caution was indicated.

All was satisfactory but for Angelo's comatose state. The EEGs, the electro-encephalograms, that Erv and the neurophysiology consult had ordered, continued to show some low voltage activity. Not brain dead, but not normal activity either. Not bad news, but not good news either. A repeat CT scan showed "No change, with mild contusions posteriorly and anteriorly, presumably from the old bullet wound to the posterior skull". In short, he was fine, but he just didn't wake up, and there was nothing anybody could do about it.

Chapter 20 - Two Broken Arms

"Sorry to bother you like this doc."

"No problem. Do we know each other? I'm sorry I don't remember your name." John Pullman replied to the huge black man standing not two feet in front of him.

"No, sir. You don't know me. But you be the mob doctor, don't you? I am Larry Lowance. I'm hopin' you could help me with a little problem?" He had to be at least six-five or six, and two-fifty, easily. Muscular, in his clean, stretched-tight tee shirt. A large, black version of a smiling Mr. Clean, bending slightly down to John's six-two, smiling. Trying to be as non-threatening as possible, he kept his hands behind him, and smiled, obviously smiling to please. But in pain. Pain somewhere.

"I'm not the mob doctor. Larry, is it? Is there something I can help you with?" John, perplexed by the introduction. Not worried. Just curious. *Who is this big man?*

Suddenly Larry straightened up and brought his arms forward, startling John. As a trauma surgeon, he was used to encountering strange sights, but this surprised him. Both of Larry's forearms were obviously swollen and fractured with some degree of dorsal angulation. John's first thoughts, *Fresh fractures. No splints. No support. Must hurt. Hurt like hell. But here is this apparent gentle giant, quietly smiling, asking for help by the mob doctor?*

"Oh? I'm sorry. I heard you was the mob doctor. It was the mob who done this." He said, presenting his distorted arms to John. "I was hopin' you could help me with these. See, it was the mob guys who broke 'em." The smile persisted.

"Okay," John said, putting a gentle hand on Larry's left elbow to lead him, "Let's get you in the system here. Can you walk okay?"

"Yah, doc. I got no problem wit my legs. Just my arms."

John led him down the hall to the intake clerk, seated at her desk, "Gracie, this is Larry Lowance," he said half turning to Larry, "Lowance? Is that right? L-O-W-A-N-C-E?" Gracie was staring up at Larry's deformed forearms.

Larry looked straight at Gracie, "Yeh. That be right. Larry Lowance, like the doctor said."

"Uh, Mr. Lowance," she asked, "do you have an address and phone number? I'll need to see a picture ID. Driver's license?" She immediately regained her professional composure, and started typing into the computer, then paused, and looked up with an expectant but somewhat forced smile.

"Yassum" he replied, frowning. "I got all that. Just can't get 'em." Silence. No one moving. Gracie staring at her screen. Larry staring at Gracie. John staring at Larry. Gracie broke the impasse by silently looking up, questioning, expecting.

Larry looked sheepish, "Can't git in my pockets. Hands don't work." He looked from one to the other of his distorted forearms.

"Here let me help you, Larry, can I get them for you?" John asked. "Where are they? Do you mind?"

"Yah, doc. I 'preciate that. They be in my billfold, in my rear pocket. You get'em?" Larry half turned his back toward John. "Just dig 'em out. I show you where."

John easily slid the well-worn, black leather wallet out, laid it on the counter and looked up at Larry. "Get out the driver's license." Larry said to John. To Gracie he asked, "This do?" as John reached over the counter and placed the laminated card down on the desk top.

The registration completed, Gracie reached up and very carefully placed the ID band on the big man's wrist, well beyond his fracture sites, and said, "Don't know how long that'll stay there, but it's okay for now."

A hospital security man brought up a wheelchair. Larry slowly backed into it, plopping his big frame the last six inches with a deep, painful grunt. The security man, about to push the wheelchair, asked, "He going to X-ray?"

"Yes. He needs films of these fractures," John replied. "I can take him there. I'm headed that way anyway." John was actually going the other direction, but this is what John did. Plus he was curious, more than curious. *How could this unusual pair of fractures have happened.* He carefully wheeled Larry back to the X-ray room, wondering — *How can this big man remain so peaceful and pleasant while in undeniable pain. Unsplinted fractures. Ouch!*

"When did this happen. And how did it happen, Larry." John inquired. "You're going to need an Orthopedist." Not a good time for talk as they went back down the hall.

"Gottem both on both sides." tech Lynne Nordon reported, chewing a huge wad of Juicy Fruit, as she flicked on the screen, and brought up the images.

"Jeez! That's me?" Larry could see the abnormality of the angled bones. Both bones, both sides. Right. Left.

"'Fraid so." John was stating the obvious, as he started pushing the wheelchair across the hall. "Let's go over to the orthopedics room. Thanks Lynne," then back to Larry, "You okay? You feel weak? Dizzy?" He was trying to make contact, get some history. "We'll call the orthopedist on call. That okay with you? Or do you have a choice? Here, can you sit up on the gurney?" The big man didn't have to hop or jump to ease up onto the gurney. "Want to lie down?"

"No. I'm better sittin' up. Thanks, doc. I thought you're the mob doc." Larry cradled each arm with the other, in his lap as he hunched over to relax a little, looking at John.

"No" said John, "I have my own private practice with a partner. We both work for the hospital. I don't......we don't work for the mob. But what do you mean by the mob? The Mafia?"

"Yah. The mob. The Mafia, I guess it is. I heard that you takin' care of the mob boss who go shot. That you the go-to doctor."

"Well, yes. I'm the one who operated on Angelo Ginnini. That's true. But I certainly don't work for them. Why? Did you want one of their doctors? Do they have any special doctors they use?" John was a little alarmed with this tie-in to the Mafia by an unknown from the outside, but he said nothing.

"No, doc." Larry looked straight at John, "They be the ones who done this to me."

"Did what? Broke your arms?" John was jolted, thinking of the past week with Angelo's people. The phone calls - sudden shiver. *Get control. This guy's not threatening.*

"Yah, doc. They done it. Got me this mornin' as I was comin' to work. Got me right outside my apartment. Four of 'em. The two I whacked and two more. Three with guns. Other guy's the boss, givin' orders. Pull me into the alley next door. Kicked my feet out, an' whacked both arms with a iron club. Like a baseball bat. Took several whacks 'fore they broke 'em. They seen they was broke, an' took off."

"Ouch! That's painful." John was heading for the wall phone when Molly Jakes, the ortho nurse, came into the room. Fiddling with her key-ring, she wasn't really paying attention to the two men, but when she looked up and was about to say hello to John Pullman, she spotted the two misshapen forearms.

"Oh my goodness. What have we here? Oh, ow. That must hurt. Whoa. Let me help you." She approached the gurney.

"I be okay." Larry stiffened slightly, hoping to avoid any unnecessary motion.

"Morning, Molly. Who's the ortho guy on today?" John asked the nurse.

"Uh, morning sir." She checked the wall list. 'That's......let's see. Dr. Bayard? Yah, says here, it's Dr. William Bayard", she said.

Chapter 21 - William Bayard, III, MD

William Bayard, III, MD, came from an old family in
Washington, DC. Bill, a Yale classmate and friend of both John
Pullman and Al Towns, wore Yale belts, Yale ties, Yale golf shirts,
even Yale sox - but not all at the same time. Known, locally, as
"Mr. Yale" and generating a lot of teasing by good friends, he
faithfully went to as many of the home football games as his
schedule would allow. More importantly, he was a first rate
orthopedist, who stayed up on the latest scientific literature, and
was very caring for his patients. Like John, he was a people
person. Patients all loved him.

"Molly, can you page Dr. Bayard? Larry, here's gonna need
him." John asked the nurse.

"May I page his PA? That's Shorty Buck," Molly said. "He can
get Mr. Larry, here, going, so he'll be ready for Dr. Bayard."

"Good. That'll be fine." John answered and turned to the
patient, "So they whacked you with a billy? Why did they do that?
Do you work for them?"

"Lord-a-mighty, no." Larry shifted his gaze from Molly to
John. "Two of 'em didn't like what I done to them. But I was just
doin' my job, see? Carryin' out orders."

"I don't think I understand, Larry. Explain it to me. I'll get
you hooked up with the right doctors, but I need to know why all
this came about. Can you tell me? Or is it some secret? And why
did you think I was part of the Mafia? I'm in the dark, here. Help
me out." John's arched eyebrows and squinty eyes reflected his
serious concern.

"Okay, doc. I'll tell ya. I got nothin' to hide. Ya see, I works at
the 27th Street Art Theater. That's what they call it. It's a peep-
show joint. Ya know, where ya pay ten bucks for twenty minutes
watchin' this naked chick dance. You watch thru a three inch hole
in the wall. Yer in yer-own booth, like a bathroom stall, door
closed and all. The chicks are mostly hookers who dance naked for
extra cash during the days. The clients do whatever they wanna do
there. Ya know. By themselves. There in their stall. Most of 'em in
there beatin' off, masturbatin' is yer medical term, I guess. They

s'posed to come out after twenty minutes. Time's up. They don't come, it be my job to rap my Billy on the door, and tell 'em time's up. I give 'em a couple minutes, and rap an' tell 'em again. Third time I gotta get down on hands and knees and tap 'em with my stick on the legs and ankles, under the partition wall there. That mostly gets their attention, so they come out."

For a moment Larry halted his story as he bit down on his lower lip, trying to suppress his pain. Larry continued. "Two guys don't come out last week. Three, four warnings. I s'posed to give only two, but these are big guys, and I don't want no trouble, so I give 'em extras. They don't come out, so I hadda whack 'em. Both of 'em. They come out. They don't like it none, saying I gonna pay fer that. That they gonna get me, cuz no one messes with them guys, an' all this tough talk. They be two of the four who got me this mornin'. Dirty jerks. Couldn't do it by theirselves. Hadda get two more, an' hadda use guns. Couldn't take me one on one, or even two on one. You gonna fight, least you fight fair. Not them though. Chicken. Both of 'em. Mafia goons." Larry was getting as agitated as he ever got, but, then he paused, relaxing a little, and looked straight at John, as though Molly wasn't even in the room.

"Yah. Then they pull me roun' the corner inta the alley, like I said. Guns. Three guns. I ain't gonna fight three guns. They put long-chain cuffs on my feet and one on each arm. One stands on the foot chain. The other two push me down cuz, I can't move my feet. They pull out the arm cuffs, an' the boss guy puts his foot on my neck. Then the arm guy pulls the cuff chain an' the other guy picks up the bat an' starts smashin' my arm. Then they switch sides. You could tell, they done this before, cuz they got it all worked out. The boss guy takes his foot off my neck so I can breathe, looks at the arms be broke, an' they take their cuffs, an' all walk away like nothin'.

John cupping his chin between his thumb and index finger, and Molly, her hand loosely over her mouth, were speechless. John broke the silence, "Wow. Some story. But what's the Mafia connection, and why connect with me?"

"Well, these guys was Mafia. Hoods from the Ginnini gang. An' I heard, when the Don got hit, you was the doc, so I figured you was a good one. Don't make no fuss. Don't bring in the cops er nuttin'. So I pick you. 'Cept, now you say you getting' a different doc? Why that be?"

"Larry, that's because I want to get you a specialist who fixes broken arms all the time. I used to fix broken arms many years ago, but now I defer to the guys specially trained in it, and who do it every day. I don't do fractures any more. Haven't set a fracture in years. In addition, yours will probably need to be opened and plated, both sides. Also, you're going to need special care adjusting and caring for the daily activities of life, what with both arms post-op and pretty much out of action for the next month or two. They have people up there on the orthopedic floor who can help you with that stuff. You have enough troubles, Larry, without me trying to make a mess of things for you. You're gonna be just fine. I promise I'll see to it. Is that a deal?" Larry eyed Dr. Pullman, a little doubt giving way to trust. "You have my word on it. I know Dr. Bayard. He's a good man, a square shooter. You'll get along fine with him."

"Yah, okay. I guess you know best. I take your word on it, doc. Take your word on it."

Just then a tall, lanky, young man confidently strode through the door, heading straight for the patient. "Hi. I'm Shorty Buck, the orthopedic PA." he said, extending his right hand for an introductory handshake. Seeing that both arms of the patient were obviously fractured, he quickly pulled back. Then he saw John Pullman. "Oh, hi, Dr. Pullman. Didn't see you here."

"Shorty, this is Larry. Mr. Larry Lowance. His films tell it all." To Larry he declared, "Larry I leave you in good hands. Shorty here will get you admitted. I'm pretty sure Dr. Bayard will need to operate on your arms tomorrow. You will like him. He's an old, trusted friend and a great guy. He's been around here for years. You're gonna do great. And I'll stop in on you every now and then. See how you're doing. Shorty, you're not gonna believe his story. Make sure you tell him, Larry. He needs to know."

Just then John Pullman stepped away to answer his chirping cell phone. When he hung up, he saw Shorty was already listening to Larry's breath sounds with his stethoscope. "I gotta go," he said. "Good luck Larry. I'll see you soon. Promise."

Chapter 22 – The Systems Awaken

Luckily for John and Annie B Pullman, for their children, and for Erv Anson and his family, Angelo's post-op course had gone surprisingly smoothly. Angelo's gut had started up, resolving the ileus that had temporarily paralyzed the bowel's peristalsis after the intestinal surgery. His gut was getting ready to receive food. This was good news. The primary worry had been that the remaining pancreas might leak inside the abdomen. But so far no signs of infection or leak. The patient had been started on special diabetic tube-feeding diet to deliver the balanced liquid nutrition so necessary for healing.

The still comatose, Angelo couldn't tell his caregivers of any abdominal pain. He couldn't tell them anything — almost veterinary medicine. But the team had dealt with situations like this before, and took them all in stride.

But there was an undercurrent of Mafia anxiety casting a pall over the entire hospital. Rumors of threats —death threats and other nasty calls to some surgeons. No one knew any facts — just rumors, so far. But those rumors kept everyone — doctors, nurses, ward clerks, pharmacy, even housekeeping on edge. All things concerning Angelo Ginnini, Mafia Godfather and crime boss , kept everyone ill-at-ease — everyone, except for the three RNs and the two LPNs, specially assigned to his room. They seemed totally unruffled about the fact that the patient was the Godfather, the Mafia family head man. None of the staff's undercurrent conversation seemed to bother them. Strange women, but good, professional nurses.

That he was the Godfather was pretty well established, not only by his name, by the rumor-mill, by the news media, but particularly by the statements from the series of goons, as they were known, stationed forever outside Angelo's room.

Healing of all of Angelo's systems progressed well. All, that is, except his brain. It was still shut down. Comatose. Neuropsychiatrist Dr. Mal Salteese had been asked to consult, and he reported that there was some early evidence of "lightening of the depth of the coma," a result determined from subtle neurologic tests he performed daily. That was good news to everyone. Good news to the surgical intensivists, to pharmacy in the basement, to the hospital administration, to the police who hoped to eventually question Angelo. It was especially good news to John and Annie B and to Erv and his wife. The nightly calls to the threatened four were definitely less intense. "Treatment's first class, but youse better keep it up!" To the Pullman kids in Delaware, they had stopped altogether.

A conference was held daily in the Hospital Board Room next to Olsen Albert's office. The same hospital people who had agreed that Angelo could be treated intensively in a private room on the trauma floor discussed Angelo's progress. But the three Mafioso had changed. They now consisted of the apparent leader who called himself Sal. Next to Sal was an immaculately-dressed Italian, introduced as John. The third was the guy they knew as Billy. Some days they seemed a little pleased by the improvements. Other days they tended to doubt what they were told, and repeated their ugly threats. And so went the roller-coaster. Day after day.

However, it was becoming more and more apparent to Sal and his two compadres, that Angelo was, indeed, improving on all fronts, with the exception of his cerebral concussion.

John Pullman summed up all the specialists views, "There is nothing anybody can do about the brain, except wait. No doctor. No specialist. No world's top neurosurgeon. Nobody can reverse the coma. The brain has to heal itself. Only time will tell." Mal Salteese verbally agreed.

It was reiterated that the damage was from the bullet wounds, and not by any fault of his care. The Family trio were shown pages from Angelo's medical chart. Slowly, only slowly, these Family reps began to believe in the quality of the Godfather's care. It was cautiously pointed out that, eventually, Angelo would have to be transferred to a chronic-care nursing home for his comatose care if he didn't wake up. But that would only be after he was as healed as he could be. After all his medical regimens were predictably established. Dr. Mal Salteese told Sal, John, and Billy, "the statistics show that in his comatose state, Angelo would probably eventually succumb to a complication such as pneumonia. So keep that in mind for the future, and don't blame the doctors. But he may well wake up at any time."

Chapter 23 – Coming Around?

The first overt neurologic signs that Angelo showed were twitches, called tics, of his facial muscles. That was on post-op day thirteen. Then he began to move his head, a little at first. That morning on rounds, the doctors on rounds noticed that Angelo had crossed his feet, left over right, and his lips were beginning to move. Was he trying to speak? Babble was more like it. Was he "coming out of it?" Did he have significant brain damage? Cognitive damage?

"Is he ever gonna be able to think good again?" Sal wanted to know. "Could he think like the original Godfadder?"

"No. No. No. No!" were Angelo's first intelligible words. He sounded threatened, frightened. The night shift nurse whispered this to the goon outside the door, but the policeman heard it. He told his duty officer, who told his Captain, who called Ollie Alberts, who paged John Pullman. So the word got out.

But by the next day, Angelo's speech became obvious to anyone connected to the case. Angelo moaned, cried out with slurred, nonsense phrases — something like, "No, Gah-wy", or "You gotta hep", or, "We gotta see a film. We needa info". And, strangest of all, "the plane gotta be orange." Angelo's babble was written down, analyzed, transcribed into understandable English, and shared at the morning conferences in the Board room.

Sal was troubled that some secret Family information might be disclosed, so he read Angelo's utterances first. But he couldn't make any more of the gibberish than anyone else, so it all was openly discussed. It was clear to all, however, that Angelo was probably waking up. Dr. Mal Salteese, the neuropsychiatrist, verified the signs. Sal admitted they wanted all the help they could get, so his aggressive, threatening attitude seemed to soften ever so slightly. Or so it seemed to the hospital-based conferees.

At the conference the next day, Ollie Alberts asked Broune Malcolm, the hospital lawyer, to have some research done by his firm's office staff. Browny, as he was familiarly known, was a young hot-shot, youngest full-partner in his firm, and a big problem solver for hospital legal issues.

"On the clock?" Browny asked.

"Yes, on the clock," Ollie replied.

The day after, Browny reported back to the hospital conference. "Angelo Ginnini had at one point been drafted into the Viet-Nam conflict. The draft board only knew him as a number. They knew no more than they did about Elvis Presley or Cassius Clay or anyone else. At first, Angelo fought it," Browny continued, "and I'm reading between the lines here, it would appear that his family boss had told him something like - 'Don't make a stink. Go in. Learn everything you can learn. Who's who. Where's the power lie? Who are the go-to guys. Find out who's on the take. Contacts and contracts. You gonna be our inside guy there. For the Family. Keep a low profile, and when you get out, you got a job with the Family.' Angelo agreed. He had no choice."

Browny explained that after Angelo had willingly joined the Army, he volunteered for Army Intelligence. The attorney made a smiling effort to point out the irony of that situation, which was not appreciated by Sal and his boys. But, according to the information the law firm had found, Angelo had had something to do with the CIA and the U-2 high altitude surveillance program during the Cold War of the 1960s.

"According to information," Browny continued, "previously classified, now open to the Freedom of Information Act, the U-2 high altitude surveillance planes had all been painted black to be less visible both to the naked eye and to radar. They took off from Scandinavia, flew to very high altitude, shut off the engine, and glided over the Soviet territories they needed to photograph. Once back over friendly territory, they restarted the jet engines, and landed the plane in Turkey. That was fine, except the Turks didn't like the black color of the planes. Some ethnic problem our side didn't understand."

Some around the conference table began to get restless. Billy looked out the window. "Stay with me on this." Browny requested, "It's complicated, but you'll see the point when I'm done. All this happened just about the time that Gary Powers was exchanged by the Soviets for some of their US-held spies. Research by a CIA operative named Morton Dana determined that the planes could be coated with a yellow or orange substance developed by a science research lab of one of the Fortune 500 bigs. That coating turned to black in colder temperatures."

"Aha!" Ollie Alberts interjected, "Perhaps that would tie in with words like 'film', 'info', 'help', and 'the plane gotta be orange'?" No one was certain. But no one could do anything about it in any case.

Browny said, "That's all I've go so far, but I can dig for more, if you want. Let me know what you want."

Sal was quiet, but he was thinking *All this 'psycho-babble' certainly don't seem related to any business the Family's dealin' wid. But what's all this mean? Maybe the Family needs to work better wid dese hospital people? Maybe I should call a Council meeting tonight, and bring it up.*

Chapter 24 – Whaddaya Need?

John Pullman was about to leave today's Board Room conference. A busy office awaited him, so he was hurrying, but stopped for a quick word with Erv Anson on the way out. Suddenly Sal came up from behind, and grabbed both men's upper arms with a painfully tight grip. In a voice resembling a rusty pipe, he quietly asked, "Could I see youse two gentlemen fer just a minute or two?"

Both men tried to turn to look back at the voice, but the vice-like grip prevented it, allowing only their heads to turn. A sudden scare shot through each surgeon upon the realization of the requester.

"Uh, yeah, I guess so." Was all John Pullman could get out of his tongue-tied mouth. Erv just nodded with a quiet "uh-huh" grunt. The trio stopped in their tracks, and stood, zombie-like while the rest of the room emptied.

As he was leaving, Ollie Alberts looked back over his shoulder. He could see the fear in John's and Erv's faces and the grim determination in Sal's eyes. "You guys coming? You all right? You need something?"

"Nah. They're okay, Mr. Alberts. Everything's cool, but thanks," the big rusty pipe grated. Ollie looked at the two surgeons, who returned his gaze with the mute inaction of fear. So Ollie continued on his way.

With the room empty but for the three, Sal released his grip, and walked over to quietly close the door. Was everything about him sinister - his hovering, forward slouch, his little pig-eyes, his attitude? John and Erv shared a single thought, *What now? It can't be good.*

"Gentlemen. What can I getchu?" Sal tried to soften his voice to a rasping whisper.

Silence. Stupified silence from the two dumb-struck surgeons.

"Whadda ya need? What can I getcha? Anything. Getcha anything. Anything youse needs."

Silence. Erv jerked back ever so slightly, mouth open,

clueless. John shook a tiny nod of his head, blinked repetitively, and focused on keeping cool, despite his furrowed brow and puzzled mind.

Sal saw he wasn't getting through, so he repeated himself, "I wanna gettcha something. Anything. Just tell me whatchu need. Me an' Billy can get it fer youse. Name it. Anything."

Again, silence. John's mind was racing. *What more does this guy want from us? Jeeziz!* He was about to ask Sal what he meant, but Erv, blurted out, "What do you mean? What are you talking about?"

John, cued in, "Yah, Sal. I'm not clear what you want. We've done everything you wanted. We've given Mr. Ginnini everything we've got. Like you say, first class. We've done our very best. And you know that! What more do you want from us, man? There is no more!"

"I don't want no more from youse. I wanna give......" He was interrupted by Erv.

"There is no more!" He was now clearly annoyed, despite the possible consequences. "You got it all. We worked our butts off. We save your guy from certain death. He's getting better. All the time, you and your lousy thugs threaten us. Call us all hours of the night. Call our wives and kids, terrifying us. Threatening us with unmentionable horrors beyond any civil imagination, and now you want more? Mister, you got a lot of balls. You go ahead and do what you want, but I'm done with you and your goddamn thugs. That's it mister........ mister...... mister Sal, whoever you are!" Erv was now red in the face. The veins stood out on his muscular neck. His eyes bulged. Now he was the one looking fierce.

Sal jolted back a step from this outburst, his eyes incredibly wide. Suddenly a big smile, a genuine, pleasant smile, wrinkled his whole face. With his hands folded across his chest, he bellowed a loud chortle. "Hah! Youse guys is too much! Youse don't get me. I'm not lookin' fer nuttin'. I wanna give to youse, like I said, anything youse wants. Anything. TV? Refrigerator? Mink fer da lady? Cars? Whadda ya want. I get it fer youse."

Slowly the lights began to go on for both surgeons. If this wasn't a threat, what could it be? Was this a peace offering? Had the tables turned? What the hell was going on?

Sal was no slouch at reading faces and body language. He knew he was staring at doubt and confusion. "Lemme put it like this". He said tilting the huge head on the massive, short neck, "I 'pologize fer all the tough stuff, an' phone calls, an' all dat stuff. We hadda be sure youse guys was on de up an' up, not puttin' de Godfadder down fer da DA. Ya know, like makin' him slip a little here, an' little there, till, bingo, he's a goner. That you was treatin' da Godfadder good and first class. First rate. Whatever youse guys call it. We, me an' the boys, we know dat...... now. Dat youse guys are onna up an' up. So now, we playin' ball widjahs. We all onna up an' up, da same team. Right?"

Slowly, somewhat reluctantly, both surgeons gave slight nods.

"No more phone calls", Sal continued. "Tell yer ladies, 'pologies from me an' da boys. Dey nice ladies. Youse guys're lucky. Nice ladies." He paused to regroup his thoughts. "Now, like I said, we wanna play nice, so I'm askin' youse guys whachu want. We wanna give youse a gift, a present, cuz you done good. You need it, we got it fer youse. Free. Gift from da boys an' me. TV? Cars? Jewelry? Broads?" He swung his arm out to include the world. "Naw. Youse ain't the de type go for broads. Ferget da broads. Whaddevah youse wants, we get it fer yuhs. Glad to get it. You just name it." He looked John square in the eye, and held out a right hand, smiling, almost inviting.

John held back, staring at the outstretched hand.

A peace offering? Is that it? Or is this some sort of a trap? Maybe not, because Sal seems genuine, at least at this moment. Where is this going?

All he could think to do was to stall. See where it was going?

"I really don't need anything right now, thanks. Nice of you to offer. But right now..... right now....... right now, I just want Angelo to get better and wake up. Fully wake up." He was stumbling, but that was it. Shift the subject. "It would be very nice if he were to wake up. Wake up and, uh, make sense. Show us his brain is still working. Still capable of rational thought." He paused again.

Sal shifted to Erv who was still speechless after his bold tirade. "I don't blame youse fer bein' a little sore. Like I said, me an' de boys 'pologize. Tell the little missus, we 'pologize. We're done. No more. Tell her she's okay, cuz we're on de up an' up. Lemme give her a little make up gift. A little somethin' to make nice. What she want?"

Erv was on it. He saw where this was going. *This is Sal's peace treaty, his offer of reparations. Let Sal know I got it.*

"Sal, if I may call you that?" Erv asked.

"Yah. Sure. Everybody knows me, Sal. You call me Sal. Yah." He swung his extended hand to the left, over to Erv, who looked Sal square in his little pig eyes and shook Sal's hand, firm.

"Sal. Thank you for your offer, but my wife and I are just fine right now. There really isn't anything we need. But thank you. Just stop the phone calls and the threats. That's enough. No more phone calls."

Erv continued, "I can't vouch for Angelo's future, and I'm sorry for that. But with any luck, he may just pull out of it. He may just return to normal. But it's also possible that he may not." Erv, energized with renewed confidence, realized he was rambling, but he continued. "We have no way of knowing what his mental status, his mental capacity, may turn out to be. To be honest with you, I've seen cases where the patient fully recovered and cases where they never come out of the comatose state. I've seen them wake up with a totally different personality. I've seen them wake up with the mentality of a three-year-old. That's something we have no control over. The science isn't there yet. Not today. Maybe sometime in the future we'll be able to control for that variable. But not now."

Erv realized Sal still had a firm grip on his hand and seemed to be slowly drawing him in closer. Maybe not? But Sal's little pig eyes still bore down into his, unblinking.

"I hear whacher sayin', doctor. Lemme call you Erv? Yah, Erv. You don't got no control onna future. I know dat. We know dat, all-a-us. We got dat. You done good by da Godfadder. So now we onna up an' up. Like you say, back to normal."

Sal released Erv's hand and stepped back. "Well gentlemen,

if I can't getchu anything right now, least we unnerstan' each udder. You help us. We help youse." He turned to look at John. "An', oh yah, by da way. I need yer charges fer da Godfadder. Whatchu charge fer yer care so far. If you give da bill to our guy at da door today or tomorrow, that be good. We wanna be square widjahs."

"Our bill. You mean our time and fee for service up to now?" Erv asked, "From when Angelo came in? That's over two weeks ago?"

"Yah. Dats right. Yer fee fer yer services. Onna a bill head. You got one from yer office. Ya know, on what dey call official office let-ter-head. Fer our book-keeper. Please."

John felt compelled, "I agree with Erv about different mentalities or personalities, I've seen that as well. I've seen radical changes sometimes. Changes enough to cause a divorce after thirty years of marriage. Angelo could wake up a different person. He could wake up with brain damage. I only mention this so you and your people will be aware of the possibility. Be ready, should it occur."

Sal nodded slowly, eyes focused on John.

John continued, "Whatever happens, don't blame the hospital or any of the medical staff. There is nothing any of us can do to influence the outcome, whatever it may be."

"Yah. I gotcha on that doc. I hear whatchur sayin'. And you too, doc", he said looking at Erv. "Like I was sayin', yer fee for yer services so far, on yer office let-ter-head. Fer up to now. Then, in addition, every other Friday, give to door guy a update. Onna let-ter-head office paper. Fer our accountant. You be paid reg'lar. The Family always pays."

Sal looked more at ease, less threatening, than either surgeon had ever seen him during these past two weeks. Almost relaxed. The meeting was over. That was clear. One hand on the door knob, Sal turned back, "Anythin' youse needs."

With that Sal was gone. Erv and John faced each other, speechless, wide-eyed, and smiles that enveloped both faces. Then Erv spread his arms, wider than his smile, and looking up at the ceiling, and exclaimed, "Thank you Jesus!"

Chapter 25 - Sunday Dinner

Sal was good on his word. The calls stopped. The first time in almost two weeks, the Pullmans and the Ansons slept soundly through the entire night. Both couples felt as if a great weight had been lifted from their lives. John and Annie B called their kids, rejoicing. That night, John and Annie B snuggled in bed. Snuggled and talked happy nonsense. One thing led to another, and they made long, deeply emotional love for the first time since the ordeal had begun.

The Anson children said nothing, but they, too, knew that things were better, much better. Erv's wife, Mary, was not nearly so jumpy or prone to fits of sobbing. They, also, held each other in the first peaceful, uninterrupted embrace in two weeks.

Sal made good on the surgical fees. The surgeons' standard billing rates, printed on office letterhead invoices, were given to the door guy, and the next day a different door guy stopped John and Erv to give each a plain brown envelope. Opening them later, in a private moment, each surgeon found cash. The amount was double that listed on the invoice.

Occasionally, each surgeon saw Billy in or around the hospital. He never failed to ask, "Hey doc. Anythin' youse needs. TV? Fridge? New car? Mink fer the lady?" Then one day, he stopped them as each approached Angelo's door. He had been waiting for each of them.

"Mrs. Ginnini, Angelo's wife, is askin' you and the missus for dinner, Sunday noon. You can come?"

Separately, each surgeon was taken by surprise by the invitation, and maybe a little anxious, too. But both, being the gentlemen they were, accepted with pleasure. The next day, while rounding on Angelo at the same time, Anson quietly started to ask his colleague, "You and Annie B been invited to........? Pullman's immediate nod precluded the need to finish the question. "Ya. Us, too." They arranged to go together.

"Turn right in two blocks. That'll be Ocean View Drive. Number 24 is on the left." They parked out front, behind a big, black Lincoln Town Car. In this middle-class neighborhood, colorful flower beds brightened the well-kept yard at 24 Ocean View Drive, a moderate house, similar to other unpretentious homes along the row.

Erv was about to press the doorbell, when the door was opened. "Hey. I'm Vito. Dis is the place. Mrs. Ginnini welcomes all yous." Vito stood in the door, until he stepped back and allowed the ladies to enter first. Both men wondered if perhaps they should have gone in first, just in case. Billy was smiling in the hall, with his hand out, ready to shake all four guests. He was actually cordial.

"Dis way please." he said, extending his left arm to usher them into a sitting room. Seated on a big, overstuffed couch with a somewhat gaudy floral print was the hefty woman John had met in the early morning of Angelo's surgery - Mrs. Ginnini. John stepped forward, bowing slightly, looking into her warm brown eyes. He took her outstretched hand, "Thank you for asking us." Then he introduced Annie B, Erv and Mary.

"Please sit down", said Billy from behind.

"Welcome to our home", said Mrs. Ginnini. "How is my Angelo today. When's he coming home?"

Vito brought in a gold tray with five small wine glasses, partially filled with a red wine, and dainty lace, napkins. "Chianti. La Rosa Chianti. Very nice. Very smoot", he said, passing to Mrs. Ginnini first, then to each of the others. Erv and Mary exchanged mildly questioning glances, then each took a glass.

Mrs. Ginnini kept her eyes on the glass she held resting on her lap, until John spoke up to break the silence. "Thank you, Mrs. Ginnini, and to your health, and to Angelo's recovery. We all hope we can send him home to you, soon."

"Santa Maria, Mother of God, forgive us our sins", she almost whispered as she crossed herself, then sat still for a moment, head bowed. When she straightened up, she raised her glass, looked at John, paused, then took a sip. Her four guests followed suit.

The room was lush, decorated with an Italian rococo flair. Ornate baubles — expensive, gilded, well made, but no consistent theme or motif. The four guests looked around, twisting in their seats, quietly taking it all in. Annie B turned to Mrs. Ginnini, "This room is amazing, so well, uh, decorated. You have some lovely things." Everyone nodded in agreement, even Billy, standing back under the arch to the front hall.

"Oh, thank you. Thank you so much. Many pieces from Sicily. Many gifts from my Angelo's business associates. My Angelo has a very big business. Lots of friends."

John turned ever so slightly to sneak a glance at Billy, to see his reaction, but Billy kept his poker face, as always.

"Yes, my Angelo has a good business. He is a very good provider for me and our children. Of course the children are all gone, now. Lives of their own. But, you see what he gives me. Such treasures. Billy, please show our guests around."

There weren't many rooms on the ground floor, but the space was impressively designed. Upstairs was presumably the same with the same Sicilian, southern Italian decor.

In the dining room. Vito was the waiter, serving a delicious six course meal: antipasto, soup, pasta, fish, salad, and finally, gelato. Small servings, but filling. Annie B guessed there must be a cook in the kitchen. John noted that Billy stood very quietly against the wall — unless the polite conversation came anywhere near the Mafia or its various businesses —when he'd redirect the topic.

It was apparent that Mrs. Ginnini knew that "my Angelo" had many "very nice business interests", but her main interest in life centered around the Ladies Guild at Saint Francis Holy Church. "We support the Catholic Orphans Appeal. You know of it? It's really quite famous."

She repeated, several times, that she was "so very happy that 'my Angelo' has such nice doctors. Billy says you're very famous doctors." She was surprised that neither Annie B nor Mary played Bingo. "The social life married to such famous doctors, must be very exciting."

After espresso coffees in the sitting parlor, and a little more polite conversation, "Thank you" was expressed, all around, several times.

"Our car is parked just down there", John pointed for Billy.

"Yah, I know. My man has been on it. No problems."

It wasn't until they had gone several blocks that all four let out a big sigh.

"Nice lady", said Erv to break the silence.

"Very nice, and, I think, genuine. What you see is what you get. No pretenses", said John.

"Very content with her life in the church. The orphans' guild, or whatever it was", Mary suggested, "Not my cup of tea, but obviously good for her, don'tcha think?"

Erv said, "She sure doesn't know anything about his businesses."

"That's for two reason is my guess," said Annie B, always the analyst. "First, Angelo, in true Sicilian fashion, is a male supremacist. Women belong barefoot, pregnant, and in the kitchen. Second, for her protection, he doesn't want her to know anything if the Feds ever nail him."

Chapter 26 – Angelo Talks

John Pullman came striding up to the Trauma Unit nurses' desk, his eternally pleasant and optimistic self, whistling "Va Pensiero" from Verdi's opera "Nabucco". "So what's the word today?" he asked Penny Field, Head of Nursing, who also was usually eternally pleasant and optimistic, but not at this moment. She was making her rounds, concerned about the nurses caring for Angelo.

"I dunno. They're as tight-lipped as ever. Strange hires. Still don't know anything about them. Where they came from. No C-Vs. Nothing. HR said they had seen their state licenses. But that's all they told me. Rumor has it they're Mafia hires. But really, Doctor Pullman, no one knows for sure. It's a big mystery." She picked up her clipboard. "Of course, if you want everybody to talk about it, just make it a mystery. Nothing like a secret to get the grapevine hot."

"Penny, you're the original hospital philosopher." John said with a grin, "Plus you run a good ship here. What goes on down there," He pointed down the hall, "is beyond your control. We all are well aware of that. You're the best, so keep it up." She melted under his warm smile and crinkly eyes. Resuming his whistle, he strode down the hallway.

"Well, what's he been saying today?" John asked the day nurse as he entered Angelo's room.

"Shhh!" she whispered. "Listen. He's been going on, some nonsense about this Gary guy. Again. And yellow planes, or orange planes."

John did not approach the bedside. He just stayed where he was and on the nurse's suggestion, listened. "Cold made it black. Gotta tell Morton. Tell Morton. Gotta tell Morton. Tell Morton now. Gotta." Angelo, obviously wrestling with something in his delirium, turned and twisted so vigorously in his bed, that the nurses had put a body restraint on him. His eyes were still closed, but his his head thrashed side to side, and beads of foam at the corners of his mouth accentuated his discernible frown.

"How are his sugars today? They any different when he's like this?"

"His sugars are within range, Doctor: 120, 150, never over 200. Pretty well controlled. Pretty stable, Doctor."

"He's burning a lot of energy like this. How much of the time is he like this?"

"Not much. He usually goes on like this ten, maybe fifteen minutes. Then he quiets down for a couple of hours. Then starts up again. Slow at first. Then gets more agitated."

"You giving him anything for it? To calm him down before he hurts himself? Reminds me a little of the DTs."

"Yes, Doctor. That's what Dr. Anson said too. But Dr. Salteese said not to give him any sedatives. Not unless he develops something like seizure activity, or something like that. He said he wants the brain to control its own healing speed. We should stay out of it. Not impede it."

"Huh?" John Pullman just rubbed his chin thoughtfully, as was his habit when he met with something medical he didn't know. He pulled out his stethoscope and approached the bed, bending over to try to listen to the belly for the tenor of his patient's bowel sounds.

As soon as he touched Angelo, the patient stopped his writhing and mumbling, and lay flat on his back. He opened his eyes, looked straight at John, and his gravelly voice barked "Who the hell are you?" Then with head cocked at a slight tilt, and with both eyes wide open and fixed on this stranger, he growled, "Who the hell are you? What the fuck you doin' here. Git away from me, you bastard! Can't you see I'm busy!"

John jumped back. "What the..... what the heck?" The nurse rushed up, but there was nothing to be done. With John now away from the bed, Angelo grunted as he turned onto his side, closed his eyes, and lay still once again. John and the nurse, both wide eyed, jaws half open, just stared at each other.

Angelo lay comatose for the rest of the day. That evening he began the babble again about "the orange or yellow plane", and the same men named "Gary and Morton", "asking for help", and three new items about "a top secret" and "the plane turned black" and "classified". The duty nurse recorded it all, thinking it might be important, and reported it to Rick McIver, the chief resident.

"Dr. Pullman, Rick McIver here. A quick follow up on Mr. Angelo Ginnini. The nurse reported that he had started the babbled stuff again about the orange-yellow plane, Gary and Morton, help, and three new bits about top secret, classified, and the plane turned black, sir. I don't know what it means, but I thought you might want to know."

"Has he opened his eyes again or turned himself in bed again?" John asked.

"No sir. Not according to the nurses. I have not noted anything like what you described this morning, and I listened to his chest as you did. Nothing, sir."

"Well, thanks Rick. That is very interesting. Strange, but interesting. Erv Anson doesn't know what to make of it either. Mal Salteese said he thinks Angelo's about to regain full consciousness. Thanks for your help. Keep me posted."

John decided to run it by Broune Malcolm, the hospital lawyer, even though it was after hours. Browny, as he was known answered on the third ring.

"Hey Browny. John Pullman here. About that..."

"Hi John. What's up? How's that wonderful Annie B?" Browny was smart, sometimes cagey, but always a friend.

"Great, thanks, Browny. How's Weesie? Annie B says she saw her the other day." Getting to the point, John continued, "Hey Browny, that research your firm did on our patient, Angelo Ginnini, when he was in the Army Intelligence? Do you have any more info on that? Any more details?'

"No. Nothing new. Haven't tried."

"Can your people dig up any more data on Ginnini at that time of his life? The reason I'm asking, is that Angelo's mental status looks like it's getting lighter. He seems be waking up, because he's making more of the same partial phrases and allusions to that info that you gave us the other day in the Board Room. He seems to be tormented by this stuff, whatever it is. We were hoping that more info might help us get into his stream-of-consciousness and perhaps, bring him around a little better?

"Very interesting."

"If I get a meeting scheduled, you available?"

"Yah, I'll get on it, in the AM. Isn't that fascinating. Some of the things that you guys do and run into are so interesting. A lot more fun than all this legal stuff I'm confronted with day after day. I'll get back to you soon as I've got anything.

John's cell phone rang that afternoon. It was Broune Malcolm, "Hey Browny. What's going on? Come up with anything new?"

"Yah, John. Quite a bit, actually. Apparently your patient was a military aide to this guy Morton Dana, a civilian in the OSI. A part of the CIA. A fascinating guy. Dana, that is. It's a rather long, complicated story, and we don't really have much on your guy Gininni, himself, but we can give you quite a bit on where he was, and what he was a part of during those times."

"Yes, sure. That would be great."

Browny continued, "He was attached to Dana during the late 60s, but apparently stayed in contact with him for a decade afterwards. Let me make a suggestion?"

"Certainly. Go ahead." John's hopes brightened.

"Can you arrange a conference in the Board Room on this subject. Just this subject. Get the facts straight, as we know them. Include more people, anybody who might be part of his care. I'm not a neurologist or a psychiatrist, and it might be a far reach, but knowing the background for all his ramblings might help you guys take care of him."

"I agree", John answered. "Tomorrow good for you? I'll try to round up the troops here. Ollie will be there for sure. How about the Mafia guys? I suppose we better include them. I sure as hell don't want to stir up trouble with them again."

"Absolutely. I totally agree. Make sure they're there, too. Noon good for you? Maybe have some sandwiches and drinks?"

"Perfect. See you then."

John had some trouble sleeping that night, wondering what Browny and his people had turned up.

Chapter 27 – Morton Dana

The Board Room was packed. The padded captain's chairs around the big mahogany table were reserved for key administrators and medical staff. Ollie Alberts and John Pullman with Erv Anson were seated either side of Browny Malcolm, at the head. Three seats at the table were reserved for Sal and his usual two companions. But Sal showed up with John and Billy, and two more, somewhat older men, immaculately coiffed, impeccably tailored in dark pin-stripe, and dark glasses.

Quickly, Ollie had two more executive chairs hustled in, closer to the head of the table, next to Sal. There was a lot of mumbled introductions, bowing and nodding and quick handshaking. John couldn't quite get the names, but they certainly commanded attention. *Ominous forces, John thought. Will they be a problem? I surely hope not.* Angelo's nurse-caretakers and several surgical residents involved in Angelo's care, sat in side chairs at the distant end of the table.

Promptly at twelve noon, Browny asked for quiet. On Ollie's suggestion, he announced, "Everyone grab a sandwich and a drink, then please take your seat. I will start with my presentation, followed by a time for questions and answers."

Browny stood at the head of the table, and the room quieted. He took a sip of water and cleared his throat. "My firm has been engaged to research some historical information on your patient Angelo Ginnini. A disclaimer: I have never met Mr. Ginnini, and have never had any dealing with him. I was told that the patient has been uttering names and phrases that didn't make any sense in a semi-comatose state. This research has been requested only to see if there might be a tie-in with events in his past life, and, as I understand it, to put his utterings in some sort of context that would psychologically help him awaken." Browny looked at John Pullman, "John, have I got this right?"

"Yes, that's my understanding of the therapy plan, too. Wasn't this your suggestion?" John directed his question to Mal Salteese. "For those who are not familiar with him, Dr. Mal Salteese is a Neuropsychiatrist consulting on Angelo Ginnini since the start."

Browny continued in a serious tone, "This is confidential information relating to the recovery of our patient Mr. Angelo Ginnini, and will be conducted as a medically-related conference, just like any other medical conference in this medical center. May I remind you that this conference will be governed by the HIPPA federal regulations. Violations of which may be a Federal offense."

Sal and his team seemed to shift a little uneasily inter seats.

Browny continued, "All of the information I'm about to give you was collected via the internet. None of this data is any longer classified, though it was until a few years ago. We are presenting it now solely in the hopes that it may benefit Mr. Ginnini in his fight to regain any or all of his former cognitive functions. I have to advise you that any other use of this data could be subject to disciplinary action. That includes gossip of any form." Browny looked down to the foot of the table at the five women assigned to Angelo's care. John settled comfortably back in his chair. His index fingers steepled under his chin.

Browny continued, "We all know Mr. Ginnini. May we call him Angelo?"

"Dats his name." growled Billy. There was a snicker or two. One of the two older gentlemen looked sharply at Billy, who slunk back into his chair.

"A very young Angelo, we know, was inducted into the US Army, June 12, 1969. After basic training he requested assignment in Army Intelligence, and was assigned as an aide to a Mr. Morton Dana, a civilian working for the US Government in ORD, the Office of Research and Development, a branch of the CIA."

A little background on Angelo Ginnini's new boss to give you some idea of just what Angelo was getting into: Mr. Dana, first name Morton, graduated from college with a degree in physics, when he was introduced to the CIA recruiters. That day, Morton Dana had been out in the woods deer hunting and was covered with deer blood. He was one of fifty-two prospects, and selected because they were looking for a physicist with woodsmen's skills. During his interview, a younger recruiter asked the questions, but the head guy just sat there continuously staring at Dana, completely silent. It was unnerving, but the kid didn't crack."

Morton Dana was hired as a technical analyst to work for the US Government in overt intelligence. That's overt as opposed to covert, and required clearance for access to classified information. He studied photographs of Russian, Chinese, and Indian nuclear programs, obtained from both satellite and U-2 photographs. He would find a hydro-electric dam and follow the power lines, photograph after photograph until the power line entered a fertilizer or a nuclear plant. These would have waste pools, some of which were found to be radio-active by infra-red sensors.

By the way, Morton helped develop these sensors. He was partly trained under the command of Neils Bohr and Edward Teller in Los Alamos and Kirkland Air Force Base in Albuquerque. Pretty high-up stuff. Using a tool called intercept telemetry, they could watch Soviet launches from Tyuratam, and see the rocket stages separate. They watched Soviet atmospheric nuclear testing. This was all in the early sixties, but — here's the point, everyone — this was history that Angelo would have had to learn, both as background for his Army job, but also, we think, as info that his Family back in the city wanted".

Sal and both the pin-stripers were paying close attention, very close attention.

"During Angelo's time working under Morton Dana," Browny referred to his notes, "the team was tasked with developing a nuclear powered radio-sensor device that would run itself into Soviet territory and send back data. Unfortunately, it was discovered and had to be discontinued. This was under NPIC, National Photographic Interpretation Center. In those days, some of the surveillance satellites were the size of a Greyhound bus. The satellite, if you can believe it, would collect a grouping of sensitive photos, put them in a can with a parachute, and eject it from space. A special Air Force plane tailing a wire loop would then snag the can. This was all stuff that Angelo worked on with Dana. Angelo must have been very bright, because he worked with all this highly technical information without any formal training, at least no training that we have uncovered. It was all OJT."

Browny noted that one of the Mafia men to his left was

staring out the window, and the nurses at the other end were whispering amongst themselves, so he altered his voice. "This is all fact. Not fiction, gentlemen..... and ladies", staring at the nurses. "Top secret then, but a matter of public record, now, and, as I said, all stuff that Angelo Ginnini apparently learned about and worked on."

"The U-2 project was also under NPIC control. Gary Powers, as some of us may remember, along with other U-2 pilots, flew very high. Dana would watch the films of the Soviet missile trails as they fell short of the U-2s. Gary Powers' problem was that he flew too low, and the Ruskies got him in 1962, ending the U-2 program. That was before Angelo's time. But when Powers was released and traded back to the USA, he returned to NPIC to work for Dana, and had personal contact with Angelo on a daily basis. It's my guess that this is the Gary that Angelo has been verbalizing."

"Dana was later advanced in ORD, Office of Research and Development, taking Angelo with him. By this time, Angelo, probably on advice from the Da Capo, re-upped his enlistment, to stay with Dana. We are only guessing that he was so advised, but we do know that he chose to remain in the Army." Browny pointedly looked at the Family representatives, but they remained silent.

"This is when Dana and Ginnini worked with the yellow and orange that the patient has been apparently babbling about. These were coatings for the second generation U-2 planes. The coating was based on technology developed by NCR, National Cash Register, the non-military company. They made carbonless copy paper, using micro-cells of ink. Dana and Ginnini used a similar principle that was temperature sensitive, so that it was orange or yellow at ground level, but at the low temperatures of the high altitude, it turned black. Apparently, Gary Powers was the test pilot for that first run, and he radioed back to someone, screaming that the coating had indeed turned black. That someone may well have been Angelo Ginnini, who then called Morton Dana with the success. At least that's what the data insinuates."

"Morton Dana was then moved up to become a DDS&T,

Deputy Director for Science & Technology, one of twelve, taken all over the country to train in everything the CIA did. They were in charge of ORD, OEL, Office of Electronic Intelligence, NED, Nuclear Energy Division, and FMSAC, Foreign Missile and Space.

"By this time Angelo's second term of enlistment was up, and the Family called him home, probably because Dana had to leave him out of much of this new higher level stuff that required higher security clearance than Angelo was cleared for. There was also some hint in the Army of something about his family's connection with organized crime." Browny paused as he tried to look innocently around the room, then he kept going, "Angelo, himself, was not suspected. There was some data suggesting that Ginnini and Dana kept in friendly communication for years after that until Dana's death, but no hard evidence of that.

"So that's the story of Angelo's connections with the CIA and Morton Dana, and some of the events he encountered. Are there any questions?"

No one said a word. John looked over at the two older Mafia men. One was staring at Browny. The other was slowly nodding his head, almost imperceptibly. Sal was focused on the older men, John Dominicci was scowling as he tapped his finger tips together, and Billy was looking around the room.

People began to get up, and some low conversations could be heard, but most of the group was pretty much shell-shocked. Slowly, the room emptied without any questions or comments. Some people were shaking their heads in disbelief of the magnitude of the information they had just heard. Erv overheard one quiet aside from one of the private-duty nurses to the other, "and look at him now."

Chapter 28 – Ben Blagden

Ben Blagden was riding his bicycle to class at the university when Allison opened her Lexus door without looking. Ben was pedaling fast with his head down because he was late this morning. He slammed into the door, brushing Allison's left leg causing a mild scrape. But Ben shot over the door catching his left knee on the door top, causing him to start to somersault through the air at twenty-three miles an hour. It was a warm morning, so he had left his parka home, wearing only his logo tee-shirt and jeans. He hit hard on his right shoulder, just as Allison began cussing "the stupid fucking kid! Why doesn't he watch where the hell he's going!"

Ben bounced to the left, out into traffic, where the side of the next passing car knocked him with a loud "whump" back toward the curb. He slid halfway under the car in front of Allison's Lexus, and lay there immobile.

Allison drew a sharp breath, "Jeeziz!........oh......my......god!" She tried to get out of her car, but the bicycle was in her way. The car that had whumped Ben, jammed on screeching brakes. Traffic behind that car jammed on screeching brakes. Cars behind swerving. Chaos. Traffic stopped. People rushed to Ben.

"Don't touch him! Wait for the EMTs." Cell phones punched 911, police, Haz-Mat rescue, EMTs, Ambulance, huge crowd gawking, police holding back, Allison hysterical in a police cruiser.

"Airway clear. Breathing regular. Pulse present. O2. No response to verbal. Careful traction. Stabilize neck. Spine precautions. Strapped on spine board. IV started. Obvious fracture of the right upper extremity. Probable left knee. Questionable abdominal trauma. BP 90 over 57, pulse 158, respirations rapid at 38/min, shallow. Pupils not dilated, reactive to light. Mild response to painful stimuli. Load and go. ER contacted. IV Ringers lactate, wide open.

Arrival at ER dock, met by full trauma team. Full trauma protocol. Additional IVs started. Bloods drawn. Quick ABCs physical assessment. Airway clear, functioning. Bleeding – nothing externally. Breathing spontaneously. Cardiac – regular sinus tachycardia on the EKG monitor. No audible murmurs with the stethoscope. Circulation - peripheral pulses weak but present in four extremities. Carotids – no bruits. Chest – bilateral breath sounds. Fracture of the right humerus. Possible fractures of ribs eight, nine, and ten on right. No crepitus. Abdomen – slightly full. Active bowel sounds. Not apparently tender, but patient not fully responsive. Checking the neuro. Unconscious, at least a major concussion. No helmet.

John Pullman strode into the room with practiced urgency. He stopped to assess the situation. The residents and nurses had things under relative control. At least they weren't pumping the patient's chest. "Whatta we got guys?" he asked.

"Bicycle-auto collision, sir" replied Deb Matthews, second year surgical resident. "Responding after two liters of Ringers, 105 over 65, pulse 118, Glasgow Coma scale of 7 out of 15. Obvious right humeral fracture. Possibly a couple of ribs on the right. Chest clear though. Moving air well. Possible pelvic trauma. Contusion left patella. No gross external hemorrhage. Labs sent. Cardio-thoracic probably okay on the prelims. Abdomen unclear as yet. X-ray on the way. Probably gonna need Orthopedics and maybe Neuro, sir."

The left subclavian IV central line, its tip in the heart, was all taped in securely, as were two other peripheral lines. The foley catheter was in place, draining 50ccs of clear urine, after the digital rectal exam. The gurney was pushed over to the X-ray table, and cranked up so it slid onto the table. The films were taken; chest, abdomen, pelvis, extremities.

Four days later, Ben Blagden was resting somewhat comfortably in Room 505, in the Trauma Unit. The dim night light under the sink gave form to most of the things in the room, but it was still pretty dark in there. The Toradol was wearing off, and he, though groggy, was awake and lying still, with his right arm secured to his right side by the big six-inch Ace bandages wrapped around his arm and chest to hold the humeral fracture in place. Any movement of his sacroiliac sent spasms of immediate pain all over. He was basically a prisoner in this hospital bed. He didn't like the situation, though he guessed it was necessary. At least temporarily. A trapeze fixed to the frame over the bed could help him shift himself using his left hand and arm, but any mobility was minimal. Minimal, and slow, and painful. His mind wandered as he dozed off again.

Suddenly he was chasing. Or was he being chased? No, he was chasing Tom. Tom? Was it Tom? Yah, Tom. His fraternity brother. Tom was on a unicycle, a high up unicycle. He was going through doors. The doors all opened into the light, where it was good. But every time he, Ben, came to a door to try to catch Tom, the door slammed shut, and he'd bump into it. He turned to his right. To an open door. To more light. Following Tom. Then, slam, the door would shut. Suddenly these were now car doors. No longer square rectangles. Car doors. The situation was frantic. He couldn't catch Tom, and he had to catch Tom. Not for any reason, but he had to catch him. Still, car doors kept slamming on him. Harder and harder. They hurt. They hurt his shoulder. And something was pulling on the cord from his left chest. Was there a cord attached to his left chest? He didn't know how it suddenly got there. But it was there. Attached. That cord pulled on his left chest. Couldn't get loose. Tighter. It pulled tighter. The cord and the door were going to swallow him. Envelope him. Smother him. Getting worse. Terrifying. Oh, my god he tried to scream, but nothing came out. He gave a massive wrench, and awoke with intense pain in his arm.

Slowly Ben realized he was okay. He saw the ceiling, though the room was dark, as usual. But the IV line was still tugging on his left chest. He put his hand up as he regained reality. It was his IV line. Yah, his IV line. The central line, they called it. They said it went right into his heart from his left chest. He didn't remember when they put it in, but it was tugging now. Something pulled it. Something from his right side. He looked to the right. A man was there. A man in a white coat. A man in a white coat fiddling with his IV line. Doing something with his IV line. And even though it was dark, he could see that the IV tubing was dark. Not clear with fluid. Dark. Dark, like blood?

Chapter 29 - Hey, What're You Doing?

Where did this guy come from? Who was he? What was he *doing?* Ben never heard the guy creep into his room on silent sneakers. He never saw him. Of course Ben wasn't looking for anybody. *I was asleep. Yah. That nightmare. With Tom and the slamming doors.*

Ben tried to focus, to wake up, fully. He knew he was awake. He knew he was not dreaming any more, but alert enough to be surprised by somebody in his room at this hour of the night. *What time is it?* He was confused. That hot-bodied nurse had checked on him, he guessed, about an hour ago. He wasn't sure. *Was it an hour? Or was it more? But I'm sure I remember her. Her name's Louise. Am I confused? Maybe a little dizzy?*

Suddenly this guy was there, fiddling with his IV line. "Hey, what're you doing?" Ben demanded.

"Whaaa......uh...oh! You startled me. I thought you were sleeping." The voice was high and worried. The two men locked eyes in the semi-darkness. "Uh....I'm......uh......I'm drawing some blood. Ya know. Blood fer the lab. Yah, drawing blood fer the lab. I'm the night tech...."

"I'm not due for any blood tests. My next hematocrit isn't till 7 a.m." Ben was fully awake now, and remembered clearly asking earlier that evening about all the blood they were drawing from him. The hot-bodied nurse had told him, "Four days post injury now, bleeding from your fractures, multiple contusions, and abrasions have all stopped. You've stabilized. You don't need your blood checked so often." Ben clearly remembered the conversation. So what was this guy doing?

"You're Mr. Blagden, right? Yah. I'm supposed to get your blood. Yah, room 505. That's you, right?"

"Yes, that's me. But no more blood drawing. Not now." Ben insisted. "I've lost enough, and I don't want to have to have a transfusion." Ben was beginning to get more worried than annoyed.

"It's okay, sir. You just go back to sleep," the stranger said. From what Ben could see in the dark, the guy seemed to be rushing the procedure, with a guilty look. Ben was immediately suspicious, but the guy just kept working with the IV, apparently drawing blood, a lot of blood. Ben felt his heart start to race. *What the hell is this guy doing with my blood.* He raised his head to try to see more. Something was very different. He was drawing out the blood with some sort of tubing, then switching something, and pumping it into another tube down out of sight.

"Hey, what are you doing. Stop that. No more blood. They told me no more blood. My blood count goes any lower, they're going to give me a transfusion. I don't want any transfusion."

The guy paid no attention. He just kept on doing what he was doing. "Stop what you're doing! Stop it now!" Now Ben was scared. Something told him this wasn't supposed to be. Something was wrong. Really wrong. Increasingly anxious. Increasingly angry. He searched with his left hand for his call bell. *Where is it? Damn. Should be right here. Where is it? Damn. Damn just when I need it. Where's my damn button.* He was getting panicky. Short of breath. *What's this guy doing?* But there was nothing Ben could do. The guy was on Ben's immovable right side, the side all bound up. *No damn call button.* The guy just kept pumping the blood.

"Listen buster, you stop that right now!" he yelled as loudly as he could, but he felt himself getting weaker, and what should have been a loud shout, came out as a loud whisper. His throat was closing up on him, and as a cold sweat broke out, his pulse was pounding fast in his ears. Close to full blown panic. He felt like he was going to black out.

Just then, over this stranger's shoulder he saw the nurse with the hot bod, Louise, in the hall. His only hope. Trying to gain some strength, he took a deep breath, and with his head back and his neck arched, he gave it the strongest blast he could muster, "Help! Help me now! In here!" Immediately he collapsed back into his pillow, and the room went black.

"Mr. Blagden, how can I help..........Hey! What are you doing? He's not supposed to have any blood work........"

Steve Wojek turned. Saw her coming in. "Shit!" He froze, dropped his equipment, stared at the nurse for a few long seconds, and ran out of the room, almost knocking her over as he brushed past her shoulder. She watched as he ran down the hall. She instinctively turned back and looked at the monitor. Marked dysrhythmia, no BP, Pulse 230, irregular. She ran out into the hall, and yelled "Code Blue in 505, Code Blue in 505. Code Blue! **Noise and confusion. Something going on** in the hall. Larry Lowance had not been sleeping all that well anyway. He got up to pee, which wasn't easy. Getting up was hard enough with limited use of his hands or arms, but peeing was a real task. They told him to use his fingers as much as he could, but peeing still wasn't easy. Took a while, but since he was awake, he stayed up to see what the commotion was in the hall. He poked his head out. *Must be coming from that kid's room, three doors down.* He stepped out into the hall just as this guy, running down the hallway, ran smack into him — into Larry's tender, very tender forearms. Both of them.

Larry was a large man. Steve wasn't. Most of the kinetic energy of the collision was absorbed by Larry's mass, the rest caused Steve to bounce back. He almost fell, but caught himself, and found he was looking up at a black giant in a hospital johnny-shirt that was way too small. The two men stared at each other.

Steve blinked first, stepped back, dodged around Larry, and ran down the hall, disappearing through the stairway door. Larry's frame stood still, but his face contorted, "Wouch! Shit. Sheee-it........Ooooohhhh. Groaning, he crept back into his room, clutching both arms to his chest.

Chapter 30 – What's Going On?

John Pullman hurried into Trauma 505, just behind Erik Cromwell. Residents and nurses crowded the room, mostly all busy. Some were watching the monitor, waiting. The EKG showed the cardiac rate slowing, and still in normal sinus rhythm, as it should be. John stepped up behind the group of residents crowded around the bed, where the patient was half off the spine board that had obviously been hastily shoved under him. He wasn't intubated, but his head was turning side to side, trying to shake off the O2 mask the CRNA was trying to manually clamp over his nose and mouth. It looked like he was waking up.

Erik Cromwell was gesticulating over in the corner with Rich Percy, the Internal Medicine chief resident. Rich had been leading the Code Red resuscitation effort. It was Rich who had called both Erik and John in the early morning hours. An unusual situation — very unusual, what was security doing here, at a Code Red?

"When I got here," Rich was telling Erik, "the code was in full swing. The airway and respirations were fine, so no intubation. Sonny Webster was pumping the chest, but stopped when the EKG showed a spontaneous rhythm. There was blood hanging already, which I couldn't quite understand. How did they get it here so fast? That's when the night nurse, told me the story."

"What story? What's going on here? This looks like a major catastrophe." declared Erik Cromwell, not his usual calm self. "Jeeziz, the whole hospital is on alert. Five o'clock in the friggin' morning. Security everywhere. What the hell's going on?" Erik looked over at the patient and the bedside activity, which was beginning to ease off. The scrub suits were starting to straighten up, and observe the monitor. Rich looked over, too, as did John.

The patient was clearly waking up. He still had a little tachycardia, but his pressure was up, and he was breathing on his own. The bag of blood was almost empty.

"That's the second bag, Rich. Wanna hang another?" Sonny asked over the general hubbub.

"The repeat hemoglobin come back yet? What were his latest blood gasses?"

"Ten point five. Same as the blood in the bags. Gasses good." Sonny answered.

"Why don't we hold for now and see how he does. The bed in ICU ready yet Louise?" Rich asked, looking over at the nurse.

"Ten minutes. Transport's here with the monitors." She turned toward the door, pointing with an index finger.

Rich paused while both Erik and John studied him. The resident scanned the room with a confident, practiced eye, and turned to the two senior attending surgeons, "Yes, sir. Let's go down the hall." He said. He called to Sonny, "Your team all set?"

"Yah. We got it from here. Thanks for your help." Sonny turned back to monitoring the patient. The three doctors brushed past the crowd, out to the hall, and down to the small conference room., where they each took a chair, facing each other at angles across the table. John sat with his hands folded on the table, looking at Rich.

"Lemme get security in here too." Rich said as he started back toward the door.

"Security?" Erik barked and John asked at the same time. They looked at each other. "What the hell? What's security got to do with this? I got called for a code, not security." Erik exclaimed, hands upturned.

To add to the confusion, Al Towns, the Trauma Head Nurse, burst into the room. "What's going on." He jerked to a halt, astonished to see both John and Erik there. "What're you guys doing here?" And Rich returned, sat down, and was followed a few seconds later by Jacob Madecz, the assistant chief of security for the hospital.

"Jeeziz, what they got you in here this early for, Jake?" Al asked when he saw the big, familiar, hospital cop. Jake topped six-five, hard bodied, topped by a mop of thick, white hair. Everybody knew Jake, and everybody liked him, maybe because of his perpetual smile. A great guy, but a ferocious hospital cop, when he had to be. He yanked a chair back and slung himself into it sideward. His knees never fit under the table. No friendly smile this morning. Jake looked serious.

"Will someone please tell me what's going on here?" Erik snapped and sat abruptly forward. John, his cooler temperament keeping his profound concern subdued, leaned in, elbows on the table, as he studied Rich, awaiting his words.

"Gentlemen," Rich began. He was older than most chief medical residents. In his fourth year of training in Internal Medicine, he had been a very successful business entrepreneur for six years before entering medical school. Mature, intelligent, usually calm and measured in his approach to even the most pressing problem, Rich now looked agitated. His troubled frown alerted the already anxious men. "Let me start at the beginning." Everyone focused on Rich.

"At about 3:30 this morning a code was called by the nurse in 505. She's Louise Strang. You all know her, and she knows everybody. Married to Tim Strang, our resident. She's been here for years. Good nurse. She said that as she was passing 505, the patient called out for what sounded like help. She went in. This other nurse, his ID badge said Steve Wojek, was supposedly drawing bloods on the patient, Ben Blagden. Except Louise knew that the patient didn't need any further blood drawing, hoping to avoid a transfusion. Plus, this Wojek had filled one bag, a big bag, with blood, and was working on filling the second from the patient's central line. She asked him, this nurse, a stranger to her, what he was doing, knowing that something was not right. He said something to the effect that he was drawing blood for a trauma research project that Dr. Thornton Brooks was doing. She didn't believe him, especially with a bag and a half of blood already, which, she said, were much larger than the usual blood banking bags. She said no one ever took that much. She tried to arouse the patient, when she noted the hypotension and tachycardia on the monitor. She ran out into the hall, to the desk, to call the code."

"Jeeziz! This is weird." Erik burst out.

"This is nothing, yet. It gets worse." Rich cast an eye to Jake before turning back to Erik. "This nurse, Steve, took off, almost knocking Louise over as he bolted for the hall. There he ran into another patient, then ran down the stairs. The code response was swift. Even for 3 a.m.. Gotta hand it to our guys. They did a great job." Both John's and Erik's jaws dropped and their eyes widened. Al was speechless, and Jake's face reddened with tension.

"Louise told Dr. Upson Webster, who was the first to arrive, about the blood this Wojek guy was withdrawing from the patient. Sonny, as he is known to most of you, was the one who put two and two together, and started to re-infuse the blood back into the patient, adding a pressure pump, to run it in ASAP. We used the usual pressors and more IV lines, presuming this was hypovolemic shock. But it was the quick re-infusion of the patients own blood that did the trick. Luckily we were right. Or, rather, Sonny was right. Smart kid. He made the call before I got there.

"Anyway, the patient slowly came around. The shock hadn't become irreversible. Not yet, thank goodness, and lucky for him."

Chapter 31 - Wojek

"So who's this Wojek guy? Don't know him. Not on the surgical service, is he? I thought I knew them all?" Erik Cromwell asked, annoyance replaced by a frown creasing his forehead. John Pullman was still sitting forward in his chair, taking it all in, contemplating this strange situation.

"Well, that's where Jake takes over", Rich said. Both surgeons blinked in surprise.

"Jake? What's security got to do with a code?" Erik asked Rich.

"Wojek", John said slowly. "Wojek.......Wojek's the problem. That's my guess." John leaned back slightly as he spoke for the first time. "So, Jake.....Wojek? Who is he?"

Jake Madecz looked at John with studied intention, and with a slow smile replacing a straight, tight mouth, he said, "Always thinking, John. Always two steps ahead." He looked back at Erik Cromwell, "This Steve Wojek, of record, isn't Steve Wojek. It's an alias. He doesn't live at his given address, which is a fake. We really don't know who he is. We pulled his file this morning. We do know that he works nights on Oncology. Good patient care. Very attentive. Good nurse, only there is no RN under his name registered in the state."

Well, who the hell is he?" Erik wondered out loud.

"Good question, Erik", Jake said. "We're working on that as we speak. My team is all coming in early. I hope we'll have an answer for you in a few hours. Gotta wait for public records to open up, and get the police fully involved. They're already sending over an investigative team to work with my boys."

Just at that moment the conference door flew open and a breathless Olsen Alberts burst through the doorway. He was dressed impeccably, hair was combed back, as usual, but that was the only semblance of calm in this normally cool, unflappable hospital CEO. Desperation was etched all over his face.

"Good morning, Mr. Alberts," Jake said softly. "Have a seat.

I was wondering when you'd get here. Welcome to the chaos."

"What's going on here, gentlemen?" he asked as he sat, looking from man to man.

"I was just about to explain to this illustrious gathering what we have so far." Jake was not only being his usual understated self, but he was also trying to defuse the general anxiety around the table. "As I can get it from the medics here, and Rich, please correct me if I'm wrong, this Steve Wojek was found withdrawing blood from a post-trauma patient. A ......" He glanced down at his note pad, "a Mr. Ben Blagden. Something, I gather he was not supposed to be doing. Wojek, that is. He was discovered by Louise Strang, one of your nurses....."

"Everybody knows Louise. She's been a steady here for years", Erik interrupted.

"It was Louise who called the alarm.......the code red. This Wojek guy, or whoever he really is, fled. Down the rear stairway to the basement. Through to the garage. The surveillance cameras picked him up just as one of my guys there on the floor called the desk. The exit gates were lowered, but......."

"So you've got him?" Rich asked.

"No. He calmly rode his bike out around the gate, up the ramp, and off into the night. We dispatched a car to follow, but we lost him." An exhale of annoyance was heard from all in the room. "Now," Jake said, looking around at each man, "I have a question for you. Why was Wojek drawing blood on Blagden, and how does that enter into the problem? Why the code red? Are they connected?"

The three physicians started to answer at once. All three stopped. Erik then looked at Rich, "You tell it Rich. You were there. You ran the code."

"Okay," Rich shifted up in his chair, took a deep breath, "Okay. This Steve Wojek, a nurse from Oncology, was found withdrawing blood from the patient who was.....what, four days post bike accident with several fractures, with a good deal of internal bleeding, which, fortunately, had stopped. What I could get from your resident Sonny Webster, was that the patient had been considered stable, hemodynamically at evening rounds."

Rich looked at Dr. Pullman.

"That's right." John agreed. "The orthopods have been handling the fractures. Trauma was just overseeing the case, having admitted him with questionable abdominal problems, none of which panned out. The orthopods had him pretty well trussed up, and arrangements were being made to transfer him to rehab. But my name was still on the chart."

"Right," said Rich. "Anyway this Wojek bled the patient down to a shock level, when he was discovered. Dr. Pullman, I gotta give the credit to your resident, Sonny Webster. As I was saying before, he's the one who had the brains to give the patient back his own blood right away. I'm thinking that's what saved his life."

"So the patient is doing okay......so far?" Ollie Alberts asked with a worried frown. "I take it then, that this Wojek guy's actions were not the result of an order? Not an order written by one of our physicians? Was he acting on his own?" he asked. "Not following hospital protocol?"

"No sir. Definitely not hospital protocol." Rich responded somewhat forcefully. "No one in his or her right mind would draw down a patient to a shock level. This guy had over, I'm guessing, over 1500 ccs of blood in those two bags. Like I said, it was Sonny Webster's quick thinking that......."

"Yah, we got that. And God bless Sonny for his actions." Erik interrupted again, "But to answer the question, no, Ollie. We would never draw blood from a patient who had undergone a significant trauma. Small aliquots for a blood test, maybe, but certainly nothing even approaching the amount withdrawn in a standard blood donation. That's only 400 ccs. Not 1,000."

John Pullman had quietly been taking this all in. "Do any of you think this might have somehow been a criminal action? Something completely outside the hospital rules and regs. Something illicit? A black market for fresh blood, perhaps? Or some other non-medical, possibly criminal purpose?"

"Yes, I wonder the same thing." Ollie Alberts added, hoping that perhaps the hospital might not be so liable after all.

"I say that purely as a wild guess, what with the invasion of our hospital trauma unit by one of the city's crime families." John added, turning to Jake for an answer. "They certainly are a presence here. On a daily basis. I wonder if one of their operatives decided to do a little side business. Something to do with blood? Or, perhaps the sale thereof. Or maybe some other horrendous activity? Who knows what they are capable of." John was still smarting from those first ten days of Angelo's admission.

The police did come in. A special committee of the Medical Staff was appointed to look into the matter in conjunction with the police. Was this a criminal act or not? That was the question of the day. The word, unfortunately, spread like wildfire throughout the hospital community. The general opinion was that the Mafia was not involved. That it was the act of a solo lunatic. This was even further confirmed when Wojek didn't show up for work that next night. Or the night after that. In fact, he never showed up again. The gossip soon lost interest, and turned to other unsubstantiated rumors and hearsays.

The special medical committee formed did not lose interest. John Pullman and Erik Cromwell, together, verified the fact that there had, indeed, been a string of unexplained deaths on the trauma service over the past two months. All the deaths had several things in common: one, hypovolemic shock, associated with very low blood counts; two, no overt blood loss found on autopsy; three, all incidents had occurred on the trauma floor around 3:00 to 4:00 a.m. This caused some discussion among the committee members. The Internist on the committee stated that he couldn't understand how there could have been an anemia so severe that it caused hypovolemic shock without any evidence of external blood loss, unless this suspect had pro-actively extracted the blood, himself.

A side comment by the Oncologist on the committee was missed by everyone but John Pullman, who was sitting next to him. This cancer specialist rather quietly remarked in his unaggressive way, that there had been almost as many unexplained deaths on the Oncology floor during this same time frame. Unfortunately, his comment was lost amid the flurry of theories being expounded by others who knew little of the facts or details. Finally, Erik Cromwell called the group back to order. They decided on a date to resume discussion, and adjourned.

Chapter 32 – Hi There!

Surgical resident Will Lain went in to check on Angelo
Ginnini. He was between cases in the OR. Easy cases this morning,
so he had a few minutes to catch up on some of the details he
hadn't time to attend to before the 7:30 OR start time. The usual
day-shift, "hired" nurse was there. They had become known as the
"hired nurses" because no one knew where they came from. They
weren't the regulars called in for extra load times. They weren't
travelers, who, on contract, moved to a distant town or city for a
three or four month sign-on. They were strangers, who made no
effort to join and mingle with the regular staff. Strange set of
women. Of course the rumor was that they were Mafia-based
people sent in by the Ginnini family business to take care of the
Godfather, to make sure all was done right. "No monkey-business"
with the Godfather, as Drs. Pullman and Anson had been
relentlessly warned. As the guys stationed at the door said, "First-
class. Nuttin' but first class fer de Godfadder!" No one knew that
the "hired nurses" kept a small hand gun secreted in the
Godfather's room.

Will, like the rest of the surgical residents, was on a perfectly
friendly basis with Angelo's nursing team. No problem there, so
with his usual inviting smile, he asked, "So how's our patient this
morning?"

"Stable" came the hired nurse's answer. Then softening a bit,
but still no smile, she added, "No change doctor. Everything the
same as yesterday."

Will quickly scanned the chart, the latest labs: Hgb
(hemoglobin) 12.3, Hct (hematocrit) 43%, WBC (white blood cell
count) 7,300, blood sugar 143. The rest revealed no change. All
normal. In fact, everything about Angelo appeared to be normal
except for his comatose status. The hired nurse was right.

Will pulled his stethoscope out of the side pocket of his
stained white lab coat, and stuffed in the ear pieces. Bending over
the still, supine form, he carefully pulled the fresh white sheet

down, and placed the bell of his stethoscope over Angelo's heart. He expected Angelo's heart sounds to be normal, but John Pullman had taught him to listen, to try *not* to expect everything to be normal. "Listen to the heart, to the lungs, and to the abdomen," Dr. Pullman would say. "Try to find that hidden abnormality that would eventually trip you up as the treating physician. A detective's game. Find it before it finds you. Keep the art of medicine in your practice", Dr. Pullman always stressed. "Sure, you need the science of the labs and X-ray to help you, but never forget the physical exam." He was right. It was surprising how often the younger docs got caught short when they skipped the basic physical exam.

In a calm, soothing voice just above a whisper, Will said, "Hey, Angelo, Morton Dana says hello. Morton says you do good work there with your pilot buddy, Gary. Gary Powers. You remember Gary Powers don't you?" All the surgical residents rotating on the Trauma service currently had all been briefed on the information Broune Malcolm had given at the conference. They were advised by Mal Salteese, the neuropsychiatrist, to gently mention some of the story connected to Angelo's ravings. Erv Anson had agreed. But so far, these Dana references had fallen on deaf ears. Angelo's deaf ears.

The hired nurses made it a point to overhear everything the surgeons said to Angelo. In fact, they quietly wrote it all down — later. Everything: routine or not, medical or not. However, they did it subtly, avoiding other staff's eyes. These nurses, obviously well taught and well practiced, were good at deception..

Will continued his low discourse to Angelo: "Your pick-up on the yellow U-2, turning black was a big help, Angelo. Morton said you did good, Angelo. Good job, Angelo." Angelo seemed to give a little jerk with his whole body. Maybe not. Will wasn't sure. Concentrating on his stethoscope, Will didn't see Angelo's eye-lids flutter. For just a second. Just a short flutter. The nurse saw it though. She said nothing.

Will was about to move his stethoscope bell around to the other side of Angelo's chest, when Angelo lifted up his head, and with eyes wide open and looking at Will, said in a clear, cheerful voice, "Hi there. How are you?"

Will jerked up straight, stethoscope dangling from his ears, mouth agape. "Wh.....what?" Staring at Angelo, Will took a small step back, to catch his balance. Both individuals appeared equally surprised. The nurse immediately was at his bedside.

"Mr. Ginnini, good morning", she said, hustling to be involved. "How are you feeling today?"

Angelo, also with mouth open, looked from Will to the nurse and back to Will. Confusion written all over his face. Where was he? Who were these people? What did they want? Why did they wake him up? The silence was almost palpable for a full minute as the two medical people stared at Angelo, and he looked back and forth at the two of them. He tried to sit up, failed, and flopped back down.

"Here let me help you, Godfather", the nurse said, arms extending.

Angelo swung wildly at her hands, "Don't touch me. Who are you?" His face covered with fear and confusion. "How do you know me?"

Will, slowly, gently reaching towards Angelo, immediately regained control. Calmly, in a low voice he said, "It's alright Mr. Ginnini. You've had an accident. You're in University Hospital, but you're alright. You're getting better. Much better. It's okay. Everything's okay."

Angelo looked at Will, "Who are you? Why am I here?" He looked briefly at the nurse, but then quickly back at Will.

"Mr. Ginnini, I'm Dr. Will Lain. I'm a surgical resident. I'm helping to take care of you. You had an accident, and you......"

"This is a hospital?..... Accident?...... I've had an accident?" The patient brightened perceptibly. "Who are you? No, you just told me. Will. You're a doctor. Dr. Will. Got that. Okay, okay. Dr. Will. And you say I'm in a hospital? Right?" Will nodded. "Which hospital, and what for?" Angelo paused, looked around, wondering, but not angry.

"Did you say an accident? Dr. Will, did you say I had an accident?"

"Yessir", Will replied. Then he waited, giving Angelo plenty of time to absorb the answer,

"Yes, Mr Ginnini, you were shot in two......" the nurse began to announce in rather strident tones. Will held up a hand to the nurse. She stopped abruptly, but it was too late.

"Shot? Shot? A gun shot? You say I was shot?" Angelo's face suddenly clouded with fear. "Why was I shot? Who shot me? Why was I shot? I haven't done anything."

"That's okay, Angelo, Mr. Ginnini. You are okay. Everything is okay. There is absolutely nothing to worry about. You are all okay. All healed up. Nothing to worry about. May I call you Angelo, or would you prefer Mr. Ginnini?" Will asked.

"No, Angelo is just fine, son. Are you a doctor?" Angelo looked up at Will. "I guess I'm a little confused by all this. Yes, of course you're a doctor. You introduced yourself as a doctor. What kind of a doctor are you, Dr. Will?...... Yes, you're Dr. Will. Got it. Got it now. Okay. So now, fill me in on what's what here. I seem to be a little behind the ball here. Can you fill me in?"

This is not a thug speaking, Will suddenly realized, rethinking the situation. *This guy is clear. Intelligent. No accent. Confused, but not aggressive. Nothing threatening. Very different from the men at the door. But what should I do? How much should Angelo be confronted with at this time? How do I handle this?'* Surgical training kicked in. *When in over your head, call for help.* And that's what Will was about to do when his beeper went off.

"Dr. Lain here." Will straightened up, looked away at the wall. "Be right there." He hung up. "Mr. Angelo, I'm afraid I've got to go right now."

"Yes, Dr. Will, we need to talk, but not right now. I feel tired, so I'll take a nap. Then you come back? Please?" the look he gave Will was pleading.

"Yessir," Will responded. "Take a little rest and I'll be back. I'll bring some of my fellow doctors to meet you."

"Yes, that would be nice, Dr. Will." Angelo rolled over on his side and closed his eyes.

Will gently took the nurse by her arm, moving toward the door. "Not a word to him or to anyone else about this. Certainly not to the patient. Call if he reawakens. I will get Dr. Salteese, the neuropsychiatrist, as well as Dr. Pullman and Dr. Anson. We need to deal with this very delicately, with kid gloves. We don't want to shock him back into a coma again."

"Yes doctor", the nurse nodded her head. "Whatever you say, doctor." She, of course, had no intention of obeying Will's order.

Chapter 33 – Hiding

Steve Wojek rode his bike for all he was worth, in the dark, early morning hours just before dawn. His mind was churning, *What should I do? Where should I go? Not home. No. Not now. Scout it out? Maybe? Guess I better change these clothes. Where?*

Passing a row of darkened stores, he noticed lights on in one — a laundromat. He stopped and peeked in. One dryer working, but no people visible. *At this hour? What the hell. Worth a try.* He went in. Just the one dryer and two washers going round. He yanked on the dryer door handle. Locked. He yanked harder. Nothing. Then he noted the lever behind the handle. Pushed it. The dryer stopped, and the door popped open. Wojek pulled the contents out on to the floor, and ruffled through them. A blue work shirt. *Perfect.*

Quickly, he pulled off his white hospital coat and green scrub shirt, and put on the work shirt. *A little big, but okay. Pants,* he thought, *pants. Gotta be some pants in here. Sox, no. Don't need them. Men's boxers, no.* He discarded a towel, a dress or skirt, another face towel. *Ha! A cotton sweater, dark brown. Good! A little large.* He put that on over the shirt, anyway.

Pants. Pants. Come on, some pants. Something dark sticking out from a twisted bath towel. He undid the twist as quickly as he could. *Shit, shit, shit, loosen up. Come on, gimme this thing, whatever it.....Ha!* He pulled out a pair of grey shorts. Male? Female? He tossed them. *Damn. Gimme some pants. Shorts won't do it. What's that?* He reached across the pile. *Khakis? Yah, khakis. Lookin' good. Not too big.* He dropped his green scrub pants, but had to pull off his sneakers to get the scrubs off completely. Shoving his right leg first in the almost dry khakis, then balancing, he jammed in the left and pulled them up. A little tight over his butt, he could barely button them. *They'll do.*

He started to leave. Stopped and stepped back in a hurry. *My friggin' sneakers.Gotta get outta here before someone comes. Owner will be back.* He shoved his foot into the sneaker. Wouldn't go. *Damn. Come on, come on. Don't screw with me. Not now. Gotta go.* He bent, undid the lace, widened the opening, and shoved his foot in, pulled the lace tight, and tied it. He tried to do the same with the other sneaker, Speed made him fumble. *There, done, goddammit. Outta here.* He started to go, but stopped again. With three fast swipes, he gathered up his white lab coat, the scrub shirt, scrub pants, winding them into a bundle and ran for the door.

A big guy coming up the cement walk to the laundromat was looking down at the walk. He didn't see Steve rushing toward him until the last second as Steve brushed past. "Hey", the guy, both surprised and annoyed, blurted, "Watch where you're going". As the big guy reached the door, he saw the pile of clothes outside the dryer. That was his dryer. Those were his clothes. He turned toward the door. "Hey! That's my sweater." He ran to the door. The kid — he thought he was a kid, was mounting a bicycle and getting away. "Hey, buddy, stop", he yelled. "That's my sweater." But the kid was gone, round the corner, into the darkness.

"That's....my.....sweat....er. Son-of-a-bitch", an astonished, fading voice. He went to the pile of laundry on the floor. "That sonofabitch. Dumped my clean stuff on this filthy floor, and stole my sweater, I think?" He bent to sort out his things, and tossed them, one by one, back into the dryer. "Yah. My sweater's gone. So's my work shirt, and Skipper's chinos. That little prick! Damn him. What a little bastard." He stood, hands hanging at his sides, shoulders slumped, slowly shaking his head. *Sure wish I'd gotten a better look at the little bastard.* He slammed the dryer door shut.

Steve rode, quietly, keeping to the back streets, hoping not to be seen. At one corner, he stopped to search in his lab coat. Whew! *Okay. There it is.* He pulled out his wallet. *Only cash I've got. At least until I can get back home.* He stuffed the wallet into the tight left rear pocket, where it bulged.

He had ridden the opposite direction from his apartment, into a poorer part of the city. *This here isn't so bad, not the worst part.* In a particularly dark, narrow alley, he got off his bike, and, with mixed emotions, pushed the bike into the deep recesses of the alley, knowing it would be stolen. *Too bad. I liked that bike. Someday get another. Someday.* Getting tired and hungry, he looked at his watch. *Ten of five. Go back to that 'Dunkin'.*

A block later he passed a dumpster outside a construction site. He rolled his lab coat into a wad and stuffed it into his scrub shirt, which, in turn, he stuffed tightly into his scrub pants, tying the empty legs around the whole mess. He looked over the edge into the dumpster and saw some dark fluid-looking crud in the corner. Purposefully he chucked his hospital clothes into the puddle and watched as the fabric absorbed some of the fluid, turning them a foul, dark color not easily distinguished in the semi-darkness.

The lights were bright in the Dunkin' place. "Coffee, blond and sweet, large, and three crullers and three glazed".

"Eleven sixty seven." The Latino-accented clerk took the twelve dollars, and without bending forward at all, he half-way handed the thirty-three cents and the bag of purchases to Steve, who had to reach across the counter. The clerk looked hard at Steve — at his forehead, eyes, and on down to his shoulders, as though memorizing. A sudden chill went up Steve's back. *What is this guy up to? He can't know anything.* Steve took a step back, his stare fixed on the Latino. *Get outta here. Leave this guy. Move it!* Steve turned and fled, feeling the guy's eyes still on the back of his head.

Chapter 34 - He's Awake

"Dr. Pullman, Will Lain, here. Your patient, Mr. Ginnini is awake. At least he was when I left the room."

"Awake, you say. That's good news."

"Yessir, but there's something strange." Will had his hand cupped around the mouthpiece, his back to the ward secretary. In hushed tones he said, "Something strange about him. Mr. Ginnini. I think I need to tell you in private. He's not what I expected."

"Where are you, Will?" Pullman asked

"The nursing station on Trauma Seven, down from his room."

"Stay there. I'll be right down." Ninety seconds later John came striding down the hall. Will led him into the small dictation room. The resident quietly shut the door, looking out through the door window at the empty hall.

"So he woke up, Will?", John asked the young resident .

"Yessir. I was checking on him between cases. I was talking that stuff they told us about Gary Powers and all that, and he woke up and answered me. But two things happened. Not what I expected. So I'm looking for help, and mostly, you need to know."

John's curiosity was aroused. "Okay, Will. Talk to me. What don't you like?" John sensed from Will's expression that it was something unpleasant. Not to his liking.

"Well you see sir", Will searched for the proper words. "He's not what I, what we, what all of us figured he'd be like. Ya know? We all thought......kinda, I guess, he'd be like one of those tough guys outside his door. Tough, gruff, dictatorial, ...uh, just nasty."   "Okayaaaay" John nodded. "Go on."

"No accent. No gruff tone." Will decided to let it all hang out. "He's just a confused, nice old man. No cussing. No tough stuff. No threats. Totally unaware that's he's in the hospital. Unaware of any gun shots. Very anxious, worried, a little upset. Don't blame him though. I figured I was outta my league here, so I called you. Also, I took the liberty of calling Dr. Salteese . I hope you don't mind?"

124

"No, that's good, Will. You did just right. Let's go look at him. I want to see this. As you say, not what we expected from a Godfather type."

"Plus there's this other thing", Will added hesitantly. "The nurse there. The private duty nurse. That we're not quite sure about?"

"Yes. What about her?"

"Well, she witnessed his talking, too. I told her not to talk about it. Not to tell anyone. At least until we had a plan on how to handle the situation." "Good advice, Will."

"Right after I left to call you, I saw her come out into the hallway. Very suspicious-like. Looking all around her, over her shoulder. Sneaking. Talking on her cell phone with her hand covering, so no one could hear what she said. I was sitting down in the nursing station. She didn't see me, I guess. But she sure looked suspicious. Obviously telling somebody something. I'm guessing it was about Mr. Ginnini."

"Huh. Suspicious. I thought we had all that secrecy stuff settled with them", John looked puzzled. "Good observation, Will. We'll add that to the big picture. Let's go see the man."

"Yessir. I hope he's still awake."

Angelo looked like he was sleeping when the two surgeons entered his room. The nurse raised her index finger to her lips for quiet. They stopped at the bedside. The patient, lying on his side, gave a small twitch, and rolled over onto his back, looking up, first at John, then at Will. "Dr. Will. Are you back? Nice to see you." A wide grin crinkled his black eyes. He looked back at John who responded by bending forward.

"I'm Dr. John Pullman, Mr. Ginnini. Nice to meet you", John said with his usual welcoming smile, holding out his right hand. "I'm one of the surgeons taking care of you, along with Dr. Will, here."

Angelo looked back at Will for reassurance.

Will said, "Yes, he's my boss", which caused Angelo to look back at John, and smile.

"Oh, I'm so glad to meet you, Dr. John Pullman. I'm afraid I'm a little out of my element, here. A little confused. Dr. Will told me I had some surgery, but, I don't seem to remember what for. The nurse said something about my being shot, but for the life of me, I don't remember anything about it." Will, turned his head to check on the nurse who was standing apart, halfway across the room, hands pressed to her mouth, eyebrows arched with worry.

"Yes, you did sustain two gunshot wounds. One in your abdomen, and one to your posterior scalp. You had a concussion, from which you are just waking up. You are perfectly fine and mending very well. Out of danger." John wasn't sure whether the law and the police would agree he was out of danger, but John wanted to reassure his patient, medically.

There was a knock on the door, and Mal Salteese came in. He crossed to the bedside and introduced himself, lightly describing his specialty. Angelo grinned as they shook hands. "Mr. Ginnini, Dr. Pullman.... and Dr. Lain, here, filled me in on your case." He turned to John, "Do you have a few minutes we might spend with Mr. Ginnini?" Mal asked. "And you, Dr. Lain?" Mal rechecked the name on Will's hospital badge.

For the next twenty minutes, the three physicians gently and cautiously filled Angelo in on what had happened to him, his current status, including his diabetes and memory loss of the event, and some suggestions as to the next few weeks. Angelo interrupted them with questions. He was fascinated, most eager for every detail, and for the meanings and intricacies of some of the medical terms.

Angelo insisted that they call him Angelo, not Mr. Ginnini. To John and Mal, he was quite delightful. A lovely, intelligent gentleman. He seemed to have a good grasp of all this new information. New to him. He remained polite and rational throughout. He was really quite optimistic about the future handling of his diabetic status. He asked if his wife might visit him? And his family?

"Certainly, by all means", Mal reassured him.

Will's beeper sounded. He excused himself, shook Angelo's proffered hand, and left, dodging to avoid the hovering nurse, who had taken in every word.

Chapter 35 - I Need A Priest

John and Mal told Angelo that they both would be back every day, and, in addition, whenever he called or needed them. Angelo shook both their hands with a big smile, said, "Go well, my friends, and God bless you. I thank you so for the care you have given me. My family and I shall never forget it. I am deeply in your debt. I shall see you tomorrow."

In the little dictation room, down the hall, at the nurses' station, John closed the door and said to Mal, "Boy-oh-boy, that's not what I expected from Angelo Ginnini."

"Me either. Not at all. A clear personality shift. I never knew him before, but this is not the Mafia Don personality that one would expect. I've seen this before. A marked personality shift into a totally different persona, usually associated with a severe head injury. It could fit here. Patients sometimes take on a personality diametrically opposed to the previous one. We're not quite sure how or why this happens. Probably something to do with the subconscious and its effect from the ego. Not to sound too much like Freud, but that's some of the current thinking. It probably happens in the amygdala part of the brain. It may last, or he may revert to the old self, or even take on a third personality. A change may occur as a result of a further trauma or severe outside pressures from family or environment."

"That's helpful, Mal", John said. "I've never seen this before. Heard about it happening, but never seen it. Interesting. Really interesting. How far divergent will he be likely to go?"

"No way of knowing. Only time will tell. But if he turns into a goody-goody, he could be in trouble with his business colleagues and peers."

"You mean with the Mafia crime business?"

"Only time will tell, but you could have a real problem on your — our — the hospital's collective hands. Look, I've gotta run, but let's stay in touch about this. And", and looking John squarely in the eye, he added, "be careful, yourself."

Mal followed John out of the room, turned toward the elevator and pushed the button. Down the hall the nurse came out of Angelo's room, and looked up the hallway, and down. She saw John, and walked briskly toward him. *Is she coming after me?* John wondered. *This is unusual.*

"Dr. Pullman, uh, the......the, uh.... Mr. Ginnini would like to see you. He has a question for you. Wouldn't tell me. He wants you."

"Sure. Thanks." Pullman followed the nurse back into the room. When Angelo saw John, a big smile came across his face.

"Nurse, would you excuse us for a few moments, please." Angelo said, turning back to John, the smile gone.

"Yes, certainly, Mr. Ginnini. You just call if you need me. I'm out in the hall." She left, closed the door, slowly, and turned to the thug guarding the door.

"Dr. Pullman, may I call you John?" Angelo questioned.

"Yes, certainly, Angelo. May I call you Angelo?" John stood next to the side of the bed.

"I am coming to remember things. Things that give me a big problem. Business things. I don't know if you know what kinds of business things I have been involved in, but..."

John felt suddenly nervous, "I have heard of some things. I mean, some businesses you may be involved in, but I'm not sure...."

"Yes, you probably know of my legitimate businesses, but there have been some others as well." Angelo said, looking seriously into John's eyes. John felt a sudden chill, and broke into a cold sweat. *I'm not sure I want to hear this,* he thought.

"John, I need to confide some things to you, confidentially. Doctor-patient relationship, you know? I also need to have a priest here. There is a Catholic priest in the hospital, I presume?"

"Yes there is. Father James Gibbons. I know him well."

"Good. Would you call him, please? Oh," Angelo said, stroking his chin. "How rude of me. Do you have a few minutes now? Or is this a bad time for you? I don't mean to take your time, but this is important."

"Sure. Actually this is a good time. I have a break in my

schedule. Serendipitous." John took out his cell, dialed, waited. Angelo could hear the ringing buzz in John's ear.

Click. "Father Gibbons. How can I be of help?........Is this you John?"

"Good morning Father. How are you? Busy, I'm sure, but do you have a moment you could spare?"

"You mean right now?" the voice paused, "Yes, as matter of fact, I do. What's on your mind?" Father Gibbons knew John well, and assumed this might be an issue of some importance, some gravity.

"I'm with Angelo Ginnini, my patient. He has an issue he would like to discuss — to discuss with me in confidence, and he would like to have you present. He has requested you, if you have a moment." John's mind was racing. *I have no idea what Angelo has in mind. I know Father James is wondering the same thing, considering who Angelo supposedly is, and things he has supposedly done. He is the Godfather of one of the biggest crime families around.*

"I'll be right there. I'm only one floor down." Two minutes later, a soft knock on the door, and in swept Father James, his big, friendly smile greeting the doctor and the patient. His outstretched hand reached straight to Angelo, as if they had been parted friends. "Father James, Mr. Ginnini. I'm so glad to see you, my son. May the peace of Christ be with you", he stated as he made the sign of the cross, "And with you, Dr. Pullman."

Both Angelo and John felt as if a breath of fresh air had come into the room, but their faces remained serious . Father James' smile quickly faded. "How can I be of help, Mr. Ginnini?"

"It's Angelo, Father", he said. Then, pointing a finger at the standing doctor, he said, "Bring some chairs, please, and sit." motioning to the seats in the room. "I want to make a confession, Father."

John straightened, "Then I'll be going. I'll leave you two alone." Father James looked at John, as did Angelo.

"No, please, doctor," Angelo pleaded. "I want you to stay. I want you both to hear what I have to say. I need you both. The Church and the medical. Please." He looked from one to the other.

"And bring the chairs, please."

Angelo was sitting upright in bed, unshaven, hospital johnny, but in control. He looked from one man to the other, and back again, both seated by the bedside. His face grew dark, forehead creased. "I have had a very bad past. Evil. Things I have done." He paused, obviously thinking for the right words. "Let me say, I have been told. Father Perez at Our Lady of Sorrows has told me. Told me many times, from way back. He told me that God would give me a chance. A second chance, if I changed my ways. I could still come back. I could do good. The right things. Amend my ways. He said God would do that for me." Angelo looked at Father James.

"That is so, my son. God forgives those who repent the error of their ways. Those who....."

"Father, I think God is giving me that chance."

"Yes, my son........"

"No, I mean since I had my accident. When I woke up. When I could think straight, again, I see that chance."

"Yes, my son."

"So I need to come clean. I need to set some things right. A lot of things that I need to set right. But, I'm going to need help. A lot of help. The things I've done. I'm going to need a lot of help."

"Yes, my son. We're here to help you any way we can. Trust in the...."

"Father, I'll get to the confession, my Catholic confession, in the Church, full thing, all of that, later. But now, I need you to help me with the real world. I gotta deal with the real world, first, and with the problems from my family and my business associates. I need help with some bad people, doing bad things. Like me. Doing bad things for a long time." He paused, looked down into his lap, silently reflecting. "Sins. Sins in the face of God. For a long time. And I need help to clear the air. Then, when that's done, I'll be on my knees before the altar, Father. You have my word on that." Angelo's stare penetrated Father James, who was speechless.

Chapter 36 - Father James Gibbons

Angelo turned to John with the same intense stare of his black eyes under heavy, furrowed, black, bushy eyebrows. "You too, Doctor John. You both. Both you on the medical, and Father, with the Church. I need both of your support." His mouth was dry. He had a little trouble getting the words out. John noticed.

"You okay, Angelo? Can I get you something?" John asked. "Want me to get the nurse?"

"No! Don't get her. Can't trust her. She's not part of this."

"What do you mean?"

"I hired her and had her trained. Specially. The bunch of them. Couple years ago. For the Family. For the Family ways. For just the stuff I want to discuss. Go public with. Get out in the open. My second chance with God." He turned to Father James, "Right Father?" Then to John he said, "Don't trust any of them. They all work for the Family. Keep them out of it. They'll find out soon enough." John got up, went to the wash stand, and came back with a glass of water for Angelo.

"So how do you want us to help you, Angelo?" John asked, sitting down again, earnestly leaning forward toward his patient.

"I want you to get the district attorney in here. Court reporter, stenographer, whatever you call her. Complete with video. I figure I've only got one chance on this. To make it right. One chance. I think they're gonna get me next time."

"Who's going to get you?" Father James asked with obvious concern in his voice. "What do you mean?"

"My enemies, Father. My enemies. I've got a lot of enemies. In my business there are lots of enemies. Lots of friends, but lots of enemies. Deadly enemies. They almost got me this time. Right Doctor John? Almost did it this time."

"Yes. You're right there. You were a very lucky man. An inch or two either way, and you would never have made it to the hospital, much less through your big surgery."

"Yes. I remember now, it was Herbie the waiter at Pasgucci's. He must have been set up by the Gambinis. That's my guess. That's past. They're looking for me to get even, now that I'm still among the living. And, yes, I'm going to get even. But not the way they think I will. And, I'm not doing any of this to get even. I know my time has come, or almost come, so I want to make good on all the bad I've done." He looked at Father James. "I want to come before God and right my wrongs. But I need to right my wrongs with society first, and if I live through that, then come to confession in the Church, Father. But God will know that in my heart, I have already started."

"Yes, my son. I truly believe you have it in your heart, if all you say is true."

"But living through it will be a real challenge. That's why I need the DA. In here. Now. Soon as possible. The word will get out, and that will be that, for me. So the DA with the video."

"I understand, completely, both what you want to do, and the ramifications." said John. "I happen to know the DA, personally. J. Edwards Baird. Angelo, he's a straight shooter. I can honestly attest for his honesty and competence."   "I need to talk with him, on the record, as soon as possible." Angelo leaned forward looking hard at John. John dug into his pocket, pulled out his cell phone, a hit a few buttons, and listened.

"Hi Molly, John Pullman here. Is Jeb around?..........Good.......May I speak to him? It's rather urgent........thanks........Hey Jeb, John here." John Pullman spent the next several minutes telling a very silent, very receptive J. Edwards Baird the particulars of the phone call. "And he wants it all on official video record." John looked at Angelo with raised eyebrows, and asked him, "Something that will stand up in court?"

"Absolutely. That's the point", Angelo answered.

"Okay. That will be good......Yes...... Hang on. Let me check." Speaking around the phone to the other two, John asked, "Five-thirty okay for you two? Here in Angelo's room? I can make it back. That okay with you Father?" John turned to Angelo, "You want Father here for this?"

"Very most definitely. I'm going to need God on my side.

Father'll make sure I do. He will add big credence to the testimony I'll be giving."

John swiveled the phone back to speak, "Five-thirty then, Jeb......Good. See you then."

Chapter 37 - Billy's Mistake

After John and Father James left, the nurse came back in immediately, looking all around the room. Angelo, resting on his pillow, was sleeping. At least he looked like he was sleeping. She watched him for at least a minute. Nothing. *Asleep* she assumed and tip-toed to the door. She opened it crack and whispered to the thug standing watch, "I gotta see Billy. I need to see him now. Today. You got that. Now."

The uniformed city policeman standing guard on the other side of the doorway didn't move a muscle, as if he never heard a word. When the nurse closed the door, he slowly, casually glanced down at his watch. *Twelve-forty-five. Remember that. Gotta tell Sarge. Something's coming down.* He shifted his weight, and glanced down the empty hall towards the Nurses Station. He was one of the few not on Sal's payroll.

Joey, known as "Li'l Joey" to differentiate him from "Big Joey", had this watch on the Godfather's door. He looked up the deserted hallway. He looked down the deserted hallway. He looked at his watch. He looked at the city patrolman, who looked bored and spaced out. *Nothing happening. Nothing. So's nows a good time.* He stepped away from his side of the doorway and crept down the hall a dozen, two dozen paces, maybe. He dug deep in his voluminous black trousers pocket, pulled out his cell phone, and punched a quick-dial key. "Yah, dis is me. Nurse needs words wid-cha....... Yah......Now. She said now......Dunno......didn't tell me. Wannsa tell you. Personal-like........Yah." Click. Phone back in pocket. Back to the doorway. The door cracked open just an inch. It was the nurse, again.

"You tell 'im?"

"Tell who?"

"Did you tell Billy what I told ya to tell him? That's a simple yes or no. No rocket science here. So, yes or no. Didja tell him or didn' ya?"

"Yah, so I told him arreddy. So there."   "What did he say?"

"Who, Billy? He didn't say nuttin'. Asked what it was all about. I told him I didn't know from jack-shit. Just come see youse. Like youse said. Dats all. Nuttin' more." She was pissed, but she shut the door, quietly.

Billy didn't make mistakes. Not in his business. Not in his position in the Family ranks. He was a Sargent, a Da Capo, in charge of a bunch of soldati - soldiers in the business. There were half a dozen Da Capos, and almost a hundred soldati taking care of the organization's many businesses, including those nurses and nurses aids caring for Angelo. Billy was fairly high up, with only a few more levels above him up to the Boss, the Godfather, the Don. So when he decided not to interrupt the important meeting to go see that damn nurse, he didn't know what he would be missing. *She's gettin' to be a real pain in the ass. Always, whining about dis er dat little thing. The Boss, he's gettin' better. Waked up and talking. He even talked to me after lunch. Short chat, 'bout nuttin' in particular. But he was sittin' up and talkin'. Dat's good, like I told Sal, the Underboss. No need to jump cuz de dumb broad sez come. Dis here meetin's important. Talk to her later. When I got time. Yah. Tonight, maybe.*

So Billy never saw John Pullman return at 5:25, along with his friend, District Attorney J. Edwards "Jeb" Baird, and an assistant DA, carrying a fat briefcase, a big woman with a little machine in a case, and a guy with a professional video outfit. They all went into Angelo's room. The nurse had been excused.

"Go to supper. I'll call you when I'm ready for you to come back. I wanna be private till then", Angelo had ordered. She obeyed and passed Father James as he hustled toward Angelo's room.

"Good evening" Father James said to her. But she didn't know who he was, so she pretended not to see him. She didn't know who any of the others were either, coming in with Doctor Pullman. He never came in at this time of day.

In the cafeteria, the nurse quick-dialed her phone again. Spoke briefly. Ended the call, and shrugged her shoulders, pouting her lips, pissed off. She didn't eat much; too worried. *Something's going on, and I should know what it is and tell them. But if they don't wanna listen, screw'em.* When she finally did return to Angelo's room, she checked everything. Normal, including the hidden gun. *Angelo's sleeping. Nothing's been moved. The meds are all there. No one touched them. Nothing changed. Nothing new. Maybe it's all just my imagination. But what's with the three-plus-hour private time. What's he doin'? Something's goin' on. Gotta be. Who were those people with the doctor? They part of the Godfather's private? Gotta be. But who? Never seen any of them before, an' I know all the Godfather's talk-tos, or at least most of 'em. Huh?*

Chapter 38- Al Towns, RN, MSN, MPH

Al Towns, RN, MSN (Master of Science, Nursing), **MPH** (Master Public Health), the Head Nurse for the Trauma Unit, was smart and quick. Way back when, he and John Pullman had been buddies at Yale. John had been on track to Medical School, while Al had enlisted in the Marine PLC program. But they were pals, each respecting the path the other had chosen. They had tossed back more than a few beers together, had gone to football games and movies together, and had double dated. They had compared varying courses they were taking, concepts and philosophies they were learning. So it was with some sadness when they said good-bye at graduation, knowing that their separate paths might not meet again for some time.

Al went off into active duty with the Marines. Quantico, Virginia. Second Lieutenant, waiting for orders for flight training at the Naval Air Station, Pensacola, Florida. Fixed wing aircraft at first, then helicopters. He had always been a good athlete. The girls all called him "big, black, and handsome", well over six feet and hard. His buddies on the Yale lacrosse team used to call him the next Jimmy Brown.

The physical training the Marines required delighted Al. Nothing was too much of a challenge. The longer, the harder, the steeper, the tougher, the better for Al. When some of his buddies caved beside him, he kept going, encouraging them, pushing, bolstering. He loved the challenge, the discipline, and especially the guns. Writing to John, he claimed, "The ability to put an M-1 rifle bullet through a two inch hole at a hundred yards, really appeals to my sense of precision and engineering perfection. I've gotten pretty good at it. It'll probably save my life someday."

But flight school wasn't enough for Al. In off hours, he continued his training in several different martial arts. Tae Kwon Do, the ancient Korean art of self-defense, meaning, "foot, hand, art", was his favorite. "He's a natural", the instructor had told the rest of the class. Brown belt, then Black Belt. Physical as well as mental growth. Third degree was all he had time for before being shipped out. He had tried some of the other self-defense arts as well, but favored Tae Kwon Do. Where one of the arts lacked, another filled in. Al called it "total defense training."

The Marines taught him all he needed to know about offensive combat. He was one of the few second-lieutenants in his group who could disarm, and if necessary, kill an opponent in a few, quick, decisive moves. Everyone said, "Don't piss him off, if you're smart." But Al's low burn point, his easy going way, rarely raised more than a frown, occasionally a "Watch it, buddy."

Even if you were unaware of his lethal skills, you never wanted to tangle with him. Six foot-four, two hundred twenty-five pounds of unsprung steel, buffed and toned by the military physical exercise, stretching most tee-shirts. He cautioned respect across the street and down the block.

One of his buddies, another young, second lieutenant in his group, a guy named Baird, was getting the worst that a couple of fat-fisted, local bullies had to offer. Al just happened to come around the corner. Recognizing the unfair circumstances, he commanded, "Hey, fellas. Lay off. He's with me."

Both bullies, big men, each, maybe six feet, and heavy, fat-heavy. They spun around facing Al. "Sez who!" one spat.

"Well lookee here, Butchie", the other bragged. "We got us a even bigger prize."

Al stopped a couple of yards away. He sized up the situation. *About two good steps. They'll undoubtedly stick together, as bullies usually do. That's good. Piece of cake.*

"Sez me", Al challenged. "Leave my pal alone. You want fair odds, you try me." The two hunched to fighting stance, as he knew they would, and glowered. Al taunted them a little more, "You always go two against one?"

"Bet chur ass, buster. When we done wid-ju, black-boy, we gonna eat chur whitey pal for dessert. Ain't we Butchie."

"Are you sure you wouldn't rather just go on your way, now?" Al asked in a kindly, earnest tone, ignoring the racial insult. They glowered even harder. "Okay, then..." he smiled.

The two shifted foot to foot. They were so predictable, like bulls pawing the ground.

Al decided to make it fast and simple. He moved the two steps and with lightening speed, grabbed both by the neck, jerked them apart, off balance, and with a grunt, crashed the two heads together with an audible 'clonck'. He let go, as both hulks of flab collapsed to the ground, senseless.

Ed Baird stood frozen, staring at the two unconscious heaps. He shook his head, and stood straight. "Jeesis, Al. Thanks, buddy. You really saved my bacon. I owe you. Big time. They'd have cleaned my clocks. Probably would have knocked me outta MP-police school."

"Think nothing of it. Let's go have a beer. The O-Club is open. First round's on me."

About a year after the six months of Operation Desert Storm, Al decided enough was enough. Non-combat assignments in the States were pretty boring, and Desert Storm was over. He had been flying both fixed-wing, single engine reconnaissance, and helicopter missions into the desert, rescuing fellow Marines and Army guys, wounded or in a tight situation. Getting shot at was no fun. His good fortune finally ran out , and he was shot down, just as his tour was ending. He credited his survival to sheer luck and a little training, and figured he'd spent most of his nine lives. So, now bound to a desk, he resigned his commission. Highly decorated. With much hand shaking, "thank-you from your Government", and "gonna miss you around here, buddy", Al became a civilian, looking for a new career.

First thing he did, was call his buddy, John Pullman.

"Doctor Pullman is in the OR", the voice said, "Do you wish to leave a message?"

When John called back, he was delighted that Al was back in the USA. He was even happier to hear that he was a civilian again. They arranged to meet on the next weekend that John had off. "Let's go back to Morey's, in New Haven?"

"Yah, Morey's, in New Haven." It was farther for Al to travel, but he had plenty of time. It was a trip for John, too, with each coming from other direction.

Chapter 39 - A New Career

They drank a lot of beer, and each wolfed down a sixteen ounce steak, rare, and more beer. Maybe one or two too many?

"So, tomorrow, whatta wanna do?"

They talked and they walked, and they talked some more. "Like a couple of old women." Al said. John told Al of the planned surgical course before him. Al said he had no idea what to do. They fell silent, all talked out. Then John said, "Lemme call Annie B We're engaged, you know."

"Yah, you told me, maybe fifty times. Wanna meet her."

"I'll get her to bring a friend. We can see a show or something. Annie B will know what to do. I'm clueless, as usual. Spend all my time in the damn hospital."

Annie B did bring a friend. Barbara Painter. "I'm Al. Al Towns. Where you from?" The small talk was hesitant and shy, at first. But a couple of drinks helped the situation, and by the time the salad course was finished, it was obvious that Al and Barby had each found something attractive here. Very attractive.

The weekend was over way too soon. Each went back to work, except Al. First, he got into insurance. Then he tried selling "these new personal computer" machines. That lasted a little over two years. He made money, but boring. After active duty with the Marines, this life was too dull. Same old, same old, day after day. Nothing new. Nothing stimulating. He called his old friend, John.

"We've been friends a long time, so tell me honestly, what would you think if I went into medicine? I mean, do you think I'd fit? You know me pretty damn well. Think it would work for me? I've watched you. I know it's a long process. You still love it?" He realized he was nervous, spewing out words, and Al never did that. "What do you think? Think I could do it?"

"Slow down Al, and damn straight I love it. Couldn't, wouldn't do anything else. It is absolutely the best. At least the best for me. What are you thinking? You're getting a little old for medical school, ya know?"

"Yah, John, I'm very aware of that. I was thinking more of trying nursing than med school. Shorter apprenticeship. A good deal of independence. Involved in critical decisions. Save a few lives, perhaps, and helping people to better health, better lives. Is that too Pollyanna?"

"Hell no", John was getting excited for his friend. Al sounded more enthusiastic than he had in years. "Go for it man."

"I worry a little that it might get to me, always having to follow the doctors' orders, and not thinking it through myself? Woman's work?"

"Al, a really good nurse, a well educated go getter, is always out ahead on the patients under his or her care. There's always gonna be those who follow the crowd, who follow the orders, and not much else. But that's not you. You'll always be a step ahead of everyone else, and that would be particularly true for a guy like you in a field like nursing. Gee, Al, now that I think of it, I think it would be a great field for you. And no, it's not woman's work. Far from it. You'd rise to the top fast."

Al relaxed his death grip on his telephone, let his shoulders go, and took a deep breath. "Thanks, John. That's what I'd hoped you'd say. I'm going to give it a try. I've already got my application in to a couple of places." He paused, swallowed, cleared his throat, and asked, "You don't think it's too sissy, do you? You know, a male in a mostly female profession?"

John smiled to the phone. *Typical Al. Always the self-doubt, despite his physical size and warrior capabilities.*

"Al", John said, "Lemme tell you a short story. They made a TV documentary last year at University Medical Center, and interviewed this male nurse on the ER evening shift. The interviewer tried to embarrass him by asking why he wanted to go into "this female dominated profession?" He kicked his head back, snorted a quick laugh, gave a wide toothy grin, and boasted, 'Because that's where the chicks are, man.'"

Al graduated first in his class with a combo BSN/MSN. He and Barbara got married. She was the smart, sweet, six-foot lady from that double date years ago. She was a lawyer with a particular talent for mergers and acquisitions and, eventually, a seven figure income. At a young age, she became the first black woman partner in her firm. But her first love, by her own admission, was Al Towns. She had been smitten from that very first of many dates.

Al went on to earn his second Master's degree, in Public Health, working the evening shift on the surgical floor, despite his wife's more-than-adequate income. The Nursing Department at University Medical Center hired him the day he applied. In six months, they made him head nurse on the Trauma Unit. After a year, they wanted to elevate him in the nursing office hierarchy, but Al refused. He told them he preferred to stay on the floor, working with patients, which was his true professional love.

Chapter 40 - Larry

"Good morning Larry. How you feeling this morning? Get some breakfast?" Dr. Bill Bayard burst into the room, with Shorty Buck, ortho PA close behind. Larry Lowance was sitting up in bed, his food still on the tray on the bed-straddling service table in front of him. He looked a little sheepish. Such a big man, stuck, helpless.

"Mornin' Dr. Bill. Good seein' you, and you, too, Dr. Shorty. Feelin' pretty good, but seems I got a little problem here." Larry's left arm was in a posterior molded splint, triceps to hand. Kind of a semi-cast. Wrapped up, it felt pretty good, but the arm was useless. The right arm was free, but for a light dressing, however, he didn't want to use it because it hurt like hell, even with the pain pills the nurse gave him. "Nurse told me to feed myself, but I can't do it. Hurts. Don't wanna do no harm to what you fixed last night."

"Larry, I'm sorry. That's my fault. I tried to tell you all about that last night, but I guess you were still too spaced out from the fentanyl to remember."

"Yeah, doc. I don't remember nothin' from last night. No pain, no nothin'. Nice job. Didn't feel a thing." Larry said, resting his right arm over the left semi-casted one, looking at one then the other.

"Okay, Larry. No problem. Here's the deal. Both bones of both forearms had transverse fractures which required plating. You've got a twenty centimeter metal plate screwed onto each bone. Two right and two left. They required two longitudinal incisions on each forearm to mount the metal plates onto the bone, but they are good and stable. It would take a lot of stress to mess them up. You can use your arms normally for light work activities. No heavy lifting. It's going to hurt, particularly these next few days, but not from the fractures or plates. They'll be okay. The soft tissues in there, the muscles, tendons, nerves were badly bruised by the beating they gave you to break those bones. That's what's going to hurt. Not the fractures. It'll hurt to move your fingers, as I'm sure you've found. But you should move them as much as you can. That will help against the swelling in there. We put your left arm in that plaster splint there to give you some rest, and less pain on that side. That's purely for comfort. It won't help the healing any. You don't need it, unless you want it."

"I wanna get better quick as I can, doc. Need to get back to work, make some dough to pay for all this."

"Don't you have health insurance? A plan where you work? To cover you for things like this?" Bill asked.

"Hell no, doc. That outfit is so tight, they charge us a buck for a cuppa coffee. No. No health insurance. No bennies of any kind. Straight hourly wage. Eight-fifty an hour. Got a raise to ten. My rent takes half of that. No, I gotta pay this myself." Larry looked Bayard straight in the eye. "Both you and the hospital."

Bayard turned to Shorty, "Make sure the social workers see him. Today. Get the Medicaid application papers going."

"Yah, right." Shorty answered. "I'm on it." He made a note on his iPad.

"I'm gonna need Medicaid? Larry looked puzzled. "I only been here one night."

"I don't want to alarm you," Shorty said, "but Larry, what with the OR, X-rays, hospital room rates, and all, I'm guessing your hospital bill is already up to twenty thou, give or take a few thou."

Larry looked panicked, "Dr. Bill, that be true?"

"Yes, Larry, I'm afraid Shorty's about right on that, and there's more to come. At ten bucks an hour, you're certainly going to need financial assistance." Bill looked over at Shorty who took up the discussion.

"Our Social Workers will get you on Medicaid which will not only bring down the charges the hospital will accept, but will help you cover most of the fees and charges."

"I'd be much obliged if you could make that be." Larry looked from Shorty back to Bill. "And you was sayin' about movin' my hands and fingers?"

"Yes, use your arms and fingers much as you can. Especially your fingers. Light activities, much as you can tolerate. It'll be sore, but you won't damage anything. In fact, you'll help heal everything by keeping them going. That's why we want you to try to feed yourself. Clean yourself at toilet. Bathe yourself. For the next week, you'll have to cover your arm dressings with plastic bags when you shower. The therapy people will get you all that."

Bill turned to Shorty again, "Shorty help me remove his splint." Shorty came around the bed, and together they slowly, carefully unwrapped the ace around the plaster on Larry's left arm.

"Woooh", Larry let out a long breath. "Feels weird. You're right, though, doesn't hurt much." He wiggled his fingers just a little. "Different feeling, but not bad. How much I gotta wear that", Larry asked nodding toward the splint.

"Only for comfort. At the end of a long day. It's not therapeutic. Comfort only. Won't affect the bone healing. Now, today the therapy people will come in to work with you. Then tomorrow they'll transfer you up to the rehab unit." Bill paused as he scrutinized the computer.

Shorty continued the information, "The physical therapists will teach you and help you with exercises to help you keep and maintain motion and strength in your arms. In the long run, the exercises will help decrease the pain and help return you to your normal, pre-injury status." Then he dove into his iPad, and Bill took over again. A well rehearsed team.

"The occupational therapists will help you regain what they call your ADLs, Activities of Daily Living. You know, feeding yourself, bathing, toilet, caring for yourself at home. It'll probably take a couple of days to get where you can do that by yourself. Then we'll follow you in the clinic. So get up and walk around. Ask the nurses to help you put your splint back on, if you want it."

"Yah, and walk around a lot. Much as you can." Shorty said. "Keeps the blood flowing. Good for healing."

Larry, slightly overwhelmed by all this information, thought about his situation for a minute, staring blankly at the opposite wall. Dr. Bayard and the PA stood together at the foot of the bed, checking the medical record computer, entering orders and necessary data.

"You're right on schedule, Larry. You'll be getting antibiotics for twenty-four hours. Regular diet. Pain meds. Ask the nurse for the pain pills before the pain begins so they have time to kick in before the pain gets bad."

"Oh, I won't need much of them", Larry stated. "I'm pretty tough if I know the pain's expected, and not a sign that something's going wrong. Besides, I don't wanna get hooked again, like I did when I was a teener."

Shorty looked up, "You had a drug problem?"

"Yah, we all did, back in those days. Everybody did it. Pushers everywhere, tellin' you it's good for you. Glad I never got as bad as my mother. She was hard core. I was lucky. I kicked it in the Army. Stay away from it now, for sure. Both ways."

"Both ways? Shorty asked, "Whatta you mean both ways?"

"Using and dealing. Both ways. Stay away from all of it. Road to hell is covered with heroin an' that new stuff fentanyl. Seen it end a lotta lives. Not for me. No-siree.

Bill punched the computer a last jab, and came closer to Larry, "I've written for some Toradol. It's a non-opiate, non-addicting. One or two are not very powerful, and, as long as you are having pain, they are not likely to addict you. So take one when the pain is really uncomfortable. Which it will be for the next few days. Those forearm soft tissues took quite a beating. They looked badly battered when we were in there plating the bony fractures. It'll be a week, maybe ten days until you loosen up the muscles and other soft tissues. The bone won't hurt at all. Its stable. Trust me on that."

"Oh, I trust you all right. You and Dr. Shorty, here, and all the docs. And Doc Pullman, too. He's the one who got you to fix me up. I'm mighty obliged to all of you wonderful people. You take good care of ol' Larry. You sure do." Both Shorty and Dr. Bayard noted the small tear welling up in the corner of the gentle giant's eye.

Chapter 41 - Trouble

"The doctors all done? All gone? For now? I gotta talk to the Godfadder. No inneruptions", Billy stared down at the nurse. "You got dat? No inneruptions. No one goes in. No one goes out. No one. Goes for you too, Fats." Billy looked over at the thug who was standing his watch outside the door. The city cop, standing watch, on the other side of the doorway, pretended not to notice or hear. His Captain had told him to notice everything and report it all, but he was also being paid off not to. So he didn't.

Billy went in and shut the door hard. The lock clicked. Angelo, sitting in his soft, padded, orthotic chair, looked up and smiled. "Hello Billy. Nice to see you. What brings you in on this fine day."

Jeeziz, Billy thought, *Whats dis? Sure ain't the Godfadder. Musta took a pleasant pill, cuz he sure as shit ain't gettin' laid. Not in dis place.*

"Hello Godfadder", he said as he took off his narrow-brimmed fedora and bowed slightly. "How you feelin' today. Yer lookin' good, Godfadder."

"And I'm feeling good too, Billy. What's new?"

"I just come in to see howsya doin', Godfadder. Could I sit?" Billy motioned to the empty chair, and drew it up to Angelo, but without waiting for an answer.

"Business going alright, Billy? Things running smoothly, I hope?" Angelo smiled as he asked in a very civil, pleasant tone.

"Yah, everything's good, Godfadder. Goin' good." Billy didn't know what to say. *This ain't the Godfather. He's nice at me. Funny accent. Talkin' like some college guy. Not the Godfather. Smilin'? Bein' nice? Somethin's wrong here...... He's up to somethin'. Testin' me? Looking for somethin'? I done nuttin. Nuttin going down bad.*

"Tell me Billy, income steady? Businesses all in order? Anyone disobeying the law?" Angelo, still smiling, seemed obviously very happy.

Jeeziz, this ain't good. "Escuse me, Godfadder. Gotta do somethin'. Be right back." Billy lifted out of his chair, and lumbered across the room to the door. "Be right back, Godfadder. Don't go nowhere." He was out of the door, which he closed softly but firmly.

Billy checked that no one else was in the Men's room, looking under the stall doors. "It's Billy", he whispered into his cell phone....... "Yah, I gotta talk to him." Tapping his foot nervously, and trying to bite his already chewed fingernails. "Yah...... Can ya come now?....... Good...... Meet me there. I'm goin' back to his room now.........yah.......see ya then." He put his cell back in his pocket, and left the men's room.

Walking toward Angelo's room, a perfectly manicured gentleman, Italian shoes, beautifully shined, grey silk suit, obviously custom tailored to fit his slight frame, greying hair coiffed back from the high, Italian forehead. A menacing air about him was not helped by the two thugs following, at a respectful distance. Outside the door, he nodded to the current guard, who knocked five raps, then opened the door.

"Juanito, my boy, how good it is to see you." Angelo's smile was genuinely warm, inviting. He leaned forward, holding out his right hand. Billy jumped from his chair, and looked around, checking the room.

"Godfather, so good to see you. You look so well. They must be treating you well, here." But Angelo's welcoming smile was not returned. Juanito's name was really John. Just John. Formerly Johnny. He was called Juanito by Angelo. By Angelo only. The last person, other than the Godfather, to call him Juanito was no longer living.

Chapter 42 - John Dominicci

Born in Palermo, Sicily, Giovanni Dominicci was brought to New York by his mother, Bella after his father had been removed by a rival family. A puny kid from the start, Giovanni had to grow up tough to hold his own against the kids his own age. At eight, he had roughly the same stature as his neighboring paisani, but by ten, he began to notice he was falling behind. By twelve even his closest friends were bigger. He was shorter and skinnier, and this bothered him. A lot.

One Sunday morning, on his way to church, lagging behind his mother and sisters, he was snatched by three big kids — bullies. He knew who they were by reputation. After binding his hands and feet, they stashed him in a metal garbage drum. Giovanni couldn't move. Couldn't get out. Couldn't tip the barrel over. He was stuck until someone heard him yelling. At that moment he decided he'd get a weapon. Something that would equalize the odds that his lack of physical size couldn't. That changed his life remarkably.

A little over a year later, he wasn't supposed to be there, but he was. Three soldati were arguing over "who had to do the job". He knew they were soldiers from the Family. Inside men, men who had been *made* into the Ginnini family. A hit. They were planning a hit, but none of the three wanted to do it. Too dangerous. Too many repercussions. Too big a risk.

Giovanni stepped out from his hiding place, and blurted, "I can do that. You want him hit. I can do it." They spun around, took one look, and started to laugh. Giovanni was pissed. He growled, "Shut da fuck up." The little guy had a big voice. "Get me da gun, an' I'll take care of yer problem for ya's." They did shut da fuck up. They gawked at one another.

"Hey, why not."

"Yah, why not."

"Yah. No skin off my balls. Let him do it. Worst he can do is miss. Then it's not our problem no more."

"What's the Boss gonna say?"

"Da Boss don't need ta know. Capisc? Job gets done. We get da credit."

"Yah, I'm for it."

"Yuh, okay. I guess so."

"Okay den. Hey kid, com'ere." They told him who, when, where, and gave him a pistol. "You use one of dese before?"

Yeah, he had. His uncle had showed him. Lots of times. Shot beer cans lots of times. Him and his cousin. Lots of times. He was a pretty good shot.

So he did it. He did it, but not like they told him. He did it smarter. He waited till the guy was taking his afternoon nap, there in the sun. On his back patio. He snuck up, put the muzzle to the back of his head, and pulled the trigger. Blew his face away. His entire fucking face. Jeeziz, Joseph, and Mary. Easy to do. So easy to do. Quick and easy. The first of many.

The gun — his gun — was a great equalizer. Equalizer, hell. It made him superior. By the time he was eighteen, he was known, respected, and feared. He told everyone to call him John, and they all obeyed. The kid had been "made" by the Boss himself. Yah, the Boss, the Godfather, who kinda adopted him, and called him Juanito. A special name.

There were two of them made into the Family. They were called the Enforcers — the hit men. Even though he was only nineteen, John liked being called 'a man'. Five foot five, 121 pounds. Wiry. Wiry, maybe, but fast. Fast like lightening. One second you were there, The next second you were dead. Ruthless, they said. Yah, ruthless. He liked ruthless. Gave him stature and respect. "No one fuck with John no more."

Yah, he got respect. He liked respect.....and stature. So he decided to get more respect, better respect. He studied how educated men spoke. How they used language. And business men — how they dressed. And manners. Yah, manners, too. "Manners make the gentleman" he heard them say. He learned those too. *I'm savin' my dough. No*, he corrected himself, *I'm saving some money*. At that fancy men's shop down in the business district, he told them he needed a "wardrobe". It cost a lot, but he bought himself a wardrobe. Then he enrolled in night school to get a college degree in business.

His life changed even more. People considered him a gentleman. Even the Boss said so. He was glad the Boss liked it. If the Boss liked it, then everybody liked it. That was the way it was.

That didn't mean he had gotten soft inside. Quite the opposite. He was tougher, and faster, and colder. When they caught Vido with his hand in the numbers till, taking more out than was called for, the Boss called John, his Juanito.

"Aw come on, Johnny. It was only a few thou", Vido was scared.

"Yes, I know Vido. You know it's not the money. It's the trust. The Godfather can't trust you anymore, so it's time, Vido. It's time. And just so you know, you call me John. You haven't earned the right to call me by any other name. So for you, it's John."

"Yah, sure, John. Anything you sez, John." John took two steps forward and shot Vido up through his nose. One single shot.

John's "boys", the two goons standing quietly ten feet behind him, stepped forward, their eyes questioning John. "In the dumpster. In the alley next door." John answered.

Chapter 43 - The Positive Good

John Dominicci delicately seated himself with precision in the hospital chair Billy had just vacated, and turned to Angelo, "You need to see me, Godfather?"

"Juanito, my boy. You know you are my pride and joy. My trusted and dear friend. It's always good to see you." Angelo was still smiling like a child at Christmas. "So how's business, Juanito. They keeping you busy? Things go well while I'm staying here?"

"Yes, Godfather. Things are good. We had to let one of the pimps go other day. Kept a little more for himself than our contract allowed. I helped him out of his difficulties. Took care of him for you Godfather. Good and quiet. The way I know you like it."

"Yes. That's what I want to talk to you about. I want to change our business plan."

"Our business plan? Change it? How change it? It's working very nicely the way it is". John couldn't help looking a little uneasy. "Like they say, a well oiled machine. Everyone in line. The cash flow is good. Even the legitimate businesses are doing well. What would you want to change, Godfather? I, for one, wouldn't change a thing."

Angelo sat in his orthotic chair, fingers interlaced under his chin, nodding ever so slowly, lips pouting just a bit, thinking.

"Godfather? Change what? What do you want to change?" John shifted uneasily in his chair. Billy, equally perplexed, waited behind John, shifting from foot to foot, cracking his knuckles, peering down at the Godfather.

Silence. No clocks ticking. No oxygen hissing. No monitor buzz. Silence. John tried with all his cunning to keep his poker face, but worry was creeping in. And Billy noticed it.

Angelo wasn't looking at him. "Yes, change the business model", he said barely above a whisper. He blinked, and looked up, across the room, paused, cleared his throat, and focused on John. "It's time to change the organization. We get out of the criminal business, and put it all into the legitimate side. I been in here almost two weeks, they tell me. Lucky to be alive, they tell me. Time to make amends. Time to shift to the positive good."

"The positive good. What do you mean, the positive good? Godfather, I don't understand positive good. What do you mean, Godfather?" Angelo remained silent, but now he was staring at John. Angelo's black eyes, unflinching, unblinking staring directly into John's eyes. Very few people got to John, but the Godfather was one of them. That's why he was the Godfather. He was the one individual in the organization with a more murderous past than John's, and John was well aware of it. Perhaps the Godfather was physically a little slower than he once was, but smarter, and much more powerful.

"Did the District Attorney talk to you about the positive good?" John asked, knowing he was treading on thin ice. "I heard he was here...... with the court reporter. Is he bothering you, Godfather? Did he come barging in here to talk to you when you are not feeling well? Do you need me to get our lawyer in here to protect you?" John was getting steamed, leaning forward in his chair, trying to glare back at Angelo. "What's this positive good? What did you tell him? I don't understand, Godfather. What questions did he ask you?"

"Juanito, my boy. You've always been a good boy. A good, dutiful son to me. True, I have no male heirs, but you are my boy, Juanito. You've always been my boy. Someday this business be all yours." He paused to let it sink in. "You're smart. You've got a good head. You've gotten a good education. You know right from wrong." John's eyebrows arched involuntarily.

"What do you mean, Godfather? This is not you talking, Godfather. They give you something make you talk like this?" John was afraid he'd lose it. "You sure you're okay. You're not making sense to me, Godfather. No sense." John looked over at Billy, who, standing feet apart, hands on hips, slowly shook his head, then shrugged his shoulders.

"See why I called you?" Billy mumbled barely above a whisper. Angelo glared over at Billy, then back to his Juanito, then back to Billy, adding to the discernible tension.

"Why didn't you come to see me before this, Juanito, my boy? What keeps you away, from your old Angelo, who loves you so?"

John, at first confused by the change in topic, tried to regain his self-confidence. "I was here. Just the other day, I was here. Wasn't I Billy? I was here at a meeting......They called a meeting, ah..... to discuss you. How to, ah...... treat you. Like when you were starting to wake up from your concussion. Just like the doctors said you would." John knew he was talking too fast and too much. But he couldn't stop himself. "We were talking about your time in the Army, working with that CIA guy with the U-2 spy plane stuff. Remember? From years ago? The spy plane, U-2 stuff, you were involved in?"

"Yes, I remember Major Powers, and all them. I need to take a little rest now, Juanito . You come back to see me tomorrow. We'll talk some more." Angelo leaned his head back, folded his hands across his still ample belly, and closed his eyes.

"What the fuck's going on here, Billy? I told you to keep an eye on things." John whispered harshly, as they walked down the hall, away from Angelo's closed door. Then he stopped short, stepped in front of Billy, rose up on tip-toes, trying to get into Billy's face. Billy, ramrod straight against the wall. He found himself looking down his nose at the much shorter man.

"Naa.......nothin', John. You heard what I heard. First time I heard this stuff. First time he's talkin' funny. Sayin' stuff..... Not Godfadder stuff. Not like he usta talk....I mean, dats why I call you. I call you right away." He dipped his head with a dry swallow. "You know what I know. But, I gotta agree wid-jas, dis here ain't de Godfadder. Not de Godfadder I know."

"Billy, get this, and get it straight. You make a meeting for me and the doctors. Tomorrow morning. Private conference room. No more fuck-ups. Call me what time. You got me on that?" John whirled and left. Billy shrank. He wiped the perspiration off his oversized face.

Chapter 44 - What next?

Steve Wojek was alone and confused on the street. His mind galloping in every direction, compelling him to stop and try to think it all through. *Okay, what next? Get logical. Fact: they're gonna come looking for me. Fact: they don't know where I live, not really. Fact: they'll find the address I gave them is a phony, like my name, so buys me time. Supposition: My apartment should be safe. But only for a short while. Fact: Some patients died, had to be sacrificed to run the research. Supposition: they're gonna call it homicide. No, probably murder. Homicide's if they catch me and I cop a plea...... no, stay focused, here. Fact: they got my photograph. They will circulate it. My neighbors might see it and ID me, so I better move fast, and clear out. Shit, that will be a hell of a hard job. Not only get my stuff outta there, but wipe the place of my prints. Never thought about that. Shit, shit, shit.* He picked up his pace, heading toward his apartment.

He walked fast. *Don't run. Too noticeable.* No one else was on the sidewalk, and only a rare car on the street, so when the police car slowly rolled by, he almost froze, but he kept walking. *I'm okay, I'm okay. They didn't stop or slow down. Hey wait, they're making a U-ey, coming back, slowing. Shit. Okay, okay, okay, just stay cool.* The police car stopped. Window rolled down. "Everything alright?" the cop asked, looking intently at him.

"Uh, yeah. Just walking home from work. Need the exercise. Know what I mean? Sitting on my ass for eight hours. Like I need some exercise, ya know?" His mind was racing. He didn't know what to say. The words just spilled out.

"This ain't such a hot neighborhood for walkin' alone this time of day. You need a ride? Can I give you a lift?" the cop asked.

"No thanks. I'm almost home. And like I said, I need the exercise." Just then another car came squealing around the corner, way too fast, and shot past the police car. It took about half a second before the flashing blue lights lit up, and the police car took off in hot pursuit. *Whoa, thank you buddy. Last thing I need is a cop checking me out.*

It was mid morning before he got all his portable belongings out of the apartment and into the big SUV. He had to leave the big items, bed, couch, stuffed armchair, rugs. *The damn centrifuge takes most of the room, but I can't leave it or any of the research equipment. Way too damning. Not sure what I can do with it all. Maybe dump it someplace. Maybe start again, someplace else. My whole idea, my basic concept is still a truth that needs discovering. The tumor necrosis factor will work just fine. That's not the problem. I just need to refine the methodology a little. Probably take a little less blood from the trauma patients, and infuse it more slowly into the tumor recipients. Probably too much too fast. Huh? I wonder? What the hell am I thinking? I gotta get outta here. Now.*

It took until past noon to wipe down the entire apartment, as best as he could. He remembered they took everybody's prints when they got their Nursing licenses. *I don't know where or how they might look for prints or other evidence, but I'm guessing they will.* His brain felt like it was exploding with all the thoughts and ideas of how to perfect the clean-up. *Gotta beat the system.* All the china, glass ware, and cooking utensils he put in the dishwasher, and started a full cycle with extra soap. *That ought to take care of any prints there.* He looked around one last time, and walked out, closing the door and locking all three locks.

Driving west, mostly on back roads, avoiding the Interstates, at least at first. *They'd be looking for me there, if they are looking for me, yet. Nothing on the radio about any of it. Okay, okay. Think it through. They're gonna expect me to go west. Everybody goes west. So I'll go east, or maybe south. They're not as sharp down there, maybe.*

By six o'clock, he was creeping along with everyone else in the rush-hour jam up on the beltway around whatever city this was. *"C"-something? All the same. What state's this? Got a couple more hours before I'll stop. Find a cheap joint. Pay cash. Got plenty of cash. Should be several grand in my box there. Damn good thing I didn't succumb to that ad for the Credit Union and open an account there. Stay in cash. No card, no trail. Cash only.*

It was almost ten-thirty when he pulled into the nondescript Uncle Harry's Motel, five miles off the Interstate, in some podunk town. Neon sign blinked half the letters. Thirty-five bucks, cash. He tried to crash, but his mind racing with the what-ifs swirling around in his brain, searching for possible answers? Were there any?

Steve arose early the next morning pecked at the biscuits and gravy at a near-by greasy-spoon, but he wasn't really hungry, just worried. *What do I do next? Unload most of my stuff. If and when there comes a time that I will need it, or need to explain it as part of my research, then I can get it. But until then, it could cause some unnecessary questions. Store it. Someplace.*

The sign said he was coming to a small town. Just what he needed, Howie's Storage: Cheap rates, Monthly, Yearly. *Perfect. Where is this place? Better write it down. Never remember.* And cheap it was. He paid Howie cash for a full year. Howie said he'd get a refund if he pulled his stuff earlier than a year. Steve said he was being sent to Switzerland on a medical research project for a year, and wouldn't need his equipment. Howie was impressed. "Y'all a real live sci-en-tist? Never had one a thems before. Git all types, but no re-search sci-en-tist. Yer stuff'll be safe wi' ol' Howie. You betcha."

Steve told Howie thanks, pocketed the key, and asked, "Where's the nearest hospital?"

"What'sa matter? Y'alls sick or somethin'?

"No." Steve said, realizing his mistake. "Just looking for an old girl friend supposed to be working around here. In the local hospital."

"Yah. The County's down the road, oh......I'm sayin' sebenteen, eighteen miles, be my guess. Cain't miss it. Biggest thing 'round here. County hospital. They handle all kinds o' stuff. Got a whirlybird fer accidents, an' all that fancy stuff. E-M-Ts too. My sister's boy's one o' them. A E-M-T, ain't he just. Good job. Real proud o' him. First one in the family to go medical. They can fix anything there. Had my 'pendix out there some twenny year ago, give or take a few. Course that was before it got big. Gov'ment money. That Sen-a-tor got the money fer it. Some say he made a bundle from it. Good job though, God bless him. Sure helped the 'conomy here-'bouts."

He was about to ramble on, but Steve, getting restless, wanted to get going. "Thanks a lot, Howie. Gotta shove off. I'm sure we'll be in touch. You run a good show, here. I know I can count on you. Thanks a lot."

"Yah. See ya 'round. Say, I don't know your name. What's your name? Need it for my records."

"Neil. Neil Armstrong. Named for my uncle, the first astronaut on the moon. See ya later, Howie." Steve hit the gas and sped off. About five miles down the road, he pulled off in front of a boarded-up shack, and reached over to his backpack. In the second pocket he searched, he found his brand new ID, perfect condition, but made to look old, worn. Neil Armstrong, 22 Reacher Road, Athol, Massachusetts, 01331, his photograph smiling back at him. There were several others, too. Cost him fifty bucks, each, and worth every penny. He started up again, and soon found the hospital complex. *Perfect. Just perfect. Gotta be a level one trauma center.* He took out his Steve Wojek license along with his jack knife, and cut it into pieces. He locked the car, and dumped the cut-up Wojek license into a trash barrel. *So long Steve. Nice knowing you. Fun while it lasted. Hello Neil, leading mankind into the future, once again. Maybe a little delay at first, to get resettled, then on into the future and a place in history.*

Chapter 45 - Two Meetings

The hospital Board Room was nearly filled. Factions sat on opposite sides of the big conference table, facing each other: Ollie Alberts at the head, John Pullman, Erv Anson, Erik Cromwell, Mal Salteese, Al Towns, Rich Percy, Broune Malcolm, George Emmely, and Jake Madecz lined one side and around the end. On the other side sat John Dominicci and two men also in double-breasted suits, one of whom was introduced as Sal, Mr. Ginnini's assistant, and the other as his attorney, Izzy Stein. Next came Billy, with two of his soldiers, Gonz, and Li'l Joey in shirtsleeves. Subdued conversation hummed from each side.

John Pullman leaned over to Ollie Alberts, and quietly said, "The man on the right is John Dominicci. He's the Enforcer, the top hit man. The next guy, in the double breasted suit is Salvatore Ucciderita, the Underboss. The next guy's the lawyer, called the Consigliere, Izzy Stein. He was here last week. Then, Billy you know, and two of his soldiers."

"Yes. I've seen them on the door-guard duty the past week," Ollie replied. "Let's get this going." Alberts stood up, and in a loud voice, announced, "Gentlemen. May we come to order?" The room became quiet. "I've been given to believe," he said as he scanned his audience, "that our patient, Mr. Angelo Ginnini, who has awakened, is doing well. But he has been exhibiting behavior that is somewhat unexpected. From our point of view, he has been cooperative, polite, and a delightful gentleman to care for, not unlike many of our other patients." Focusing on Sal, the Underboss with a slightly pleasing smile, he added, "I've been informed that you have noted a change in Mr. Ginnini, as well. One that is troubling to you. To address this issue, may I ask Dr. Malcolm Salteese to speak to this issue." He sat down, and Mal rose to his feet.

"Gentlemen", Mal said with a slight bow, "I am Mal Salteese. I'm a board certified Neuropsychiatrist. I study brain injuries. In my opinion, Mr. Ginnini has suffered a classic TPS, a traumatic personality shift. To put that in everyday English, the concussion, caused by the posterior gunshot wound, has resulted in a personality shift. This is not a common phenomenon, but it is not rare. Medical science has not elucidated the exact mechanism of this conversion, but there is no known treatment for it. It is not uncommon for the personality to shift to an opposite type. Sometimes, just the passage of time can reverse the syndrome. It sometimes reverts due to a severe emotional shock, a subsequent concussion, or some other trauma."

"Question, please." John Dominicci interrupted. "How long is what you call a passage of time? How long can we give him, you know, before we say he's going to stay like that forever?"

"Can't answer that. Could be a week or two; could be months; could be forever. The condition is highly variable, and there's no...."

John Dominicci interrupted again, a belligerent tone creeping onto his voice, "I heard electro-shock can fix the problem. We were thinking you ought to try that for the Boss.....uh, for Mr. Ginnini."

"Good question, Mr. Dominicci. Electro-shock therapy was tried forty, no sixty years ago. The effects were worse than the symptoms, and the method was discontin........"

"Well try it again." John rasped. The Underboss in the double-breasted suit, turned his large frame slightly toward John Dominicci, and put a big, beefy hand on John's forearm. "That, plus the DA talked to........"

"It's okay, John. It's okay. Not now, John." The Underboss whispered, and turned back to face the opposite side of the table.

"Gentlemen, please continue with your information."

The hospital team spoke one after the other. John Pullman gave a brief discussion of Angelo's abdominal expectations. Rich Percy spoke to his diabetes management, possible insulin shock, hyperglycemia, and other issues. Erv Anson said, neurologically Angelo was stable, and that he concurred with Mal. There were no more comments from John Dominicci, who sat staring at his hands folded in front of him, a scowl on his face, a particularly ugly scowl.

Angelo's Family associates sat listening in silence, and displayed - to a man - a dead-pan poker face. Whether they heard or understood what was being said was not clear. With not much more to say, the meeting was adjourned, in silence. The Family filing out first, followed by most of the hospital team.

Jake Madecz took both John Pullman and Ollie Alberts by the arm, and blocked Al Towns from leaving. Jake looked at each of the three, "Gentlemen, we've got a major problem developing here."

"Who were these guys?" Ollie asked the group. "John tried to tell me their names, but who are they in the hierarchy of the organization? Does anybody know?

"Okay, Ollie, I can lay it out for you", Jake said, closing the meeting room door. "Angelo is the head guy, who is usually called one of several titles: the Boss, Capo Famiglia, Godfather, Il Padroni, the Don. They mostly call Angelo the Godfather. Under him is the Underboss, or Capo Bastone, or simply Number Two. That was him, the big guy in the dark pin stripe who quieted John, the hit man. His name is Salvatore Ucciderita. In Sicilian, uccidere means to kill. I'm guessing he's acting number one right now until Angelo resumes command again, if he ever does.

"Next to him was John Dominicci, the hostile one. He's the chief hit man. They are all killers, don't get me wrong, but John Dominicci does the contract stuff, officially. He's not officially in charge of anybody, but he has a lot of power and influence. He has the Godfather's ear. Stay away from him. They say he's got a quick temper.

Under Sal Ucciderita are the Lieutenants, variously called Captains, da Capos, or Capo-regimes. Your pal Billy is one of them. There are several of them. They usually handle the money, the cash pick-ups, and lower level transactions in the neighborhoods and on the street. They run the Soldiers. They report to the underboss, or sometimes to the Godfather, himself.

"The lower level are the Soldiers, maybe a hundred of them, who do most of the actual physical work, running the prostitutes, pimps, drugs, money laundering, protection schemes and shakedowns, racketeering, and collect the protection money from the neighborhoods. They do the beatings, local enforcement, and so on. Any questions, so far?" Hearing none, Jake continued, "All the guys in these ranks have been made, swearing an oath, a promise of complete allegiance to the Family. Break that oath and you're a dead man. Other allies who work for the organization, but who have not been made, are considered Consiglieres. They are lawyers, like Izzy Stein, bankers, police, even police chiefs, occasional doctors, maybe a priest or two. These men are advisors, and not officially part of the Family. They work usually on salary or on fee for service. They are not made. No oath of allegiance. They can quit the organization in some circumstances, especially if they don't know much of the inner workings. Some, if they quit, will disappear. The men under oath are serious, ruthless people. So don't mess with them, if you can help it. John, you and Erv Anson have had a taste of that. But, from their looks and actions at the meeting, we've got a problem on our hands. A problem with Angelo. They're gonna kill him, or at least try."

"Okay, now that you're all experts, I suggest we have a private meeting of our own", Jake said as the other three nodded. "You three free tonight? My place? Seven-thirty good for you? I'll get George Emmely, too. We've got to get our act together, now. Move quickly on this!"

Chapter 46 - The Families Meet

Three big, black, Lincoln Town Cars did not go to the
Ginnini home in Brooklyn. They stopped at 10 Church St., a rather
old and undistinguished row of shops not too far from the Ginnini
place, in the neighborhood. Six men entered a worn, obscure
doorway, down a long, dark hallway, three raps on a door,
followed by two more. When the door opened, the six men, still
silent, filed into a smoky room. There was light from 60 watt bulbs
under the Tiffany-style, glass shade, centered over the pool table,
an old Brunswick. Several men of varying sizes and shapes stood
to the side, out of the way, watching the six suits come in. The six
continued around the pool table and side-stepped a card table with
stacks of chips and cards of a game interrupted. Another door was
centered in a wall of plush red velvet, hung with 1890s-style
photos of mostly naked, well-fed women, with ornate, gilded
frames, with a dim light on top of each frame.

On the walls of the next room, also covered in the same
plush, red velvet, hung gilded frames surrounding lithographs of
Sicilian country scenes with peasant women, fully clothed,
working. Each of the wall's gold sconces held three low-watt bulbs.
The large oak table in the center, ornately carved in a heavy-
Victorian style, set the pattern of the eighteen chairs, nine on each
side, cushioned with the same plush, red velvet as the walls, some
with seats exceptionally worn, some with old expunged blood
stains. The chair at the head of the table, more like a throne, was a
larger, heavier version. Eighteen small lights with gold,
translucent shades, hanging from the ceiling, centered just in front
of each of the eighteen side chairs, shone with just enough light to
illuminate the chair's occupant with a shadowy glow. No light
illuminated the throne. Ash-trays, large enough for cigars, were
empty and polished, as were the nineteen cut-glass tumblers, full
of ice water, at each place. Beyond the foot of the table, against the
wall, rested an odd-looking old, Panama wicker-style chair with a
wrap-around high back. Covered with a red, thick, plastic sheet,

tailored to the large, surrounding back, the chair looked well used.

Three Consiglieri filed to opposite sides of the table, and sat in chairs on either side of the throne. John Dominicci sat next to the throne on the right side. Billy, the only one seated at the table not in a dark, pin-striped suit with a gaudy tie, took his seat in the last chair at the foot of the table on the right. The rest of the seats were occupied by serious-looking men, dressed in expensive-looking, double-breasted, dark suits of similar fashion, but with markedly differing faces, body size, and body language. The last one in, Sal, the Underboss, strode straight to the throne and seated himself with a smug look on his face. He waited until all eyes were on him.

"Gentlemen, we're all here," Sal rose as he spoke.

"All here 'cept Gambini. Guess we know why that's for." The speaker was a little rat-like man with a pointed face drawn up into a snicker. He was about halfway down the table. There were a few similar snickers around him.

As he waited for everyone's attention, Sal thought to himself: *I'm the Boss, here. In charge. I ain't never done this before, but they don't know that. Get control, n'keep it.*

"Gentlemen," he repeated a little louder, fists clenched by his sides, "the Ginnini family thanks you for being here today on such short notice." The place quieted down, all eyes on Sal. "You all know why you are here today for de info on Angelo Ginnini. His condition." He paused. "Angelo is doing good. His body is doing good, and maybe he gets moved outta de hospital to a nursing home. No problem there."

"That ain't what we heard," fourth seat down on the left interrupted.

"Shaddup, Louie." commanded the third seat on the right. "Let'im say his piece." Nods all around — saggy, blood-shot eyes and pouty lips concurred.

"As I was about to tell ya's, the docs say Angelo got changed. They used some fancy word, but they say Angelo has woke up as somebody else, different, which is what makes fer dis here meetin'. He got different talk and attitude. Me and John Dominicci, here, both talked to Angelo, and he's talkin' funny, fer sure. Not talkin' the old Angelo we know as Boss. Stuff about peace, friendship, makin' amends. Pretty stuff like that. Don't make no sense. Them docs say they dunno if this is forever, or how long it gonna last." The Underboss paused to take a drink of water.

"The positive good is what he said. He wants the positive good." John interjected.

"So what's dis we hear the DA paid him a call?" asked the fourth seat opposite.

"Yah, what's dis wit de DA stuff, we heard." called out someone near the foot of the table. A demand not a question. "We heard he sang to the DA, on da record. Tape and all."

"I was gettin' dere....." The Underboss put down his glass with a malevolent stare at the questioner. "We, uh, got a tip from one of de nurses." He looked around the table. "Billy, here knows. Heard it straight from de nurse, herself. Billy, you tell our guests, here, what you got."

Billy started to stand. "Siddown an' just tell it, Billy. You ain't voicin' no opinion, here. Just tell the facts," the Underboss commanded. Billy sat back down, slowly, embarrassed.

Billy cleared his throat, and sat straight up trying to look important. "The nurse we hired to work the Godfadd.....er, the Boss, comes up all bothered. Sez she's tryin'a get me, wit stuff I should know. Sez, de udder day, she was sent on break, even though it's not her break time. The doc sez to take dis break. An' dese guys walk in. She sez she seen one of 'em inna papers. Thinks it's someone big. Sez she's on break for two anna half hours before dey call her back. Sez........"

"Billy, just tell what she told you. Forget the break shit. Just the facts." The Underboss was still standing, fists still clenched.

Billy was sweating now, his knee nervously jouncing under the table. He leaned forward, looking as serious and hard-eyed as he could, "She tol' me dat de men who went into de Godfadd......er...in the Boss's room, was one of them the DA........" He swallowed, "The DA, some docs, and some guy wid a video set-up. She said she thought it was no good, an' she thought I should know. So that's what she said." He sat back, pleased with himself, but still on edge.

"Nuttin' more than that? That's what you got? Some nurse thinks she seen the DA. So she knows the DA? That's what you call us for?"

"Yah, but, if that's the DA. If it was the DA, and Angelo's talkin' to him. Talkin' funny to him, whadda we got here? Huh? Whadda we got?" The room exploded into as many disorderly opinions as there were voices.

Fifth seat right said, "I heard on good source it's da DA, hisself, for sure."

Seven left, "Give him some time."

Seven right, "Don't give him no more time.'

Four right, 'Knock him off'

Four left, "Can't knock him off."

Three left, "Get him get home, see if he gets right."

Eight left, "Can't let him rat us out to the DA."

And so it went, with Sal beginning to lose patience.

Eight right, "What if they grab him first? Witness protection."

Three left, "It ain't just yer family involved here. He knows us, all da families. He knows too much."

"Quiet down, all youse!" Sal tried to be heard over the noise.

Seven right, "I owe him, big time." No one listening to anyone else.

Another, "Cement shoes, inna river."

"Gambinis aint here." from near the bottom of the table.

"That's cuz they put up dat waiter-guy, Herbie to make the hit," growled someone across the table.

"Yah, but Herbie aint been made to anybody. He's just a dumb shit. Don't know from nuttin'", someone said, but nobody heard him.

"Shaddup! Shaddup, all a youse." The Underboss shouted, and banged his glass, denting the table where multiple dents had preceded. "Shaddup, and sit down." The room finally quieted. "We gonna do dis the regular way. Like Angelo would do if he was here."

"Who put you in charge here?" someone challenged.

"I put me in charge here, an' that's the way it is." The

Underboss looked around the table, staring at each man, his ugly, little mouth a straight line hiding broken little teeth. Finally he spoke. "We gonna vote. One man, one vote. Everyone, 'cept you Billy. You don't got no vote. Not on dis here. If dis was reg'lar, da Boss be here, an' da Boss makes da decision, himself. But da Boss ain't here for dis, so I'm sayin' we decide for him. Anyone sayin' different?" He paused. "Thumbs up er thumbs down. Up, we give him a week er two to see if he's on the up and up. Thumbs down, he's done." Heads nodded around the table, and the thumbs came out. The Underboss counted out loud, pointing to each thumb. John Dominicci had already done the count in his head, and let a small, sly smile curve his lips. "Nine to eight. That's it. Thumbs down takes it," the Underboss announced. "John, you handle it."

"One of our boys. Back him up.....fer security," said Al Doretti, one of the suits. Sudden silence. Most eyes turn to John Dominicci.

"I work alone, Al. You know I work alone. Keep yer backup for yerself," John was glaring across at the offender. "You fuck with me, I fuck with you, so hands off, you motherfucker."

"Go fuck yerself, an' yer sister,too, you little weasel-pimp," Al snarled.

John was on his feet in a flash, reaching for his gun.

"John, shaddup an' sit down.......now," the Underboss slammed the glass tumbler. John shot a look at the Underboss, ticked his head back as he flicked his long finger up from under his chin at the offender, and slowly, giving the eye to the suit, put his hands on the arms of his chair, and, even more slowly, lowered himself into it.

Addressing the whole table as if nothing had happened, the Underboss, in a hoarse whisper, said, "We got a little business problem here. We come togedder here. All de Families represented here. We take a vote. We got a answer, here. Our Family, we take care of the business ...the problem... fer all the Families." He looked around the table from man to man. Most of the heads were nodding slightly. "Okay, now. We got no more business for outside the Family? Anybody?" Silence. He waited another ten seconds. Silence. "Okay then, no more business. We done. Like Angelo sez, we be adjoined. Yer free to go. Only our Family stay. We got anudder matter. We gonna take a five minute break, here."

Chapter 47 - Packy

Many of the chairs emptied, and their former occupants filed out, some back to their big black Town Cars, mumbling among themselves. When they all had gone, the Underboss said, "Billy, bring the special chair up. Den bring Packy in. He's sittin' outside. Den youse can leave."

Billy looked worried, but obeyed, silently, while all eyes watched his every move. He brought up the special Panama wicker-style chair with the red plastic lining, disappeared for a few seconds, and returned with a thin, slightly stooped, dull-eyed man in his fifties, wearing the usual tee-shirt and suspenders. The little man exhaled a cloud of grey cigarette smoke as he entered the inner sanctum, and stood there. Billy, quietly, slowly shut the door behind him. The Underboss, eyes on Packy, barked "Over der", pointing to the special chair.

Packy looked puzzled. Then the lights came on, and he jerked his head back, straightened his slouch, and stared wide-eyed, reflecting the terror that had seized him. "No, not da chair", his voice choked in a whisper. "No. Please no. I ain't done nothin' wrong."

"Packy, sit down.... Now..... Like I tol' ya." Packy, rigid with fear, moving stiffly, shuffled to the special chair. He ran his hand around and over the large back, as though admiring it. He had never seen it before, but he had heard about it. Now he was touching it. "Siddown!" barked the Underboss. Every eye in the room silently followed Packy's every move. Packy looked up at the Underboss, pleading. Turning slowly, he sat down, hands on the chair arms, and pushed and shifted back into the chair's recesses, as if trying to hide, but still staring at the Underboss. "Packy, you know why yer here. In that chair." Statements, not questions.

"No, I ain't done nothin'. I ain't...." Packy's lower lip was quivering. "I ain't....."

"Number one, Packy, you didn't report the change in da Godfadder. Number two, when da nurse tol' ya to call Billy, ya didn't."

"Yah I did. I called'm. I couldn't leave my post, so took a while..."

"Number three, you fucked up before. Takin' money wasn't yers. Couple times."

"Yah but I'm willin' to pay for it. I needed da dough, but I'm gonna be good for it. Da Godfadder said I was okay. He likes me better'n you do."

"Da Godfadder said it was on yer record, an' yer arreddy on probation. Number four, you been messin' wid dat Muslim woman who...."

"No, I don't do her no more. Dat's done. No more. I'm on da up an' up. Live wid my uncle other side of town." "Mebbe so, but not before you tol' her about dat business wid dem Irish, an' she ratted youse out. You know what dat cost the Family?"

Packy was mute, frozen.

"Do ya, hunh, Packy? Do ya know how much? Hunh, you sleazy little rat. What about yer pledge? Hunh? You ain't no use to the organization, Packy."

"Yah, but I'm tryin'. Gimme anudder chance, will ya, hunh? Please, anudder?"

"And number five, Packy, number five. Most games it's three strikes an' yer out, Packy. Dis is number five. Five times you fucked yer pledge, Packy. Five times. De fifth one you tol' the City cop on the door 'bout the Godfadder's change. You might as well tol' de Gambinis. You tol' de cop before ya called it in."

"No, I didn' tell no cop. I wouldn't tell no cop..."

"Packy, don't lie to me. Yer so fuckin' dumb. Dat cop is one of ours. He ratted youse out, you fuckin', lyin', little rat." The Underboss's voice was intensifying from a low growl up to a mid-range rasp. His face screamed hate.

"So, Packy, whatta we do wid fuckin', lyin', cheatin', little rats? Rats who fuck de pladge? Huh? Whadda we do?"

Packy, visibly shaking, staring at the table, wet himself.

"Packy, I'm talkin' attchu. You look at me when I'm talkin' attcha." Packy looked up, lip quivering, shoulders slumped, his pants crotch darker.

170

"So now, Packy, you done good for us before." The voice was softer, smoother now. "Yah, you fucked up five times. You shouldna talked to da cop 'bout da Godfadder an' den udder things, an' sometimes you done some good shit. So I'm gonna go easy on ya." The Underboss turned to John Dominicci. "John you got Packy a present for being good, yah?"

John smiled as he got up, and walked slowly over beside Packy. Calmly and softy, he said, "Yes, Packy, I've got a little present for you. Your favorite candy bar." He reached in his coat pocket and pulled out the gift. "Three Musketeers, your favorite. Right?"

Packy sat up straighter, trying to manage a small smile, exposing his broken, brown teeth. John paused, carefully unwrapped the candy bar, and extended it toward Packy with his right hand. Packy focused intently on the candy bar, watching it inch toward his face. John paused, "Open your mouth, and close your eyes, and I'll give you something to make you wise." John waited. "Close your eyes, Packy, close them.......that's it, Packy. Now keep them closed." In one swift movement, John's left hand was in his pocket, gun out, under Packy's nose, 'Thwup' from the silencer. The back of Packy's head exploded. Blood and brains all over the red plastic back. Not a drop elsewhere. The Three Musketeers bar was tossed into Packy's lap.

"Gentlemen, I believe that's all the business we have for today," the Underboss announced. He stood up to leave, "Meeting adjoined."

Chapter 48 -Mr. Lincoln's Boots

Larry Lowance, familiarly known as the gentle giant, stood six foot five, two-fifty stripped, with an easy, perpetual smile on his handsome thirty-five year old African-American face. He looked closer to fifty according to what the social workers had called an undirected, unstable, un-parented younger life. His mom was still alive and functioning when he was a kid, but most of her cerebral axons involved in critical thinking had been diminished by a variety of illicit drugs. This had been particularly true in her teenage years when she was pregnant with Larry. The social workers said Larry was a bright child, with good common sense, despite his mother's toxicology.

Yeah, it's true, thought Larry. *I know most of the stuff the social worker ladies used to say, and I still believe life is a wonderful gift from God. We're supposed to be here to enjoy His gift, and to help others enjoy it, too.* He had learned all that after his mom had found God and Jesus, and had straightened herself out. She took him to Sunday School at the Baptist Tabernacle Altar every Sunday and Wednesday evenings for prayer service and bingo. That was when he was eight.

All the guys, his teen-age buddies were doing it, and a lotta the girls too. They all agreed, "try it, you'll like it." And he did. He didn't use so much he couldn't function, like some of the gang, but he liked it. Liked it a lot. Problem was, he knew he couldn't quit. He felt real bad when he tried to quit, so he didn't. Like he told the social worker lady, "It don't seem to make no difference, and buyin' and sellin' it, an' I could make a little cash on the side. And everyone was doin' it. What's so bad about it, anyways?

Larry finished the PT group session, and thought he'd go down to see how that kid Ben was doing down in the Trauma Unit. Ben was supposed to be coming up to rehab, but Larry hadn't seen him. He found Ben in his room, sitting in a chair, reading a play by a guy named A. R. Gurney. Larry never heard of him.

"Thought you was s'posed to be comin' up to Rehab." Larry

said.

"Yeah, tomorrow." Ben said. "They came to the room today, and got me walking without a walker. It hurts only a little in my lower back area."

"Hey, progress. That's good. Me too. Today, I could finally wipe my own ass."

They quickly got into how and why each of them had ended up on the trauma floor. "Nice people here. Good takin' care of me." Larry said.

"Good and smart, too," said Ben. "One really smart resident saved my life. Great care here."

From completely different backgrounds, they bonded as their hospital stories morphed into life stories. Ben was fascinated by Larry, who had never had anyone interested in him before.

"I was on drugs as a teen," Larry admitted. "Not one of my better times, but God bless the US Army, they got me off the stuff, but good, once and for all. Loved the Army. Shoulda stayed in. Shoulda been a lifer. But they asked me to leave after I hit a guy. Ya see, he was a big guy pickin' on a friend of mine, little Joe Creek, with a broken beer bottle. Hurtin' him. So I told the big guy to quit it, and he came after me. Cut me here onna shoulder, so I hit him one, hard. They said I broke his neck, cuz he's still paralyzed in the legs. Can't walk. So the Army asked me to discharge.

"So I come home to take care of my mom anyhow, before she passed. Yes-sir, she had the breast cancer. They worked like hell to try to save her. For a year and a half they gave her all kinds treatments, but The Lord called her Home anyway, God bless her."

"My father and my grandfather, they was workingmen all their lives, bless 'em, but my great-great-grandfather, he was a slave who was freed. He lived to one-hundred and sixteen years, yes-sir, he did." "A hundred and sixteen years?" Ben didn't think he'd heard correctly."

"Yes-sir, he was born in 1796, and he died in 1912.

"Well, that's a hundred and sixteen years. Holy cow."

"Yes-sir, he lived in the White House upstairs."

"In the White House? As in the Washington DC White

House?"

"Yes-sir, he used to shine Mr. Lincoln's boots."

Chapter 49 - Privately

The door to John Pullman's office suite opened into the pleasant, inviting waiting room. The three people sitting there all looked up. "Sorry to keep you waiting," he said, making smiling eye contact with each as he came in.

The matron in the floral-print dress and matching sweater, smiled as she announced, "Oh no, doctor. I'm early. We're all early. We all came to see Annie B, but as long as you're here, we'll be glad to see you too." The fifty-year old business suit and the twenty-something construction guy both chuckled quietly, wishing they had said that. They all watched John disappear down the hall into his office.

It was a typical afternoon, almost thirty patients. Gall bladders, hernias, breast masses, rectal problems, lumps, bumps, sores, aches and pains. The usual gamut. As the last one left, both John and Annie B sighed and looked understandingly at each other. "I've got three phone calls to answer, then we're outta here," he said.

"Four. Mrs. Myers is on line one," Annie B countered. When John finished the last of the calls, Annie B challenged, "I'll beat'cha home." She had come into his office room and was stroking the back of his neck.

"And I'll give you a half-hour to stop that." He looked up lovingly. "Actually, I won't." Now the grin gone, "I gotta call Jeb Baird back. Privately."

"Privately? Privately? You having an affair?" she said with a smirk. She knew it wasn't true, but she was slightly annoyed by the "privately". They had no secrets from each other. She moved her hands down to massage his shoulders. "This about that Angelo? Or the Mob?"

"Yes," he replied, his deep-chested voice sounded tired.

"What's going on. Not more trouble. Don't tell me, more crap from those goons!" She stopped the massage, and took a sharp step back.

"No. This could be serious. Too early to tell yet. But it's not something you should know. Not because I don't trust you. You know that, sweet girl. But if you don't know, then you can't tell. If bad goes to worse, and you don't know anything, they'll leave you out of it. It's the only way I know to protect you."

She was alarmed now. A passionate but heady woman, she was well trained to take alarming news seriously. "Are they giving you more trouble? What's the problem now? I don't want you shielding me. I'm a grown woman, and I can take anything you can. We've always been stronger together than separated."

He swiveled his chair to face her. Looking up with a tired worry at her frightened face, he quietly said, "You're right. You're absolutely right, Annie B But this is not about us, like it was before. We......I am only a collateral player. I'm not the one in danger here. If there is any. There might be......sometime...... But not me. Not directly anyway. But, if they decide to involve me in some way, I don't want you in any part of it. But I'm not going to let them get me into it, so it's a non-issue. Anyway, I gotta talk to Jeb, so please go home. Let Luther out so he can pee. I'll be home in a half or less."

She bent down with a sad worry, and kissed him lightly on the lips. "Okay, I trust you on this. But I'm here, always here for you. And be careful. You're the dearest thing in my life and I don't want you hurt or in trouble. Promise?"

"I promise," he whispered. She grabbed her coat, and left. He turned back to his desk and speed dialed, "Hey Jeb, its John."

" Tomorrow? I'll take. Hands up. Okay?"

"I thought you needed, tonight?"

"No go. Don't know what they might have tapped. Hands up, Browny one, two, three." Click. The phone went dead. Jeb was speaking code. 'I'll take' meant Jeb would pick up John. 'Hands up' meant noon. 'Browny one, two, three' meant his nondescript white '87 Chevy, that he called 'Browny', at 123 Hospital Road, an apartment building three blocks from the hospital which had a secluded driveway behind some aged arbor vitae trees. Not a super secret deal, but enough to throw off a tail or confuse a bugged phone.

Chapter 50- JEB

J. Edwards Baird was the new DA in the city. Relatively new, he'd been recruited half a dozen years ago when the previous DA had been busted in that nasty cocaine business.

J. Edwards Baird, "Jeb", as he was known to good friends, was a popular success. He was well-liked by everybody. Well, almost everybody. The current "guests" of the Federal or State penal systems were not his biggest fans. But the rest of the city loved him.

Jeb, along with the new Chief of Police, John Redman, had really cleaned up the city. Not just the downtown business section.The whole city. Some neighborhoods infested with drugs and dealers had been miraculously cleaned up by a simple maneuver that Jeb had discovered in a brain flash while playing Hearts with his son on a Saturday. On Monday, he called both Chief Redman and the Mayor. Three days later, the public works guys put jersey barriers angled out onto the worst of the drug-infested streets, spaced apart on opposite sides, so that users could no longer whiz up the street, do a deal from the car, and speed away onto the freeway and be gone. Now they had to creep, zig-zagging sharply up the street at three miles an hour. The dealers, the druggies, and the drugs promptly moved. The mothers of the altered streets were ecstatic. The kids were happy to have their sidewalks back. No more drive-bys. No more murders. Bad guys all gone from the hood. There was only one minor problem— street stick ball was impossible.

After Phi Beta Kappa graduation from a small, prestigious northeastern college, Jeb earned his Master's Degree in Criminal Justice, and was on his way to his PhD, when he suddenly enlisted in the Marine Corps. After OCS training, he requested criminal justice school and became an officer in the Military Police, stationed at the Pensacola Naval Air Station. There he met a young Marine, named Al Towns. One day Al Towns had saved Jeb from a nasty scrape with a pair of bullies, which he often recalled.

Jeb was married to Molly Baird, nee Shaun, a community
stalwart involved in almost every positive cultural event and
valuable fund-raiser of in the city, i.e., Garden Club president, Art
Museum Board member, League of Women Voters member,
church flower guild, and the list went on. Strong, tall, tough, from
a family that went back to the Mayflower, she was as much
admired and liked as her now famous husband. And their kids
mirrored the successes of their parents: an architect, a lawyer,
computer entrepreneur, and an up and coming concert pianist.
Solid citizens, all.

Twenty-plus years later, surprisingly, or maybe not so
surprisingly, Jeb and Al met up again, right there in the city, at a
Christmas benefit the hospital was holding for autism. Molly S.
Baird was, of course, on the planning committee, as was Barbara
Towns.

"NAS Pensacola? 1990?" asked Al pointing a finger at Jeb.

"Yah. 1990. Al? You saved my butt from a couple of dick
heads just outta the brig who were gunnin' for me."

"Oh yeah. And the beer at the O-Club was fifty cents a
pitcher." They did a high five. "Small world", they agreed. Over
several beers that evening, they found they had a lot in common.
One of them was a friend named John Pullman. Another high five.

"Yah, after I separated from the active duty, I realized if I
was gonna continue in criminal justice, I needed to go to law
school. So while Molly worked to support us, I hit the books again.
We used to joke 'I was living off the sweat of my frau'." Another
beer, another fist bump.

"I did the same to Barb. She worked while I got a couple of
masters degrees," Al laughed. "Ha. I like that, living off the sweat
of your frau". By the end of the evening they were thick as thieves,
old buddies, still Marines, because once a Marine, always a
Marine.

Chapter 51 - Safe House

Jake Madecz brought the group to order. "We gotta move him to a safe house. The Mob's gonna kill him, especially when they hear he's talked to you, Jeb. There is no way they will let him live to testify." Jake Madecz's booming Polish voice filled his modest-sized living room.

Jake looked around the room, from man to man. Everyone was nodding slowly, knowing Jake was right. John Pullman was silent, as usual, when trying to solve a problem. Ollie Alberts, hands on knees frowned, George Emmely was staring at the floor, and Jeb continued to nod. Al Towns broke the silence, "I know what I'd do if he was a Marine, but he's not, so that shoots that idea."

George Emmely lifted his bowed head, and said, "If he were on a submarine, I could handle it, or even on shore, but....." He paused, stroked his chin, and brightened, "Hey wait a minute, I've got an idea." All heads turned to George. "Dusty Reade. Yah, Dusty. That could work."

Ollie Alberts asked, "Do I know Dusty? Do we know Dusty?"

George, thinking it through, said "Okay, Dusty's retired. He was Navy, an MP. Good man. Tough, and knows the game. Accepts need to know situations. He's about an hour east of here."

"Yeah, I know him. Call him. See what he says." Al said.

"Hang on a second. This could get someone cooperating with us in a heap of trouble." Jeb said.

"Dusty eats trouble for lunch," George replied. "Thrives on it. Very capable in that regard. He'd love something like this. In addition, he'd be a big asset to an untrained team like us. Not to insult you guys, but if we had six guys like Al, here, on this team, instead of old broken down retirees like me, we might handle what the mob is likely to throw at us."

"George," John said, "if you're an old, broken down retiree, then what does that make me. You're trim, fit, and harder than nails. I wish I was half as fit as you". He continued, turning to the group, "I like George's idea. If Dusty can get us a safe house and a staff to look after Angelo, I'd vote for it. A medical staff to look after him will be the challenge, but let's find out. I agree with Al, George give Dusty a call."

George got up and went into Jake's dining room across the hall. Jake spoke up, "Anyone want a cuppa? Bettye put the pot on. It's hot and ready."

"Yah, I'd love one," Al said, straightening up.

"How you like it?" Jake asked.   "Like my women, hot and black." Al joked as he got up. "Lemme help you."

"Who else?" Jake looked at John, then Ollie, then Jeb.

"Had one at supper. Won't sleep if I have another." Ollie said.

"John? You want one?"

"Oh, no thanks. Never drink it. Never have, but thanks anyway." John said. Jake and Al disappeared in the direction of the kitchen.

"How do we get ourselves into these messes?" Ollie asked John.

"I dunno, Ollie, I dunno." John looked over at Jeb. "I guess it's because we are willing to take all comers, and not screen out the riff-raff and non-payers, like some hospitals do." The men sat slumped forward, elbows on knees, hands clasped, out front, each pensively contemplating the difficulties ahead.

Jake and Al came back into the living room, and a few minutes later, George returned, announcing. "Dusty loves it," he said. "He says he's got just the place, and he knows the business. I told him the basics, and he's on board. He says it'll be ready by midnight."

"Midnight? Tonight?" Jake asked.

"Midnight tonight," George confirmed. "He says we should supply the medical aides for the patient, but if we're in a jam, he can...."

"Yah, I think midnight is good." Jeb said. "The sooner we get the defendant, I mean, Angelo, out of the hospital and away from the mob, the better. I need this guy alive. I can't tell you how important his testimony is gonna be."

"Oww. Damn. Burned my tongue," Al said, "I got a suggestion. There's four people I know in one of my martial arts groups who might work. All young, in their twenties. All single. No tie-downs. The one guy's a nurse. The other three women are all PAs."

"Jeezis, I don't know," Ollie exclaimed. "Getting four young people involved with the Mafia. That's a tough order for them, isn't it?"

"There certainly would be risk involved," George agreed.

"Al, how do you always seem to know all the great young chicks?", Jake asked with a big grin. Jake had a way of relieving the down side.

John Pullman sat up straight, "Yes, for sure, there would be risk, but there is also significant risk if we don't monitor Angelo, closely. He's brand new at his diabetes management. His abdomen still isn't healed completely. He's psychologically vulnerable. I like Al's idea of the four, young, supposedly capable, medical, hot-shots who can handle the situation both medically, as well as physically, if it comes to that. If this is a good location, then the latter shouldn't be an issue. But if there's trouble, Al, you're saying that they can handle themselves?"

Al set aside his coffee, "Yes. What I was about to add, is that the guy, Chick Morella, and one of the gals, Peggy Handleman, both are also in my shooting club. All three women are ex-military. Short timers, but they can handle themselves. Trust me on that. They hang out together a lot. They're a pretty savvy group. I'd trust them for a mission like this."

George declared, "Go get them. Think they'd be able to do it on such short notice?"

"One way to find out." Al stood, pulled out his cell, and left the room.

General discussion about details buzzed among them: transport, how to sneak Angelo out of town, following up, legal issues, and financing of the whole thing.

Jeb said, "I can get the financing through the witness protection program. I've got a budget for just that sort of thing. It's legal as long as the clien.....uh, Angelo agrees to the witness protection, then it's totally legit."

"He's done that already," John replied. "He asked for it the other day when he was requesting that meeting with you, Jeb. Both Willie Lain and Father James Gibbons can verify that. And, if I'm not mistaken, he mentioned it with you, in your interview with him. You got it on video."

"Yeah, you're right. I remember now. It's all right there. We've just got to keep him alive till we get a trial date. Soon as the judge can clear a spot," Jeb said just as Al came back into the room.

"They're all set. They love it. Very excited, and up for the mission," Al put his cell back in his pocket. "There's only one wrinkle. They, none of them, can start till the morning. I can cover the night shift, but I'd like an assistant. Ya know, in case of some unforeseen problem. Two's better than one in most cases."

"I'll cover your butt, Al", John said. "Annie B's got me going over to Carol and Don Knecht's place tonight, but she can go without me. No big deal. Plus, I'd rather watch your bony ass than Don's, any day." John said with a grin.

They all had ideas on how to move Angelo: timing, logistics, methods. How could they attract the least attention? Divert focus? First priority: get Angelo out of the hospital, unnoticed. "Okay, gents," Jeb stated. "We've got ten and a half hours till midnight." Jeb checked his watch. "I've got 1:28. Set your watches."

The meeting broke up, each man with a part to play in the unfolding drama. Thanking Bettye and Jake, five of the men departed. But Al paused on the front walk, and subtly stopped the other four. "Act natural," he whispered, "and check out the black sedan. A Lincoln Town Car, parked across the street, way down near the corner, on the right. I think we might have some eyes. They can only follow one of us. Stay in touch."

Chapter 52 - Back to Work

It was a clear, sunny afternoon. The traffic was light as John and Al left Jake's place and headed back to the hospital in Al's car. The big black sedan followed at a discreet distance. "They know we've made them. Not tailing for any purpose other than to annoy us, is my guess." Al said. "And how interesting is it going to the hospital?"

They rode in silence for a way, when John asked, "Ollie is supposed to call in the rental, right? Did he say when he expected it delivered?"

"Yah, 6:30", Al said. "He's driving straight home and is going to get his wife to drive him over to the car wash near Main. The rental's supposed to be delivered to the car wash. He'll get out and take the rental to a parking place he likes, and leave it before 4:00. The rental company is one of the mob's legitimate businesses. Ollie said he couldn't help the irony of the situation." Both men smiled. "Probably the car-wash, too."

"And Ollie's supposed to act as command central for all this, in case there's any screw-up, or we have to call it off, or whatever." John added. "He says he has plenty of work to do there, anyway, so two birds, one stone, according to him. He's got everybody's cell number." John paused, thinking, "Next, Jeb's arranging for the witness protection. He says he knows the police chief up there where the house is. Says the department's clean. Doubt many on the take way up there. Jeb said he'd back up Ollie and be available. He said to call him if we have any problems on the way. He's gonna have his cell on all night, just in case."

"You'd be surprised," Al commented. "The damn Mafia has tentacles out everywhere. If not on active take, they'll probably have a mole there in the PD." Talking out of the corner of his mouth, Al kept one eye on the road ahead, and the other on the black sedan in the rear-view mirror.

John said, "I've always wondered how they have protection for a safe house. Gotta be discreet, so they don't give it away. But people have to know. At least the ones involved. What about a mole?"

"They've got their ways." Al said.

John continued, "George is working with this Dusty guy. Does Dusty get paid for this? I presume he must."

"Yah, my guess he'll be on contract. It's his job to keep the place safe." Al emphasized the word "safe". "Jeb's office pays for it out of the witness protection program."

"And Jake is arranging the hospital end of it. I need to call in for the special procedures room now," John said as he reached for his cell.

Al said, "Jake is arranging for the hearse. His brother runs the funeral home, so that's tight, there. And he'll have the pathology stretcher there, too."

John was on his phone. "No, it'll only take about forty-five minutes..... No, 5:30 is better. No, I can't get there before then.......yes, ma'am. We'll be out before 6:30, I promise.......No, thanks. I've got the pump. It came today. Fed-Ex.........Yes, right, I know the day crew will be gone. I'll bring my own help. Yes, thanks. Be there at 5:30. Thanks. Bye." He turned to Al, "Got the room, so we should be all set."

"You talked to Willie Lain? He's ready?" Al asked as he looked over briefly.

"Yes. Talked to him earlier," John said. "He's such a great guy, good common sense. Ya know, he was a successful business guy before med school. Catches on right away. Gung-ho. I hope he decides to stick around when he's done training. I'd take him on as a partner in a heartbeat. But that's a few years off. We gotta get through tonight and the next week or two, first. I have a feeling this is not going to be easy or routine." John stretched back in his seat, and folded his arms across his chest. "He still with us? The tail?"

"Yup. Right on schedule." Al pulled into the hospital staff garage drive, swiped his ID badge on the gate, and disappeared down under. The big black sedan just kept going.

Chapter 53 - The Other Plan

John and Al separated. John went to the record room to dictate a few charts until the set time. Al took the stairs up to his locker, got a few things, then continued up to the Trauma floor, where he busied himself with the next month's shift schedules for the nurses, LPNs, nurses' aides, secretaries, cleaning people, night shifts, social workers, OT, PT, volunteers, maintenance people, security needs, and the multitude of others who were needed to run a Level-One Trauma Unit. It was his job to coordinate them all. No hint of any mob thugs following him into the hospital, but he did see the thug still on duty at Angelo's door, along with the cop.

Ollie was back behind his desk in the hospital. He called the car rental place they usually did business with, an agency used to last minute deals, so this one was no surprise. "Yes, please," he said into the phone. He had dialed the number himself, rather than let Martha, his ever-efficient secretary, get involved. *She has no part in this. The less she, or anyone else for that matter, knows about this cabal, the better,* he thought to himself. "Yes, a plain VW-bug for overnight.....Yes......Yes, and deliver it as soon as you can to the car wash place couple blocks down from you. Yes, that's the place........Yes the usual deal, please......Yes, add the GPS. Might need it. Thanks."

John Pullman left the Record Room, and went up to Angelo's room. The nurse was surprised to see him this late in the day. He looked straight at her, and said, "Slight change of plans. His insulin pump just came in, so we want to put it in tonight. Keep him NPO, nothing to eat or drink, for now." He went over to Angelo who was sitting in a chair watching the TV. John positioned himself so his back was to the nurse. Angelo looked up.

"Angelo, we've ordered an insulin pump for you. It'll control your blood sugars much more evenly. We'll teach you how to use it. It's very easy. Doesn't take long to put in. I'll do it under local."

"Jeeze, doc, that's sounds good. When we gonna do that?"

Angelo was looking up into John's face. John gave Angelo a big wink, and rolled his eyes as though looking back at the nurse. Angelo didn't flinch. John winked again. Angelo's eyebrows rose just a fraction. "The unit came in this afternoon, so we thought we would put it in tonight, if that's good for you." A half question. Another wink.

Angelo gave a very slight nod of comprehension. "Anything you say, Doc. You got me this far. I've got complete faith in you, Doc." Angelo gave the nurse a brief glance.

John turned to the nurse, "Have you got a permit form, please." She went to a pile of papers under the window.

"Here, Doctor."

John filled it out and signed it. Angelo signed it. The nurse witnessed it. All normal protocol. The nurse relaxed, somewhat.

"They'll be bringing the gurney to get you any minute now. See you down in the Special Procedures Rooms."

The gurney stopped outside the OR, where the sign said

Special Procedures - Authorized Personnel Only

in big red letters. John came around the corner dressed in scrubs and his white lab coat. The nurse stepped up, "I'm coming in. I wanna watch," she said.

"I'd love to have you watch all of it. It's a great new device. You'll love it. So will you, Angelo." John said. "Unfortunately, only the special procedures team is allowed in the room. The sterility is of the utmost importance, here, as you can imagine. If one of these babies get infected, it's a disaster. So, I'm afraid I'll have to ask you to wait outside here, or go on break, or go back up to Angelo's room, if you have anything to do up there." John was taking a chance, but he figured the last thing she'd want to do is to go back to that room and hang around with nothing to do, especially when she would be getting off in an hour and a half.

What John Pullman didn't know, was that she had already been ordered by John Dominicci to leave early at 6:00, because he "had some business" with the Godfather, before the 7:00 nurse came in to take over. The Enforcer had told her she had been doing an exceptionally good job. And if she had anything to report, she could call him, anytime. This personal compliment from this important man, the Enforcer, really pumped her up, making her feel real good. *To hell with this asshole doctor and his special procedures, anyway.* Arms defiantly across her chest, she strode out of the room, visibly pouting.

Inside the Special Procedures Room, Al, Jake Madecz and Willie Lain were already waiting after Jake had unlocked the door. No one else was around, all other personnel having gone for the day. John Pullman approached Angelo's gurney and thanked the transport man, who left for his next assignment. John pushed Angelo on the gurney into the inner sanctum, explaining, "Angelo, this is all a ruse to get you safely out of here. Can you sit up? Need help? Swing your legs over the side." John pulled on Angelo's hand, helping him up. Willie rushed over to help. Angelo looked a little puzzled.

"Here's the plan", John said. "We're going to have you dress as an Arab woman for the next half-hour, till we get you out of the hospital proper."

"Sounds good to me," Angelo agreed. "So far anyway. And you're right, I need to get outta town - soon."

"If you can do it, we'll have you transfer to another gurney. One from the morgue." Angelo looked startled, then relaxed, again, as John continued, "The morgue gurney will have a sheet covering all of you, including your head and face. Is that alright with you?" John asked.

"Yah, sure. What then?" the senior mobster asked, smiling benignly.

"You will be transferred to a hearse, to drive out." Al stepped in.

"Trying to get rid of me, right?" Angelo said with a huge grin. "Just kidding. Then what?"

Willie Lain had opened his back pack and was pulling out some long, black garments. "Borrowed these from an intern on pediatrics. I told her it was part of a trick we might pull on some friends tonight. Promised I'd give them back tomorrow, washed." He handed them to Angelo.

"Is this a burqa?" He studied it and then put the long flowing gown on over his shirt and pants. Long full sleeves.

"No, it's called a chador, the gown part. Normally open in the front, but this one's got a zipper. Not allowed by Sharia law. The hood part is called a niqab. It's open over the eyes. A real burqa would be one piece, top to bottom, with a screen in front of the eyes, so the woman is completely enshrouded. But we can call this outfit a burqa if it's easier."

Angelo studied the niqab, turning it this way and that, figured it out, and slipped it over his head. The black Sicilian eyes peering out from the eye slit were perfect.

"Your second career." said Al, and everyone laughed, Angelo harder than the others. Then abruptly stopped, and held his abdomen.

"Stitches pulling." Angelo said. He paused, got serious again, and asked, "Okay, we're at the funeral home, right?"

"Right", Al answered. "The hearse drives right into the home, and we.....you transfer."

"Which funeral home? We own a bunch of them. Not ours, I hope. They all know me," Angelo said.

"No. This is Madecz's place. It's my brother. It's okay," Jake said as Angelo took the burqa off and laid it in his lap. He shook his head, glad to be free of it.

"From the funeral home, you transfer with us into a little VW beetle. Think you can do that? In a burqa?"

"Yup. No problem. It's with one of you guys, I'm guessing?"

"Three of us", John said. "Jake's staying behind. Besides, he's too big to fit into a beetle." More laughter, but edged with a little nervousness.

Chapter 54 - John D's Plan

John Dominicci had to make a plan. He always made a plan. He didn't want to make this plan. He didn't want to do this job, but he had to do this job. Conflicting facts made the situation difficult. *The Underboss ordered the job. The families had voted at the meeting. I don't have any choice. I have to do the job. But it's the Godfather..... The Don. I have to do the Don..... The Godfather. My Godfather. The man who was so good to me. Took me in when I left home. Made me what I am. Respected me. The Godfather, my Godfather gave me class. Taught me style. Taught me about the Family. How it operates. The Family pride. That Family is the most important, above all else. I took the oath of loyalty from him. He was looking me right in the eye when I took that oath. And now the Family says I've got to do him.*

John was sitting in his big overstuffed chair in the second-floor living room of his townhouse. Professionally appointed in modern Danish - except for the overstuffed chair. Liz Long was expensive, but she was the best: high reputation, high price. She was the decorator he had picked to do the job. *Too bad she's a lesbo, I could have liked her,* he thought, trying to interrupt his confusing thoughts about the Godfather.

No, the plan should be easy. Send one of our nurses home at six, and tell the other that she doesn't have to come in that night till seven. Tell whichever of our guys is at the door to go get a cuppa. Most of the city cops assigned are on payroll, so no problem there. I slip in at 6:15, and bingo with the silencer. Point blank. I slip out. Go right to Tony's. I palm a c-note to Jack the bartender, and tell him, I'm here at five forty-five, right? First drink half price, happy hour. Right? Right! One scotch. Maybe do a steak. Then watered tea to look like scotch. One after the other with buddies and pals. All witness I was there, and pretty drunk, too. All evening, till 11:00, 11:30. Solid alibi. Too drunk to shoot anybody. Maybe I'll meet Kitty there.

He changed into a pair of sport slacks and a Polo shirt, and went out. *See and be seen, all day. Busy. Talk to everybody.* "Yah, I'm good. How are you doing. You're lookin' good. Work must be agreeing with you. Family good?" And so it went, the hours dragging by. He just couldn't keep the Godfather off his mind. *Anybody else, no problem. Ten anybody elses, no problem. But the Godfather! I took the pledge, and I have to uphold the family honor. It's too bad, but the Godfather's lost it....... He's gone...... Not the same guy. Talking to the DA! Hard to believe it. Jeeziz. I'll call Kitty.*

He reached in his pocket for his cell phone. "Hey, Kitty. It's me........Yah......Good......Say, if you're not doing anything tonight, let me buy you dinner......Yah......Good. Tony's. Five-thirty, quarter of six. Meetcha there......yah.....good. Oh, say, I might be a minute or two late, but I'll be there. Tell Jack to start a tab for me, and put yours on it. I'll be there quick. We can make a night of it......yah, my place......yah......the maid. She changes the sheets twice a week. You know me. I'm a cleanliness freak......yah, see ya, five-thirty, quarter of six......Good.......Yah sure, love you ,too." John bought a hot dog and a diet-Pepsi from a street vendor, and went home for a nap.

The clock in John Dominicci's head woke him at 5:00. He dressed in one of his older suits, possible blood spatter might wreck a good one. He took an Uber to Tony's. Then walked the mile or so over to the hospital. He waited in the men's room on the floor below, by the stairs until 6:05. He screwed the silencer on his Glock 9x19, put it back in his pocket, and took the stairs, two at a time. He came through the fire door and looked down the hall. The Trauma floor was busy for a late afternoon. Nurses and LPNs seeing to their patients. Ward secretary at her desk as expected. All normal. He stayed out of sight, no witnesses, and rounded the corner to the Godfather's room and stopped. *No one's there! No soldier from the family. No city cop. Door's open. What the hell?*

He slid silently into the room. *No Godfather. No Godfather equipment. Whaaaattt? No one, nothing? I expected the nurses to be gone, but.......* He rushed back out the door and checked room number. Right room. Right floor. He went back inside.

"Nothing. Not a fucking trace. Like he's never been here.

Cleaned out. No equipment, bed made. Probably wiped for prints, too," he whispered to himself. He was alone. "No one here. What's this......the gun we signed out to the nurses, here on the table. That a message?" He went back out again. *Looks normal at the nurses' station and the rest of the rooms. Just this room deserted. Like it never happened.* He returned to the room, pocketed the gun, and shut the door.

He quickly pulled out his cell. "Hey Billy, where's the Godfather?'

"Whaddaya mean where's da Godfadder? He's inna fuckin' hospital. Where you think he is?" Billy's voice was high and whiney, like he was nervous, covering something up?

"Listen, Billy. I'm at the fucking hospital. I'm in the Godfather's fucking room. There ain't no fucking Godfather in his fucking room." John's whisper screamed into the cell, looking all around him, twisting, seeing nothing but a clean room waiting for the next patient. He anxiously tapped his left foot, something he rarely did..

"Whadda you talkin'. I just seen Vinnie. He said Sal was gettin' Franco to replace him at da Godfadder's door. Vinnie's goin'a dentist. Sal called Franco. Special request."

John stopped twisting. Looked at the hospital phone on the empty table. "Jeeee-zizzz. They've done it. They beat us to it. Shit, Billy. They got him. They beat us.....at our own game. They got him. Damn......"

"Whadda ya talkin' about? You talkin' about da Godfadder?" Billy whined.

"Billy, you dumb shithead. Get the Underboss and all the upper level, including the consigliere, and lawyer Izzy what's his name, Izzy, Izzy Stein." John had his palm hard on the side of his face, as he stared at the floor, concentrating hard. Then he growled at Billy. "Tell them we need a sit-down. Now! Right fucking now. Church street. Tell them, meet to me at the office. One hour. Seven thirty. You got that."

"The Underboss is up at his mudder's place. Went up dere lunch time." Billy was scared of John when he got like this. He didn't know what to say.

"Listen up, you dumb fuck-face. You get them to the sit-down or you won't have any ass left to sit down when I'm done with you." He punched off so hard, he almost dropped the phone.

Chapter 55 - The APB

Neil Armstrong, RN. That was the name on one of his Nursing Licenses, as well as one of his diplomas. He had several versions of both, having anticipated that he might need them, depending on his various aliases. They matched his various valid IDs.

Steve, now Neil, looked at his watch. *2:45. Plenty of time.* He marched right in like he owned the joint, checked the Directory board to the left of the Information desk. *No sense getting in front of too many people. At least until I get the lay of the land here,* he thought. Scanning the list, he came to H R. *That's it. Room 136, Admin Wing.* He found it, easily, and smiled at the cute blonde clerk seated behind the sliding glass panel.

"Kin ah hep y'all, sir?" she asked, looking up at him. He was in the South, no doubt.

After several forms, an official photograph, which he didn't like, and offices with people with questions, he sat facing the Director, himself. This no-nonsense guy, complete with a Wharton MBA on the wall, deep voice and a seemingly embedded frown, punched his computer a few times, and studied Neil's face. After a long pause, he announced. "Neil Armstrong, your creds look in order, and we happen to have an opening on Oncology nights, as we speak. When would you be available to start?"

Neil, couldn't believe his luck. *I'll need a day or two to find a place to live, and maybe set up my lab, and check out the countryside, the culture, the roads, in and out of the area.* "How about Monday?

"That would be just fine." The Director started to push his desk chair back as though to stand, then rolled it back in again, and looked hard at Neil, then at his computer, then at Neil again. "Do you know a nurse named Steve Wojek? he asked.

Neil froze, *Holy shit! Where'd that come from. Is he on to me? Shit. What the hell? Damn. Shouldn't have come here.* He swallowed, hard. *Trapped. Okay, now. Stay cool. Find out what he knows. Where he's comin' from.* Neil sat up straight, and looked the Director right in the eye, "Steve Wojek? Yah, sure. Is he workin' here? Haven't seen him in years."

"No, we don't know him here", the Director answered. "We got an alert that a nurse named Steve Wojek was wanted by the authorities." Neil stayed still, unflinching, staring at the Director.

"Who wants him?" Neil asked. "What they want him for? Why ask me about him?"

"It says that you both went to the same nursing school, same year. Same class? You in the same class? There's a photo of him here, and he looks a lot like you. Maybe a year or two younger. Striking look-alike."

"Uh, yah. We were in the same class. He's my cousin. Mom's sister's kid." Neil paused, mind racing. *Cover him with bullshit, but stay cool. Flatter the son-of-a-bitch. Divert his attention. Stay on Steve and find out what gives.* "And a good eye on your part, sir, we do look a lot alike, at least we used to. He was a couple years younger than me. I took a few years off to work to pay for school, ya know? Where is he now? Does it say? What they want him for?"

"I'm not at liberty to discuss any of the details, but I will tell you this. The notification number came from the American Nursing Association's Credentials Committee. It was sent to all the State Boards and level one trauma centers, looking for this guy." The Director continued to study Neil's face, looking for a change. Nothing. No frown, no guilt, no fear. No change. Both stayed silent.

Neil felt like screaming inside, but didn't move a muscle. *Holy shit. The ANA. He knows. What'll I do now? Get the hell outta here. But get out easy. Slow. No-suspicion slow.* "Yessir, Steve was always kind of a loose, looney guy. Couldn't trust him. Our side of the family kinda lost track of him. Who should I call if he turns up?" The Director stayed silent, staring. *Is he on to me?*, Neil wondered, *He's on to me. He knows. Gotta get outta here. But don't run. Get out clean.*

Grabbing control, Neil flashed his best, wide smile. "Well, sir, as I said, I can start Monday morning, orientation, if you'll have me." Looking enthusiastic about starting, "Could you or someone here recommend a place to rent? Or a realtor? I'd like to settle in a little before starting work. The night shift doesn't allow much time to see the area. And this is such a pretty area." He figured the Director must live near here, someplace. "That's why I stopped. As I told the other lady, I was on my way west. No destination in mind. Just getting to know my fellow citizens in this wonderful country of ours." Neil's smile was almost genuine.

"Okay, Mr., uh, Armstrong. Interesting name." The Director's stare never wavered.

"Yessir. Our national hero. The first man on the moon. He is supposed to be a distant uncle or something, on my father's side. My father died twelve years ago, so we aren't too clear on the exact connection. He committed suicide". Neil figured this guy might try to check on this connection, which, of course was a falsehood.

"Monday. Miss Anderson, the head nurse on oncology will be glad to have you. She will handle the rest of your paper work, your three week orientation and probationary period, and assign you to the night shift, if you are ready." The gaze was still set in steel.

Neil rose to go. "Yessir. Monday morning, 8:00 a.m. Oncology Unit. I'll be there. Thank you sir." Neil extended his right hand. The Director's eyes stayed on him, and though he remained seated, he did slowly extend his right hand. The handshake was brief. "Thank you very much sir. I'll be there Monday morning."

They both knew he wouldn't.

Chapter 56 - A Ride in a Little Car

It was a tight fit. And the heavy load on the little car's springs gave the passengers a bumpy ride, but they were out of the City. Angelo, from the back seat, directed Will's route. "Turn here. Double back." It didn't look like they were being tailed, but if they were, Angelo was able to shake them. And Will, a good driver, was an eager pupil for the old master. Al, in the front passenger seat, nodded in agreement with each of Angelo's directives.

Now, the only light in the small town was the KFC. Al went in and came back with a bucket of chicken and fries and cokes, the All-American grease load, but quick and filling. Will suggested they peel off the fried skin and just eat the meat. "Healthier. No saturated fats," he advised, disregarding the hormones and antibiotics. But most of the skins were eaten anyway, because they were so tasty. *Thank you, Colonel Sanders.*

They were out in the boonies, so John watched the GPS and advised Will where to go to avoid toll roads and interstates. Just dawdling along, in the pitch-black night. For long stretches they saw no other traffic. Will suddenly broke the silence, "Looks like we got company." He was looking in the rear-view mirror. "Cops. Pulling us over."

"What for?" asked Al.

"Not supposed to happen," said John. He punched a quick-dial in his cell phone. Will pulled to the side of the road, and reached for his wallet. The police car's lights lit up the night around them.

"License and registration, please," said the uniform, leaning to look through the opened window, shining his LED light from one face to another. He stopped at the burqa. "Hey Louie. Over here." A second uniform crowded into the window. All he said was "Yup."

"Would you all please step outta the car," the first uniform demanded.

"What for, officer? Why have you stopped us?" Will asked.

"We certainly weren't speeding."

"Don't get smart, sonny. I said outta da fuckin' car.....now!" Both uniforms had backed away from the VW, hands on hips, looking tough, confrontational. "Come on, come on.......move it. Out!" Will and Al both maneuvered to get out opposite sides of the little car. "Face da automobile. Hands on the roof."

Will and Al did as they were told. Al's eyes watched one uniform, then the other, noting details. "You two, outta da back......yah, you, too, Queen-a-Sheba....out. Hands onna roof." the first uniform barked, "Come on, come on sister, or whatever youse calls yerself. That's it. Hands onna roof."

The second uniform was making a big deal of examining Will's license and the registration. "Hey, dis here's a rental."

"No shit, Sherlock. Tell dat from da plates", the first uniform sneered.

"Who are you?" the second uniform had put down his papers and was looking hard at the black burqa, trying to guess what was inside it.

"She's a visiting professor of microbiology from Pakistan. She's lecturing at University Hospit.........", John Pullman started to say, but as he turned sidewards, lifting his left hand off the car roof to explain, he was suddenly whacked in the left kidney by the first uniform. "Oooofff."

"Hands onna roof, an' shut up, asshole. We ain't askin' you," the first uniform spat.

"Hey Benny," said the second uniform from the other side of the car, "Think there's a hot bitch here in dis here Ay-rab outfit?"

"I dunno, Lou. Why don'tcha find out. Squeeze her tits. See what she's got. Maybe a pair of forty-fours. Give ya a cheap thrill."

"Yah, good idea. I'll just do that. See whatcher made of sister." The second uniform stepped forward, hands reaching out.

"Don't you lay a fucking finger on her!" Al snarled, looking hard at the second uniform. Everyone froze.

Everyone but the first uniform. "And who the fuck do you think you're talking to, asshole?" He was around the little car in a flash, eyes squeezed in fury, stained teeth bared. He bumped hard into Al, screaming into Al's ear. Al never flinched, but his mind was in overdrive, planning his next move.

"Officer Collins, and you, Officer Moody, you need to know that every word you say, everything you do is live to J. Edwards Baird, the DA. You, or at least your department was given word earlier not to stop us or interfere in any way." John Pullman said. He had carefully put his cell phone on the car top when he first got out. The uniforms were so busy, they hadn't even noticed. "And now, Officer Collins and Officer Moody......is it Louie Collins and Benny Moody? Or the other way around. In any case, you got it, Jeb?" John spoke forcefully toward the phone.

"You dickhead fuckface," said the first uniform, and both of them reached for the phone on the car top at the same time, sending them off balance, and distracted.

Chapter 57 - The Take Down

This was just the moment Al was waiting for. His right hand swung up and around with a karate chop that snapped first uniform's ulna neatly in half, and immediately followed with his left elbow smashing into the officer's face, driving his nose back into his oral cavity.

"Hi-hok!, Al yelled as the two blows landed, one — two, sending the man staggering back. Without a pause, and using the momentum of his left elbow coming around, Al leaned back just enough to lift his right leg and send it crashing into second uniform's knee, ripping his medial collateral ligament to shreds, tearing his meniscus and his ACL, and sending the second uniform to the ground also, screaming, as he grasped for his knee. Al took one step, and placed his boot hard on second uniform's neck. He turned to look over his shoulder to see the first uniform was out for the count, choking on the blood pouring out of his mouth.

"Collins or Moody, or fuck-face, or whoever you are. Who you working for?" Al raged. Not that he was expecting an answer. He was bending slightly, looking down into second uniform's bulging eyes as the supposed cop gasped for breath. He let go of his knee to clutch the boot on his throat, but the knee flopped sidewards with searing pain, and he quickly re-grabbed it with both hands. Al pushed a little harder with his boot, "I asked you, who are you working for? Who sent you?"

"De-pee-prmn. Cnnbeet."

"Oh, I see. You're having a little trouble breathing?" Al tried to put on his best smirk at the quivering flesh on the ground.

John and Will had come around the car, and were standing, jaws dropped, behind Angelo, who also faced Al's grounded captives, speechless.

"Let's try that again, shall we? Here, this might help a little." He lifted his boot just a little, just enough. Second uniform inhaled sharply. "Who you working for? Who sent you? You obviously targeted us. Why?"

"You wa' spee-din", he choked out.

Al bent a little more, checkin out the name badge, "So you're Moody, huh. You're no cop. That's for sure. So, who sent you. Huh, Moody, huh?"

"You wa' 'pee-din. 'topp ya's. Ssshhh-peee-din."

"Okay, smart ass", Al was smiling a rather malevolent grin at Moody, "You know why they don't send donkeys to college? Huh, do ya, Officer Moody? It's cuz nobody likes a smart ass." The grin vanished to stone-cold, "I'm gonna ask you one more time. You give me the right answer, and maybe we'll be in a position to get you some help......way out here, in the middle of nowhere. You give me the smart ass answer again, and I'll simply put your other knee out of commission, and leave you and Collins here for the vultures to find you in the morning. That might be tougher on you than Collins here, cuz he won't last much longer without some oxygen and some TLC. But you. Think you can drag yourself five miles to the nearest house?"

"Faaaack youuuuuu."

Al immediately pushed his boot down harder. "Can't say as I blame you though Moody, cuz anything I can do to make you uncomfortable is nothing compared to what the mob will do to you....that Johnny Dominicci or the Underboss, what's his name? Uccidera, or is it Ucciderita? Sal, I think." Moody's eyes widened, fear creeping in around the pain. "You'll be okay. The cross road is back a couple of miles. Someone's bound to come by at some point. Of course the train tracks are a lot closer, if you think you can stop a train." The sardonic grin was back.

Al looked up and said, "John, get his gun. He won't need it." John stood frozen in his tracks, still staring at Moody. Al waited, then said, "Okay, you, Will, get his gun." Will carefully pulled the gun from the holster, and held it aside. "Good, Will. Now shoot his right hand."

Will stood, frozen, "Whaaat?" was all he could muster.

"Shoot him in his right hand. That's his shooting hand. It won't kill him, but he won't shoot worth shit for the next few years."

"Oh, shit, Al. I can't do that. I don't care what you say......I can't....I....", Will mumbled, backing away slowly.

"Here, give me the damn gun." Angelo interrupted, having pulled off the niqab, "I got no hang ups with this guy." Angelo came around Moody's head, and glared down in his face, but Moody wasn't looking at him. "Do I know you? You work for us? What, you one of the newer guys? I know you? I don't know you." He took the gun out of Will's hand, and tapping his toe, sticking out from under the black gown, said, "Put your right hand out here." Moody didn't look, didn't move. "Okay then, I'll just shoot your hand, and I'll blow your knee, too. Worse." Moody let go of his knee, and moved his hand out from his side, eyes squeezed shut, teeth clenched, face turned away. Angelo, bent forward and unceremoniously shot Moody's right hand at point-blank range, right in the center of his palm. Al watched, and thought to himself, *This guy's done this before. Probably many times.*

Angelo tried to hand the gun to Al, but Al said, "Keep it. Might need it."

So Angelo turned to John, and said, "I'm done with these things. Here, you take it."

By this time, John had unfrozen himself, grasping that immediate danger was past. He took the gun, and gave it to Al, who tucked it in his back belt.

"Get Collins' gun, John, while you're at it," Al instructed.

John following the order, straightened and said, "Here, this one's yours." Will, instinctively obeying his mentor, took the gun, and like Al, tucked it in his back belt.

"Let's go," Al said. "We're gonna be late. Back in the car." He took his foot off Moody's neck, who responded with a deep inhale, followed by wracking, prolonged coughing. Al said, "Moody, when you get back to your mob....if you get back to your mob, you tell them to lay off. Your amateur bullying tactics won't work with this crowd. So, lay off. That's an order. And Moody, just to keep you quiet for a while, so we can leave in peace, I'll leave you with this", and he kicked Moody's deformed knee a savage blow. Moody rolled onto his side with a howl, then quietly passed out.

"Watch 'em. Be right back." Al said, as he strode over to the cop car. Got in, took the keys and popped the hood. He got out, went around, and reached into the engine compartment, pulling some wires out in a series of jerks. Then coming back to the VW with the handful of wires, he noted that both bodies were still breathing, but otherwise, motionless.

Back in the car, no one spoke. But Will couldn't contain his astonishment any longer. "Al, how'd you know they weren't cops. I mean, real cops. They sure looked....... legal."

Al smiled, wondering when they'd get around to the questions. "First of all, cops, real cops won't stand right outside your window. Big target. He, or she, doesn't know who you are. He or she, will stand off to the side and behind the window, so he-she can still talk, from behind your shoulder. Try to get at me when I'm behind your shoulder. Can't do it. Safe place."

"Second, two cops never stand next to each other like they did, looking in the window. Bigger target."

"Third, cops don't use foul language. That's a misdemeanor. Don't use it with the public, period. In the back room at the barracks, that's a different story."

"Fourth, they had no cause to order us out of the car. And what did they stop us for? Certainly not speeding. It's a clean, new, rental, so the chances of having a tail light, or a brake light out, are negligible. No other traffic. No other cause."

"Fifth, why the big interest in the lady in the burqa? No, I knew soon as they reacted, they were Mafia." He turned back to Angelo, "Sorry, buddy, but that's who they were."

"Oh, I know. I know my boys, or who used to be my boys. I know how they operate. I know their language, the way they talk. Yah, I'm with you on that. No doubt", Angelo admitted easily.

"And sixth, cops don't carry the V 90-9 millimeter Gloc that these guys had. They usually carry thirty-eight specials."

Will, still in awe, asked, "And how did you know you could take them both down?"

Al just smiled.   "Yah, he's a champ. A tournament champion. Medals and trophies", John said from the back seat.

"Okay. Got that, but how..... both of them?"

"I waited for them to bunch together again. They do it once, they'll do it again. Two in one place is a cakewalk. Separate them, and you got a problem. Look at your opponent. Study him. The way he moves. Which are the weaker parts of his body. He may have arms like a gorilla, but if his knees are weak, that's what you go for. Forget boxing, fisticuffs. Go for the weak, vulnerable points. Knees, elbows, noses, eyes, sometimes, feet."

"Jeez, I never figured it that way. And you got them both." Will could hardly keep his eyes on the road.

"Will, you get one chance. These guys were easy. Bunched together. Arms outta play, reaching for John's phone. That phone, by the way, was a great move, John." Al looked back at Will. "Both of them were off balance. Totally non-professional. Ducks on a pond. There for the picking." Al went silent, looking out the window at the passing black night.

John was starting to doze in the back seat. He'd heard it all before. Angelo unzipped the chador, and let out a long sigh. He sat there contented, a smile across his whole face. But Will was still concerned, "Think they'll make it?"

"Oh, sure, Will. They'll do fine. They look worse than they are. I just needed to stop them temporarily, not kill them." Al affirmed. "As you know, the nasal bleed'll quit. Clot up, hopefully before he chokes on it, but it'll quit. He'll wake up from the pain in his arm. The other guy, Moody, a bit of a problem. Bad hand and bad knee, same side. Hard to walk on one side alone. They'll be there for a while..... until someone comes along and sees them."

Chapter 58 - At the House

Finally, after what seemed like hours, and the adrenaline had been metabolized, the VW slowly rolled in the dark through the residential section of a small town. Just a few lights. No traffic. No people. *All bedded down,* Al said to himself. *Kind of cozy.* Then he broke the silence, "There's the house", he said pointing down the street to the left, "Third one. There", as they rolled past, slowly, all looking through the black night.

"Drive around the block," Angelo said. "No, to the right. Everyone drives around the block the house is set on. Don't do that. Drive around the opposite of what they might suspect. Then go up a block and a half."

Al said, "Dusty, George's buddy Dusty Reade, said there's a covered garage. Hides the car. I suggest we put it in there." Everyone agreed.

"Do it", said Angelo. "Is it connected to the house or do I have to wear this dreadful costume?"

"Attached", Al assured him. "There's supposed to be shades, according to Dusty, so we can turn on the lights."

All four were blinded by the light when they opened the door from the garage into the kitchen. A man got up from a kitchen chair, facing them. Stunned, all four bumped into each other. Al reached for the thug's gun.

"Welcome, gents. Dusty Reade at your service", the stranger said with a big smile and a slight bow. "You must be Al Towns. You can put the gun away. You're safe. You're all safe, and, as I said, welcome to my humble safe house."   "I'm John Pullman, Dusty. " John, the first in, extended his hand. They all shook, each in turn, introducing himself. After checking the place out, each looking at different parts of the house, each for differing reasons, they settled around the pale blue, Formica, kitchen table. Dusty poured coffee for everyone but John and Angelo. "I'm planning on sleeping tonight", Angelo said. "Gotta tell you, I'm tired after all this sneaking around. I never thought I'd be having to sneak around to avoid my own people. But then, I never thought I'd have to confess my crimes and ask God for His forgiveness. Or the DA, either, for that matter." The room was dead quiet. The five other men all stared at Angelo.

Finally Al spoke up, "Yah, I imagine this is a real tough time for you. This can't be easy. This on top of the medical stuff you've been through already. My hat's off to you, Angelo. You're one tough mother. You got my vote." "I agree", said John, "Al's right. What you've been through. An assassination attempt, alone, is enough to uncork anybody, but then, two serious bullet wounds, and you wake up with a whole new disease...... and a new personality. That diabetes. Changes your whole life. And, now, with the DA and all. It's a wonder you can sleep at all."

"So you say, Doc, but I sleep very well. Always have. Doesn't mean I can't wake up fast if there's a problem, but I sleep fine. In my business......well, in my old business, if you get things right in the daytime, you can sleep all night. Sometimes you have to work all night, so you sleep in the daytime. Doc Will knows that. Right, Dr. Will?", Angelo said with a nod toward Will who was draining the last of his coffee.

The amiable chit-chat continued for another few minutes before they all decided to turn in. Angelo had been assigned by Dusty, to the large room at the top of the stairs. Quick exit, front and back, if needed. That room was designed so that opposite the metal, multi-locked door at the top of the stairs, was a large-size window over a three-foot drop onto the sloping porch roof, then a seven-foot drop to the ground. The big window also had an iron grate across it that opened from the inside, only. The room was cluttered with heavy, dark, wood furniture — a massive bed, two chests-on-chests, a large chifforobe, and several high-backed over-stuffed chairs — all of which would take time to search, and would be slow get around, unless you were familiar with the layout. Good cover. There, you had the advantage over an intruder. The rest of the house was less impressive. Maybe even normal.

They settled in. Will called in, changing his unexcused absence to an excused one. "Yah, I'm on a special project with Dr. Pullman." Mention Dr. Pullman, and you could do almost anything, as long as Dr. Pullman was behind it. And he certainly was behind this cabal.

John Pullman called in, too, to David Allen, his young partner. "Hey Dave, what's up? Say, I've run into a little problem keeping me out of the city tonight. Should be back tomorrow. Any chance you could cover my butt tonight? Annie B will deflect what she can, and the PAs will handle most of it, but if there's a problem....?" He listened, nodding, then smiled. "Yah, thanks buddy. I owe you......Yah, right. I appreciate it. Thanks, see ya." John disconnected, then called Annie B All was okay, he assured her, but he'd not make it home tonight, and he'd be back in the office in the morning after making rounds. Al called Barbara, "I'm good. Can't get home tonight. Got an all nighter.........love you too."

Angelo wished he could call Mrs. Ginnini, but it was better to keep her quietly at peace. If she knew nothing, then they couldn't get anything out of her. But he felt sad, because he missed her. He hadn't seen her since before he was shot.

The next morning, 7:00a.m. sharp, Dusty had made a diabetic breakfast for the whole team who were busy devouring it, when four young people knocked on the back door. "That'll be your nurse team," he said as he rose to open the door.

"No thanks. We've already eaten", the male of the group answered. All nine of them were standing around the table, and had shaken hands — a large group, of large people, in a small kitchen. The four new-comers wore professional nursing scrubs. The male, Chick Morella, RN, hard-bodied and almost as wide as he was tall, obviously pumped iron. Two of the women, Cindy Keefe and Cindy Kingman, were sinewy and alert. The third woman, Peggy Handleman, was taller and fit. Al introduced them, listing their creds. "A formidable team....on several levels. I suggest you don't try them out. Any one of them," he said with a sly smile, "you'd lose."

John Pullman, with both Al's and Will's help, instructed the four person team on the care of Angelo's insulin-dependent diabetes, his diabetic, low-fat diet, and all-round nursing care. The three PAs and the male nurse worked out a shift schedule and various duties. They chose the male nurse to be the head, as it were, not because he was a male, but because he had the most training and experience of the foursome. John approved of their grasp of Angelo's various problems. Al approved, Will approved, and Angelo, particularly, approved, with a jovial slap on the back for each, smiling as if they were long-lost buddies, reunited, once again.

The plan was for Dusty Reade to stay living in the house, as usual. He said, "Should anyone ask, I'll introduce you four caregivers as two of my own kids, a niece, and the niece's friend." Looking at Angelo, he added, "And this is my former father-in-law who's in failing health. He's here due to family circumstances." He went on to say that he would not go out of his way to get them well known, but he didn't want anybody to think he was hiding anything. So "the kids" were free to come and go, hang out in the yard on sunny days, and chat with neighbors, if the occasion arose. No obvious secrets. "Grandpa" was too ill to go out much anymore, if at all.

Jeb had two disposable cell phones delivered to John's and Al's homes by secure courier, which had unregistered numbers, and were to be used only by the safe house team to call for medical problems, should they arise. But neither man had any way of knowing that neither of them would be getting to their own homes. Not, at least, for a while.

The whole set-up looked "clean", as Dusty called it. Both Al and Angelo could find no loopholes, and both agreed to implement the plan. "Take care of you, and behave," John said to Angelo as they parted. John, Al, and Will got in the little VW, Will driving, Al riding shot-gun.

"See you soon", Al called out the window, as he waved.

"Yah, see you soon", Angelo, smiling, as he waved back from the garage door while the car backed down the driveway. None of them knew how soon that would come true.

"Where we headin'"? Will looked in the rear-view mirror at John.

"Hospital, don'tcha figure, Al?", John answered, leaning forward to be heard.

"Yah, my car's there, and I've got some stuff to do."

John paused, thinking for a moment, and suggested, "Will, could you drop us off at the hospital, then take the car back to the rental place. I'll call Annie B and ask her if she could pick you up there and bring you back to the hospital. That work for you?"

"Yessir. That's good. I don't even remember who's on call tonight, but I'm sure they'll need me in surgical clinic this afternoon. So, yes that's good. Be glad to see Mrs. Pullman again, too. She's such a nice person." Will, keeping an eye on the road, turned his head slightly to be heard over the engine noise.

Chapter 59 - A Few Questions, Please

Rosy cheeks and the creamy complexion accentuated the policeman's boyish face. The rookie cop was looking up, way up at Larry Lowance, and Larry Lowance was looking down, way down at the young cop. The officer said, "A couple of questions, sir, if you don't mind." Larry was a little surprised by the high voice.

"Sure", he said, "What's this about, sir? If it's about who attacked me, and why, I ain't pressin' any charges, so there shouldn't be any trouble."   "No sir. I'm Patrolwoman Sally Smith. This is not about your....er...." She looked at the two bandaged forearms folded at eye-level in front of her eyes. "Er....your accident, or about you. Early this morning, you saw a hospital nurse. Somewhere around 3:00 or 4:00 a.m. A young man. He came out of the room two doors down from yours, and ran into you here in the hall?"

"Yessir, er ma'am." She blushed. Larry thought, *she's a real cutie.*

"You remember him.....the incident?"

"Hard to forget. Ran right into my sore arms. Post-op, ya know. Had to have plates put on....."

"Yessir, but can you describe the young man who ran into you?"

"Well, I'm guessing he's about seven or eight inches taller than you. White kid. Looked scared as hell...... He in trouble? Looked like trouble. I can smell trouble. It's my business to...."

"Yessir. Age? What age, about?"

"Me? I'm 47 come next month."   "No sir. The perp. I mean the young man who ran into you? How old, would you say?"

"Between 23 and 25. That puts him at 24. Yah, I'd say 24. I'm a pretty good judge of age. In my job, I gotta guess people's ages. Can't let any juvvies in, ya know. Against the law. Close us up, faster'n a flea can fart........oh, excuse me, ma'am. Yes, to answer your question, 24."

The young officer was busy making notes in her notebook, and not really listening. She stopped writing, and looked up, "Twenty-four, you say? Could you identify him? From a photograph?"

"Yah, sure."

"How about in a line-up? You know what a police line-up is? It's when...."

"Oh hell yes. I sure as heck know what a line-up is. Every time you guys get a tall perp, who's black like me, for ID, they ask me to stand in. Down at the Twenty-sixth Street Station, ya know."

"Eh, yessir." Her neck was getting a crick from looking up.

Larry saw the problem, and smiled at her. She looked puzzled. He asked, "Officer Smith, would you be more comfortable sitting down? I'm going to sit here in my special chair, and you sit there, on my bed. That way you'll be higher. Might be easier."

"No. I'm fine, thank you." She was obviously flustered. "I'm just fine. It's okay."

"Well, I'm gonna sit, if you don't mind." Slowly he lowered himself into the high-leg, padded chair, using his finger-tips on the chair arms. A painful procedure. Larry rested back, and blew out a relieved sigh. He looked up at Officer Smith who had changed her mind and had tried to hop up on the hospital bed, but had slid off. Larry smiled, "Try the stool", he said.

She looked over at the footstool, slid it between them, and started to squat down on it. "No", Larry gently said, "Use the stool to get on the bed." She blushed again. He was beginning to like this hapless rookie. Probably one of her first solo assignments. He tried not to laugh. She did as he suggested, and with an audible "Humph", made it onto the bed. Her face was beet-red and serious. She leaned hard to her side, and pulled out a vinyl pouch from under her butt, all business. As she was pulling out a wad of paper, a scrap broke loose and fluttered down to the floor. They both looked at it, then looked up, at each other, and both broke into a smile at the silliness of the situation. She finally found what she was looking for. Regaining her serious-cop face, she asked,

"This him?" It was a small two by three.

"Yup. That's him. That's the nurse who ran smack into me.

Almost knocked me down. Almost knocked us both down. He bounced off me and had to get his balance. That's when he looked at me. And I looked at him, ya know. One of those times when everything stands still, and you never forget it? Yah, that's him for sure. Ask me again in ten years. Answer'll be the same. Never forget that face. Sometimes I see it when my arms hurt."

Officer Smith was writing in her notebook again, nodding at everything Larry said. Putting down her notebook, she looked up and asked, "Do you have a picture ID of yourself? If so, may I see it?"

"Yah, sure. It's right there in the....... No.", He paused, "I'm s'posed to be doing this stuff myself." He lightly put his fingers on the chair arms, leaned way forward, and with eyes squeezed shut and teeth clenched, he slowly rose out of the chair. Officer Smith's instinct was to help, so she slid off the bed at just the wrong moment, tripped on the foot-stool, and thumped rather unceremoniously into Larry. A full frontal collision. Ooomph.....Luckily for Larry, his arms were still behind him on the chair rails. Her nose pushed his hospital johnny into his navel. They both recoiled back a half step, hers larger than his, almost tripping over the foot-stool. A moment passed. They looked at each other. Another moment passed, then Larry broke into a loud guffaw, and Officer Smith into a slightly embarrassed snicker, face still bright red.

"It's okay," he said, "I'll get it. She stepped back on the footstool and hopped back onto the bed. He went to the bedside table drawer, carefully opening it with his finger tips, found his wallet, and, gingerly, pulled out his state-issued photo ID card. "This do it?"

"Yessir. That's perfect, sir. Let me just copy the info, if you don't mind."

"Be my guest," he said, "Nothin' there ain't legal. Two bucks every three years. Get it from the state. Best investment I ever made."

Chapter 60- The Snatch

Will drove the VW Beetle, with Al and John back to the hospital, on the straightest, most direct route the GPS had to offer. Sure enough, as they had already guessed, they picked up a tail about three minutes inside the city limits. A big, black Lincoln Town Car, as expected. At the hospital the two older men got out, and Will turned back, heading for the car rental place to meet Annie B

John and Al were walking across the parking lot, but the big, black Lincoln Town Car cut sharply in front of them, with tires squealing to a stop. Two big men in black got out, "Dr.Pullman, and Nurse Towns, would you please get inna car."

"Well, actually, I was heading into my office to do some work", Al said with a sneer, "How about later?"

"De boss wants-ta see yuhs." Their faces were shadowed beneath wide-brimmed fedoras. "He sez he needs to see yahs. Sez it's important."

"If your boss would like to meet with us, we'd be very glad to do so", John said, not wanting to meet any of them at all. It could mean nothing but trouble. He tried to swallow with a dry mouth, and, looking at the goon, tried to suggest, "Have him call my office. I think I've got some time tomorr......"

"The Underboss, Mr. Sal, he wantsa talk. Now." A beefy hand came out of the coat pocket with a big, black Smith and Wesson, held close to his side, not moving an inch, pointing directly at John. No doubt about its message. John froze. Instinctively, his hand already in his pocket, fumbled for a second, then feeling his cell phone, pressed the speed dial to his office. At least he was pretty sure he had hit the right button. He'd done it before. He quietly took his hand out of his pocket, and tried to look over at Al. *How is he handling this?*, John asked himself, but his gaze stopped at the other thug's gun, pointing at Al. He didn't dare look further. Couldn't see Al anyway. A cold shiver ran up his back. John stood wide-eyed, feeling like a lost child, not knowing what to do, so he did nothing. His mind raced: *Please God, not more of their nasty behavior. Not again. Please no. Just let me....*

"Inna fuckin' car, like I said. De underboss wanna see yahs. He don't care if yah got a slug in yer or not. One way or de udder, yer gettin' inna car." The gun waved side to side, just enough to make his point.

John tried to calm himself, *Get control. Do what he says, but stay calm. Don't freeze up.......follow Al. Yeah, follow Al. He's done this stuff before.* John forced himself to turn back, to look at Al. *Al is stone-faced. No anger. No hate. No fear. Nothing.* "Whatta you say, Al? What do you want to do?"

Al shrugged, "Guess we get in the car. Let's go see what the Underboss wants," and he moved forward to duck into the big sedan. *Say nothing more. Show nothing.* John did his best to do the same, but his heart was thumping in his chest.

The day had become overcast, but they could see that they were heading out of city center, toward the suburbs.

The goon in the front passenger seat stayed half turned, keeping the big, black gun pointed over the seat back at first one of them, then the other. Back and forth. The driver goon kept one eye in the rearview mirror, and the other on the road.

John shifted a little in his seat, just enough to sneak his hand under his left thigh, behind the cell in his pocket. Slowly and carefully, he slid the pocket contents to the front of his thigh. He realized the car was going out to the area where Angelo's house was located, where he and Annie B and the Ansons had gone for lunch with Mrs. Ginnini. Trying to be casual, he said to the front seat goon, "Doesn't Mrs. Ginnini live out here, somewhere? Is that where we're headed. It would be nice to see her again. She's such a nice...."

"Shut de fuck up. It's none of yer business where we's goin'. An', no, we're not goin' to bother Mrs. Ginnini. Youse got a appointment wid de unnerboss."

Al figured out what John was up to. *He's sending someone a message. Clever old bastard. Keep up the message.* He said, "That's right, you told me you had dinner out with Mrs. Ginnini. You and the Ansons. Am I right?"

"I said shut de fuck up. Save yer kibbitsin' for de unnerboss."

The third goon, in the left rear seat, sat forward and also half turned, also pointing his gun. *In his left hand,* John noted, *must be a lefty.* "You a lefty?" he asked, "one of my surgical buddies is a lefty. Great surgeon."

"I told ya, shut de fuck up." The gravelly voice was getting higher. Annoyed. The gun was moving faster, back and forth, back and forth.

Chapter - 61 Annie B and Jeb

Annie B and John actually made a pretty good detective team. John, occasionally, managed to get himself in trouble, while Annie B sitting in the office, watching the crisis unfold, and using her keen, logical mind would figure it out, notify the proper people, pull the proper strings, and set things in motion to bail John out. So when the phone rang unexpectedly, her first thought, *John's in trouble.* Twenty-five-plus years as soulmates had fine tuned her instinct, and she wasn't all that surprised when she heard mostly static with some distant voices in the back ground. Pressing the phone to her ear, she heard something about ".....underboss......wannsa talk...", static or a rustling motion, a pause, then ".....Inna fuckin' car....Shut de fuck up.... No, we're not goin' to bother Mrs. Ginnini..... Youse got a appointment wid de unnerboss." This part came in really clear for some reason. Annie B recognized one of the same gravelly voices that had been so threatening last week in those nasty phone calls about John's patient. She also recognized John's voice....something about Mrs. Ginnini. Then she recognized Al's voice, unmistakably answering some more about Mrs. Ginnini

She straightened in her chair. *Okay, okay now. He's in trouble. They're both in trouble. Okay, rule one, keep the line of communication open.* She laid the phone receiver on her desk blotter, and punched the speaker button. The voices and the motion noise came through diminished, but audible if she listened closely. Then she punched the record button. *Don't know how long the tape will last, but we'll see what we get.*

She pushed away from her desk, went into John's office, and using his phone, she punched in a well-known number. It rang, once, twice,

"The District Attorney's Office. If you are looking for J. Edwards Baird, press one. If you are looking...." Annie B pressed one. "Mr. Baird's office. Whom may I ask is calling?"

"Molly, hi, it's Annie B Pullman. Is Jeb there?"

"Oh, hi, Annie B Is there something I can help you with?"

"Molly, aren't you a sweetheart, but no. This is something I need to talk to Jeb about, personally, confidentially. Is he very busy? This is quite urgent."

"Sure. Hang on. Let me interrupt him." Annie B waited for less than ten seconds.

"Hey Annie B, how are you?" Jeb answered. "What's going on?"

Annie B told him what she knew. He caught on right away, as if he knew more than she did. "I can't tell you much about it," Jeb said, "because it might put you in danger."

"Me in danger? What about John? And Al? I'm getting a little anxious."

"I can tell you this. We have put Angelo in the witness protection program. He's in a safe house. It's my guess the Family wants to find out where, and go bust him out. They'll most likely silence him. They must know that he has testimony against them. So they're going to try to get Angelo's location from John and Al. You said Al was taken with John?"

"Yes, I'm pretty sure. They were on some project together last night. From where, to where, I don't know. Most likely the bad guys got John and Al in or near the hospital, because that's where they were supposed to be left off by Will Lain, and I'm pretty sure I recognized both their voices on the open phone line."

"Will Lain? Who's Will Lain?" Jeb asked.

"He's one of the surgical residents at the hospital. He was driving a VW rental car, and is on his way to returning it to A & J Rentals, over on Renell Street. I am to meet him at the rental place and take him back to the hospital. But I can't do that now."

"Open phone line? What open phone line?"

"John called me on his cell, and left it open on purpose, cluing me in."

"Okay, Annie B I can take it from here. I'll alert the police. Set up a man hunt. We'll find them. Tell him to leave his phone on. We can track it, and find him, both of them, if they're still together. You go take what's-his-name back to the hospital." "I can't do that. I've got John's phone live on the other line, here in the office. I've got to monitor it. Follow what's happening to him."

"Jeeziz, got it on live? That's great. Don't lose it. Annie B, I'll send over a cop to mind the phone. We'll cover that for you."

"Edwards Baird, you know me well enough to know that there is no frigging way you're going to budge me from this phone. John's in deep trouble and I'm staying right here."

Jeb knew she wouldn't move, couldn't be moved. She only called him Edwards when she was really intense. "You stay right there. The cop won't bother you. We will need to stay in touch. You got my cell number?"

"1776USA?"

"That's it, and don't let that phone connection break."

"I won't break it, and John knows enough to keep his phone live. We've done this before. The only question is how long his battery will last."

"Right", Jeb said with some worry. "I'll get things moving from my end. Stay in touch."

"Right", she said. They hung up. The transmission from John was getting worse. More garbled, more dead spaces, harder to follow. More noise, like car noise. Not much talking. Then a brief clear bit. It sounded like walking, feet on pavement, then "Inna door." That was all. Static.

Chapter 62 - The Board Room

But the car turned away from the area John remembered, and
pulled up to the curb in a run-down commercial area he didn't
know. Garbage piled up on the sidewalks. He saw that Al was
watching even more intently, as if he were memorizing this Church
Street location. The back seat was tight with the three of them. No
room for any maneuver. John knew Al wouldn't try anything in
these close quarters.

"Okayee-doakee, assholes", Front-seat said, "enda da ride.
Out." The black coats climbed out, their guns now hidden by bulky
coat pockets, but still aimed to stop any nonsense. The driver went
ahead and opened a shabby, unpainted door.

"We going inside?" John asked as loudly as he dared, hoping
his phone would hear it. A coded knock on the door, and they were
ushered into a dingy hall, the front-seat-thug leading the way.
Back-seat brought up the rear, as they were led through a door
into a smoky pool-room. *A gaming room,* John noted, as they
were led past a table with cards thrown down in the middle of a
game. Half a dozen, maybe eight variously sized goons, some
lounging, others standing, remained perfectly still. Every eye
watched in dead silence, as they were herded through another
door. This room had red fabric walls. *The meeting room,* John
realized *where they have their "sit-downs." The mob's version of a
Board Room. Chairman there, at the head. Looks more like a
throne.*

"Siddown. You here", John was shoved against a chair on the
near side. "You, over dere", Front-seat shoved Al to the chair on
the opposite side of the table. "Siddown an' shaddup." The voice
was deep and nasty. John and Al, obediently took their places.
John slowly shifted his phone to the front of his thigh again.

"What are we here for?" John asked. Al gave him a stern,
negative look, just as Front-seat barked,

"I said, shaddup." The goon had backed up to the wall, arms
folded across his chest, stretching the black overcoat fabric over

thick arms, eye-slits staring, pug mouth down turned in a sneer. John looked at Al. But Al was very subtly, looking carefully around the room, taking in every detail. John tried to do the same thing, but he knew he wasn't seeing all that Al saw. They waited. Silence. The goons were staring at Al, who was almost motionless, while slyly observing. Suddenly the door opened, and a goon came in. John turned to see him, a shorter, thinner, wiry guy, carrying what looked like a lap-top. 'Whack!', someone hit the back of John's head.

"Mind yer own fuckin' business. Eyes front, dickhead", the gargled voice grumbled. The skinny guy opened the lap-top at the head of the table, and booted it up, then went to the foot of the table, and stood silently, hands behind his back. The door opened again.

Annie B was focused on the phone static. Then, just as abruptly as it had died, the reception erratically returned. She was scared. Scared for John, and for Al, too. But mostly for John. Al was trained in self defense, well-trained, but not John. There hadn't been any open hostility since the phone calls stopped. But Annie B knew this was bad, and she feared it was going to get worse.

"That's okay, Gonz. No more rough stuff. These gentlemen are our guests. Our friends. Good morning, gentlemen." It was Sal, the Underboss. Both John and Al recognized him immediately as he rolled into the room like a tsunami. "I said, good morning, gentlemen." He turned a sharp eye to John, visually boring in to him, then doing the same to Al. Staring at one, then the other.

"Good morning, Sal, is it?" Al said as he started to stand, but was immediately shoved back down by the goon behind him.

"Gentle, boys, gentle. Like I said, these gentlemen are our guests. I have a favor to ask of them, and I don't wanna piss 'em off." Sal looked at each of his goons in turn, then focused on John and Al again with long burning stares. After silence for what John guessed was about a minute, Sal asked, "Would-chu gentlemen like a drink of somethin'? Soda? Beer?Whiskey? We even got water. What's yer pleasure?"

Al responded, "Good morning to you, too, Sal. It's been a few days. A nice clean glass of pure, potable ice water, if you please", he paused for the effect, then added, "with a wedge of lemon in it." Al returned Sal's stare, not taking his eyes off the mountain standing at the head of the table.

Sal broke first, "And you?", he said turning to John.

John steeled himself, trying to follow Al's lead. *Show-down time,* he told himself. With his purposeful, easy smile, John said, "Yes, please, Sal. A glass of water would hit the spot," but the controlled rise in the pitch of his voice kept Sal waiting, suggesting John had more to say. A short pause, and John then declared, "But, Sal, no ice. Don't like ice." John was trying to play Sal, and Sal knew it, and John knew Sal knew it, so he continued, "And, Sal, a wedge of lemon, also. That would be very nice, Sal. How thoughtful of you." John's smile never faded, never changed. But only his lips were smiling. His stare continued, cold, unwavering.

Al watched the whole exchange without moving a muscle, staring hard at Sal. *Attaboy John. Keep it up. Don't let him in on you. Keep it up. Piss him off. See what he's up to.*

Sal slowly sat his large frame into the throne at the head, and nodded to one of the goons who then went out. Sal, then, turned to the lap-top. He didn't say a word as he pecked with his index fingers, paused, and pecked again, for at least two minutes. It seemed like more to John. The door opened and a guy in a tee-shirt, baggy black pants, and suspenders came in. *A regular goon,* thought John, *except this one is only average size, both in height as well as girth.* He placed the waters in front of each man, straightened up, and looked at Sal, who merely tossed his head toward the door. The man left as quietly as he had entered. Sal, finally, looked up, first at John, then at Al. "Thank you gentlemen for agreein' to meet wid me."

John was about to say something, but he looked over at Al, who was staring at Sal, jaw clamped shut. *This is Al's type of game , John said to himself, one he's played before. Silent, hardball stares. Follow his lead.* He took a small sip of his water. Tasted a little funny?

"I'm hoping that we could work togedder." Sal's rough voice was almost even toned when he spoke, more pleasant this time.

218

"We need each udder's help." He paused, fingers fiddling mindlessly with the pencil in front of him. Silence. Al continued staring at Sal. John did his best to keep from squirming in his seat. "Yeh. We needa work wit each udder, here, on dis here problem."

John couldn't help himself, he blurted, "What are you talking about, Sal. May I call you Sal?" He looked over at Al whose eyes were still fixed on Sal, lips tightly sealed. "Enlighten me.... us."

"You know what I need, what I'm talkin' about. You got him. Where-izz'e?"

"Where is who?" John immediately regretted the response. He'd been played. One point for Sal.

"Come on Mr. Pullman......" Sal leaned forward, fingers clutching the pencil tightly. " 'Scuse me. I should say 'doctor'. Doctor Pullman, you know 'xactly what I'm talking about. I needa know watchu done wit da Godfadder....... wit Mr. Ginnini........ wid Angelo." His jowls shaking as he spoke, his angry little eyes almost hidden in the slits. *Could Sal be losing his cool?* John took another sip and just sat there. He felt himself withering under Sal's glare, but said nothing.

"Mebbe youse didn' hear me. I ast-chu whatchu done wit Angelo? Hunh? Whatchu done wit him?" Voice rising, he stood up, leaned big beefy knuckles on the table, face reddening by the second. "Where-izzy?"
Sal kept looking from John to Al, but mostly at John, who felt himself trying not to cave. He hoped Annie B could hear this.

Al remained a brick wall, rigidly upright in his chair, mouth clamped in a scowl, eyes unwavering on Sal. John glanced briefly at Al. *Military training,* John thought. Sal straightened, hands at sides, obviously forcing himself to calm down. Then he sat down.

"Dere's a diff'rnce 'tween me an' Angelo," he said, "Me, I got a short fuse, ya know. Angelo, he got patience. He don't get hot so quick. 'Spose 'ats one reason why he's da Boss over me. Dat, an' he's older. Been 'round more den me. So lemme ask youse like he woulda." Feigning a smile and raising the pitch of his voice, he said, "We know you got Angelo stashed somewhere. Somewhere outta town. Inna safe house. We know dat. His room in da hospital is empty. Empty like he was never dere. We seen it. Empty an' cleaned up, wiped down. No prints. Nuttin'. Nice job." Sal now focused on John, his voice calmer and trying to sound soothing. More of a condescending smile than a smirk. An in-charge adult coaxing a child to spit out his disallowed chewing gum. "So where-izzy? Hunh? Not down in special procedures, neither. Checked dat too. He's not inna hospital, no place. So if he's not inna hospital, he's somewheres else. So if he's somewheres else, just where is he at?"

Sal paused. Waited. John didn't trust himself to look Sal in the eye, so he focused on the grain in the table, hands seemingly relaxed, folded in front of him. He swallowed, and swallowed again. He looked at the water. Reached for it, and took a sip. *It does taste a little funny. Stale? Chlorine?, Amobarbital?, Something else?,* But the water eased his dry throat. He looked over at Al. *Looks like a statue. Hasn't moved a muscle. How's he do it?* John said nothing.

"I didn't say I want to know where the Boss is," Sal spoke again. "I said I <u>need</u> to know where he is." Breaking his gaze on John, he concentrated on the open lap-top in front of him, pecking in some data, waiting, clicking some more. Sighing, he sat back, and looked up at John, "Mebbe dis will refresh yer mem'ry. Look at dis here. You recognize dis here picture?" He turned the lap-top to face John, and pushed it in front of him. John jerked back when he saw the screen.

"Jeezis no!" His face turned white as his body tensed. "Where'd you get this?"

"You recognize Wilmington?" Sal growled, no longer Mr. Nice-guy. "We got friends everywhere, even in Delaware."

"You leave my family alone, you son of a bitch!" John seethed through clenched teeth. "They have nothing to do with any of this."

"So you recognize your grandson. Nice picture. No?"

"You lay a hand on him and I'll......"

"You'll do what. Hunh? Do what? Hunh? You do nuttin'. Ain't no need to. He's only gettin' onna school bus."

"You bastard. Yes, that's my grandson, little Jack. He's in

Kindergarten. You leave him alone! You leave his family, alone."
John rarely spit out hard, but this was a rare situation. Even Al
flinched slightly at this out-break.

"Like I said we got friends in all sortsa places." Sal was
sitting back in his throne, a nasty smirk spreading across his face.
He looked over at Al, and noted his attention had been diverted to
John as well. *Good. Got him too. Tough, but not that tough,* he
thought. Sal turned to one of the goons standing behind John and
said, "Give 'em da word."

The goon stepped forward, and talked into his cell phone,
"Go ahead wit de plan." Leaning over John's shoulder, he punched
half a dozen buttons on the lap-top. then stood back and waited.

The screen jumped, animated. Young Jack trotted to join
friends in line to get on the school bus. Any other time, a great
video. Not now. Jack climbed on with the rest of the kids. The bus
doors closed. Seconds passed. Not a sound in the red-walled Board
Room. The school bus pulled in its stop signs and metal
barricades, and started off in a small cloud of diesel exhaust, the
photographer followed for about thirty seconds.

"Enough, arreaddy. Turn it off." commanded Sal. The goon
stepped forward again and swept the lap-top from the table. "You
seen enough. You got da picture." Sal, hands folded across his
ample belly, content, relaxed, and sporting a mean smile, "So,
now, mebbe youse can tell me where is the Boss, Angelo." John
and Al looked at each other, tension. Stand-off time. No one
moved except Gonz, who, nonchalantly leaning against the wall,
shifted one leg to the other.

Chapter 63 - Time for His Task

Annie B couldn't hear every word, but she certainly heard enough to know exactly what was going on. She quickly dialed Jeb's cell, and the second he picked up she blurted, "They're going after my grandson Jack, outside of Wilmington, Delaware." She told him everything she had heard. Then she told where Jack lived, and where his school was. She'd been there and knew it well. He asked details and she answered, them all.

"Got it", Jeb said. "Lemme get on it, right away. Talk later." He switched off. Annie B sat back, a deep frown etched into her forehead. She picked up a pencil and tapped the eraser lightly against her teeth. *What's he gotten himself in to now. Himself and the rest of us. Damn!* She slammed her palm on her blotter.

Gonz's birth name was Peter Kannes. He didn't look like the Ivy League wasp of his heritage. He worked for the FBI. Having been undercover for the past nine months, he was waiting to be "made" by the Mafia. That required successfully carrying out tasks on orders of the Godfather, taking the pledge, and being allowed inside. There were varied levels of assigned tasks, and not everyone was "made". You had to become a trusted insider, a member of the family.

Known as Peter by his friends of pre-FBI, pre-Mafia days, Gonz was the promising product of a high quality private school education. He had been recruited by the FBI during junior year at his Ivy League college, and encouraged to continue his major in political science, but, they suggested, he should minor in theater. "Play as many varied roles as you can. Get used to living in a different personality," they had said. He was going underground.

After training at Quantico, Peter spent several years doing covert work, often assuming borrowed personalities, infiltrating minor criminal enterprises in different sections of the country. He was always carefully "extracted" before the arrests were made and the case became public knowledge. As far as the general FBI or anyone else snooping around went, Peter Kannes had moved away. Only a very few of his high level handlers knew the truth.

Worming his way into the Mafia had been easy. Using his martial-arts skills, he bested Mafia goons on several occasions, as they were making their weekly rounds collecting protection money and pimp-money. He reduced the "tough-guy" they sent after him, to a bloody, unconscious mass on the sidewalk. Billy had "a little talk wid dis here new guy. Calls hisself Gonz", he reported to Sal. "Nobody knows him, but the word is he done time. He sez his mudder was Flora, a junkie-whore. Never knew his fadder. Grew up onna street in LA. Doesn't know where he was born or when. Done some schoolin', but not too much. Street smarts. A survivor."

Sal offered him a job, doin' what the guys he had smacked around done, collectin' protection money. See what's he's made of.

Gonz "done good". Better'n good. He rose up fast. Became Billy's best soldier. Sal said he should be made. The Godfather agreed. That was before the Godfather had been shot when things were put on hold for a while, but, now, Sal figured, it was time for Gonz to do his task. This situation might be just the one.

Chapter 64 - The School Bus

Finally, after what seemed like a long time to John, Sal sat forward, elbows on the table, fingers meshed, index fingers pointing at John. "I'm gonna ask youse guys one more time, eidder youse or yer black-ass buddy here, can answer." He looked over at Al. "Where you got Angelo? We know you got him. We need to know where. We need to know where, now."

Silence. John looked at Al. Al never flinching, glared at Sal. Sal looked from one to the other with increasing malice. Silence. One minute. Two minutes. More. Nothing. Sal balled his fists, and slammed them into the table. Then looking over at the goon with the lap-top, he demanded "Part two. Show 'em."

The goon said something into his cell phone, opened the lap-top, and placed it near the foot of the table so both John and Al could see it. He tapped a few more keys, and the image, obviously shot through a windshield, came up,. There was one car between the camera and the big, lumbering school bus. No other traffic. They watched in silence, as the bus turned right. The car following it went straight. The camera moved closer to the bus. Twenty-five, thirty miles an hour? Empty road, residential suburbia.

John eased up a bit until Sal said, "Unless I tell 'em udderwise, in the next minute, my friends are gonna have-ta pull alongside, cuz they got a little fire bomb they needa get rid of. Like under da bus. At the stop sign. You know them bus drivers make a full stop at every one of them stop signs. It's a state law. Only my friends never stop. They keep going. Ya see what I mean. They keep going, one way or the udder. I get told where the Boss is, an' that bomb stays in the car, save for anudder day." Sal looked purposefully at John. No word from me, an' people maybe get hurt." Sal sat back, smirk in place, eyes intentionally widened, eyebrows up.

John couldn't stand it. He blurted, "You'd do that to little children? You'd actually do something like that?" Sal just sat there, resolute. The only sound in the room was the school bus rumble. Then a higher whine from the down-shift as it approached the stop sign fifty yards ahead.

John leaned forward, mouth open, about to tell all, when, suddenly, there was a different sound. Faint at first. Then louder. A siren. Sal's smirk disappeared, confusion, replaced by a grimacing frown. Not just one siren. Several. Getting louder. The picture on the screen sped up. No longer smooth and steady. Bumping. Jarring. Out of focus. Passing the bus. Stop sign blurred as it sped by. Then the picture went dark. The video goon rushed to grab the lap-top, "What da fuck?", he mumbled, scooping the computer off the table.

"Get it outta here!" Sal growled. "Get it the fuck outta here." All eyes were glued on the video goon. Even Al watched as the goon rushed out of the room. The door slammed behind him. Sal pounded the table, "Where is he. I wanna know. Now. Right now. Where is Angelo Ginnini. Where you gott'im stashed." Demands, not questions. His little mouth slobbering, white froth at the corners.

John saw a slight curl at the edges of Al's lips, but Al's face said nothing. He tried to do the same. John's brain working in over-drive. *What to do next. Something. Do something. What to do. Deny. Try denial.*

"Sal, I'm afraid you're over-estimating me, us. I can't tell you where Angelo is. If he's not, as you say, not in the hospital, I can't tell you where he is. I put in that insulin pump last night, and far as I know, he should be back in his room. I haven't made rounds yet, but he should be in his room. Isn't that right, Al? He should be in his room. I sure as hell haven't discharged him. He's not ready."

Al's face softened immediately, appearing almost sympathetic as he looked at John, "Yeah, like he says, the patient should be in his room. You want me to call over there?"

Sal looked away from his two guests and over at the smallish goon standing against the wall, closest to the door, and nodded ever so slightly. The goon left the room, but returned a moment later with the goon called Gonz, who, with the toothpick in the corner of his mouth, looked questioningly at Sal. Sal paused a moment, scowling. His scarred eye-lid drooping, he shifted back in the throne chair, looked over at Gonz, then back at John, then Al, not saying a word.

John knew it wasn't over yet.

Chapter 65- Wanna Job ?

Steve Wojek, alias Neil Armstrong, plopped himself down in
the McDonald's booth farthest from the order bar. He dumped
some of the fries out on the paper covering the tray, and shoved
several into his mouth. *These are the best fries anyplace. No one
beats them.* He took the Big Mac out of its box with both hands,
opened his mouth as wide as he could, and bit into the warm,
mushy, familiar taste. Of course, as usual, some of the pickles,
onions, and special sauce oozed out the back of the triple-decker,
onto his fingers. His tongue shoved the huge mouthful into his left
cheek and he commenced chewing, slowly, savoring. He put the
burger down, and licked the oozing mess off his fingers, one at a
time.

He was happy. Happy he had decided to head out. He didn't
know why, just happy. Anywhere, just away. *I'm smart to leave the
research gear back there in storage. The blood drawing
equipment is all neatly packed in those brown boxes.
Nondescript. No damning evidence there. Not as long as no one
opens them. But the centrifuge. Can't really hide that. The guy at
the storage place didn't hardly notice it, and never said anything.
Yah, so I'm gonna let myself be happy.*

He didn't see the three men entering the restaurant, and
coming deliberately toward his booth. He aimed the straw in his
Diet Coke toward his full mouth, concentrating on the maneuver,
when the mass of cheap, dark suits stopped at his booth. Quickly,
easily, and silently, they slid into his booth. Two across from him.
The largest, next to him, tight up against him. He almost choked
on the mouth wad, but it slid down with the help of the DC sucked
in. He froze. All he could say was, "Hey!"

"Hey yourself", said the mean-looking one across from him.

"Whaaa.......?" Steve gargled, beginning to choke.

"Take it easy, pal. Finish yer lunch. We got time," mean-face
said.

Steve cleared his throat with a big swallow, dipping his chin and raising back up. He nervously grabbed a quick suck of his drink, and looked at the intruders. Fear froze his face. He could feel it. For a guy who considered himself cool under pressure, he tried to relax, relax everything, especially his face, but he couldn't. *Who the crap are these guys? Why are they here? Shit!*

"Steve. Steve Wojek." A statement, not a question, from mean-face.

"Steve.......? No. I'm Neil. Neil Armstrong. Don't know any Steve...."

"It's okay, Steve. We ain't here to hurt you. We're here wid a offer. We wanna make nice."

"No, no.......I'm Neil Armstrong. There must be, um, some mistake. You got it..... you got it wrong...." Steve sputtered. "You guys the Feds?"

"Steve, we got the right guy. We been followin' youse. We got sumpin' youse should be interested in. Relax. Youse ain't in no trouble. Not wid us. At least not yet. You got sumpin' we're innerested in. An yah, we know about Steve and Neil, an' all that shit. So we're gonna settle fer just Steve, Steve Wojek. Iffin' dats okay wid you."

Who the hell are these guys. Not Feds. No one else looking for me, that I know of. An' how they know about me, anyhow? Slowly, Steve's face faded from fear to question. "Okayaaaay", he drawled

"Steve, lemme 'splain. We're businessmen, an' you got sumpin' we're interested in. You got a special talent in a area we'd like to see developed." Mean-face softened just slightly as he rested back in the booth, hands folded on the table, the other two nodding just a little as he spoke.

"What are you talking about? What is it that you want? What could I possibly have that you'd be interested in? I don't know you." Steve tried to force himself to try to relax even more, but he knew he still didn't feel normal, still on his defensive guard.

"Steve, as you know, there's some money to be made in blood. Human blood. For-sale blood. It's a good market. An' we know you know how to get human blood in good, clean amounts, wid very little fuss or problem."

"What're you talking about. I'm just a nurse. A floor nurse. I don't work in the blood bank. Never have. Don't know nuthin' about it."

"Steve, let's stop kiddin' ourselves. We know who you are. We know what you done at University Hospital. We know who's looking fer you. So stop bull-shittin' us. We want you to work fer us. We take good care of you. Pay you good. Give you protection. So stop da bull-shit, an' lets us talk. On da level, like."

Steve knew he'd been had. He looked from one to the other, and to the third. A nerve tingled up his back through the cold sweat. *What the hell is this? What's this all about? I dunno these guys. Dunno them from Adam.* "Okay, you say you know who I am. So who are you? If you wanna talk, I got a right to know who you are since you know me." He kept looking from one to the other, to the other. Stone faces stared back. No clue. Tough. Menacing. Waiting.

Chapter 66 - An Offer You Don't Wanna Refuse

"**Steve, we represent a business** that is innerested in a new line of product, like I said", said mean face. We work for a large, legitimate business that is always lookin' fer new ways to sell products, of which we have a very wide range. We're looking to start up a new product line. A very profitable line. An' we'd like you, wid yer special talents, to work wid us in dis here new venture. Pay's good."

"Okay, so what kinda business you talkin' about. I'm just a nurse. Is this some sort of a medical business? You need help with a clinic, or something? I told ya, I don't do blood banks."

"Yah. It's a business in yer area of expertise. Blood drawing. Ya know, like fer a blood bank. Youse was drawing blood from patients at University Hospital fer yer research project. We know all about it. Youse was doin' good, only youse forgot to pass yer research through the big boys, an' the hospital took a dislike to it. Am I gettin' close?"

Steve was now sweating visibly, his stomach in a knot. *How did these guys know about this. Whoever they are. Jeezizmurphy.* He tried to answer, but his dry mouth wouldn't work. *They got me boxed in here. Can't run. Can't even move. Shit. Damn. How do I get into these things. Not my fault. They're all against me.*

"Steve, don't get us wrong." The big guy next to him spoke for the first time in a voice that was three octaves below the table. "We're here to help you and get you to help us. We like what you did. You had a good idea there. We need you to change it a little, and redirect it some."

Steve took a shaking sip of his diet coke. "Okay what do you want from me?"

The mountain next to him continued. "We're gonna take youse back to the city. Getchu set up in a safe place. Wid good protection, an' good pay. An you gonna work fer us. Fer our business. Inna city, there."

"No way. No way I'm going back to that place. Not to the hospital. Not to the city. No. Not going there." Slowly the mountain next to him moved. A big arm lifted up and over Steve's head and around behind him. A big hairy paw gripped his left shoulder like a vice. Not painfully, but totally controlled, drawing him in to the mountain's armpit. The big face wasn't ugly, but it was far from handsome. It was smiling in a sly way.

"We're gonna make you an offer you don't wanna refuse", Biggie said as he squeezed Steve's shoulder. Now it hurt.

Steve got the message. *He's got me pinned. So, okay. Calm yourself. You gotta try to play ball with these guys. At least for now. What's he want?* "So, okay. Maybe I go back there. Then what?"

"We gonna set youse up in business. Blood drawing business."

"But what if I can't do what you have in mind? I'm only a nurse."

"We think you'd be just right for it."

"No, I don't think so. I don't want to go back there."

"You're gonna give Carlos, there, your left hand," he said nodding to mean-face across the table. Steve felt the vice tighten on his left shoulder. It was really beginning to hurt.

Steve hesitated. "I really don't want to."

Biggie squeezed a little more, and pulled him in tighter. "Go ahead. He teach you something. Just put it out there." Biggie pushed Steve's whole shoulder forward. "That's it."

Steve had no choice. His left hand was already halfway across the table. Faster than a snake, his hand was grabbed and pulled savagely across the table, a vice-like grip encircling his thumb and two fingers. Carlos's other hand ripped his ring finger backward with a loud snap. Steve screamed. Lightening pain, over-whelming. His hand was just as quickly released, his ring finger was pointing backwards. He screamed again. And again. Desperately, he clutched his wrist with his other hand. Clutched it tightly to his chest. Grunting, teeth clenched, he tried not to scream again. Loud grunting. Repeated loud grunting.

Every face in the restaurant was turned. The manager

rushed around the counter toward their booth. "Hey. What's going on here?"

"It's okay, sir. Everything's okay. My cousin here has Tourette syndrome, an' he sometimes has these seizures like this," the mountain said, shaking Steve gently, calmingly, with the arm around him. "Makes him yell out like dat. We're sorry fer dat. He's gonna quiet down now, ain'tcha Stevie. "That's the boy Stevie. Get control. Take it easy. Quiet down now Stevie. Yer okay", he said soothingly, almost as if he'd handled this situation before. The manager, feeling somewhat intimidated by the three men in black, tried to lessen his presence there.

Steve was reduced to a weeping rag beside the mountain. The manager saw that quiet had resumed, so he turned and left them to their own business. The rest of the clientele, quickly bored, returned to their Big Macs.

"Steve, give Carlos yer hand again. He'll fix it fer yahs."

"Whaaa.......oh my god. Jeeziz, look at it. It's killin' me...Aaagh, shit, no. Whaddya think I'm crazy?" Steve clutched his hand against his chest, his left hand cradled tenderly by his right.

"Give it to him again."

"No way. Oh my god, it's killing me."

"Go on. Give him yer hand. He was a medic in the Army. He can fix it. Give it him." The mountain reached across, his big beefy hand encircling Steve's wrist, and slowly dragging it across the table. Steve couldn't resist.

"Yah, here. Give it to me. It'll help the pain." Slowly, shaking, Steve's hand and arm were out, across the table, once again. And again, with lightening speed, Carlos grabbed the thumb and first two fingers, then the damaged one. With a quick yank, Steve heard a 'thunk', and saw that his ring finger, once again was straight. Or, at least, relatively straight, and, remarkably pain free, until he tried to flex it. The pain returned, but not so bad.

"Yer goin' to need a splint on that fer the next month or so. Then milkin' cows will get yer motion back better'n anything else. No cows? Okay then, try jackin'-off wid it." The three guests laughed. Steve slumped, utterly defeated.

"What do you want from me?"

The mountain removed his arm from around Steve's shoulders. "Steve, you're gonna work fer us, one way or anudder. You do it the hard way or da easy way. Yer choice. You got my drift?"

Steve slowly nodded. "I'll do what you want, just don't hurt me."

"Wise decision, Steve," Carlos said.

"Yeh," the mountain agreed. "Here's what's goin' down. Yer gonna finish yer meal, here, an'..."

"I'm not hungry anymore, and my gaddamn finger hurts. Hurts like hell. Or at least it's gonna hurt when........"

"Don't innerrup him when he's talkin' at-cha," said mean face.

"It's okay. Steve's hurtin' right now, but he's listenin'. Ain'tcha Steve."

"Yah, uh-huh", Steve whimpered, head bowed, right hand holding the left by the wrist, just under his chin.

"Steve. We're gonna leave here now. Yer ridin' with me," Carlos said, "inna back. Biggy, here's drivin'. Benny gonna drive yer car fer ya. Give him the keys." Carlos saw Steve look up, sharply, "Don't worry, Benny's been jackin' cars since he could see over the steerin' wheel. He ain't gonna hurt it." Carlos looked at his partners, "We gotta get movin'. Long drive."

Chapter 67 - The AW Treatment

Sal's face was ugly to begin with. Born ugly, and then, too
much good Italian cooking, contributed to the flab. Creases
deepened from years of angry, tough-guy scowling — his way of
life. Little pig eyes revealed a left upper lid turned up slightly by an
old knife scar. Little yellow teeth that hadn't seen a dentist and
only rarely, a tooth-brush. He was ugly-mean even when he was
relaxed, which wasn't often. When he was displeased, his whole
persona was worse. When he was angry, evil. At the moment, evil
was what impressed John Pullman as he looked at the Underboss,
sitting at the head of the table in what he guessed was the mob-
family's board room. John didn't like it. Didn't like him. But John
was working hard not to show it. He looked at Al, who remained
stoic in the silent room. *Deadly silent,* John thought, *Jeeziz,
wrong word.*

Sal, sat immobile, in the throne, giving off major bad vibes.
Only his eyes moved, from John to Al and back. *Nasty.
Threatening,* Al thought.

Sal broke the silence. "So I'm gonna ask youse one last time.
One last time. Where's Angelo? We know you got him stashed.
Prob'ly some safe house. Only there ain't no safe houses, safe from
where we know. So we gonna find him. It's only a matter of time,
but we'll find him. So just tell me where, an' youse save a lotta pain
and trouble. Last chance."

John believed him. He remembered the phone calls. He
looked at Al who remained stone-faced. John faced Sal, fingers
splayed flat on the table, he answered, "Like I said, Sal, if he's not
in his room, room 739, I don't know where he is. But I'll tell you
this. It'll take a day or two to get his new insulin pump stabilized,
and get him totally familiar with it, so he can run it. Okay?" John
looked hard into Sal's eyes, hoping for a response, a comment, a
miracle. But nothing. "Then he can be discharged, ya know. He
can return home. To Mrs. Ginnini. She's anxious to get him
home." No comment. John waited. "Okay, if he's not in 739, you

tell me where he is." John paused, and then turned to Al, "You know anything different, Al? He's not due for anything else, is he? Have I forgotten something?"

Al softened the stone-face as he spoke. "No, you're right. He should be in his room. What makes you think he's not?" looking directly at Sal, he added, "In his room, unless you've done something to him. Like moved him, Sal?" Al's face was tight, lined, every inch of him focused. John almost believed him. "You tellin' us something, here, Sal? Did you and your boys move Angelo? If you did, that could be very dangerous with that new insulin device. He could go comatose."

Brilliant, Al, thought John. *Turn the tables. Attack. The best defense...* But Sal sat immobile, protoplasm cast in stone, ugly, threatening. John stared, waiting. Al stared, waiting. Sal stared, waiting. *Show-down time.* John sensed..... *Damn. Not working. Now what?*

It looked like Sal might have started quivering with rage. Were his jowls shaking just a little? Was that froth at the corners of his mouth. Fury clearly building, he smashed back into the throne, slapped his fat hands on the table before him, looked sharply at Gonz and jerked a nod. Gonz flipped his head at the smaller goon by the door, and started toward John. The smaller goon punched in his cell phone, said something incomprehensible, then went over and stood behind Al. John's gut tightened. *Trouble coming. Damn, what's he up to?*

The door opened again, and in came Billy, who, immediately sensing the tension in the room, stopped and froze . He looked around, and moistening his dry lips with his tongue, he sputtered to Sal, "You lookin' fer......"

Sal growled, "Billy, Gonz is gonna take 'em down for the full AW treatment. No cuffs." Gonz stiffened slightly. He looked at Sal. A question? Sal was annoyed, "Full AW treatment. Now! Gett'em de fuck outta here. Now!"

"No cuffs?" Billy asked. Gonz looked equally puzzled.

"No cuffs, no nuttin'. Put 'em in alive. I want 'em awake goin' in. Let Gonz, here, work it out. It's his task." Sal got up, stormed out of the room, and slammed the door.

Billy nodded at Gonz who pulled out his cell, made a call, looked at his watch while talking. When he hung up, and motioned to the smaller goon, each came up behind a captive, Gonz behind John and the other behind Al. "Get up. We're goin', now." Gonz leaned back slightly, glaring down his nose at John. The smaller one looked meaner. He had a large black stick which he smacked into his left palm, repeatedly. Al recognized it. *Standard, solid oak, police-issue, night stick, aka billy-club.*

Al said, "Do what he says. Better chances if we're not all beat-up." John nodded.

Gonz led them out, the other goon following their two prisoners closely, also whacking his club with each step. They went through the pool room, where those loitering stopped talking, even stopped chewing gum, and whatever else they were doing to gawk at the procession.

Our last mile?, thought John. *A parade to the execution? We certainly have their attention, but whatever they're going to do to us will probably be pretty unpleasant.*

Down on the street, it had gotten a little warmer in the sun. Not hot, but certainly warmer. No breeze. Gonz had them wait. He was just standing there, toothpick hanging from the corner of his mouth, nervously tapping his foot. Waiting. Waiting. Waiting for what? By the curb of the empty street, next to a pile of garbage. It stank. And they waited. When Billy came up to join them, John stared at him, trying to get him to say something, at least to show some sign of recognition. But Billy purposefully ignored both captives.

Al leaned over to John and whispered,"I could probably take out two of them, but now there's the third, and they've got sticks and probably guns. It's a no-go."

"Shaddup, an' move apart." Gonz barked, shoving John away. But he couldn't budge Al.

It was warm, and flies were buzzing the pile of trash. John started watching them, but was distracted by an approaching engine. A big red sanitation truck must have stopped down the block, at a brightly painted "Pre-school-Nursery" sign, and was now slowing toward them. An 'AW' logo, in yellow, was clearly

visible. *AW, American Waste. This must be the AW treatment?*,
John guessed. Air-brakes squeaked a hiss. Two men in the cab.
Neither one moving. Eyes of both staring straight ahead.

"Git in."Gonz ordered.

John's head snapped around. "What?"

"Do what he says", Al said, moving toward the rear of the
truck. "No sense getting beat up."

"Yeh. You must be de smart one. Smart fer a nigger. Nuthin's
I'd rather do than smack the shit outta you, nigger boy", Gonz's
sneer framed the yellowish teeth. Now he was the one smacking
the stick into his left palm.

John's face flushed, his fists clenched into balls, his abs
tightening. He was ready to tear into the goon, but Al showed no
response. None at all. John knew Al could have taken Gonz out,
along with Billy, but, as he said, the guns said otherwise. Al
vaulted, easily, into the catchment-pit, and squatted down. He
looked at John, and waited for him. Still angry, John looked again
at Gonz, then at Billy, who was pretending to look the other way.
"One of these days you'll get yours", he muttered, and slowly
climbed into the pit, one leg at a time. The goons started throwing
the curb-stacked trash in on top of them, penning them in. John
put up his hands to fend off the debris.

"Ball up, grab your knees", Al said to John, "like if you got
tossed out of the boat into white-water rapids. Tuck your chin.
Hands cupped in front of your face. Breathing room. Stay balled
up. Less apt to fracture something. They're gonna try to crush us
with the load."

"Shaddup in dere. Don't even think about tryin' somethin'."
Gonz shouted over the mounting debris as it smashed in. Then it
stopped. Quiet, for a moment. "Push the lever......dere onna side,"
the goon's voice was muffled by the garbage and the truck's motor.
"No, push it, dumbfuck." The hydraulic whine started.

Chapter 68 -The Task

Gonz knew his task was to kill John and Al. But he also knew that there was no way he going do that. They were caught in Sal's wrath. Gonz wasn't going to kill them, but he had to do his task. Had to go through with the sentence. To refuse, would mean the end of his mafia career, the end of his covert op, and probably the end of his life.

But for all the tasks he could have been saddled with, this was a good one. He knew he could carry out the task as ordered, because the chances were John and Al might survive the ordeal. It wouldn't be pleasant, but they might survive, probably.

Pete Kannes was no dope. Gonz, his alter ego, certainly appeared to be one of the dimmer bulbs in the candelabra, but Pete had done his homework. He considered it blind luck that he had been assigned this AW Treatment. He knew that the garbage truck would be picking up the nursery school trash immediately before the mafia trash. He also knew that, even compacted, there would be plenty of air pockets. They might break a few bones. It would be really nasty and cause a lot of pain, but, in all likelihood, John and Al might well survive the ordeal.

Pete knew Sal would be furious when he learned of their survival, but it was Sal himself who had ordered the AW Treatment, the full treatment, in a fit of rage. He had ordered it, and Gonz had only carried out his orders, "to put 'em in alive, no cuffs, not already dead." What Gonz didn't know, was if the task would be counted, if it was enough to allow him to be made, to be allowed to take the oath. He watched as the big hydraulic gate swept the two men and the other trash up, out of sight, into the belly of the truck. *Good-bye, and good luck,* he thought.

John felt himself sliding up and forward, into the bowels of the truck as the hydraulic did its thing. Dark. Getting denser. He balled himself, as Al had said, as he'd done several times when he had been dumped out of the boat, running class four rapids. *In the water, I toss and spin, but here, I'm just sliding sideways, still*

upright, I think, which helps a little, but it's closing in, tighter.
It came in on all sides. He tried to wiggle, but couldn't. Garbage pressing down on the top of his head. On all sides. Nothing moved, but the hydraulic had stopped. *Damn, it's tight. Hard to breathe.* His thoughts raced, *We gonna die? We both gonna die? Like this?* He felt his heart pounding. *At least it's still pumping. Nothing else is moving. Think positively,* he warned himself. *Illigitimi non carborundum....don't let the bastards wear you down, from that General in World War Two. I've got to keep control of myself. Stay calm. I'm trying.*

Suddenly, incredibly, the fear was gone, and a sense of calm overcame his rattled nerves. It was tight, so he no longer had to hold himself in. *It stinks. But if it stinks, it means I'm still breathing. Not easily, but moving air.* He sniffed. *Huh? It stinks.... like..... like shit, feces.* John took a couple more slower breaths, trying to slow everything down. *Am I losing it or just confused? Maybe low O2 or high CO2. Is it getting harder to breathe, but I can still sniff. Is that enough, or is this gonna do it?.......Don't panic. Stay calm. At least there's nothing painful. Squished tight, yes, but not painful. Nothing busted. Not yet. Thank you, God. No pain. No light. But the ride's bumpy. Can feel it. Makes me jiggle. I'm not dreaming. I'm awake. Brain's functioning.*

Then the odor barged back in. *Feces? Feces and urine.....Baby shit?..... Baby shit, that's it.* He kept sniffing, curious. It was easier than full breaths. *There's gotta be all sorts of stuff in here....stuff making smells, but this reminds me of soiled baby diapers. Baby poo and pee, not adult - different smell.....and.....maybe..... a hint of something sweeter.* He tried to concentrate on the question, and continued short, quick sniffs. *Sweet? Baby shit and sweet. What the hell am I thinking of? Maybe I'm getting hypoxic? No, don't think so. Not short of breath. No air hunger. At least not yet. Concentrate, focus, keep you brain going......Okay, we've got sweet baby shit..... and pee, and, and, something else. Like Annie B?.....Talcum?....... Of course, talcum powder. Okay, stop this. Let's get back to a little reality. Focus on reality. You're alive, awake, and rational.....probably rational, and breathing. Can't move, but can initiate motion. Get connected with your situation. Get smart. Al, contact Al.*

"Hey Al..... Al, can you hear me? Al. .....Al," his voice getting louder with each call. Louder than the noise of the truck on the highway. *We're moving. We've been moving all this time..... Moving..... Going someplace.* "Hey Al...... Al can you hear me?...... Al?....... Al! You there. I know you're there. Can you hear me?"

A voice? A voice over the truck's rumble. "John..... can hear you just fine. No need.....shout." His voice was near, muffled. "Don't yell. Don't know...much air...have..... Try...relax. Don't over breathe....only a few feet away." *He's trying to keep me calm. but I am already calm,* John thought. Then he heard Al again. "Can't move...ch...not crushed. Truck mov.... Go... som.....re."   "Yeah, I feel it too. On the road."

".......next compaction, if....is one....get tight." John knew what he was really thinking. What they both were thinking. What Sal and his goons expected. The diesel whine lowered. The truck began to slow, then stopped.

Both captives heard the crashes of garbage being dumped into the rear pit. Several loads. Then nothing. Then the whine of the hydraulic started again. John thought he heard Al say, "Sh.... Here comes.......get tight. Say....prayers, ol...buddy."

Chapter 69 - The Blood Business

The three Mafia thugs, Carlos the mean face, Benny the car
jacker, and Biggie the mountain man, were good on their word.
They returned Steve Wojek, and his car to the city, set him up in a
"safe apartment", showed him just what their bosses wanted him
to do, and even gave him a cash bonus. A "signing bonus", they
called it, but he never signed nothin'.

It was a good, job, whether he liked it or not. He didn't have
any choice in the matter. The hours weren't so good, because Steve
found that he needed to be at his most operational in the very
early morning hours. But that was okay since he was used to the
night shift in the hospital, anyway. In addition, they gave him all
the equipment he needed to conduct his business, and drugs, and
wine, too. He didn't have to steal any of it anymore.

He would rise an hour before sunrise, and be out on the
streets by dawn, roaming sections of the city where the homeless
tended to hang out. Loners were best. No witnesses. With his
equipment in his back pack, he'd find a proper subject. "Hey
buddy", he'd say, or "Hey Madam," as was appropriate. Sometimes
hard to tell, but his subjects often were quite particular on this
distinction, so he tried to get it right.

"I got a little something for you."

"Yah. Whachu got?"   "Your choice. A little wine, a little
upper, a little downer, or maybe you like a little vodka, or gin?
Your choice." Steve had few rejections, very few.

"Whadda I gotta do fer it? You ain't no Santy-Claus."

"All I want is a little of your blood. You know, like for the
blood bank."

"The blood bank never wanted me before. Never let me in."

"This is for charity. Poor people overseas. In Bangladesh", he
lied.

"Yah? Fer real? Yah, okay, I guess. Just a pint, right?"

"So what's your choice?" It was usually the half-pint of cheap wine which was chugged in one breath.

"Which arm you prefer?" The bared arm would be proffered. The needle would be inserted, and the blood begin flowing into the liter bag, which was more than twice the size used by the blood bank, but the victim never noticed it. All sterile. All clean and professional-like. The victim was usually impressed. It didn't even hurt — this warm wine was beginning to take its effect. Good wine, great wine, guaranteed result. But it wasn't just the wine causing the vic's brain to swim. He or she never tasted the rapid-acting fentanyl. No taste, but quick.

After extracting the first liter, hypoxia began to take effect. But it was painless, and the donor never noted the difference. These street people, usually anemic due to poor nutrition, unsanitary conditions, and chronic ill health, could afford to lose less blood than the healthy, non-anemic blood bank donor. When more, often much more, than twice the safe amount was "donated", the consequences resulted quickly. But it was a peaceful death. A belly full of wine, and, although they didn't know it, a brain full of fentanyl, relaxed, sedated. *Sleepy, no problems, very sleepy. Could use a good sleep.*

When the venous pressure in the victim's heart fell below the pressure in the arm and in the IV line, the blood ceased to flow, and Steve removed the needle. He pressed the venipuncture site with a gauze for a full minute. No further bleeding, with the vic sleeping peacefully in a deep sleep. A very, very deep sleep.

Biggie even got Steve a freezer, which he carried into the apartment himself, without any help from Steve. "We pick up every Friday noon. Keep it froze. We 'spectin' six to eight quarts a week. More, you get points fer a bonus prize."

The business was good. Easy. No problems for Steve. Lotta free time on his hands. *I should be doing something. Something like working toward my goal, proving my truth. Show the world the true value of Tumor Necrosis Factor. My Noble prize.* But there was no way he could figure out how to get the trauma blood full of TNF, and no way to get the TNF into *the oncology patients who so desperately needed it.*

Bored, he talked Biggie into supplying him with regular

500cc blood bank bags, some tubing, and blood typing reagents. In return, he told Biggie that he could return the purloined blood, typed and ready for transfusion. Biggie thought this was great because he didn't have to pay a blood bank techie any moonlighting fees to do the same thing. Gave the product more value on the black market. Great profits, and it was semi-legit. Of course, there was no screening for AIDS or Hepatitis A, B, or C, or any of a dozen other diseases and problems, but no one cared about that. Steve got a raise.

"Hey, Biggie, who you got puttin' the dope in the booze we give out? Why can't I add it in for you, instead? Save you some more dough." Steve was proud of this new idea. He had the time. He was bored. Why not.

"Yah. We can do that. Lemme show youse to Da Chemist. He's our guy. He's an outside employee, a Consiglieri, like you. Not made, not part of the family, but a trusted guy we do business wid. He's Enrico, or somethin' like that. We just call him Da Chemist."

Chapter 70- Compacted

It did get tight. Worse than tight. Compacted. With the hydraulic whining again, and the mass of garbage in which John was immersed squeezing him unlike anything he had ever felt, intense pressure mounted. Pressure all over, but more from the back than the front. He felt like the whole mass was moving forward, deeper into the truck. *Damn. Ouch! Something's sticking me in the back. But the front is soft and mushy, almost like Jello. Not liquid, not solid, mush. Some sort of soft garbage. Old food? Something rotting? Glad Al told me to cup hands over my face. Helps. The smell's familiar.......baby feces, and urine....and, and, talcum. Baby diapers. Now, I remember.*

He tried to move. Couldn't. Couldn't even wiggle. *Softer in front than in back.* "Owww", he heard himself moan, "Damn thing's getting tighter. Can't take a deep breath. Can't move..... Al, you okay?" he yelled.

"What?" John had trouble hearing Al's muted voice, which came through just as the whine of the hydraulic quit. He could hear the higher pitched sounds, but not his lower tones. "Maybe.......the end of......run.......hope so.......next......get uncomfortable," or something like that.

Typical Al. We're close to lethal compression, and he's talking uncomfortable. John raised his voice again, "We got a problem if they squeeze again. Don't know the P.S.I. Probably up to forty or fifty. If it goes over seventy it will shut down our venous return. Cardiac arrest."

Al thought he could hear most of what John was yelling. He answered John, "Pressure....... like deep water," Al's voice was muted, but John could still understand most of it. "Keep... here..... long, problem....... bends.......get out."

Get out? That's Al. The eternal optimist. Get out. Shit. How are we ever gonna get out. He tried to speak out around his hands, but they were pretty-well smashed against his face by the soft stuff, and he could only take a half-breath to make it louder.

"You think they're gonna let us out?"

"They...... dump...... end...run", Al spoke as clearly as he could. "...less Sal made arrang.....ments.....park it. We........from dehydration."

"Jeeziz, I never thought of that." A sudden cold shiver ran through John's gut.

"Not.......favorite." Al shouted both at the dark and at John. "Rather ....home watch..... Jeopardy." The truck started moving again. After a minute, Al yelled over the rumble,

"Hope......next......ount Trashmore."

The truck slowed. John didn't know if he was happy or terrified, but it felt like a turn, and sped up again. At least the pitch of the engine suggested slowing and accelerating along with the automatic-shift gear changes. Seemed like several more turns. "Where are we? Where we were going?" John wondered aloud.

"No f.....in' idea," Al answered.

They rode on in silence, each man thinking over his situation, his life, his family and home. Blackness and mush squeezing in from all sides, along with the ever-changing rumble of the truck. Acutely *depressing,* John thought. *Hunger, thirst, and cramped joints......and the damned whatever sticking me in the back. If I could only move it, just a little. I'd give Sal a thousand bucks to move it just one inch.....Sal. Damn Sal. That son-of -a-bitch. That miserable son-of-a-bitch. He really is miserable. Miserable and nasty. With his shitty, rotten life.* John felt his anger rising. *He's a dirty, nasty, son-of-a-bitch.....lousy Mafia prick.......maybe Angelo's testimony will drag him down with the rest of those miserable bastards......*John couldn't keep his thoughts straight, *Angelo, Angelo? Haven't thought about him all day. Hope that nurse can handle his insulin. He's pretty brittle. Sugars all over the place......what the hell am I worrying about Angelo for......swap places......places.....places. I'm supposed to be in a different place, and Annie B knows I'm not, and Annie B's worried. She's working on it, though. She's so damn clever. She'll probably have the cops looking for this truck right now......yah, sure. Don't I wish......what am I thinking about this stuff for. Al's probably over there thinking up survival* *techniques......yah, that's what he's doing......*"Hey Al. How you doing? How we gonna get out of here. You got a plan? I'm getting a little emotional over here. My mind's racing.....all over the place. I'm getting a little psycho."

John didn't hear anything for a minute, then he heard Al's voice, "Don't know....any plan. Right now gotta pee.......haven't peed my jeans in years. How 'bout you?...wet.....Gotta go?"

That's Al for you. Talking ridiculous stuff. Taking our minds off the problem. Calming, avoiding panic. Keep calm....Keep sane..... Keep focused......on things that matter......on the escape.......what escape, no escape.

"No, Al....... haven't peed my pants. Not yet. But I gotta go. Thanks for reminding me."

Chapter 71- The Chemist

Jeez, you got everything here. Steve was impressed by the Chemist's lab. "I had a small lab, but nothing like this. This is awesome."

"Yes, I can do just about anything here as far as mixing pharmaceuticals goes. I do a lot of business for your company, and a lot of others. Got a bunch in the city, here. Plus, I ship all over the U.S., and some overseas, too.

"Nice equipment. What's this do?"

"That's a pill presser. Put in the proper mix and close the lid. Push start and in three minutes it kicks out your batch." The Chemist patted the machine.

"How many does it make?"

"Depends on how much you put in, how dense it is, and the pill size. You can do from a couple dozen to over a thousand if you push it." The Chemist gave Steve a complete tour of his lab, explaining how each area was for a different category of drugs.

"The big drug today is fentanyl. You probably know that already. Strong stuff. More than a hundred times as strong as heroin and so much easier to work with. You take thirty grams of relatively pure heroin. That's a full tablespoon. It's gotta be grown on several acres of land, poppies harvested, processed, packaged. Takes a lot of time and labor. It's shipped, usually by the kilo. About the size of a shoebox. The middleman's gotta break down the brick......"

"That's called a rock isn't it?" Steve interrupted, trying to show he knew something about the business.

"Yeah, it can be, but a rock is usually a kilo of cocaine. Heroin is called a brick. The middleman's gotta cut the pure product. More labor. Usually sugar, talcum, or chalk. Something cheap. Special orders may take some cocaine. Custom made, party drugs'll add all kinds of stuff. Uppers, downers, psilocybin, LSD, ecstasy, whatever you want. I make a lot more for the sophisticated, adult party groups than for the kids' street stuff. The party crowd is where the money is, where most of the trade volume goes. Of course, a lot of the adult party stuff ends up at the teeners' parties."

The chemist moved Steve along to the next bench, "The size-density of the final product is what determines the ease of the distribution. Small, light-weight orders are easier, safer to ship. Go right through the mail. First class, no inspection. Quick and easy. Higher doses of heavier combos are harder to distribute. Gotta pay a mule to run it to its destination."

"Yeah, that makes sense. Increases the risk, like." Steve nodded, trying to appear with-it.

"That's what's so great about fentanyl." the Chemist continued uninterrupted, "It's so strong, it only takes a little for a big kick. A tablespoon of relatively pure H'or horse, that's heroin......"

"Yeah, I know", Steve added, butting in.

"Like I was saying, a tablespoon of H is equal to fentanyl the size of a dozen grains of table salt. It adds a little kick to the high, and causes less nausea. But it's a more stable molecule and takes longer to metabolize out of your system. We get it mostly from pharm labs in China, where they make it legit for the big U.S. drug companies. In its pure form with tightly controlled doses, it is a very good medical anesthetic drug. Widely used legally. The Chinese make way more than the medical profession needs. You start with a compound called NPP, which they send to a finisher who makes it into 4ANPP, and then into pure fentanyl."

"What's NPP and 4ANPP?", Steve asked.

"I dunno. You can look it up on how to make it on the dark-web, but it's so cheap and easy to get, I never bothered. You can get a pure kilo from the Mexico boys. Comes across hidden in trucks down on the western California-Mexico border from Manzanillo in Colima State. Mostly from the Sinaloa Cartel or the Cartel Jalisco Nueva Generacion. They get it from China."

Steve was impressed, taking it all in. For once, he had nothing to say.

The Chemist continued. "The packages are so small, hard to detect. A kilo might cost you anywhere from thirty-five hundred to five grand. You dilute it for sale, nets about three hundred grand. Or better, you make a hundred thousand pills from your kilo. They sell for ten to twenty bucks apiece, that's one to two million in your pocket.....or somebody's pockets. And you wonder why it's become a booming industry?

"Jeeziz, that's beginning to sound like some real money."

"There's over twelve different analogues of fentanyl out there on the market. There's one called Carfentanyl. It's a hundred times more potent than straight fentanyl. That's ten thousand times stronger than pure heroin. A finger tip of dust will kill ya. It has to be handled with latex gloves and you wear a respirator. I won't touch the stuff. Too dangerous. Put a few grams of this stuff in some water system, wipe out an entire office building before they knew what hit 'em."

The Chemist shifted to the other foot, with arms akimbo, he continued, "Straight fentanyl causes more respiratory depression and less of a euphoric high, but requires more, much more NARCAN to reverse the depression. That's why there's so many deaths from the opioids these days. Over seventy thousand last year alone. That's one death every twelve minutes, round the clock. They tell me eighty-two percent of the opioid deaths are due to unregulated fentanyl."

They moved on to an open area. The Chemist, alone most of the time, was obviously enjoying giving his lecture. "Most of those usin', have no idea what's in their purchase. They're partyin' and wanna get a little high. Maybe mix it with a little booze, along with everybody else. Only this kid's pill, that someone at the party bought from a street kid named Joe.....that kid's pill, for some unknown reason, is from a different batch or dealer, and not the same as the rest. That pill has two micrograms of fentanyl instead of one. By the time the rest of the crowd wakes up in the morning, this kid has been dead six hours already. Stopped breathing. Just that easy."

"You never know who is mixing what. In what doses. Not carefully measured. Ya know, a pinch of this, a shake of that. Not like the big, legit pharms. They're very precise, highly regulated and monitored. The underground labs don't give a shit about exact dosages. Profit, only interested in profit."

He turned and started a slow walk. "Like me. I'm interested in profit, but I'm also very careful about my ingredients and dosages. Look who I'm doing most of my work for. I'm the guy who puts that grain of fentanyl in your booze samples that Biggie gives you. And I make his pills, too. That's a much bigger business. He orders it special."

"I'm just a little guy in this business. But I got a wife and two kids, and we do okay. I used to work for one of the big Pharms. Production mill. I like workin' for myself, and life is good."

Steve looked around, "You ever think about taking a partner, or an assistant?"

"No. Why? You lookin' for work?"

"Not actually, but I could always do more, and I like drugs. Drugs on the medical side, not recreational. I shoulda been a doctor, but I couldn't swing it, quite."

"Well, now you've seen my shtick. Hey, I been talkin' way too much. You probably knew all this anyway."

Steve, realizing his tour was over, started for the door. "No. No I didn't. It's fascinating. Lotta people dyin' so's a few can get rich. Same old story." "Yeah, you're right........Hey thanks for coming. Come back anytime or call if I can do anything for you.

Steve stepped out into the bright sunshine. He thought, *one of these days, I'll take a few days off and go down to get my centrifuge and stuff out of that storage place, and bring it back here. Maybe do a little work of my own.*

Chapter 72 - Still Stuck

"I think the on-load they got just before us is saving our bacon." The truck had stopped which meant that John could hear Al's voice more clearly now.

"The load before us?", John asked. "Did I hear you right? Are you as tight as I am? I can't take too much more of this."

"Shut up and listen to me," Al snapped. "Can you hear me? I can hear you fine. Calm down and listen."

"Yah. I can hear you okay. What are you talking about?" They both were still shouting to be heard.

"I don't know this for a fact," Al shouted his words distinctly, "but I think they took on a big load of soiled diapers just before they loaded us." "Yah, so?"

"That's the soft stuff you feel in front of you. It's taking a lot of the compression, instead of us."

"Diapers?"

"Yah, soiled baby diapers. Smell it?"

"So what. How's that helping us right now?"

"The soiled and wet diapers are very malleable and compressible. If that was all non-compressible hardware trash, we'd most likely not be having this conversation right now."

Just then the truck rumble restarted. John thought, *It's turning, slowing, bouncing on a rough road, then it stopped. Hard to tell, but probably stopped. Doesn't seem to be moving or bouncing, plus the engine sounds like it's idling.* He waited. They both waited, sensing the same thing.

Al confirmed it. "I think it stopped."

"Yah. I think so too. What now?"

"Dunno. Haven't got a cold beer over there, do you? That'd be kinda nice right about now. Let's go get one when we get outta here." Al felt his voice straining.

Then the truck engine did stop. They both heard it. Two cab doors slammed, at least that's what it sounded like, the sounds stifled through the surrounding insulation. Then silence. Silence and more silence. John waited. And waited and waited.....and waited for something. For anything. John stopped thinking for a time. How long a time, he didn't know. Did he nod off for a bit? Probably, but he wasn't sure. He tried to shake himself awake. *I'm getting too used to the cramped confinement. Not bored, exactly, but less tense.*

"Hey Al." John shouted, too loud. "Al, what are you thinking. That's the only function I have going right now. I think we need at least some auditory input to keep ourselves focused. Keep from going nuts."

"Good idea, John. I was just thinking through our situation. This is an American Waste truck. They're not just going to leave it out here to rust."

"Yah, they could. Our friend Sal and his Mafia pals have undoubtedly gotten to these guys. Or, maybe they own the whole damn business. Did you see the guys in the cab when Sal's thugs loaded us. They never looked at us. They tried not to see what was going on. I know. I saw them."

"Okay, I'll give you that. So what."

"So what?", John said incredulously. "Al, the loading guy in the rear never gets in the cab. He stays in the back. Dumps in the trash, and rides back there. In the back. He's never in the cab."

"Yah, so what?"

"Al you okay? You getting enough air?"

"Yah, buddy. I'm just fine. And you're just fine. Let yourself relax. Stop all this wild thinking. But, to be honest, yes, I agree we're in a bit of a sensory vacuum. We've got sound. Also, I think I can move my toes inside my shoes. Try it, you'll like it."

After a moment, John answered, "Yah, you're right again. I can move my toes. And I can move my fingertips. Not much, but they move. And I think I can move my eyes. Can't see anything, but I can feel them moving."

"Right. Keep everything you can think of moving."

"Hey, what are you talking about? You playing games with me?"

"What do you think?" Al answered.

John thought it a bit. "You got that training in the Marines, didn't you."

"Yah, we had some in special training, but to be honest, most of the mind control came from the martial arts. And, yah, you're doing fine. We've got time on our side. I keep you thinking, and, as you've discovered, you keep me thinking. This is a mind game. Perhaps, the ultimate mind game."   "Now I know how John McCain and the other POWs in Nam must have felt in their four or five foot cages," John said. "Only he had more air......... but I guess he was in there for a lot longer."

"Don't get all excited. Just sit there, calm. Don't use so much O2. We're gonna get out of this.......somehow." They both sat there in silence for a while, tired of yelling at one another. Time had no meaning. Neither man had any idea how long they had been incarcerated.

John felt himself getting sleepy. *Stay awake and alert. No sensory input. But it's just so easy to rest. So nice......Just for a minute, maybe?......No. Don't do that. You'll never wake up. Keep thinking, don't sleep. It's probably oxygen deprivation, or maybe CO2 build-up, or both. Deadly, either one. But so tired. Never been so tired. Peaceful, nice. No pain. Sleepy. No! Don't do that. No sleep! Stay awake. Keep yourself awake. Move.....at least try to move.* He pushed and felt the pressure.

I wonder what Annie B's doing right now? I don't know what time it is. Who cares what time it is. Time? What is time, anyway. Time for a smoke. Yeh, but I don't smoke. Who smokes. No one smokes these days. No one in their right mind. Right mind. Am I in my right mind? What day is it, what time. Oh, yah, time again. What about time?......What the hell am I thinking about? Jeeziz. A bunch of weird thoughts. Edge of consciousness, maybe? Dunno. So tired, sleepy. Just a little sleeeep.....

Chapter 73 - Meanwhile, back at the ranch....

Hours passed. Lives went on. Annie B was very frustrated. *I'm not able to accomplish anything positive, make any headway. I can't find John, anyplace, and the cops can't either. No more phone input. Transmission blocked or his battery dead.*

Barby Towns glanced at her watch, not really seeing it. *Al's late. He should be on his way home, or at least called by now, if he was going to be late.* Just then, her phone rang. It was Annie B

Rick McIver was operating on an emergency gall bladder, and was, at that moment, thinking only about the common bile duct which was edematous, as Thornton Brooks watched and waited, patiently, for the young surgeon to make up his mind and state what he thought they should do about it.

Mal Salteese just finished a consult, and was heading home, thinking of the dinner he was planning for Barrie, his loving wife of thirty-eight years.

George Emmely checked with the hospital security night crew. "Nothing out of the ordinary, sir. All systems go. Calling it a day?"

J. Edwards Baird wondered why he hadn't heard from the police either about John Pullman or Al Towns, or their whereabouts. He was interrupted by the phone buzzer. *Molly with an important call. Dammit, they're all so important.*

John Dominicci wondered why Sal didn't let him take care of those two bastards the proper way. *Should have gotten rid of them up front.* He was still smarting at having been out-foxed by the opposition having removed the Godfather.

Sal Ucciderita looked at his watch, thinking, *They shoulda bought it by now. If they wasn't crushed before, they woulda run outta air arreddy. Too bad. Time for dinner, anyways.*

Gonz and the other goon, who put them two hospital guys in the AW truck, were busy bent over a fierce game of eight-ball. *Wonder if they're still breathin'? Hope so. They're pretty good guys,* he thought.

Suddenly, John Pullman was jolted awake. He tried to move. *Where am I? Oh yah, I'm still here, and still can't move. But still okay, I guess.* He heard some muffled sounds, and said aloud, "Al? Oh yah, Al."

"Something's telling me, we're gonna get outta this. I don't think they'll leave this truck just sitting around for long.", Al said. Just then a loud noise. "What's that?"

"Hey Al, that you? What'd you say?"John thought he heard what Al had said.

"I wonder what that noise was. You hear it?" The noise again.

"Yah, I heard it. What is it?"

"That the truck door? Someone in the cab?"

More noises. The big engine starter whining, the diesel catching. Clearly evident to both Al and John. Al tried to say something, but John couldn't make it out over the increasing engine rumble. Then, a force that made his body jerk. *Motion? We're moving. Feels like bumps. Makes me a little dizzy.*

They rode in silence for a few minutes, or what seemed like a few minutes. John wasn't sure of the time. He wasn't sure of anything, just the engine rumble. Then more motion. *Bumps. Seems like up and down, and side to side.* "Where you think we're going?" he shouted at Al.

"Dunno....... they pick.....more.....compact.....done for."

"How long do you think we've been in here?"

"Dunno.....hours.......longer. No way.....tell....nodded off..." Al's loud voice barely audible over the engine.

"Yah, me too. Sure glad I woke up again. We must be getting air in from some place, somehow, breathing's fine. Can't smell the stink."

"You mean.....baby diapers?

"Yah, I'm guessing you're correct on that. What do you think..." He stopped, interrupted by the truck's sudden stop. Then the engine revved again, and there was a slightly different pressure on both men. "Backing up? I think we're backing up." John yelled.

"I...... you're right."

"Shit, what does this mean? Another load?" Instant worry

shot through John.

"Hope not....hear hydraulic......sayonara...... kiss your ass......."

John stopped his racing thoughts. An overwhelming fear suddenly shot through his entire being. *God, please don't let me die here. If you can let us out of this mess, I'll promise to....to....* He mumbled softly, "God, please give me strength. Let me forgive......."

He was interrupted. The truck stopped. Nothing. The cab door slammed. Noise outside. Voices? Nothing again for twenty, thirty seconds. Then that familiar hydraulic whirr. John panicked, "Oh God......oh God......... our Father who art in Heaven, hallowed be thy......be merciful, dear God. Please take care of Annie B......and the kids. And forgive me the wrongs I have done. Dear God, please let it be quick."

The whirring continued, but no worse pressure. John kept waiting for the pain. *Maybe I'll black out before the pain gets too bad. Oh God, please make it quick.*

Al was waiting too. Waiting for the crushing pain, but all he felt was motion. He couldn't believe it. Motion? *Doesn't make sense. Different. Something's different.* He couldn't tell. *Tipping? Maybe?* Suddenly with an unfamiliar roar, the pressure lessened. *Something's wrong,* He almost said it out loud. *What the hell?* More loud noise. Now a crashing sound. Much less pressure. He moved. Getting free? Louder noise, screeching, moving, falling. Suddenly he was free. The blackness became grey. He could move. He was falling. No, he was tumbling, arms and legs flailing. No control. He hit something and stopped. Everything stopped. Then something hit his head. Hard. Instinctively he reached up. *Hair. Longer hair. Not my hair.* "What the fu......Jeeziz. What the......" he yelled.

"Al? That you? Al? You there? What happened?" John was in a tangle. He tried to get up, onto his hands and knees. He tried to look up. Grey light on the left. Black on the right. Dizzy. Disoriented. *I'm blind,* was all he could think of. "Al, you there? Al, where are you? Al!"

"Hey, asshole, I'm right here......No. To your left."

John looked. He thought he saw Al sitting straight up, laughing. *Al's laughing. Al's laughing. Jeeziz. This a dream? I'm here, and Al's laughing.* "I'm blind! I can't see out of my right eye." John put his hand up, but all he could feel was mush. "My face. It's crushed. Jeeziz, I'm blind and you're laughing. I don't..... this is......"

"Damn right I'm laughing. At you, you miserable old asshole. For three reasons I'm laughing. First, it's cuz you're still alive and kicking. Second, it's cuz I'm alive and talking to you. Third, it's cuz you've got a baby diaper on your head covering your face with baby shit, and you look pretty damn funny. Here, let me help you." Al leaned across to lift off the stuck diaper. "Wish I had a camera to record the event. Send it to your good friend Sal."

"And you think this is funny. We almost damn died, and you think it's funny." John looked around. The dump. The dump and baby diapers. "Those damn baby diapers, saved our lives", Al said.

"Well, now, that you mention it, I guess it is pretty funny. Thank God it's funny. It could have been worse. A lot worse." John reached up, carefully, and wiped a big glob of baby shit off his right cheek and lower lid. He flung it off his fingers, wiping the rest off on his pants, and very carefully reached up and cleaned off most of the rest. He blinked several times, mildly shaking his head. "There, that's better. Twenty-twenty, both sides." Looking hard at Al, he asked, "Jeeziz, you okay? I'm all worried about me. And here you are helping me. You okay? Nothing busted?"

"Nah. I'm fine. A little stiff. Nothing a nice hot shower and three fingers of Jack won't fix."

"Seriously, old buddy, I thought we were done for, and, and I was praying, back there, to God, and, and, and....He answered." John was so exhilarated, he could hardly contain his high pitched voice, "He answered, Al. He answered my prayers.......I think. And we're alive. We're alive. I don't know why, but we are. My prayer. Your luck. I don't know what did it, but we're here and still alive....." A lump formed in the back of John's throat, forcing him to stop talking.

Al was silent during John's outburst, silenced by John's

faith, something he had never personally had, but which he had seen before in his friend, and had always envied. *A source of inner strength, yes, which I wish I had.* As he thought about it, he felt embarrassed, and got tough again......survival tough. His training took charge again. "Let's get outta here?"

John was jolted out of his prayerful reverie. "How we gonna do that. I don't even know where we are", John could still see the mess around them in the fading light .

"I'm guessing, with any luck, we're in the city dump."

"Luck? In the dump? What's lucky about the dump?"

"Because it's big. It's huge. And they'll have a harder time finding us."

"They, who's they?" Then he knew, and John's eyebrows arched over bulging eyes, "Sal..... Damn Sal..... and Billy." He looked up the hill of trash behind them. The truck was gone. No one in sight, but his vision was limited by the hill. He looked at Al, seeking an answer.

"Still got your cell phone?" Al asked.

John frantically frisked himself. Smiling as he dug it out, "Hey, it works. It's still on. Hot-damn. Lemme try to......damn. No service, and the battery's really low."

"That's okay. Leave it on."

"Right. Leave it on. Annie B, or Barby, or even the cops are probably looking for us. They can search for the phone. That's the good news." He paused, thinking out loud, "Sal can do the same thing."

Chapter 74 - Larry and Ben

They spent a lot of time together during the next three days at rehab. Ben Blagden had been moved up to the Rehab Unit the day after Larry Lowance. They attended the same sessions, each with different exercises and goals, but in the same room, often using some of the same equipment. Ben, walked carefully within the sacral pains from his severe contusions and his fractured ribs, all without the use of his right arm immobilizing the fractured humerus. He had to learn the ADLs, Activities of Daily Living, using his left hand exclusively. It wasn't easy dressing himself, eating, brushing his teeth, writing legibly, using the toilet, among other daily performances he had always taken for granted. He felt uncoordinated and dumb, and twisting his torso pulled painfully on those broken parts.

Larry found many of the same problems. While he was encouraged to use his arms, hands, and all of his fingers, using them was painful, difficult, and slow. Both men had suffered significant soft tissue injuries with tearing, hemorrhage, and swelling of the muscle tissues. Any attempt to make a muscle fiber contract caused pain. Big muscles had more fibers which resulted in more pain. Both men had big muscles, Larry's bigger than Ben, but Ben was in great shape before his accident, and had been well muscled since puberty.

"When muscles cause pain, a reflex arc is set up that tells the muscle not to contract, so initiating injured muscle movement does not occur naturally." Both Ben and Larry had had this explained to them, and they were told to "concentrate on the action. Force the muscles involved to start the action. Once started, the motion usually becomes a little easier and less painful. Unless, of course, you overdo it and cause some more mini-tearing to the injured fibers", which both Larry and Ben, in their zeal to succeed with the program, often did. Overdoing it was followed by a wincing from the pain, and a warning from the therapist.

They worked together, they healed together, and they

bonded into an unusual and wonderful relationship.

Ben went home for two-and-a-half weeks, allowing his ribs and humerus to start the re-calcification of the fractures, and the pain to all but disappear. The Friday evening after returning from classes, he called Larry and asked him to come over for supper at his frat house. By this time, Larry had healed most of his forearm injuries, and functioned quite normally. He had tried to return to his job at the Art Theater, but they told him he was a "trouble maker. Job's been filled. Get lost."

Ben was enraged. "That isn't fair. That's not right. You were only doing your job. It wasn't your fault."

"That's how it works, Ben. In my world, them's the breaks."

"We'll see about that", Ben retorted. "The other day you were talking about maintenance? You know anything about equipment and repair and taking care of machines?"

"Yeah, I know a little about that stuff. I took them courses in High School, what I remember of it. Why you asking?"

"My grandfather's got a business that takes care of that stuff. He's always telling me he needs good, motivated guys."

"Yah? What's his company?" Larry leaned forward, eyebrows arched.

"Elton Steer and Co."

"Not the Elton Steer? Here in the city? That's not just a machine maintenance company. It's the biggest and best in the city. I read about him inna paper. Him and that nice wife he got. What's her name? Starts wit 'A'-something."

"Annabelle. She's my Gramma."

"Yah, Annabelle. They's inna social section I sometimes look at."

"Yeah, they're big benefactors to all kinds of stuff. Granddad's office is downtown on Beach Street. He's a great guy. Would you be willing to work for him?"

"Hell yah. I love a job like that. I mean, like, that would be a real job, doin' good, helpful stuff. Not like that rat-hole peep-show place."

"Lemme call him." Ben pulled out his cell. With a little awkward effort, he scrolled down and dialed. He waited, looking at

Larry.

"Hey, Granddad, it's Ben......yah, I'm fine. Only another three weeks an I get my right arm back..... yah.... Starting new therapy on Monday."

Granddad wanted to know all about it, and Ben took the trouble to explain it all, before finally turning to the purpose of his call: Larry. His new friend needed a job. Engines and equipment, either one or both........High school.......no, not since high school, I think. Hold on lemme ask him. Ben said to Larry, "Have you worked with any equipment since high school?"

"Yah, I was a mechanic in the Army. Assigned to the motor pool. Haven't done much of the kinda thing since I got out. The VA only had airplane jobs back then. No motor vehicles."

Ben returned to his phone, "Yeah Granddad, he was a mechanic in the Army." Ben listened as his grandfather said that he had heard what Larry had just said in the background.

"Granddad, he's a real good guy. A straight shooter. I can vouch for him. If he screws up, you can blame me." Ben listened some more, nodding his head frequently. Then, holding the phone slightly away, he asked Larry, "Can you be at Granddad's office eight o'clock, Monday morning?"

Larry straightened hard in his chair, almost stood up. "You be sure I be there. Yessir. You tell Mr. Elton, eight o'clock, Monday morning, bright and early, I be there. Yessir.

"Yes, Granddad, he says he'll be there. He's a real good guy. You're gonna like him. And Granddad, when you're talking to him, remember to ask him about his great-grandfather who lived in the White House with Lincoln."

Chapter 75 - Home

The four goons in the big black Town Car were closer than the cops to the landfill. Both were racing to the scene, but the cops had the advantage of their sirens and flashing strobes. The Town Car was about to careen in through the gates, but stopped hard. The landfill was closed.

"Shit! What's dis."

"Closed. See da sign, asshole. Closes at six, an' it's seven thirty-five."

"What's that?"   "What's what?"

"That siren. Couple of 'em. We're outta here."

"Big Sal ain't gonna like it. He said to finish da job if da truck ain't done it arreddy."

"He gonna like it less if'n he's gotta bail us out." He backed with a hard turn, jammed it into drive, and floored it, fish-tailing in the dirt, and squealing onto the hard top, two police cruisers not a hundred yards away.

"Here they are, over here, down there." John squinted into the blinding beam of the LED spotlight. Al raised his hand to shield his eyes.

"Hold it right there. City police. Hands on your head." A low voice of authority.

Their hands shot to the tops of their heads, "City police? Boy, are we glad to see you."

Another voice, "Dr. Pullman, is that you? What're you doing here? Hey Susie, it's Dr. Pullman, my surgeon who did my hernia last winter." The two policemen stumbled and slid down the rubbish embankment. "Dr. Pullman, it's Richard King, your patient."

"Richard King, holy cow. Am I ever glad to see you. Boy oh boy." John shoved out his hand to shake. "Perfect timing, Richard. How you doing; your hernia still good?" John stepped back, "And this is Al Towns. You guys probably know him. He's head guy up on the Trauma floor.

"Yah, sure. Hi there Mr. Towns. I'm Richard King, and my partner, Susie Scudder." They shook hands. There in the middle of the city dump, in the evening darkness, they stood, shaking hands as if old friends out for a night of bowling.

"Susie Scudder?" John asked. "Are you the same Susan Scudder who's on the City Council?"

"Yup. The one and the same. That's my other life."

"That's great. There's some things we need to talk about", John said.

"I don't wanna break up this party," Al Towns interrupted, "but what say we get out of here."

"This is so much better," John said to Annie B as he came out to the kitchen and enfolded his wife in his arms and nuzzled the side of her neck. "Oh my god, this is so much better. Hold me tight, sweet girl, and never let me do that again."

"You feeling a little better, my poor darling?"

"Yeah, that shower really hit the spot."

"Of course it did. You must be exhausted."

"Just happy to be home. With you." Jane, their yellow lab mutt pushed her nose into the back of John's knee, tail wagging full sweep. "Janie, girl. I'm glad to see you too. Yes, I missed you too." He scratched the front of her throat, her favorite place. "You're such a good dog, Janie. Good girl."

John not only had an Irish Dark Ale with supper — he had two. Both John and Annie B were worn out. They did the dishes and headed for bed.

"What night is it? I'm so turned around, I'm not even sure."

"Well, the *Dr. Blake Mysteries* are on tonight, your favorite." "No. I'm ready for bed. How about you? Aren't you tired, too?"

In bed they cuddled, in their favorite position with her head on his shoulder, his arm around her back, her free arm across his chest, and their legs entwined. Nothing sexy. They had an active, intimate sex life, but they both were much too tired tonight.

"John Stevenson Pullman, how do you manage to get yourself into these horrible scrapes." Annie B murmured in her low alto voice.

"I wish I knew", he said in an equally low, quiet tone. "I certainly never try to get into these things. They just seem to happen. It must have been you that sent the police to rescue us. Did they track my cell phone?"

"Sweetheart, I'd been tracking your cell ever since you called this morning. I could hear most of what went on this morning with those Mafia creeps. Then I lost signal for almost eight hours. Where were you? Did they have you in some kind of a steel building, or something?"

John related the whole chain of events from the kidnapping, the Mafia Board Room, the threatening of their grandson, the loading and incarceration in the garbage truck, and the rescue by the police. "You remember a patient, Richard King? He's a cop, with a hernia? He found us."

"They put you in a garbage truck intending to crush the life out of you." a statement, not a question.

"Yeah. I don't know how long we were in there, but it felt like forever. It was pretty damned tight. Couldn't move anything."

"That was probably when your cell signal vanished, which means you were in there almost eight hours. That's how long your signal was gone. I almost gave up hope. Thought you'd hung up, or battery dead. How did you breathe? I would have freaked. Too claustrophobic."

"Al. He's cool as a cucumber. Kept us both calm and rational, God bless him. We could talk a little, hear each other somewhat. But there's several things that don't jibe, that I can't figure out. One is how the Delaware cops were on to the Mafia there. They were going to firebomb little Jake's school bus."

"Yes. I know. I could hear that part from your phone. I called Jeb, and he called Delaware. They sure responded fast. Apparently, there was a police cruiser right there in the neighborhood, thank god."

"How did they know which school bus it was?"   "Jeb

said they are routinely tracking the Mafia down there. Part of some sort of a larger sting operation they're running with the FBI. Good thing. That would have been too horrible for words."

John turned his head and kissed her forehead. "I love you sweetheart."

"I love you too, and I hate it when you get into these troubles. It scares me. I don't know what I'd do if anything ever happened to you."

"Well, nothing did. Tomorrow's another day. Back to work, I guess."

"That's putting it mildly. You are booked solid for the next two weeks."

John couldn't keep his eyes open. "I gotta go to sleep. Good night lovely girl."

"Good night my sweet boy. I love you."

Chapter 76 - Angelo's Fall

It had been just over five weeks since Angelo was shot. Things had quieted down. Annie B made sure that John Pullman worked overtime and had consulted on, treated or operated on the backlog of patients, both in the office and in the OR.

During this time, J. Edwards Baird was waiting for a court date to open up within the next two months, a courtroom where one of his favorite criminal court judges presided. To any outsider, it appeared that there was no case. The word on the street was that J. Edwards Baird had failed to get any useful testimony from Angelo "the Crime Boss" Ginnini. He was okay with that. He and the FBI knew different.

Sal Ucciderita had it from a reliable source that there "ain't no case, and that all this safe house shit wid Angelo, was bullshit." He also heard from a different source that "Angelo was having 'severe complications' which the hospital was hiding from da press, and he was gonna die soon, anyways." Sal told the Family, "We should quiet down fer now, an' get on wid our regular business pursuits. An' I don't wanna hear nuttin' more about it, unless youse hears something from which I should know about."

There was no news from the safe house, either going in or coming out. Inside, Angelo, cooperative and pleasant, was getting the hang of his diabetes care. An old dog learning new tricks, he understood and cooperated, mostly, with the strict new diet and the carefully measured insulin dosages. Chick Morella, the male nurse Al had hired, carefully supervised Angelo, with the two Cindys and Peggy assisting, 24/7.

Al Towns, on advice from one of the hospital endocrinologists, had laid out a course of treatment with Chick, who worked with the three women to lay out a twenty-four hour schedule of coverage for Angelo's care. They had been recommended by Al because he knew they "could keep this op quiet". They were being paid well by the DA's office: Peggy Handleman, PA, Cindy Kingman, PA, and Cindy Keefe, PA. The two Cindys were martial arts sparring partners at the center where all four of the team trained, where Al Towns worked out.

Later that week, Angelo calculated his own morning insulin dose, finished his low carb breakfast, rejecting the OJ because it didn't taste so good, which was a mistake that no one noticed. He watched the morning news on TV, and went into the bathroom. A few minutes later, Chick and Cindy heard a moan and a loud crash. They rushed to the bathroom, only to find the door locked. Feeling over the door frame for the little Allen wrench that had been placed there for just such a need, Chick shoved it into the hole by the side of the handle. The lock clicked open. There on the floor was a bleeding Angelo, unconscious.

"Could be a stroke , but it's most likely hypoglycemia," Chick blurted. "Go get an IV, stat." Cindy bolted up and away. Chick checked that Angelo was breathing okay. Shallow, but breathing. "Airway clear, moving air", he said aloud to himself. He checked his carotid pulse. *Rapid but weak, with frequent PVCs* (premature ventricular contractions*), sweaty.* "Angelo. Angelo, can you hear me? Angelo. Angelo, open your eyes. He rubbed his knuckles hard on Angelo's sternum. No response. Cindy returned.

"Here, you hold his head, cervical traction, while I roll him onto his back." Angelo let out a soft low moan as they rolled him. "That's encouraging." Chick said. He tried to pry open Angelo's mouth with his fingers.

"Here's a spoon I brought, just in case of a seizure." She handed it over Chick's shoulder, and he used it to help open the mouth. Then he turned the spoon to depress his tongue to keep him from swallowing it. "Set up the IV with D-5/W (five percent dextrose in water)", Chick ordered.

"Already got it."

Chick saw that there was bleeding from a small gash over Angelo's left ear. Bleeding, but not bad. He reached across and grabbed a handful of toilet paper, and pressed it against the gash with his right hand. With his left, he probed and palpated Angelo's chest and abdomen, and ran a hand over those parts of the extremities that he could reach. *Cursory exam. Nothing grossly obvious.* The toilet paper finally stuck to the scalp wound, controlling the bleeding.

Cindy quickly but carefully stepped over Chick, then over Angelo, and knelt by his side. Tight quarters between the bathtub and Angelo's ample hips. She did a fast arm swipe with the alcohol, and punctured a good vein, running the intra-cath up easily. She connected the D-5/W and the IV line to the intra-cath. "IV's in and running wide open."

"Great. If it is hypoglycemia, he'll begin to come around in a few minutes. If he doesn't, we've got a problem. Did you check the glucometer?"

"Jeeziz no. I thought you did." She jumped up and ran across to the kitchen. Chick heard her banging around, then "Where is it? Can't find it."

"It should be over on the right counter, by the toaster."

"Got it." She hurried back.

"Slow down," he said, "There's no rush. The result won't change what we're doing. But it'd be good to get a reading."

She bent down again and pricked a finger. When the tiny bubble of blood surfaced, she captured it on the paper strip, and inserted it into the machine in her palm, and waited. The number came up, "Forty-one".

"Bingo. That's our problem. Hope it's the only problem. He did hit his head hard enough to get that laceration." Chick put his stethoscope over key parts of Angelo's heart. "Heart sounds okay, with considerable irregularities." He shifted the scope and listened to the breath sounds, front and sides, "Clear bilaterally. Moving air well."

Cindy put a pulse-ox (pulse-oxygen) reader on Angelo's index finger. "Ninety-six O2, pulse one hundred two," she said.

"Okay. Let's sit tight for a little bit. See if he comes around. If not, we'll not only have to move him outta here, but it'll mean he's probably got a concussion, as well. He ought to wake up in another few minutes if it's just the blood sugar."

Cindy repeated a finger stick and blood sugar measurement on the glucometer five minutes later. "Up to seventy-one."

"Okay, slow the D5/W, t-k-o (to keep open)." Chick listened to Angelo's chest again, as well as to his abdomen. He sat back, and said, "Let's get him out of here. I think the scoop-stretcher's out in the garage, leaning against the wall, if my memory serves me correctly. Probably our best gimmick to get him onto his bed. Toss me the cervical collar on your way, would you?"

"It's there behind you," Cindy said. "I brought it in last trip."

"Always thinking ahead. Thanks, Cindy." He grabbed the soft cervical collar, opened it and carefully placed it around Angelo's neck. *There, that'll give your neck some stability,* he thought as he watched for any signs of return of consciousness. *Nothing yet.*

Cindy placed the scoop stretcher one half on each side of Angelo and replaced Chick at the head, maintaining mild cervical traction. Chick moved around to Angelo's crowded side, rolled the patient towards him, and holding him with one hand, slid half the scoop under Angelo's right side, and let him gently roll back down onto the stretcher. Then he repeated for the left side and went to the foot. Together, Chick and Cindy clicked the two halves locking them together. Chick took the IV bottle, hanging on the corner of the towel rack and placed it between Angelo's legs. "Ready?" He looked up at Cindy, who was already holding the head of the stretcher in a knee-bent squat.

"Let's go," she said. With an audible grunt, they struggled to lift the stretcher with Angelo's comatose, fireplug body, up and out of the bathroom, down the hall, and off-loaded him on his bed.

Chick did a brief neurological exam, as best he could with Angelo still in his pajamas, but unresponsive. Cindy checked his blood pressure, his pulse-ox, and a blood sugar, "One thirty-eight over eighty-six for the BP. Ninety-eight percent O2, and pulse definitely stronger at ninety-three, less irregularities. Sugar up to seventy-six. Coming around, at least metabolically."

"Yeah, that's good, but on his Glasgow coma scale, I get only a six out of fifteen. Not so hot, so I'm guessing that's our major problem."

"Better call Dr. Pullman."   "Yeah, that's what I was thinking." He pulled out the special cell phone he had been given for just such occasions, and dialed.

Chapter 77- I'm Done Here!

"John Pullman, here. That you Chick?"

"Yessir. Sorry to bother you, sir, but we've got a little problem."

"Go ahead, Chick, I'm with you." "Well, sir, here's what we've got so far." Chick was standing with his back to the foot of the bed, looking at the morning sunlight blanching the drawn shade. "Angelo apparently fell in the bathroom, unwitnessed. His sugar was below forty with a shallow laceration over his right ear, comatose. We have the D5/W running. Brought his blood sugar up to seventy-six, vital signs coming back to normal, but still unconscious. We moved him to his bed. I got a six out of fifteen on a Glasgow just now, with an arm flexion response to a hard trapezius pinch. No verbal, eyes non-responsive, pupils equal and reactive. I'm guessing a concussion." "Sounds like it. Is the rest of his physical suggestive of anything else?"

"No sir. I've checked him a couple of times, and can't find anything else. We're monitoring his sugars now using the glucometer, but it s all we've got."

"Good. Sounds like you've got it under reasonable control."

"Thank you sir."

"What do you recommend we do?" John Pullman asked Chick.

"Well, sir, I was about to ask you the same question."

"You're on the scene. First hand. Tell me your plan."

"Dr. Pullman, what with a blood pressure normalizing back to his usual mild hypertensive state, no bradycardia, previous PVCs gone, normal respirations, I'm figuring that he's suffered a cerebral concussion, but not too bad a one. I doubt that he has an intra-cranial bleed. His vital signs sort of point to that. At least, I hope he hasn't had a bleed, but that comes from my basic clinical assessment, sir. Not a CT scan."

"Yes, I agree. You make a good point. We certainly have no

CT confirmation. Let me run it by Erv Anson, and get his take. We may have to come out there, but that runs the risk that we'd be tailed by the bad guys, and they'd find the safe house. One of the two of us will get back to you."

"Yessir. That would be good, sir. We'll keep a close watch and call any acute changes...... until you call back, sir."

"Thanks, Chick."

"Thank you, sir."

The next ten minutes ticked by ever so slowly. Chick and Cindy, checked and rechecked all his signs and numbers, waiting for the promised call. When time slows, important issues always take so much longer. Chick, biting his lip, was on the verge of calling Dr. Pullman again, until he looked at his watch and realized the only a few minutes had passed, and Angelo's signs were stable. No outward signs indicated anything getting worse. Indeed, Cindy thought she saw Angelo's eyelid flicker. So they patiently waited. Checked again, and waited.

"Chick, his eye lids did flutter. Just then. I'm sure of it this time," Cindy said.

"I'll check his Glasgow again", Chick said, and started with the trapezius pinch, using considerable force. Both Angelo's arms rose up, hands grabbing at the pincer. Both legs moved. "Lighter. Definitely lighter. Maybe he's coming to." Chick noted hopefully, and moved to retract Angelo's upper lid to check his pupillary reflex. When he touched the lid, both Angelo's eyes flew open, and he bellowed with a huge grunt, causing Chick to draw back fast.

"Hey, muufuuukah. Hey. Hey. Shit." Angelo turned his head, looking right then left, then back. Clearly confused, but awake. Then he closed his eyes and with a snort, went back to sleep.

Just at that same moment, the special cell phone rang. Chick snatched it up, "Yessir, Chick Morella here."

"Chick, Erv Anson here. What've you got?"

"Dr. Anson, I don't know what Dr. Pullman told you, but Angelo had a fall in the bathroom, probably due to insulin shock. We think he must have hit his head. We stabilized his sugars back up to normal clinical ranges, but he was unconscious, with a Glasgow of six."

"Yeah, Chick, I got something like that from John Pullman. The question is of an intra-cranial bleed?"

"Well, yessir, but I think he's waking up as we speak. The phone rang just as I was about to check him out, so I....."

"Good idea. Go give him a quick once-over. I'll hang on", Erv said.

"Yessir. Hang on. I'll be right back." Chick watched as Cindy checked Angelo's vital signs, again. Then Chick gently tried to raise Angelo's left eyelid, but Angelo jerked away, eyes wide.

"What da fuck! Whatta you think you're doing, sonny boy. Get away!" Angelo twisted away from Chick with a fierce, angry glare. Chick recoiled fast, hands up to chest.

"Whoa. Angelo. Hey, you're awake. Good, Angelo, good. You're awake."

"Yah, I'm awake. You betchur ass I'm awake. Whatta you tryin' to do to me." Glaring at Chick, he snarled, "Keep your fuckin' hands to yourself, sonny-boy. Touch me again, and I'll have your ass." Chick and Cindy both stood rigid, momentarily paralyzed. Angelo swung his feet off the bed. "Ahhh-god. I got a fuckin' headache. Shit.........gimme an aspirin. You", he grumbled, looking at Cindy, "Yah you, chicken-lickin, go get me an aspirin........now."

Cindy and Chick looked at each other, jaws gaping. "Angelo," Chick said softly, "aspirin's not such a good idea right now. We don't know if you might have any recent bleeding, you know, from your fall."

"Fall, my ass. Gimme a fuckin' aspirin. Now! Right fuckin' now. I got a fuckin' headache, an' I need a fuckin' aspirin, an' I need it now."

"Angelo, aspirin is contraindicated after undiagnosed head trauma."

"Who you think you are, gettin' off callin' me Angelo. You call me Don Ginnini, Il Padroni. That is until I invite you to get familiar. You got that, sonny." Angelo let out a big sigh and relaxed a bit, getting a better hold on himself.

"But, Angelo, we've been...."

"Yah, I know, sonny boy, we been livin' here, an' you and yer women-friends there been takin' care of me, an' that damn diabetes. I got that. But things are back to normal now. I took a little nap and got things figured out, so you can start showin' a little respect, seein' as you know who I am."

"You fell in the bathroom and hit your head. You were unconscious for about twenty minutes. It looks like you passed out from insulin shock. Your sugar was less than forty. We gave you some glucose IV, and you came out of it nicely."

"Huh, that right?" asked Angelo, now more pensive than glaring. "Okay, I got that. You guys are helpin' me with the insulin part, but I gotta business to run. Been away too long arready. They be lookin' for me? My boys that is?"

"Yes. You are correct in that, but they were looking for you to do you harm. They want to kill you."

"Yah, I remember all that, an' this here safe house an all that shit. But all that stuff is done now. I'm going home, back to my business. I'm thinkin' better now. I got the picture. So you'll give me a phone if you know what's good for you." He stood up, looking around, searching.

Chick and Cindy, now a bit anxious, looked at each other. Cindy broke the silence. "Don.....uh, Don Angelo Ginnini, sir, I need to check your blood sugar?........to see where we are right now.......you know what I mean?"

"I can do it, and I'll do it when I say so. Gimme a phone. I'm callin' Billy, now."

"Angelo, I got Dr. Anson on the phone. Waiting. I called him because we were worried about you. Hitting your head, I mean." Chick picked up the phone, "Dr. Anson, you still there? I'm sorry, but the patient just....."

"No problem, Chick. I heard the whole thing. He sounds pretty awake, and pretty ornery."

"Yessir. Nothing like he used to be. Strange change, but fully conscious, and seems to be moving all extremities normally, sir."

"Chick, get your ass over here, and gimme that phone. I'm outta here!" Angelo yelled, standing by the bed, clearly angry.

"You sound like you've got your hands full there Chick," Erv said on the phone, "Call me later, or sooner for any changes. I'm only far away as the phone. And, Chick, good luck." The phone disconnected. Angelo started toward Chick, fists clenched.

A sharp series of raps on the back door stopped Angelo. They stopped Chick and Cindy too. A twist of keys, the door opened, and Dusty Reade called from the kitchen, "Good morning people. Everyone up and at 'em?" He strode into the living room followed by the other Cindy and Peggy Handleman.

"What do you think you're doing here?" Angelo growled. "Your services are no longer needed here." He looked back at Chick and across at Peggy and both of the Cindys. "And you neither. You're fired. All of you. Don't need ya's no more. I'm callin' my people to come get me, so you all can go home. This game is over."

Dead silence. Angelo glowered from person to person, and all five stared incredulously back at him. Angelo broke the silence, "Go on. Go home, or wherever. I don't need ya anymore. Gimme yer cell phone there, Chick. I gotta make the call. And tell me, exactly, where am I?"

Chapter 78- Trouble

"Annie B, my sweet, what do we have scheduled for this afternoon?"   "Uh-oh, why do you ask? What's on your mind? Am I gonna like your answer?"

"Well, maybe not, but it looks like Angelo is causing more problems."

"Again?"

"Again, and still."

"What is it now? And why do you have to be involved with it, or him, or whatever? Is it surgical, or are you going to go get yourself in another mess?"

John pushed away from his desk, groaning as he got up. "I just got a text from Dusty Reade, and then a cell call from Chick Morella. Apparently Angelo had an hypoglycemic episode in the bathroom this morning, passed out, hit his head, and was unconscious for about twenty minutes. Chick and Cindy got his sugar back up, and he woke up. But......he woke up different. They say he's changed. Not the nice, reasonable, and cooperative Angelo they had been dealing with. This new guy is a tough, take-charge, take no crap dude, giving them a tough time. He's been demanding a phone to call Billy, one of his henchmen, to come get him. He won't let them check his blood sugar."

"Sounds like he's had another personality change. Could it be?" Annie B asked John.

"Yeah, I was worrying the same thing. I'm gonna call Mal Salteese. See what he says."

"Good idea, but why don't you just stay here and operate telephone central. They really don't need you out there to......."

"I dunno Annie B It's my responsibility, this whole mess. I feel if anyone should be out keeping things on an even keel, it should be me."

"John, my love, you know I admire your bravery, logical thinking, and utter fearlessness, but there are people out there who are more experienced, and more knowledgeable than you. People who can, and should be physically on the front lines." She got up out of her chair, came front to front, put her arms around his neck, and looked up into his determined but puzzled face. "I know you love the action, and your sense of justice is to right all wrongs, but just stay here.....please, John?"

"Okay, okay, okay......yeah. I know you're right. Let me see how this breaks out, and I'll try to stay here. Yeah, a phone contact, like you said. But if they need me, I'll have to go. First step, from control-central. Call Mal Salteese."

"Thank you, honey. That's a much smarter option." She took a step back, smiling, obviously somewhat relieved.

"Mal, John Pullman here. I got a new devel......."

"Hey John, what's new? How's that lovely wife of yours?"

"She's fine, thanks, but I'm calling about a new development here on that Angelo Ginnini case. You remember, the crime boss you consulted on?"

"Yeah, how could I forget. Gunshot concussion with the personality change. Sure I remember. A memorable character. What about him? Something new? He revert?"

"It sounds like he might have. At least something's up. We were hoping you might have a look at him?"

"Yeah, sure. But isn't he stashed away somewhere? Safe house or something?" "Correct. That's still on the "QT", but I can get you access if you need it. I thought maybe you'd do better talking to the team taking care of him."

"Yeah, sure, I can do that, easily. What's the number?"

"A little background. You know Dusty Reade? He's running the place."

" Yeah, sure. I've known Dusty for years. Great guy."

"And the medical bit is being handled by Chick Morella, an RN. Not sure you know him. Big self-defense Black belt guy."

"Okay."

"Dusty and Chick called me. They say the patient had, or they think he had a hypoglycemic episode, blacked out, fell and hit his head. They gave him some sugar and he woke up about half an hour later, but woke up different. Aggressive, demanding, giving orders, trying to assume command. No thug speech like his henchmen. Well-spoken, but definitely a different person."

"That's very interesting. Unexpected, but not uncommon", Mal said.

"I thought you might like to speak to them directly, rather than get it third-hand from me. Ask questions. Get a better feel for it, so we are more certain where we stand.

"That would certainly help. How about a possibly more serious head injury?"

"Chick didn't think it looked like anything more than a concussion. He did what sounded to me like a pretty thorough neurological exam on him as he was waking up, at least until he changed character. That's something you'd have a better handle on than I."

"Yes, I agree. I'd like to at least talk to them. Sounds like a personality reversion. We talked about that, remember? In fact, those Mafia people were asking about that at the meeting we had with them at the hospital. It got them all bummed out."

"Yeah, I remember all that," John said. "They wanted to know when he would revert to his old self. You told them there was no way to tell, and that little guy, the tough one, got angry. What was his name?" "I think it was John Dominicci. He is supposed to be the enforcer, the hit-man. I read about him in the newspapers."   "Yes. That's it, John Dominicci. And they all left shortly after that. I thought they figured you weren't leveling with them. Not telling when he would revert. Kinda scary for a while there, but nothing came of it. I told Annie B about it because we were worried that they would start threatening us again, but they didn't do anything."

"The whole thing just sort of went away. Go figure?", Mal said.

"Well, I think that may be partly due to Jeb Baird. His office leaked info to some of their street informers. He told them that Angelo suffered complications and was secreted, still, in the hospital, on special infection precautions, and the bit about the safe-house was a hospital cover-up. We're guessing that the Mafia guys bought it, and figured their Boss was a goner."

"Jeez, that whole business sounds like you got it right out of a dime novel."

"Truth is stranger than fiction. Anyway, that's the way it is. I'd love it if you could call up there. Talk with Dusty and Chick and his team, and let me know what you think. You can tell them your impression, too." John gave him the number.

"Will do. I'll get back to you."

"Thanks. See ya."

Chapter 79 - I Never Forget A Face

"Is Doc Pullman in today?" Annie B looked up, surprised. Surprised because she never heard him come in, and surprised because he was a giant. Well, not a giant, but a huge, black man.

True to form, she quickly regained her composure, "Hi. Can I help you?"

"Yes please, ma'am. I need to see Dr. Pullman. I was a patient of his, sort of."

"Sure. What's your name?"

"I'm Larry Lowance. I broke my arms a few weeks back."

"Oh, Larry. Yes, he told me about you. I'm Annie B, his wife. It's a pleasure to meet you. What's the trouble today?"

"See Miss Annie B, it's not me that's the trouble. I wanna tell him I seen the guy that was takin' all that blood at the hospital and ran away. Least, I think it was him, I'm pretty sure. I never forget that face."

"Wow. Hang on. Just a minute." She got up and turned into the corridor, "John, honey, Larry Lowance is here with some pretty interesting news. Let me bring him back?"

"What? Larry Lowance? News, what news? Yeah, sure. I'm just finishing a journal article," John called back.

"Come on back with me," Annie B told Larry. Do you mind if I come too?"

"Yes ma'am. Thank you so much. You and Dr. Pullman such fine people. Always helpin'. Thank you." He automatically stooped slightly as he passed through the doorway.

John met them in the hallway, his welcoming hand out to shake. Looking at Larry's arms, he paused, then asked, "Your arms healed? Okay to shake your hand?"

"Yessir, it sure is. Thanks to you, I be just fine these days. It's all good. But it ain't me I need to tell you about."

"Larry, you look good. A lot better than last time I saw you."

"Yessir. But it ain't me today. Remember that guy in the

hospital who was takin' people's blood too much?"

"Yes, I sure do. We never caught him or found out who he was."

"Yessir, the papers said he was Steven Wojak or somethin' like that. A nurse at the hospital who was doin' harm to folks."

"That's right. He was stealing blood from patients on the Trauma floor. We never found out why," Pullman said. "Probably the black market."

"John, didn't you tell me you thought they had linked it to some of those unexpected deaths there?" Annie B squinted slightly, trying to recall.

"Yeh, right. There were five patients with sudden death and no findings on autopsy but severe anemia." John turned to Larry. "Is that when you were there?"

"Yessir. I woke up that night 'bout 4:00 AM from the noise. Wasn't sleepin' good anyway. I was out in the hall, lookin', and this nurse guy came out, runnin'. He ran square into me, there, and kinda bounced off. We looked at each other, hard. I never forget that face. He ran smack-dab into my sore arms. Hurt like the be-jeeziz. Never forget that face when he look right at me."

"That was some morning. There was a young patient that nurse had been exsanguinating before he was spotted and ran.......into you." John looked up at Larry's serious face. "One of our residents was very quick- thinking and saved the patient's life. While everyone was busy calling a code, he pumped the blood in the bag back into the patient. Ben somebody."

"The resident was Ben? I thought you said it was Sonny Webster that saved the day?" Annie B said.

"Yes. It was Sonny who hung the blood, but I think the patient was a Ben somebody," John explained to Annie B

"Yessir, Ben was the patient alright.," Larry confirmed. "Mr. Ben Blagden. He's a friend of mine, Ben is. Yessir, my good friend. He goes to college. Got me my job with his grandfather, Mr. Steer, Ben did. Yessir, Mr. Elton Steer. He owns the Motor Pool and Maintenance Company. My room at your hospital was only a couple of doors down from Ben. That's why that Steve-nurse ran into me, and I saw him this morning downtown. That's what I came here to tell you. To see if you were interested in finding him?"

"You saw him? The nurse, Steve? Oh, yes, Larry. We're very interested in finding him. You say he's here? In the city? The Police said they thought he had disappeared. Down south somewhere."

"Could be, Dr. Pullman, but I know I seen him this morning. Down in old-town. I never forget that face."

"That's very interesting. Do you remember where, exactly?"

"Yessir. It was on Third, near Seymour. He didn't have nurse clothes on. Just regular. And a back pack. He didn't see me. He was walkin' fast and lookin' at the ground."

"Larry, let me call Jeb Baird and have you talk to him. He might have some questions."

Larry looked a little confused. John added, "He's the District Attorney. The top cop. He'll want as many details as you can give him."

"Yessir, I do the best I can, but I only saw him a little. Didn't follow him or anything."

John went behind his desk and punched in a number.

Chapter 80 - He's Gone

The shrill bell of John's phone pierced the quiet of his den, giving him a bit of a jolt. It was the special number from the safe house. "That you, Dusty?", he answered.

"Hey John. Yes it's me. Bad news. Angelo's gone."

"What?"

"A team of his henchmen drove up from the city. He said he was going, and he went."

"Just like that?"

"Just like that! Not much we could do about it. He was adamant about going, and they had the guns. We didn't have much of a choice." There was silence on the other end. "John, you still there?"

"Uh, yeah, I'm still here. You say he went willingly?"

"More. He was the one who called them to come get him."

"Jeezis. Didn't he know they were out to kill him?"

"Oh yes. He knew alright. You shoulda heard him on the phone, with whoever was on the other end. He scared the shit outta me, and I wasn't even talking to him. I'll tell ya, he's one tough, slick operator. Never raises his voice. Smooth talkin'. Gives orders and never asks questions. Smooth and even. The kinda guy you never say "no" to."

"Gone, huh?"

"Gone from here, and gone from the Mr. Nice-guy. It sounds like he's back in control of the whole shebang. He is one cool cookie, John. I'd never want to have to deal with him."

"What happened. He was subdued, contrite, feeling guilty, even apologetic before. At least he was before that second concussion. And now, you say, he's running the show?"

"That's right. A complete opposite personality. Chick says he woke up radically different after his concussion this morning. We weren't dealing with the same guy."

"I hear you. I guess it's what Mal Salteese calls the personality change. It sounds like he must have reverted to his former self. The Mob Boss self. I talked to Mal earlier today. He said he thought that might be what's happening. Did he call up to the house?"

Dusty turned away from the phone, "Hey Chick, did Dr. Mal Salteese call you, here?"

"Yah, he did, earlier today." Chick crossed the room to Dusty. "I told him what happened. He said he thought the personality change had reverted. Said it's not unusual, especially after a second concussion. By then Angelo was really throwing his weight around, and we didn't know what to do. Couldn't handle him, anymore. You saw that. You were here by then."

Dusty returned to the phone, "John, Mal Salteese did call, and he did tell Chick that it was probably that personality reversion condition." "Yes. I could hear Chick. Well, what do you want to do?"

"Guess we might as well fold up shop here. Better let Baird know."

"Yes, and Ollie and George Emmely at the hospital. At least alert them of possible trouble. Who knows where Angelo's headed with his new-found freedom."

"And his new-found personality. He's one aggressive son-of-a-bitch," Dusty said.

"You wrap things up there, and I'll go to work here. We'll be in touch. You wanna get Al up-to-date? He hired you."

"Will do. Talk to you later."

J. Edwards Baird looked at the caller ID, and picked up his home land line. "John, how are you, you old scally-wag, you. You in trouble again?"

"No, Jeb. For once I'm in the clear, sitting here quietly in my den. But we've got a problem, and by we, I mean all of us."

"What's the problem?"

"Angelo has escaped, back to his own people."   "What? Angelo Ginnini? The Godfather?"

"Angelo Ginnini, the Godfather. One and the same. It's a long story, but he had another concussion and reverted back to his old crime-boss personality. Not even Dusty Reade could handle him. He called up his people, told them where he was, and they came and got him. He's gone. And from what Dusty says, it sounds like he won't be coming back."

"Shit!"

Chapter 81- Find Herbie

"**Juanito, come to me.** I got a little job for you." commanded the voice, quiet, and controlling.

"Godfather," John Dominicci acknowledged, as he slowly moved into the chair next to Angelo, "for you, I do anything, but I feel I am not worthy. I have a confession to make to you, and you may not want me after you learn my error."

"And what is that, my boy?"

"I was ordered to terminate you. When you were in the hospital. When you were the other Angelo Ginnini. I went to do it, but you were not there. So I failed on two levels. I am not worthy of your trust, Godfather." John stared down at his folded fingers between his knees. "I need to tell you of this before you hear it from the others. I know I deserve your wrath."

"Juanito, my boy, I know all about that. Your actions only cement your place in the Family, even tighter than before. A distasteful task for you, yes. But you held the Family honor higher than your personal feelings. You are a trusted and valued member. When I was your age, in your position, I would have done the same thing." Angelo bent forward, jaw jutting, eyes intent on John, voice an intense whisper. "What you tried to do, and your shame at your failure only raises the esteem I hold for you, my boy."

"There was a meeting Sal called with all.....," John's throat was dry. He could hardly get the words out.

"I know all about the meeting," Angelo interrupted. "All about the vote. Sal giving you the order. Juanito, do not trouble yourself with these matters. They are from another day, and they will be compensated for later. Trust me on that. But in the meantime, I have a little errand I would like you to do for me. I ask this of you because you are like a son to me, and this is a personal matter."

"Anything you ask, Godfather. I will do anything you command of me. You know that. What is it I can do for you?"

"Do you remember a waiter at Pasgucci's Italian, named Herbie?"

"Yes, of course I know Herbie, but he's not there anymore."

"As I'm sure you know, he was the one who did me."

" Yes, Godfather. This I know. I was going to pay him a call, but Sal told me no. Said it would upset relations with the other families at a time when he was looking for unity. Herbie resided with the Gambinis for a while, until the word came out that you weren't dead, only severely injured. He's laying low over on the south side. Should I pay him a little call, Godfather? Can I do that for you?"

"You know, Juanito, that's one of the reasons I love you like a son. You think like I do. Yes, you got class, too. You know how to control yourself, and you often think like me, Juanito."

"Godfather, I will pay Herbie a brief call. Consider it done."

"Yes, that's good. Now, tell me. How's that nice girl of your's?"

"She's good, Godfather. She's very good. But with business and all, I don't get to see her too much. Enough, but not too much, you know what I mean?"

"That's good, Juanito, my boy. Don't get into too many entanglements. Keep life simple. You can go now, Juanito. I've got some work to do."

"Yes, Godfather. Thank you, Godfather. And please give my best regards to Mrs. Ginnini." John picked up his grey fedora as he turned to leave. He looked at the Godfather, who was already busy with some papers.

John Dominicci did find Herbie. Two days later. With John's reputation on the street, he had little trouble obtaining information and following it up. It wasn't hard to find Herbie. He was living in a crummy apartment, down on Seymour. John found him sitting on the toilet. He looked like hell. Life was obviously not agreeing with Herbie these days.

"Herbie, it's nice to see you. It's been a while."

Herbie looked like he was about to cry. "John, I didn't do nothin'. Why you here? I done nothin' to you."

"Herbie, Herbie. You know why I'm here. I came to pay you a

social call. You got nothing to be fearful of. Not from me, Herbie. You're sitting there, taking a shit without a care in the world. Nor should you have a care in the world. This is just a social call, and I brought you a present, Herbie. I know you like a candy bar every once in a while, so I brought you one." John pulled out the Three Musketeers bar, and extended it to Herbie.

Herbie had heard about John's Three Musketeers bars. He took one look at it and let all his sphincters go. John moved quickly and put his Glock with the silencer to the back of Herbie's head, and pulled the trigger. Thup. Herbie's terrified face blew away in a shower of blood, bone, and brain tissue. John put the Three Musketeers bar back in one pocket, and the Glock in another, looked around the room, briefly, and walked out as quietly as he had come in.

Chapter 82- Steve and Herbie

"**The District Attorney's Office.** How may I direct your call?

"This is Dr. John Pullman, and I'd like to talk to Mr. Baird. I've got some information for him I know he'll want to hear." The phone clicked in John's ear, and clicked again.

"This is J. Edwards Baird." The phone-voice was all business.

"Jeb, it's John. I'm here in my office with Annie B and a patient named Larry Lowance. Larry says he saw that nurse from the hospital, that Steve Wojek, or whatever his name was. The guy who was caught stealing blood from a patient, and who ran off. The one, I believe, your office has been looking for."

"Yes, Steve Wojek. And, yes, we've been looking for him. Hang on a sec." Jeb turned and called out the office door. "Molly, can you bring me the file on Steve Wojek. That's WOJEK., Steve Wojek". He swiveled his chair to look out the big picture window, thinking. Molly brought the file and handed it to Jeb. "Yeah, here it is. Steve Wojek, RN. He's a person of interest we're looking to question about those deaths your trauma department reported, and also some strange deaths reported on the cancer ward. As I understand it, some were severely anemic and others had too much blood that had clotted or something on the cancer ward?"

"Yes, that's the guy. My friend, here, Larry, says he saw him this morning." John said.

"We are also looking to see if the autopsy reports match those of a string of deaths of inner-city homeless victims, who also had that severe anemia and no other cause of death." Jeb was flipping through pages in the record. Suddenly he stopped and asked, "Your patient Larry saw him this morning?" "Yes. I thought you'd want to know, and want to talk to him, yourself."

"I would love to talk to him."   "Good. I'll put him on."

While Larry was talking to Jeb, John picked up the morning paper, scanning it carelessly, as he listened to Larry's end of the conversation. He was pretty sure what Jeb was saying on the other end. Something caught his eye. He called out to Annie B, who had returned to the front office. "Honey, what was the name of that guy who shot Angelo? Wasn't it Herbie someone?"

"Yes, I think, Herbie someone. The police were looking for him, but never could find him. Didn't they say they thought he had been whisked out of the area by a rival gang family, or something like that? Why do you ask?"

"There's an article in the paper that says, and I quote, 'A body identified by authorities as Herbert Raphaelo, was found dead in his apartment near Seymour Street, of a gunshot wound. The body was found after neighbors complained of an odor, causing the Police to investigate. An anonymous source said that evidence suggested it was a professional-style assassination, tying Raphaelo to the assassination attempt two months ago of Mafia Don, Angelo Ginnini'."

"I'll be darned." John scanned the rest of the article. "It doesn't say much more, but I think I remember Angelo saying something like he had been shot by this Herbie, a waiter in some restaurant."

Chapter 83- The Godfather – Returned

Angelo Ginnini slowly rose from his chair, the throne at the head of the table in the Meeting Room. Slowly, but purposefully. Everything he did these days was slow and purposeful, not because of any residual illness, but because he was the Boss again. No doubt about that. He had retaken control of the Family and all its business interests, intricacies, and secrets. Every eye in every chair moved with his every move. Aside from Angelo's deliberate moves leading the eyes around the table, nothing else in that room moved. Inside everyone's immobile chest, hearts hammered. Worried brains stimulated sweating. *What's he gonna do now? This new Angelo, I don't know. We don't know. One minute he's quiet and reasonable, almost friendly. The next minute he explodes in a rage. Shit! What's next?*

Relaxed, with the hint of a smile on his mouth but not his eyes, Angelo moved one step, paused, then another step, stopping behind each chair. Looking at the occupant of the chair opposite, across the table. Staring hard for four or five seconds, then he moved on, as though oozing through oil. One chair at a time, staring at each individual. Silence commanded. *What's he doin'? What's he up to?* He stopped behind Sal's chair. Sal was sweating. A lot. His face, tight in a grimace, exuding fear.

"I was away for a while." Angelo's hoarse voice whispered. "Sal you took over. Like you should have. Like always in the family. Yes, Sal, you took over. You held a meeting of the other families. You voted. You send John, my boy Juanito, to do his thing." Casually, Angelo took the gun from his pocket and placed it behind Sal's right ear. All eyes at the table focused on it. All eyes but Sal's. His were squeezed shut. Tears or sweat or both?

"Yes, Sal, I was away for a while and you didn't know when I was to return, so you moved ahead. You gave the orders. The orders for the gun to my head, just like this. Right Sal? Just like this." Sal felt the gun pressed hard into the back of his head.

Angelo paused for the effect. "Then on the count of three we

290

pull the trigger. Right Sal? One, two, three, and blam. Right Sal?"

Sal's whole body shook visibly, eyes, like teeth, clenched. Shirt soaking wet.

"Is that how we do it, Sal? One, two, three, and, blam? So, okay, Sal, here we go. One...."

Sal let out a tiny, high squeak.

"Two........., Sal, two, then three, and....." Angelo pulled the trigger. The metallic click pierced the silence. Every one seated around the table jumped. Sal's pants suddenly turned a darker shade just to the left of his zipper, running down to his seat in the chair.

Angelo replaced the cold, snub-nosed gun in his pocket, and calmly walked back to his Throne. Sal fluttered both eyes open, not seeing anything. His face pale grey, flaccid without expression, jaw dropping, lower lip hanging, starting to drool. From across the table, some, with their eyes still fixed on him, thought he was having a stroke. Incredibly, Sal was alive, but looked instantly aged, slumped like an old man in a wheel chair.

Knuckles on the table top, Angelo leaned into his words, "Sal, you did well. You did a good thing, the right thing." Startled, all eyes looked up, mouths agape. Did they hear right? Angelo looked out at his underlings. "You heard me right. Sal did the right thing. What is......I ask each one of you, what is the single most valuable aspect of our venerable organization? Of all our business entities? What is it that ties us all together?"

He eyed each sitting member, but didn't pause. Didn't allow an answer to interrupt. Angelo kept control, absolute control. That was his style.

"The Pledge, gentlemen. The Pledge. That's the important thing that keeps us all together. We all been made and sworn to the pledge of allegiance to the Family, to our cause, upon pain of death. Each of us." He turned slightly toward Izzy. "Except Izzy, here. Izzy's got his own reasons for staying true to de cause, dontcha Izzy." Izzy nodded solemnly. "For everybody else, the pledge makes us the Family. Some blood, yeah, but, The Pledge of Fidelity to the Family, an' our businesses. Sal did what he figured would be best for de Family, for all our businesses. He was following his Pledge. Thinkin' big. For de good of de Family, not for his own self." Angelo paused again to let his words sink in. Then he said, "I was away for a time. I couldn't be with you, and Sal tried to keep de Family together. That loyalty was to the Pledge, not to any one guy. To the Family. To what they call back home, cosa nostra. Yah, I say, thank you to Sal, and so should you." Angelo stopped and sat down, in the throne.

All eyes were still fixed on Angelo, but minds were stunned. *Sal's still sitting there. Alive. Scared shitless, but alive.....Never try to out-guess, out-think the Godfather.* John Dominicci, seated next to Sal, turned and clapped him on the shoulder.

"Shake out of it Sal. The Godfather's right. This is not a dream. Hey, Sal!"

The stunned silence was followed by, "Yah. Hey, Sal, yer good.", from across the table, jolting others back to reality,

"Yeah, Sal, you done good."

"Atta-way, Sal." Heads shook assent, general agreement.

"Yeah, he did good."

The Godfather watched from his perch, smiling on the outside, but always watching.

"We move on to more pressing matters. Get your monthly reports ready." A statement, not a question. The table chatter instantly quieted. Even Sal seemed to return to reality, shaking his head, throwing off the fog, the fear, the disbelief. He took out his handkerchief and wiped his face, jowls, and neck, then neatly refolded the white linen, and replaced it in his suit breast pocket. He wiggled his wet butt and sat up straight, eyes on the head of the table.

Angelo looked out on the attentive faces. "Banking. Pietro, that's you." Pietro cleared his throat and reported the status and profits from the various money laundering schemes across the city, across the state, in other states: Vegas, Atlantic City, several other state-sponsored casinos, as well as overseas ops.

The next reports, one at a time, went through the Lending (loan sharking) business, Community Safety (protection and extortion), Gaming and Numbers (gambling), the Escort Services (prostitution), Immigration and Adoption Services (human and baby trafficking), Tobacco and Alcohol (bootlegging), ending finally with Pharmaceuticals (heroin, marijuana, cocaine, meth, and numerous others, plus the newest and most profitable, fentanyl).

Izzy Stein, the Consiglieri was taking copious notes, just in case. Angelo listened carefully to all the numbers and dollars, and kept track of them in his head, his speciality. He never forgot a number in his many businesses.

"A second meeting to review the other (legitimate) businesses will be scheduled for tomorrow." Those included hospitals, commercial banks, insurance, REITs, hotels, fast foods, motion pictures, video, TV, publishing, and electronics. These businesses all generated good cash flow. Not as good as the more questionable businesses, but they were a great place to stash excess cash. "Diversify", as Izzy often suggested.

Angelo, satisfied by most of today's reports, reminded all his lieutenants, "the inflation rate is over two percent, and we expect a minimum of five to ten from you next month, and triple that if you are looking for any bonus money, and you want to keep your position."

The meeting was over. The various members got up and left, fear mixed with determination and ambition.

Izzy and John Dominicci stayed behind. "So Boss, how are you these days?", Izzy asked.

"Getting stronger every day. Glad to be back in the business."

"You feel strong enough to carry on?", Izzy looked up, a carefully-placed sympathetic frown wrinkling his salon-tanned brow.

"I'm gonna tell you, Izzy," Angelo said, then turning to John on his other side, "And you, Juanito. I tell you this confidentially, this whole thing has been very strange. First of all, the hit hired by the Gambinis. Of all
the people? Needa find out what's behind that and make it level. Then, what that doc, um, uh, that Salt......., Salteese guy says that it was that personality change thing. The whole time I was like in some dream. Like if I was hypnotized. I knew what was going on, but didn't have no control. It was my body, my voice doing and

saying things, but not me. Never, in my right mind am I gonna talk to a DA. And not on video-tape. Can't explain it." He turned to Izzy, "You ever been hypnotized?" Izzy shook his head. "No? Me neidder. Then I konked out from de low sugar and it all went away. Like some bad dream."

"Yeah, that's good Angelo," Izzy said. "That's very good. There's your plea. If that DA Baird ever tries to drag us into court, all you gotta do is deny. Say it was all them drugs they gave you in the hospital. You weren't, as you say, in your right mind. Like inna dream. Good term. Remember that one. Judge'll never allow that video. Obtained under false circumstances. Drugs made you do it. Inadmissible in any court." John Dominicci was nodding, slightly, watching the Godfather's every expression.

Chapter 84 - Undercover Surveillance

Ben Blagden's phone rang. "Hey, Ben. It's me, Larry."

"Hey L-man. What's up?"

"Meet me down at Dunkin's. Gotta plan to tell ya."

"In ten?"

"In ten."

"So what's up?" Ben was eager to know. Eager for anything. What with rehab only three times a week, and being limited to only one class this semester, he had time weighing heavily on his hands. Reading was fun, but he was sick of sitting around, wasting much of his time.

"I'm gonna do some undercover surveillance work", Larry said between slurps of his coffee. He liked the French-vanilla.

"Whatta you mean, undercover surveillance? You get recruited by the CIA or something?"

"I'm gonna stake out that Steve nurse guy. Find him and bring him in." "Steve nurse guy? You mean that guy who dammed near killed me in the hospital? The one who ran into your arms."

"Yah, that guy. I seen him down in poor town, near Seymour Street."

"And how you gonna do that?"

"It's called surveillance. I learned about it in the Army. I almost went into it. You know, intelligence, instead of diesel mechanics. I'm gonna do a stakeout, which means I go where I think he's gonna be, at the time I think he's gonna be there, and nab him when he shows up. I'll do it in the early mornings, before work. That's when I saw him before."

"So you think you're going to catch that nurse guy who was trying to kill me."

"Well, he wasn't tryin' to kill you exactly. He was collecting the blood for something. They think it was for the black market or something." "How'd you know that?"

"I was talking to Mr. Baird, the DA. Dr. Pullman had me talkin' to him."

"And he said for you to go stake out this Steve nurse?" Ben's face betrayed his doubt.

"Not exactly. He said he would be very eager to find him. Bring him in for questioning. He said there are a lot of questions about this blood Steve was taking. Steve, Mr. Baird told me his name is Steve Wojek, and he is a full nurse. Not just an assistant. So I'm gonna go bring him in for Mr. Baird. I got a friend who's a bounty hunter. It's sorta like that. I'm gonna start first thing in the morning."

"Not alone, you're not. I'm going with you. This sounds like fun, plus, I got nothing else to do, anyhow."

"You wanna go with? That'd be great. Two heads better'n one. Now here's what I was thinkin' of doin'."

Steve spotted the two of them. *I don't remember seeing these two before. Unusual, two together, but, hey, why not. Twice as much product. And that big one probably carries a good blood volume.* "Hello, gentlemen," he said to the two huddled masses. They were dirty and disheveled. They hardly recognized themselves after all the preparations Ben had made them do. The worn clothes, the make-up, the general filth, or so it appeared, were all new to Ben and Larry that morning.

Neither body responded, the big one still snoring. "Good morning, gentlemen." Steve said louder. Louder and closer. Ben gave a startled jump, and sat up, slowly trying to open his eyes. He wiped a dirty hand back across his mouth, and squinted as he looked up at the stranger.

"Hey, Jake, wake up. We got company", Ben said, lightly punching his companion. The big guy turned, stretched and groaned, slow to wake.

"Huh? What time izzit. I'm thirsty. You got any stuff left?" He, too, slowly sat up. He recognized Steve, but feigned surprise to see anyone staring down at them. "Whadda you want? We ain't done nothin' wrong. We got a right to be here. Same as you. Just as much right. This yer doorway or somethin', huh?"

"How would you gentlemen like a little mornin' eye-opener? Free. What would you like? A little red wine? Vodsie? Gin? Or do you like pills. I got pills." Steve was bending toward them slightly, smiling.

"What're you? The wine fairy? Whatta you sellin'?" Larry held up his hand against the light behind Steve, eyelids mere slits.

"I'm not selling anything. I'm on a research project, collecting small blood samples for study, and offering a drink of your favorite, or pills if you prefer, in exchange for a small sample of your blood. Painless, harmless. Good deal for you. A good deal for my research company. A win-win situation. How about it?"

"Let's see what you got," Ben said. "You got red wine?"

"Nice red wine. Here have a sip. Hell, take a swig, take as much as you want." Steve bent over Larry as he dealt with Ben. Ben took the bottle and made it look like he took a couple of big gulps, while only getting a tiny sip. He lifted the bottle back to Steve, just out of his reach, pretending a big swallow, followed by a large belch.

Larry was watching closely, waiting for the right moment. He grabbed Steve's outstretched arm, pulled it down, hard, and at the same time brought his knee up with a deep smash into Steve's solar-plexus. Steve fell forward, and Ben parted his knees just in time, and slammed them shut again, trapping Steve's head in-between with a scissor hold from wrestling days.

The bottle in Steve's right hand smashed on the pavement, but Ben didn't let go. Steve's reflex was to jerk back, which pulled Ben's knees up and over, twisting him half onto Larry. Ben let go. Steve recoiled further, rocking back onto his haunches. He held for a second, then stood up, brandishing the broken bottle neck. "You cocksuckin' son-of-a-bitch," he exploded in instant rage, and started thrusting the jagged bottle at Larry, who was splayed wide open to attack as Ben had rolled off.

Ben was on his feet in a flash, "You dirty prick. You might've tried to kill me once, but not twice." Glaring at Steve, crouched in a fighting stance, arms with hands at the ready, Ben fumed, "Come get me, scum-bag. Go ahead, try it." Steve's attention was diverted. He jabbed the bottle at Ben, but was too far away, and took a critical step closer. Larry saw the opening. He rolled and kicked his leg between Steve's. In one continuous motion, he drew it back, pulling Steve's right leg out from under him, then powered it forward, up into Steve's groin. Steve let out a howl as he lurched forward, bent over, clutching for his testicles. As he did so, Larry's left foot tripped his passage, and he fell into a roll forward. On his way down, Ben managed a hard jab with his foot to the side of Steve's head. He lay almost fetal on the ground, gasping and moaning.

Ben jumped around Steve, and from behind him, put a heavy foot, none too gently on his neck. Larry, up on his own two feet, was about to grab Steve, when a harsh bark stopped everything, "Freeze you motherfuckers, botha ya's, er I'll blow yer fuckin' heads off!" Ben and Larry did freeze and looked up to see two black forms, one big, the other shorter, in long black coats, black fedoras, black shades, and two, very big, black guns pointed at them. A frozen standoff for a few seconds of immobility. "Over to da wall. Hands above yer heads. Facin' the wall."

Ben and Larry, stunned, not knowing what else to do, did as they were told, with eyes glued on the guns. Steve was beginning to loosen up. Larry said "Whaddaya think yer doin'?" Larry blurted. "This ain't yer fight."

"Shut-da-fuck up. Hands behind ya's." They obeyed, and quickly their wrists were bound with plastic ties, ratcheted tight. Steve, moaning was getting to his feet, looking at his rescuers, puzzled but glad. "You too, motherfuck. By the wall, an' shut-up."

Steve, confused, slowly lurched toward the wall, next to Ben. "I haven't said....."

Whack! One of the two guns smashed into his right shoulder. "I told ya's, shut da fuck up, asshole. You hard-a hearing?" His wrists too, were bound. "Turn around......alla ya's." They turned as one, blinking in the early morning sun just topping the buildings across the street — three baffled men facing two black coats holding two black guns. The bigger of the two hulks switched his gun to his left hand, pulled his phone out of his coat pocket with the right, thumbed a couple of buttons and listened. A click and an indistinct voice. The hulk said, "Left atta corner and a hunnerd yards on yer left. Now," he growled.

The black Town Car stopped with a whoosh by the curb. The driver got out and opened the rear door. "Inna fuckin' car," he ordered. Larry got to the car in three steps, and despite his size, ducked in without a pause. Ben, with a surly sneer, took his time crossing the sidewalk, and got in.

Steve looked at the larger hulk and whined, "You don't want me. You got the wrong guy. I work for you guys. I'm on..." He was answered with a sharp blow to his left ribs.

"I wan'cher opinion, I'll ask for it. Inna meantime, shaddup an' get in, asshole."

Chapter 85 - Come for Lunch, please

John Pullman's cell phone gave its characteristic ring. Unrecognized number.

"This is John Pullman", he answered.

"Dr. Pullman", the husky but quiet voice answered, "This is Angelo Ginnini. I dunno if you remember me or not, but I'm a patient of yours. I had the gunshot that caused the diabetes."

"Of course I remember you, Mr. Ginnini. May I still call you Angelo? How are you? Are you okay? You having a problem?"

"Yes, please, Doctor, call me Angelo. And, no, Doctor, no problems. I'm doing just fine. I wanna apologize for having to leave in a kind of a hurry the other day, from that half-way house you arranged for me, but I had an urgent business matter I had to attend to. I hope you understand."

"Your appetite and digestion okay? No fever? Diabetes in good control?" John didn't know what to say. What was it about this phone call, that was making him nervous. *Something isn't right. Why my cell and not the office number? Strange. Maybe not surgery related?*

Angelo chortled at the other end, "No, no, no. Everything's "va bene, futtitinni", good, real good, Doctor. You did a good job, and I'm doing good. I'm calling because I want to thank you for all you done for me. You and Mr. Al, the nurse there. Without you, the two of you, I'm told I woulda been a goner. So I would like to buy you and Mr. Al a lunch, please."

"Mr. Al? You mean Al Towne? The head nurse of the Trauma Unit? That would be very nice, but it's not necessary."

"No, it's not necessary, but it is something that would make me feel real good, if you would accept. I won't take up your whole day, but for you two, just to share a plate of spaghetti carbonara and a glass of Chianti, together, with me, would be good."

"That's very nice of you, Angelo. I would enjoy that very much, and I know that Al would too."

"Would tomorrow noon be alright for you?"

"Hang on a second, if you will, Angelo." John replied. "Let me check my calendar. *Is this some trick? Another garbage truck ride? But this is Angelo, not Sal.* Trusting his instincts, he tried to relax. He swallowed and answered, "Yes. Tomorrow noon would be dandy. Where and when?"

Pasguccis Italian on Galileo Street, at twelve o'clock. Would that be okay?"

The food was delicious, as was the bottle of Chianti they shared. Al and Angelo were deep into a conversation about fishing - which is more rewarding, deep sea or fly-fishing? John, fascinated by the depth of knowledge each had, was mopping up the last of his sauce with a chunk of bread. He sat back with a contented sigh.

"And for dessert?" Angelo asked, "Gelato? Pie? Pie with gelato? What is your pleasure, gentlemen?"

John was about to answer, when a large fellow in the standard black pants and white shirt, came over to the table, and bowed slightly. "Scusami." He bent over whispering into Angelo's ear. Angelo's eyebrows went up as he grunted "Huh?" The whispering continued. John and Al forced themselves to look around the room at the rococo decorations, pretending not to notice the interruption. Pretending not to be interested. Pretending not to be trying to overhear the whisper, but they could discern nothing.

What they did note was that Angelo's look darkened. Eyebrows now furrowed, he grunted again, an audible "No." One more short whisper, answered with a brief, "Yes." The black and white straightened, turned, and left the room.

Angelo, forced a smile from his lips, but his brow was still wrinkled, his eyes had a hard look. Something had changed. "Please excuse the interruption, my friends. Francisco, here, has no sense of timing. Now where were we? Ah, yes. Dessert. What would please you gentlemen?" He looked from one to the other, but the smile was gone.

"Angelo, I'm sure the dessert is as delicious as the entree, but to be truthful, I'm stuffed. I haven't got room for another bite", Al said. "That pasta was the best I've had since my R&R in Italy many years ago. But thank you."

"Yes, I agree", said John, gently patting his abdomen. "Terrific meal, Angelo, but I couldn't get another thing into my fat gut, either."

"A cigar, then. Fresh from Havana."

"Ah, no thank you. Nice offer, but I don't indulge. Never have." John said.

"None for me either, Angelo. Used to enjoy a fresh Cuban now and then. Gave all that up when I reached forty." Al saw that Angelo considered the luncheon over, so he added, "Actually, I've got to attend to some things at the hospital before heading home." All three got up.

"Thank you, Angelo. This has been a very nice time. I'd like to do it again, but next time it's my treat," John said as he headed toward the door. Al noticed that two black and whites came out of nowhere, and followed them out on to the sidewalk. A big, black Town Car was parked at the curb, and a second one was just rolling to a stop behind the first.

"Gentlemen, I saw you came in a cab, please allow me to give you a lift to your homes." Angelo was all business. "It's the least I can do, and taxi cabs are hard to come by this neighborhood." Angelo was gesturing to the rear door of the second car, which had just been opened by one of the men. "Good afternoon, and thank you for coming." Angelo stretched out his right hand. They shook, a little too quickly. He turned and disappeared into the rear door of the lead car.

Chapter 86 - Not Enough

"Yer holdin' back on us. Yer not deliverin' the whole load. That's why," explained the voice.

"No I'm not holdin' back nuthin', and that's bullshit. I told you guys that before. How long I been here? I told them other guys the same thing." Steve looked up at the face barely visible beside the blinding, white light shining on him. Tied to the chair, he was sweating, profusely. "I'm thirsty. Gimme some water."

"Got a nice big glass of really good, clear, cold, spring water with lots of cold ice....... just as soon as you start levellin' wit us. What-chu doin' wit the extra?"

"There's no extra. I told you arreddy, before." His nose was stuffed with the dried blood, never mind the pain, so he had to mouth breathe. "There is none."

"Yer such a asshole. We know you been takin' some extra. We gottchu on pictures. Proof. Iron clad evidence, as your DA likes to say. So what-chu doing wit it? Huh?" He paused to let it sink in. "This is the last time I'm gonna ask you nice, right Gonz? You know Gonz, there? He likes to hurt people, don'tcha Gonz."

Gonz was pacing, unseen in the dark background, whapping a billy club into his left palm, a nasty, sly smile curling the edges of his thin lips. Since he'd recently taken the oath and been made, they treated him more important, more trust.

Steve tried to look around to see Gonz' face by the light, but couldn't see anything in that dark area.

The voice noticed. "Hey, Gonz. Come here. Over here", he said pointing to Steve's left side. The tall, thin, wiry guy in a tee shirt, a toothpick dangling from his sneering lower lip, came into the corner of the illumination. A serious dude by any description, Gonz continued whapping the billy club audibly into his left palm. "Gonz has broke lotsa bones wit his stick, ain't-cha Gonz."

"Yeh! Lots. Arm bones best. Just above da wrist. Both sides, so ya can't wipe yer ass." His short high laugh made the toothpick jiggle. He remembered, quietly to himself. *I had to break the forearms of that big black fella in the alley with Billy several months ago, when I was still being tested to see if I was tough enough? At least I didn't have to kill the guy. And now, that same guy shows up here with this guy, if it's the same guy. Can't be sure.*

Steve tried to swallow. His mouth too dry to function. He looked at his hands, both middle fingers tied to the front posts of the chair, but the arm rests had been removed. The voice noted. "That's right. No use to ya if he has to whack ya. Can't use either arm for a good three months. We'll just have to get someone else to get the blood. You want that?"

Steve knew he was in over his head. He didn't want to be hurt. "I only took a little. Less than a pint. For my research. Biggie said I could do my research. I'm usin' it for that."

"Is that why that chink, what's his name....Soo Loo......"

"Sung Long."

"Yah, okay, Sung Long. So is it that why he shows up to yer place every Friday, just after you deliver to us? What's inna bag he takes away? Huh? What's inna bag. I'll tell you what's inna bag. A half gallon of our blood's inna bag. That's what's inna bag."

Steve didn't answer. Couldn't answer. His head bent forward, looking at the floor, defeated.

"How do we know?" the voice continued behind the light. On the left, the night stick kept whapping into the palm. "We been watchin' you. For two weeks now. We got a tip, an' we been watchin' you. An' you know what else? Huh? Do ya?" The voice paused, then screamed, "Look at me when I'm talkin' at-chu, you little prick!"

Steve looked up quickly, his heart in his mouth. He was really scared. Suddenly dropping to a low, threatening level, the voice continued, "You don't mean nothin' to me. I just as soon let Gonz here, mash your skull in, but that wouldn't teach you nothin' now would it? When you gonna learn, boy. Learn you don't cheat your business partners. Huh?"

"I've learned." Steve whined, on the verge of crying. He had been threatened before, even beaten up by punks, but nothing like this. He was about to pee his pants. *These guys mean business.*

"I've learned. All you had to do was to ask. Tell me I shouldn't take a little onna side. I would-a stopped. You don't have to do this to me. I won't do it anymore. That's a promise."

"Promise, huh? Do you know how lucky you are?" The voice was completely different. Calm, almost friendly, "We came by just in time for you. Them two guys would-a done a lot worse than Gonz. Yer fuckin'-A-lucky we was watchin' you. You'd be inna morgue, downtown now if we wasn't there right behind you. Yah. Right there. Every mornin' for the last two weeks. Watchin'....... Saved yer ass, you little prick. Dunno why, but we did. Orders from above. Cut him loose Gonz."

Gonz came at him with the longest switchblade Steve had ever seen. "Just cut the ties, Gonz, just the ties." Steve froze, staring at the knife. "I know you wanna cut him, but hold it for another day, Gonz. If he fucks up again, you'll have plenty of time wit him to use both yer stick and yer knife. That's a promise, Gonz." The voice paused, "You got that Steve? Next time we get serious. Sit right there. The Under Boss wantsa talk to ya."

"Yes, I really appreciate it. I appreciate your understanding, and I appreciate your savin' me from those two guys." Steve was having verbal diarrhea, but he couldn't help himself. "Thank you Mr. whatever-your-name-is.....Were they a plant? They weren't street bums. I guess they were waitin' for me, but why? I don't know them from nuthin'. I might-a seen the big guy before, I don't know. You know why they were there? You know who they are?"

The voice had moved away from the light, answering, "We're gonna find out, soon, if we haven't found out already. The Under Boss is directin' that one hisself." The voice was fading to the other side of the room. "I don't wanna see you in here again, Steve. You got that?" A few footsteps, and Steve heard "Gonz get him outta here."

Chapter 87 - Captive

As the big sedan pulled away, Al heard a soft click from somewhere. It was dark in the car. At least it was dark in the back, which was divided off from the front, as in fancy limos. He looked around and felt around. Feeling uneasy, he didn't feel any better when he couldn't find any door handles. No door handles meant no way out. Not from the inside. He leaned over and murmured to John. "We've been taken captive."

"What......?" John blurted out.

"Shhhh", Al continued to whisper in John's ear. "It's probably bugged in here, so keep it mum. I'm pretty sure we've been taken captive. Let's see where they take us. If we go home, we're okay. If not, we got a problem."

John whispered back, "Another problem, you mean. At least there's more room in here than that garbage truck, and we can see out of these darkened windows." They rode on in silence, John thinking, *come on Angelo. Enough's enough. No more of your games. I've got work to do, patients to see......what's he doing now?*

Al decided to see if the back was miked. In his normal voice, he said, "Hey! We're going the wrong way."

Silence. Then a soft click, followed by a voice through a side speaker. "Yessir, sorry 'bout that. We, uh, we, uh, gotta make a stop...... if youse don't mind."

John leaned over to whisper to Al, "I'm thinking our friend Angelo has a very thin skin. One minute he's our bosom buddy, the next minute it appears he takes us captive. You remember during lunch he never made mention of our friendly time together, much less our saving him from his own mob execution. Something very strange."

John and Al remained quiet as it became apparent that they were heading in a direction opposite from either of their homes. **John and Al were each in a chair**, hands bound behind with the usual ratcheted strip ties. Sal Ucciderita was pacing back and forth before them, hands clasped behind him. "Let me get this straight. Yer tellin' me that you know both this Ben Bag-somethin' and this Larry guy, but yer sayin' you didn't set them up for this here street caper, with this Steve guy? Yer sayin' youse don't know nuthin' 'bout this here shakedown on Seymour Street they was doin'? Is that just a coincidence? And youse 'spects me to believe it?"

John looked up.Those were the most questions he had ever heard Sal ask at one time. "It's what it is, Sal. Take it or leave it. What would you rather have me tell you?"

"The Godfather takes youse guys for nice food, and this is how you pay him back? Nice. Real nice. And you sit there actin' like hot-shit gentlemen, all over again. I thought we was rid of youse before. But no, youse is like a bad nickel, youse keeps turnin' up in business youse got nuttin' to do wid."

"Sal", Al said, "we don't know anything about what you say those kids were doing, and we sure as hell don't want to be any part of any of your businesses. How the hell you got us connected with those kids, I don't know. Like we told you, we only know about them as patients at the hospital. They both were on my Trauma Unit, and doc, here, was assigned to them by the hospital. One got beat up, and the other, hit by a car, I think. If I got the right kids. One's a big guy, not a kid anymore."

"Yah? How come they say you set 'em up for the take-down on this Steve guy? I gotta think youse is lyin'. They say you put 'em up to it."

"No Sal, that's not it." Gonz, one of the two "soldiers" over in the dark, leaning against the concrete wall, pushed off and came toward the circle of light, tooth-pick hanging from the corner of his mouth. "I mean, it's not 'xactly what they said. I'm not sayin' youse is wrong, Sal. I never say yer wrong, but they told me different, before. They say the DA tol' da big guy, Larry, that he wanted yer guy Steve, for questioning 'bout the blood thing he was runnin'. This here Larry-guy, decides he's gonna be a hero and get this Steve-guy for da DA. It was the doc, here, that got this Larry guy hooked up wit da DA. The doc's right sayin' he didn't do no part in the sting."

"That's right. I didn't know anything about it. Did you Al?" John asked his friend.

"No. Not in the loop on this one," Al said with a frown. "Sorry to disappoint you Sal, but you're lookin' in the wrong place for this one."

"Yah, that's right," John continued. "Not until you people told the two of us all about it. I'm still not sure I understand it all."

"And now, youse know de whole routine. Can't wait to go blabbin' to dat DA friend of yers." Sal, staring at the ground, shaking his head. Sal knew the Boss still sorta-liked these two. He turned to the toothpick, "Cut-'em loose, Picky."

"Picky" was the name Sal sometimes called Gonz, partly because of the wood sliver always in the corner of his mouth, but mainly because he was skinny. Skinny since a kid, but wiry, strong, tough, and mean. When Sal couldn't think of his name, he called him "Toothpick". The nick-name stuck and was shortened to "Pick", then "Picky", because Picky was choosey about who he "messed up". So Gonz, hesitated, thought for a second, then moseyed over behind John and Al and with a quick flick of his shiv, cut the plastic ties, and stepped back into the shadows.

John brought his hands forward, massaging his wrists and flexing, and extending his fingers and palms. Al just let his freed arms hang by his sides, giving no clue to any discomfort, as usual. Sal pretended not to notice. He looked up, "Bring in that Steve guy, an' the udder two."

Chapter 88 - Do Unto Others

John looked at the three younger captives as they were ushered in by an Uzi-09 , then he looked at Sal, unsure of what was happening, glanced again at the younger men, then back at Sal.

"Over dere, behind 'em." Sal ordered with a small flick of his head. Ben, Larry, and Steve were shoved into the circle of light. Larry looked around into the dark reaches of the room. He thought he could see at least a half dozen men. He wasn't sure. *We're clearly outnumbered,* he thought. Al was thinking the same thing, *and out gunned.*

Sal broke the silence, "Steve, you tell me just what Biggie had you doin'." He was the judge, holding court.

Steve brightened up, "As you know I'm a nurse, at the hospital," he spoke to the voice behind the light, eager to be a defensive part of the team. "I was collecting blood with venipuncture, using it for my research proje....."

"Forget that shit. What was youse doin' for Biggie?"

"Uh, yessir. I was collecting blood for Mr. Biggie and his team."

Sal sat back with an unseen smirk, "So, now, Biggie, or Mr. Biggie, as you calls him, seems to have got his own team, now........Yah, I get it. Go on."

"Yessir, I trade a drink or a hit for blood......ya know, down on the street.......homeless people, mostly. They all like it. It's a good thing for......"

"And whattaya do wit all dis blood youse collects?"

"I give it to Biggie. Every Friday..... He picks it up.....either him or one of his team."

"You give it all to Biggie?"

"Yes, all of it."

"What do you do with the stuff youse don't give him." Not a question.

Steve tried hard to swallow, hard. Dry mouth. He had to pee.

Shit. What do I do now?

"Maybe youse didn't hear me. Whadda youse did with the stuff ya didn't give......"

"It was only a little. Cuz I needed it for my research. I didn't take much."

"So mebbe youse should like to give some of it back?" An answer was expected. "Huh? Whatchur plan on that? Huh?"

"Well I can't give it back. It's not useable anymore. Too old. You don't want........."

"Yah, yer gonna give it back." The voice growled. Sal's implication was clear.

Silence, except Steve thought he could hear his heart thumping. A door opened. A figure approached the light. A figure carrying something. Steve peered into the dark. *Jeeziz, it's Biggie. What's he got?* The figure shoved a small table into the light with his foot, and put his load down. *Jeeziz, it's blood drawing stuff. Just like my stuff.*

"That looks just like the equipment I use to draw blood", Steve said.

Biggie stood up, "It should. It's yer stuff. I got it myself."

"You got my equipment? How did........."

"You need a better lock, Steve. That one's easy."

"Arright, enough already." Sal looked at Ben, "Kid, you know how to draw blood?" Silence. "Kid. I'm talkin' attchu........Kid!"

Ben straightened, "Who me?"

"Yah, you. You draw blood?"

"What do you mean?"

"Can you draw someone's fuckin' blood....from his fuckin' arm, into a fuckin' bottle, or bag, or whatever the fuck they use. Simple yes or no. Either youse can or youse can't."

"I, I, I never......No. That's not something I can do."

"Steve, show him how to put in the fuckin' needle inna fuckin' artery or what ever youse put it in, and make the blood go inna bag there." A big hairy fist came under the light, with a big hairy finger pointing to the pile of plastic on the little table.

Steve jerked back to attention, "Whaaa. Whadda you mean?"

"Take yer fuckin' needle and put it in the kid's blood vessel, or vein, or what ever youse call it." Sal shook his finger at the apparatus as he growled.

"What're you talkin' about?" Steve asked, his voice an octave higher than normal.

"Just what I said. Put the fuckin' needle in his fuckin' arm. Now!"

John Pullman spoke up, "I think he wants you to start an IV in Ben."

"Hey asshole. Who asked you? What I want is this asshole"— the hairy finger pointed at Steve, "to teach this asshole"— the finger pointed at Ben, "how to stick the needle into this asshole's blood vessel" — the finger pointed back at Steve.

Steve was speechless. He swallowed and finally spat out, "You want me to show Ben how to start an IV on me? What for?"

"Yer finally, fuckin' catchin' on, asshole." Sal was annoyed.

"Come here." Steve said to Ben. Steve spent the next few minutes shaking as he explained to Ben how to tourniquet the arm, uncap a needle from its package, slap the arm to bring up a vein, swab the site with alcohol, lay the needle almost parallel to the vein, puncture the skin, and down, into the central hollow of the vein, look for the blood return, plug in the IV tubing, and tape it. He trembled so badly that he missed the first try, even though Ben's vein was a good size. He got it on the second pass.

"Good. Now, you do it on him", the voice growled.

"Me? Do it on him?" questioned, Ben, alarmed. The rest of the room focused on the action.

John glanced over at Al. Neither one liked what was going on. Sal caught John's glance. "Hey, fuckface, you want what he should do it to you instead?

Steve looked like he was ready to cry, as though he had a premonition of what was to happen. "Why do I need an IV?"

"Steve, I'm gonna give youse a short lesson." Sal, although only barely visible behind the light, looked around at his five captives. "My mudder brung me up to be a good Catholic. She told me once, she told me a thousan' times. She said, 'do unto the udder guy, as youse wants them to do to you.' So Steve, that's what we gonna do for you. You Catholic, Steve?"

No answer. Steve's eyes, wide with fear, started to water.

"Hunh? Youse Catholic, Steve? Yer mudder teach you that lesson? Hunh, Steve?" Deadly quiet.

Sal waited, knowing the fear was building, the part he liked. "Okay, kid, put the needle in him."

"Me? Why me."

"Cuz I said so." Ben was motionless. "Now!" Sal's harsh bark startled all five men, even Al.

"What about this?" Ben indicated the IV in his arm.

"Take it out." someone said. Ben wasn't sure. He thought it was Larry, or maybe the other guy. Steve was immobile, staring off into the darkness. Ben started fussing with the tape without much success.

"Here, let me help you." It was Al, who quickly undid the tape and pulled out the needle, putting pressure on the puncture site, with the skilled practice of the years.

"Enough of that. Get going, dickhead", Sal growled again.

Ben unwrapped a new needle from its sterile container. The plastic wrapper made a loud, krinkling noise in the silence. Looking the needle over, carefully, he held it up to the light in front of his eyes, trying to determine just how it worked.

"Comeon, dickhead. I ain't got all day." Ben was stymied, not knowing what to do next.

"Put the rubber tubing tight on his upper arm," John advised, his voice soothing, quietly reassuring. Ben looked for a vein.

"See that big one on the inside of his elbow?" John continued guiding. "No, the other one. It's bigger. It'll be easier." Every eye in the room was focused. The concentration in Ben's eyes could have lit a fire. He trembled slightly.

Al, just above a whisper, "No, wipe it with the alcohol swab in that little packet there."

"Good", John said.

"Okay, take the guard off the needle. That's it." John still encouraged, supporting Ben's efforts.

Steve tensed up his muscles, squeezed his eyes shut, and awaited the needle puncture in his skin. Ben lightly pressed the sharp needle bevel against the forearm.

"Push down and slide it up, through the skin into the vein underneath", John continued.

"Aaaagh. Shit." Steve's cry, just as expected, surprised no one. A jelly bean sized lump under his skin began to swell just above the needle.

"Pull the tourniquet off. Put your left finger over the site, and pull the needle out. You blew the vein," Al's voice noted, showing little concern. "Try again."

"Same needle?" Ben's question quivered with his hands.

"Might as well." Al, always two steps ahead of everyone else, was guessing that Steve wouldn't live long enough to make a new, sterile needle necessary. "Gauze and tape tight on that site. Then the tourniquet again, on the other arm."

Ben got the needle in and secured on the fourth try. Steve howled with each attempt. "Now what?" Ben asked.

"Hook up de bag." The growl came from behind the light.

"That tubing over there." Al pointed. "First, tape the needle in place. Good. Now pull the stylet out of the needle hub there, and plug in the tubing.......quickly." Blood was flowing out of the needle, expanding a pool of red. As Ben tried to plug in the tubing, Steve, eyes still closed, jerked his arm, letting the blood run onto the table. Ben, with Steve's blood all over his fingers and hands, followed, plugged in the tubing, and stopped the leak.

"Now what?" Ben turned to the growl behind the light.

"Put the bag on the floor. It'll run faster." the growl answered.

"How much you planning on taking?" Steve had opened his eyes.

"How much you take when yer collecting it?" the growl countered.

"No. You can't do that. It'll kill me. No, no, no stop it. Five hundred CCs, maybe. No more."

"Do unto the udder guy....., remember?"

Chapter - 89 Take 'em Outta Here

"Juanito, my boy. Come see your old grandfather." Angelo hung up the phone and sat back, momentarily closing his eyes. Twenty minutes later, John Dominicci knocked softly on the heavy study door, and slid in quietly.

"Godfather, so good to see you. You're looking better, Godfather. It warms my heart to see you back in your old form."

"Juanito, it does my heart good to see you looking as classy as you always do. There was a time, there, I was away, but, as you know, I'm back now. Some things came up when I was away that we need to fix, my boy.

"Someone misbehaving? Want me to eliminate the troubles?

"No, no, my boy. You always do such a nice, tidy job when you are called on. But this time, I need you to move a couple of guys out, and keep them in good health. I want you to escort my doctor, Dr. John Pullman, and his chief nurse Mr. Al Towns, outta the cellar to where they can get themselves safely home, and out of our territory."

"Yessir, Godfather, I can do that for you. Where are they now?"   "Sal's got them down at Church street, our offices. My guess is that he has them down in the interrogation rooms."

"Godfather, I do not want you to think I'm presumptuous asking you this, but why bother with them? Sal thinks they're messing with one of our businesses."

"A good question, my boy. First, Sal has got it wrong, and I was misinformed. He has not done his homework on this one, and I was given wrong information. Sal usually does a good job. Gets it right, but not this time. It's a complicated mess. Second, Dr. Pullman and his assistant, Mr. Al, saved my life. I looked into my injuries and treatments, and I probably shouldn't be here today except for what they did for me. I owe them."

"Yessir, I understand. So get them away from Sal? Yessir, I can do that."

"Thank you, Juanito. Bring me word when you're done." Angelo went back to his reading, but looked up again. "Oh, and give them that canvas package over there. It's a couple of old pieces I don't use anymore, and the missus wants them outta the house." He returned to his reading once again, a signal that the meeting was over. John left as quietly as he had entered.

"Sal, John D wansa see you."

"Yah, what for?"

"I dunno. He's in room C."

Sal turned to Gonz, "Don't let nothin' happen. Be right back."

Sal returned a few minutes later looking miffed. Retaking his chair next to the light, and satisfied that the blood was still flowing out of Steve into the bag, he pointed to John and Al, and said to Gonz, "Take dese two there, to room C. John D is waiting fer 'em."

"John D? Shit no. What they done that John D wants 'em?"

"John D dont wants 'em. The Godfather wants 'em.

"I wouldn't take any more blood than that bag there." John Pullman said to Sal as he and Al were being prodded across the room. "That bag is twice the normal amount as it is. Take much more and he'll go into hypovolemic shock, with a high likelihood of death". *A plea probably falling on deaf ears,* John thought. *But somebody's got to say it.* "So I'd stop the bloodletting if you don't want a murder on your hands."

Sal shot Pullman a vicious look, "Fuck off, asshole."

"Move it mister, 'less you wanna be next." Gonz pushed John on the shoulder, but not as hard as he might have. The Peter Kannes in Gonz was glad to leave the room. He wanted no part of this execution.

Sal turned in his chair, waited a few seconds as he watched Gonz leading the two medical men out of the dark room. He looked back into the darkness, and barked, "Hey Joey, tail 'em. See where John D's takin' them two, an' lemme know. Take a couple guys widjas. Call me when you knows." "Yeah, sure Sal."

"Please shut that off now. I'm getting dizzy." Steve was sweating, and trembling. He was starting to breathe harder.

"Take his pulse an' tell me." Sal directed his order in the

general direction of Ben and Larry, but at neither one specifically. Both men hesitated. "Take his fuckin' pulse....now!"

Ben and Larry gave each other worried glances. Larry got up and put his big, beefy hand on Steve's wrist. "Can't feel one."

Ben reacted quickly, "Try his carotid.....on the front side of his neck."

Larry moved his hand. "Yeah, I can feel it. It's real fast."

"Hey, don't push so hard. I can't breathe", Steve wheezed, twisting his head to look up at Larry. Larry brought his fingers up to his own neck, checking his own pulse for comparison, and then replaced his fingers on Steve's neck.

"Hold still," Larry told Steve. "Yah, it's fast, but not too strong."

"Schtop IV. Pleeese schtop it. 'attsanuff." Steve's face was wrenched and sweaty. "I really feel like.....shitty. Dizzzzzy." His head dropped on his chest. The blood kept flowing into the bag which was almost full.

Ben noted that the bag was much larger than the bags they used when he gave blood at the Red Cross. It was then that the reality of Steve's possible death hit him. *This gives a whole new meaning to the story of his taking my blood in the hospital. I'm not sure that Steve deserved this, despite what he attempted to do to me. He's gonna die.......like I almost did. But still.*

"Bag's full. Start the next one." Sal's rumble interrupted Ben's thoughts. "You. Big guy, Larry. You plug in dat new bag over dere." Larry did as he was told, spilling some of the red on the floor as he fumbled with the tubing. He moved to his chair and sat down. They all watched in silence as the bag began to fill, and the minutes passed.

Steve slumped forward, falling out of the chair. He'd have hit his head had Larry not caught him mid fall, and gently lowered him to the floor. Not knowing what to do next, he looked at Sal.

"Izzy dead?" Sal asked casually. Larry looked down at Steve, then back at Sal. "Izzy dead? Check his fuckin' pulse, asshole."

Larry bent to feel Steve's neck once again. He could feel a thin, rapid pulse. He looked up at Sal. "Nothin'. No pulse," Larry lied, "Can't feel no pulse." It happened that Steve had inadvertently fallen on the IV line, kinking the tubing under his body, shutting off the flow.

Ben staring at the bag, said, "Looks like the blood's stopped, too."

Sal looked at the bag and tubing, "Yah. Looks that way." Nothing moved for the next minute or two. Ben and Larry gaped at Sal, waiting for a reaction. None came. Finally, Sal sat back in his chair, rubbed his chin, got up, said something to one of the men against the dark wall, and left the room.

Chapter 90 - The Vacant Lot

John Dominicci led John Pullman and Al Towns out of the building at gun point, purposefully ordering them in a gruff tone for the benefit of the thugs they passed. "Get in the car. You drive. You in the back." he commanded first to John, then to Al, waving the gun back and forth, "And no funny stuff."

For some reason, John was not scared. Despite the gun, despite John Dominicci's reputation, something in John Dominicci's manner didn't seem so threatening.

"John? May I call you John?" John Pullman asked John Dominicci once they were in the car.

"Yes. That's my name. And may I call you John?" came the reply.

"Yeah, and I'm gonna call both of you John, that is, if I may", Al said with a smirk.

At John Dominicci's direction, John Pullman drove the car northeast, away from downtown, toward a less developed part. It had been an area of small family farms until twenty or so years ago. Now it was pretty much abandoned. They were passing a large vacant lot, partly bordered by woods, with some large boulders at one end and a decaying old shed at the other. Kids used to play soccer and stickball here until the new generation forced the kids into organized sports, complete with over-scheduling coaches and over-zealous parents. Now it was just an unused sandlot. What no one in the car noticed was that a black sedan had followed them. One of the four men in that black sedan was watching through binoculars as he spoke on the phone.

"This is it," John Dominicci said, "Pull over and get out." John Pullman did as requested, and left the driver's door open.

"What are we doing here?" John Pullman asked

"Do whatever you want," John Dominicci said. "My orders from the Godfather, your patient, were to get you away from our office area, so that's what I'm doing. End of assignment. You're both big boys and can take care of yourselves. So, until the next time, I bid you farewell." With that, John Dominicci went to the rear of the car, opened it, and took out a long thin package wrapped in canvas, and gave it to Al. "The Godfather, wanted you to have this." He turned, got in the car, and drove off.

Five hundred yards and unnoticed behind them, three got out of the black sedan and headed into the woods as the black sedan drove off.

Chapter 91 - Ben's Deception

"I don't give a fuck where da fuck youse take him. Take him anywheres. Take him back to his fuckin' hospital. He's a nurse. Take dem two dum-fucks widjahs," Sal barked at Joey and Shark, two thugs interrupted from a game of eight-ball. "Take him to da morgue dere an' leave him dere. Inna body bag."

"A body bag?" Joey was puzzled.

"Yah, a body bag. We keep a couple inna closet under da stairs. Go put 'im inna body bag. Youse can get dem udder two, Ben and da big one — what's his name? Larry? Get Ben and Larry to help ya's.

"Got it. Body bag to da hospital morgue. Where's da morgue at da hospital?"

"Ben or Larry'll know. They was dere. Patients. Now scram."

"Look, point that thing somewhere else. We're not going anywhere", Ben said to Joey, half in worry, half in fear.

"Like I said we're takin' him to da morgue at da hospital to leave him dere, like Sal said."

"Why the hospital morgue? At this time of night?" Larry asked, wedged in the back seat between Ben and Joey, who was half turned with his gun.

"Cuz it ain't as busy dis time of day as da city morgue," said Shark out of the corner of his mouth, his head twisted over his right shoulder, eyes still on the road, one hand on the wheel, the other waving as he spoke.

"Guess that makes sense", said Larry. "Where you going in? Through emergency?"

"Fuck no. Gotta key card to one of da back doors, receivin'. Go in dere."

They rode on in silence, stopping at all the lights, not speeding. "Don't take no chances", Joey told Shark when they set out. "Not wid a stiff inna trunk." It was dark in back in the receiving area. The key card opened one of the doors.

"Hey, you. Larry, Gimme a hand here. Shark had trouble lifting Steve's bag out of the trunk. Larry did just as requested. He lifted almost the entire load with one hand, and swung it up onto the loading platform, almost taking Shark with it.

"So you're going to carry this mess down the corridor, up the elevator, and down the hall to the morgue, which, by the way, will be well lighted, all this and not get caught?" Ben asked. Larry noted that Ben had been very quiet. He hoped his young friend wouldn't try anything foolish. The guns were in the goons' pockets, but would be out in a flash if needed.   "Okay, smart-ass, how you wanna do it." Joey obviously had never done this before.   "I can go in and get a gurney", Ben said, "and we can put a sheet over him, like they do with all dead people.

"Yah, so you can run off to some cop. No way, fuck-face."

"So one of you come with me."

They returned in less than two minutes with gurney and sheet, loaded Steve, the sheet over the bag, and started.

Ben knew his way around alright. Those days when he wasn't busy with rehab or shooting the bull with Larry, he had wandered the hospital, checking it all out. He led them down hallways, elevators, more hallways. They all looked the same. Another turn. Down a slight ramp. Larry sensed Ben was up to something. *Where in hell is he going?* They passed a few people, all intent on their own missions, no one noticing anything unusual. They passed by a well-lighted double door with a sign over it:

OPERATING ROOM
AUTHORIZED PERSONNEL ONLY

What the hell is he up to? Larry wondered, but he was ready for whatever Ben was planning. They passed another door, Ben out front, pulling the gurney with Larry at the rear, and a goon on each side, looking bewildered, but ready for trouble. Another sign over double doors:

STERILE PRECAUTIONS
NO ADMITTANCE

Ben swung a hard right, punched an automatic door opener, and pulled the gurney through into a new hallway, his entourage following, the doors closing behind them.

"Hey you can't be in here. This here's restricted. Sterile precautions. Hats and masks. No street clothes." It was a tall, thin male appropriately attired in a scrub suit, hat, mask.

"Fuck you! Who says," Ben yelled too loud. "Who's gonna make me. You and what army. Huh, big shot. I'm going any fuckin' place I wanna." People heard the noise and came running down the hall. Joey and Shark were stopped in their tracks, surprised first by the outburst by this mild-mannered kid, and second by the assembling crowd, gathering ten feet away from these intruders invading their holy, sterile inner sanctum. "And in contaminated street clothes!"

Ben put on his best scowling, belligerent face. Larry caught on, "Yah, we can be any place we wanna be. Free country."

"Call security", someone shouted.

"Yeah, get security down here, stat." Everyone started voicing at once. An angry crowd. Several cell phones out. All — but one — calling security. The one called 911. More staff in scrubs joined the hostile crowd.

"You can't be in here!" demanded some.

"Yah, we could, an' what da fuck you gonna do about it." Ben turned around, it was Shark shouting back. Just what Ben had hoped for.

A large, tightly-packed woman in her fifties swiftly pushed through the crowd, obviously in charge. "Just what do you gentlemen think you're doing in here. Please remove yourselves immediately. This is a restricted area."

Ben was about to yell back, when Joey pulled his gun, and waved it around at no one in particular.

"Whoa!"

"Jeeziz."

"Look out!" Everyone yelling. The crowd pressed back against those behind them.

The double doors behind the gurney opened and two hospital security men barged in. "What seems to be the trouble, here?", asked one. The other seeing the weapon in Joey's fist, quickly backed out through the closing automatic doors.

"Don't nobody do nuthin'. We're goin' to da morgue, so you let us pass, an' nobody gets hurt." Joey growled in his most authoritative voice, hoping he was sounding like Sal.

"The morgue's in the basement."

"The morgue ain't here."

"Watchout! He's got a gun."

"Morgue? Why the morgue?"

"Don't shoot."

"You're in the wrong place."

"No morgue here." All advising at once. Chaotic noise. Joey and Shark looking confused. Ben trying to look as tough and defiant as he could. Larry, trying to be serious, but letting his smile show just a bit. *Ben is so smart. He be de man!*

The automatic doors reopened. Five hospital security and three uniformed city police, guns drawn, surrounded Larry and Shark, but aiming at Joey. "Drop your weapon. Now! Hands in the air where we can see them."

Joey started to turn, "Move and you're a dead man!" one of the uniforms barked. Joey froze and dropped his gun which clattered on the hard tiled floor. "You too, buster." He was looking at Ben, whose hands shot to the ceiling. "Get your people outta here", he commanded to the burly woman in charge, who stepped into the circle and faced the crowd.

"Alright, people, back to your jobs. Security can take care of this. Come on, come on. Let's go. Back to work. This is not in your job description." The crowd began to disperse.

Running footsteps in the hall resounded. Three more uniformed city police came rushing through the door, guns drawn.

"Okay, what's this all about?" the older police officer asked, turning to Ben. Ben's smile broke into a wide grin.

Chapter 92 - Pinned Down

They were pinned down. No escape route either side or behind. The three goons, well positioned behind the equally spaced big boulders, could shoot from three different angles. John had the pistol that Al had unwrapped from the canvas, but he knew it was useless in his untrained hands. *Better to hold it for Al if, we ever get out of here. Out of here? Out of this old shed? It doesn't look so good. If they charge across that old sandlot, what's it, fifty yards? We're stuck. It would be only a matter of time. They're obviously gunning to get us both. Damn, I don't get it. First, Angelo has his assassin take us out here, allegedly to escape, and then has his goons come knock us off. Doesn't add up?* John paused, *Get a hold of yourself.* He forced himself not to think about the dire circumstances. He tried to think about Annie B, of the life they had had together. *So many good times.*

A burst of bullets splintered the wood window frame a foot from his head. He ducked down and glanced over at Al.

Cool as a cucumber, Al was sighting an old M-1 rifle, also in the canvas gift from Angelo. His head exposed over the sill, he pulled back down, looked at John with his usual half-grin, and whispered, loudly, "Got five shots. Gotta make 'em count. I was pretty good, once, but it's been a while." He eased his way up again. Another blast from an A-K rifle shattered some more of the wood frame. Splinters flying, Al ducked again. A pause. Quiet. The attackers were planning something. He could hear them talking, but couldn't make out what they were saying. He inched up again. The guy on the left was clearly visible, head and shoulders, talking to the guy in the middle. Al slid the rifle over the sill, and sighted in. Focused, jaw muscles tight, he forced himself to relax. *Let go,* he told himself. *A Marine forgets the danger, knows the details. Careful, intentional. No wasted movements.* He took aim, finger lightly on the trigger. Taking a deep breath, he held it for three seconds, then let it out, slowly, completely. Then he slowly squeezed the trigger.

Blam!

John jumped even though he knew it was coming. The head

on the guy on the left, a hundred and fifty feet away, disappeared into a cloud of blood and debris, blood shooting up from open carotids. The body dropped out of sight. Another burst from the far right. Splinters flew. Quiet.

More talk. The guy on the right and the guy in the center. Another plan. A sudden burst from the right, longer. The guy from the center charged across the open space, coming at them, with his A-K blasting rapid, short bursts. Wood flying everywhere, John ducked lower. He saw Al rise up again, sighting in, trained to be calm and composed before firing the critical, but tough shot. "Jeeziz, get down", John shouted. Blam! Smoke, dust, quiet. Al was still up. Still a target.

"Think I got him" Al said to the open space in front of him. The guy on the right came out, heading toward them. Blam! He tripped and went down. His A-K flew off to his right. Quiet again. It stayed quiet. Al was still looking down the barrel of his rifle, but not sighting in on anything. Just watching his quarry.

"Gimme the gun", he barked at John. John looked up. "What?"

"Gimme the gun. The pistol I gave ya. Quick. Give it to me."

John came alive, and shoved the pistol into Al's extended palm. Al vaulted over the splintered sill and ran out toward the goons. The one in the center wasn't moving, but the guy on the right was creeping toward his A-K some eight feet away.

John, eyes glued on Al, watched him run toward the goon on the right, toward to A-K in the dirt. The goon was struggling toward the A-K, but Al got there first. The goon stopped, rolled over onto his back with obvious pain. His left lower leg did not roll with him. As the goon grabbed for what had been his knee, John could see, even from the fifty yards distance, the mess of the shattered leg.

John ran out to join Al. Blood was oozing from shredded back of the goon's pants at the knee. Clutching the leg just above the knee, he rocked back and forth, moaning in agony.

Al gave the goon's A-K to John. "If he moves, pull the trigger", Al told John, then bending toward the goon, "You hear that! You move, he pulls the trigger. Blow that fuckin' excuse of a head of yours off the fat blob of a neck. You got that? One move."

The pistol still in his other hand, Al walked over to the other goon. When Al nudged him with his foot, the goon made an attempt to roll onto his back. He made it halfway. Al's foot shoved him the rest of the way. The goon, in shock, looked up at Al, questioning, confused. The blood bubbling out of his mouth which made his attempted words a slur. Trying to lift his head, he gave a weak cough, spraying bright red blood all over. His squinting eyes tried to focus on the pistol Al was pointing at his head, but he coughed again, and collapsed back down, his eyes rolling up. He lay completely still. Al, motionless himself, watched him for another two minutes. The blood had stopped oozing from his nose and mouth. Flies began swarming and buzzing around him, landing in his bloody, open mouth. They knew death.

Al returned to John standing guard over the goon, clutching at his knee and moaning. "Gimme the A-K", he told John, "and dial 911. Give them the location, details. No names."

John dialed and spoke the details. Al could hear the reply: "Stay on the line, please. It will help us track you, sir. Please stay calm. An ambulance is on its way. Please stay on the line. Don't hang up." John hung up, and put the phone back in his pocket.

Looking around, Al ordered, "Let's go. We're outta here pronto, partner. Bring the A-K. It's got your prints on it. I'll get the rifle from the shed."

Chapter 93 - He May Still Be Alive

Ben, turning to the cop who seemed to be in charge, rushed his words. "The kid in the body bag may still be alive, so we really ought to take him to the ER. He's gonna need some blood transfusions."

"Turn around, and hands in the air", the younger cop ordered.

The senior cop was more relaxed, "Cuff 'em, all four of 'em."

"Officer, this is not only a medical emergency, but it is not what it seems. Please have your men check the kid in the body bag to see if he still has a pulse. We can explain it all later."

"What nonsense you talkin'?" This cop, a black female, was shorter than the others, but just as strong.

Ben persisted, a pleading look on his boyish face, "You, officers....... trained in CPR. Please check his pulse. See if he's still got a carotid pulse. Please!" he begged.

"I can do it", one of the hospital security said stepping forward.

"You four, move away. Give him room", the senior cop said.

The hospital security officer, unzipped the bag part way, revealing Steve's ashen face, unresponsive. He carefully placed his fingers where Steve's carotids should be, and looked up, surprised. "Jeezis, he does have a pulse. Weak and rapid, but he's got a pulse. Ted, help me get him to the ER. Stat."

"Officer, have one of your men take me to the ER with Steve. I can give them information which might just save Steve's life, here", Ben said.

"Yessir", Larry added, nodding his head vigorously. "Ben's right about that. He's telling you the truth. He had it done to him."

"Yah, and I'm the Pope's cousin", scoffed the young cop next to Ben.

Three of the hospital security men quickly wheeled the gurney out of the double doors. They had done emergency runs before.

"Let him go with them, officer", Larry said to the senior cop.

"Shut up, bozo", the lady cop said.

"There's a chance they can save his life, if they know what the problem is," Ben told the senior cop. Everyone started talking at once.

"Okay, okay, pipe down, everyone", the senior cop bellowed. "Okay, junior, what're you talking about?

"The Mafia, these guys", Ben said pointing at Joey, "had us, Larry and me", Ben nodded his head toward Larry, "captive with Steve there. They took a lot of Steve's blood in a bag. Until he passed out. They thought he was dead."   "Dead? Whata ya mean they thought he was dead?" the lady cop asked. She was behind Shark, her gun aimed at his back.

"Just what I said", Ben said. "They had Larry check his pulse."

"Yeah, I checked it. He had a weak, fast pulse, but I told them there was no pulse, so they thought he was dead and made us bring him here, to the hospital morgue," Larry explained.

"So, when we got here, I led them up here, on purpose, knowing that there'd be a lot of people who could do something", Ben said.

"Sounds like a bunch of bullshit to me", the cop behind Joey mumbled.

"Okay, okay. Maybe you're legit, may be you're not", the senior cop said. "Officer Thomas, take this one down to the ER, so he can tell them whatever it is they need to know. I've got no idea what the crap he's talking about, but we'll give him his chance. Then out to the squad cars. We'll meet you there in ten. Take all of them downtown."

The ER team had Steve out of the body bag and stripped naked. Full resuscitative measures were well under way as Ben and Officer Thomas reached Trauma Room 3.

"Labs sent yet?" Rick McIver, chief surgical resident, asked.

"Yeah, they're gone. Looks like a fairly dense coma, but no other overt evidence of the cause to the hypotension-tachycardia.

It's acting like a severe blood loss with no apparent cause", Gordy Duke, third year resident, announced, busily rechecking the physical exam. "Ninety over fifty BP, and one forty. Weak."

"Excuse me, but I might be able to help you", Ben offered.

Rick's head whipped around, surprised to see the intruder, hands cuffed behind him, with a uniformed officer. "Who's this guy?", he asked Liz Johns, the charge nurse, her scrub suit still covered with nine-and-a-half hours of other people's secretions.

"Dunno", she said turning to Ben, "Who are you?"

"This person is Steve, and he's had his blood removed. He should respond to blood transfusions. His blood tests should show a really low level. Believe me. I know what I'm talking about. This happened to me a couple of months ago, right here in this hospital." Ben hoped he had it right.

"What do you mean? Where'd you get that idea?" Gordy had doubts. "You a new guy?" Then he saw the handcuffs. "Who the hell are you?"

Officer Thomas saw the resentment building. He said to Ben, "Tell them the whole story." Both Rick and Gordy stopped and listened.

"This is Steve," he began. "Don't know his last name. He was caught stealing from some Mafia guys, so they made me put an IV into him and sucked out a lot of his blood. Enough so he went and passed out. Larry and I were also their captives, but that's another story."

"Sucked out his blood? What'd they do that for?"

"That's a long story. What I'm trying to tell you, is that Steve needs blood. He lost blood. A lot. He needs some back. That's what they did for me. No, not what they — what you, you hospital guys — did for me. That is also another story."

Liz, on the phone, broke in, "Jeeziz, his hemoglobin is two point two!"

Rick looked incredulously at Ben. "Tell me that again. Someone drew off some blood from the patient. Enough for him to pass out?" He paused and looked at Gordy. "Whatever the story, he may be right. Liz get four units here stat, and stay four ahead."

The blood was started, pumped in through several IVs,

through large-bore catheters, as Ben was questioned. Slowly his story came out. By the time the second unit was in, and the third started, the blood pressure slowly came up, and eventually the pulse slowed over the next half hour.

Meanwhile, Dr. Thornton Brooks, the surgical attending on call, had arrived. Rick interrupted his questioning of Ben to bring Dr. Brooks up to date on the case. Brooks thought about it for a bit, he turned to Ben, and asked, "You're not medically trained?"

"No sir", Ben replied, "I'm a college student.....was a college student. I had to drop out this semester because of my injury."

"Injury? What injury, and why do you look vaguely familiar to me?"

"I was knocked off my bike, and was taken care of here at University".

"When was that?" Brooks scanned Ben, looking puzzled.

"I was the one in the hospital who had that nurse, who turned out to be Steve, here", Ben explained, indicating the comatose body with a finger wave. "He was illegally drawing my blood, and Dr. Pullman told me I almost died before they gave it back to me. And this person here is Steve, the guy who did the bad blood drawing on me."

"Right. You were a patient of John Pullman's? Yeah, I think I remember your case." Speaking to Rick, "He was presented at Trauma M&M."

"Yessir. There's more," added Ben. "The Mafia people had Dr. Pullman and his nurse, Mr. Towns caught, right there with us, too."

"What do you mean by that?" Brooks asked. "The Mafia people? What Mafia people?"

"These two guys here, Joey and Shark, and a bunch of others. Billy is their boss, and Sal is even......"

"That's okay. Never mind," Brooks interrupted. "The police will get all that. How much blood did you draw off," Brooks turned toward the body, "from Steve, here?"

"Not me, sir. The Mafia boss, Sal ordered the blood drawing. I'm guessing that one bag was more than twice the size of what you give at the blood bank, and the second bag was started when Steve passed out. That's when Sal told his men to make us take Steve to the hospital morgue, except I didn't take them to the morgue. I took them to the operating room, where I knew they would be caught."

With this, Officer Thomas jerked his head up. He had been writing notes, focusing on the conversation. "Wait a minute. This is getting complicated. Weren't those other men back there, Mafia? In the operating place?"

Another half dozen uniformed policemen crowded in the trauma room door. Everyone started talking at once — to each other and on cell phones. Questions. Opinions. Chaos.

Liz hung up and shouted, "Everyone out. Not a physician involved in this case? Then get out." Sudden silence. All eyes on Liz. "Go on. Outta here! That means you!" The veins were standing out on her neck. "Chester, take them to the conference room." Chester, the little, old, hospital security man, sitting quietly in the corner, as he usually did, leapt to his feet.

The room cleared but for Thornton Brooks, Rick McIver, Gordy Duke, Liz Johns, and Steve, whose blood pressure and pulse after six units, had begun to normalize. Officer Thomas ushered Ben out. The physicians reviewed Steve's most recent results: EKG normalized, blood gases normal, hemoglobin ten. Good breath sounds, bilateral chest. Abdominal exam benign. Urine output picking up. Only outstanding abnormality: Steve was still comatose.

Chapter 94 - The Mini Dictator

Annie B had delayed the three patients scheduled for the late morning until later that afternoon. They were to see John for post-op follow up. Nothing urgent. She had cancelled the rest of his morning: Infection Control Committee meeting, and an hour and a half preceptorship with fourth year medical students, which David Allen, John's partner, had volunteered to teach. The only other item on his schedule, a Medical Records Committee meeting, had been canceled anyway.

So John, in a very unusual move, obeyed Annie B and stayed home. Annie B covered the office on the computer at home. John, true to fashion had been ready to go, but Annie B had been adamant that he stay home, "You're to do absolutely nothing but relax. You can go have lunch with the boys, if you really want to. Until then, mister, you sit right here and tell me all about it." She had been right; he had to admit it. The shakes, starting in the shower that morning, were quieting down. The terror of the day before had finally gotten to him, but Annie B always had the answer.

The night before and seen a quiet, simple supper at home, the TV news, and early bed. John had cuddled with Annie B, reliving the harrowing day's trials, as he unloaded his burden to her in the private, supportive closeness of their nightly ritual.

"You knew about the luncheon with Angelo at Pasgucci's Italian," he spoke quietly, "but something happened to Angelo. One of his men came up and whispered something in his ear, and his whole attitude changed. I could see it come over his face. He tried to act natural, but I could tell something was wrong. Next thing I knew, Al and I were locked in the back of one of his sedans."

"My god. Why would he do something like that?" she asked, looking at her husband there in the dark.

"Wait, there's more, a lot more. We were questioned by Sal, Angelo's Underboss. Then Al and I and Larry, the big guy, and that kid, Ben, had to watch as the Mafia Underboss, Sal, had Steve, that outlaw nurse, exsanguinated. Steve was the one who was supposedly stealing blood from trauma patients in the hospital last month, causing those unexplained deaths on Trauma I told you about. Sal bled that poor, dumb kid of what must have been more than three to four liters. He passed out, in shock. He made us watch."   "Watch his murder? That's horrible!", she said.

"There was nothing we could do but watch. That's when John Dominicci, the Mob's assassin, came in and took Al and me out of there. I'm not sure why, but it seemed like Angelo had another change of heart, or new information, or something. He had John take us to a vacant lot outside of town, and damned if he didn't give us an old M-1 rifle and an old six-shooter before he drove away."

"He let you get away?"

"Not quite. It was more like he abandoned us. There was a carload of goons following us. Maybe his, maybe Sal's. We'll never know, but these three guys started shooting at us. Al spotted them, figured we were set up. If it wasn't for Al, I'd be a dead man. He had us run for cover to this old shack on one side of the clearing when the shooting started. I've been shot at before, but never by three guys with automatic weapons. But, once again Al, once a Marine, always a..... He saved our bacon. He got all three of the attackers. He had me call 911. Then we took off. It was after that, that I called you."

"My god, what a terrible ordeal. My poor sweetie, my poor, dear sweetie. I'm so glad you're here now. Safe and sound. With me."

"I've been thinking about it. It doesn't make sense."

"Of course it doesn't, but what do you mean?"

"It's Angelo. I don't understand Angelo. Angelo and the whole Mafia mind set. For a guy with his talent for leadership, and organizational skills, he comes up so shallow. He seems so easily misled. Too quick to react on the latest information, without checking the veracity. You'd say he's just a bad seed, but that personality change in the hospital, showed that deep down, there is basically a decent person. Good, honest, even moral. Yet he runs extortion rackets, sells protection against his own thugs, addicts young girls to drugs and prostitutes them as sex slaves. If they get pregnant, he sells their babies. He runs money laundering schemes, drugs, extortion, and more. All sorts of other illegal scams that punish the innocent. What kind of person does these things?"

"Yes, I know. You read about this stuff, but when it hits close to home....", she said, trying to calm his mounting anxiety.

"What kind of person? Is this the dictator personality? Never completely sure of himself. Covering up insecurities with bluster, force, and fear. Murdering any who cross him. It's almost as if he, and those like him, had varying levels of reaction. Varying levels of brute behavior mixed with intermittent forgiveness of some sort? One minute he's my buddy, all fun and gratitude. Takes me, takes us to lunch. The next minute he's got us locked in his car and interrogated in his cellar."

"That's an interesting insight. I never considered it in that light," she mused.

"What a miserable way to have to live your life. All based on hate, fear, rumors, uncertainty. Constant defense, constant lying, never knowing who is out to get you next. He's quick to anger with violent actions, often based on hear-say without proof. Fake news, as they say. Destroy your enemies, or those you perceive as your enemies. Murdering, stealing, cheating. Constant doubt. Completely callous to the lives of others that you mess up."

"I'm afraid you're right about most of this", she said, "but quiet down now. This is our time to relax. Let it go. Bury the world's problems, my sweet boy. You're safe here in our home, in our own bed, with me."

John took deep breath and slowly let it out in a long sigh. "Yes, Annie B, my love. As usual, you're right. You make the world right for me. Every day, every hour, year after year. Thank god, you never change. My strength, my stabilizer, my love. I love you, sweetheart."

"I love you, too. It's been a long day, but it's time for sleep."

Chapter 95 - I Want To Call My Lawyer

Joey sat, handcuffed to the metal chair, chest against the metal table. The police interrogation room was decorated in concrete. Shark, also cuffed, sat next to him. Looking the detective in the eye, Joey blabbed, "We ain't done nuthin'. It was them guys Ben an' Larry. They was callin' all the shots."

"I see. That's why you an' him had the Uzis, and them two didn't."

"Yah, they was takin' us to de morgue. They was leadin'. Me, I'm just followin' orders. Me an' him." He tossed his head in Shark's direction.

The thinner detective leaning against the wall said, "Yeah, and I'm the sugar-plum fairy. Why was you guys in the hospital in the first place?"

"I tol' ya. We was followin' orders. We don't got nuthin' to do wit dis guy there. An' that's all I got to say. Followin' orders."

"Guess they need to refresh their memories. Put 'em in cell five with that gang of Jamaicans. They don't like wops. Soften 'em up a little," he said to the other cop.

"I wanna lawyer", Shark barked. "I ain't goin' nowhere widout my lawyer."

"You can call your lawyer soon as your memory gets a little better. Meantime you can tell it to the Jamaicans."

Two rooms down, Ben and Larry had better memories, but their answers were no more credible. Both detectives were pacing the room, one staring at the floor, the other looking from Ben to Larry and back. Hard eye contact.

"I been a cop a long time, and I heard a lotta stories, but you guys ought be writin' novels. I never heard such a pile of bullshit in my life. I'd say you're wastin' my time, but that there is a great story. Too fuckin' bad I don't believe a word of it." Then he turned to his partner, "I say stick'em inna cell an' let the day shift deal."

"What is it with you guys?" The second detective stopped pacing and leaned both hands on the chair back opposite Ben and Larry. "Ya-know, if you had some real smarts, you'd level with us, and cut out all this Mafia shit. It's gonna go a lot easier on you if you tell the truth. Tell us what really happened. Ya-know."

Ben looked at Larry, confused, not knowing what to do next. Larry had nothing to add to Ben's retelling of the previous events. He had told it like it happened. But Larry had been in police stations many times before in his checkered career. He looked up at the cop, "I want to call my lawyer."

"Yah, sure, and who's your lawyer?" said with a sneer. "Melvin Belli?"

"No. I want to call Mr. J. Edwards Baird. "

"The DA. Yeah, sure, and I wanna call J Edgar Hoover."

"Mr Baird, this is Larry Lowance. I'm sorry to bother you. We talked on the phone the other day, when I was in Dr. Pullman's office, about that nurse Steve who was stealing Ben's blood in the hospital, and I told you I saw him on the street, and you said you wanted him for questioning."

At the mention of Dr. Pullman, the officer leaning on the chair straightened up, questions written all over his face.

There was a moment of silence before J. Edwards Baird's voice answered, his reply amplified over the room speakers. "Hello Larry. Sure I remember. Have you some additional news for me? Did you find him?"

"Yessir. I found him alright, but it's kind of a long story, sir."

"Well, Larry, I want to hear every detail. Can you come to my office first thing in the morning?"

"Yessir. I'd like to very much, but I can't."

"Okay. When's better time? I want to get you on a recorded statement. Would you do that for me?"

"Oh yessir. Be glad to. Just can't right now because, I......."

"Name your time, son. Want it sooner than later."

"Yessir, but you see I'm in the police station, and this is my call to my lawyer, they let me have."

"The police station? What happened? Why are you in the police station? What did you do? You in trouble?"

"Um, yessir, and no sir." Larry was so anxious, he was both sweating and trembling, almost tongue-tied, "We escaped from

Mr. Sal, the Mafia guy with Steve the nurse who you're looking for. Mr. Sal took his blood like they do at the Red Cross, except more, and he passed out, so we took him to......"

"Wait a minute. Wait a minute, Larry. Hang on a second. You've lost me. Have you met Steve, the nurse, or not?.........Where are you?.....Now?"

"Yessir, Mr. Baird." Larry paused to collect himself. "The Steve guy is in the hospital where we brought him from the Mafia......"

Ben started tapping Larry on the shoulder. Larry turned to him. "Tell him you've been arrested at the police station, and you need him to please come down to clear up the situation and get us released."

"Yes, Mr. Baird, Ben said to tell you......"

"Yes, Larry. I heard him. Let me talk to the officer there."

Larry shoved the phone toward to cop facing him, "He wants to talk to you."

"Officer King speaking."

"Good evening Officer King, this is J. Edwards Baird. I'm the DA......"

"Yessir, I know who you are, sir. These two......"   "Keep them right there. All of them, if there are some others. I'll be down in about twenty minutes. Lets see if we can get this cleared up."

Chapter 96 - Another Lunch

"You know, you're right about that, Dave", Al Towns said as he watched David Allen take a gigantic bite of his BLT.

"Yeah, you are right. His is a very unstable personality type," John Pullman added. He was sitting to David Allen's left, the third person at the table for four, opposite the vacant chair. "You know who would know a lot about that, Mal Salteese. It's one of his areas of speciality."

"And speaking of the devil, here he comes now," Al Towns said, shifting in his seat to pull out the vacant chair. "Come, join us, Mal. We were just talking about you."

"Well, in that case, I guess I better sit down.... keep the gossip to a minimum", the neuropsychiatrist said with his smile so big, his teeth looked like a Colorado ski poster. "Or is this something I shouldn't be a party to?"

"No, no, no. You're the expert on this. You're the guy we all quote," David half rose in his seat to greet the older physician, who looked a little perplexed. "We were trying to psychoanalyze Angelo Ginnini."

"What I'm having trouble with, is his inconsistency," John said after Mal was seated. "One minute he's your friend, warm, welcoming; the next minute he's holding you prisoner with murderous intent. Or at least letting his subordinates do so. An hour later, he has you escorted to freedom with a personal gift of some old, but serviceable guns. The next minute, some of his goons try to gun us down. He seems to bounce from one extreme to the other, depending on the latest information or accusation he's heard."   "Yes, well that would be consistent with what we already know about him. What brought this lovely subject up?" Mal asked, looking around the table, particularly at John and Al Towns.

"John started it all," David said, "Of course he's been out of our office a lot recently, most of it as Angelo's guest, so I guess he has a right to bitch about it."

"I'm not really bitching about him, but I was thinking about him last night in bed. About how inconsistent his reasoning seems to be. It's hard to know if he has an overall plan or agenda or if he just reacts to the cards with each new deal. Does he really know what's going on?"

"Yeah. That's what he tries to present himself as, the big deal maker. Big hotshot. Bigger and better than anyone else," Al Towns said. "You cross him, or if he thinks that you've crossed him, he strikes mercilessly. Starts lying about you. Or worse, annihilates you on the spot, without thinking through the consequences to you or anyone else. He lies all the time. He's basically a bully, skating on thin ice. He creates half the crises, himself, then lashes out. At least that's how he appears to me."

"Al, that's a very accurate description of an active-aggressive personality," Mal Salteese said. "These types, unfortunately, are often educated but poorly read, or poorly informed by their colleagues, particularly with regard to the power they wield. They gain the power by out-blustering and out-acting their opposition on the way up. It's true in many types of situations where power is involved. All the way from the man in the streets, to politicians, to Mafia bosses. That doesn't mean that all who achieve power do so with this methods. Far from it. This is only a small fraction of those so involved."

"Mal, that's fascinating. I know a guy like that. He's a minor-league politician, but fits that description to a tee," David said. "He holds on to his seat mainly with bluster and deception. Half the people want to impeach him, and the other half love him. Those who love him say he may be unorthodox, but they say he gets things done. He's kind of their folk-hero, can do no wrong. He does get things done, changes made, but they are mostly the wrong things, done the wrong way."

"History is full of these guys," John said. "Think of Huey B. Long. Think of the leadership in Tammany Hall. Jimmy Hoffa. Whitey what's his name up there in Boston years ago. Same type of modus operandi that we read about with these Mafia bosses.....all those crime bosses, whether they be Italian, Jamaican, Oriental, Irish, you name it. All work the same way, telling the populous what they want to hear, to win favor and power, and disposing of their opposition."

Heads nodded around the table. Al Towns said, "It's a pretty fine line between the legal and the illegal action path they take against those who oppose them."

"That's true. Some are farther from the fine line on the negative side. You kill one guy, it's murder. You kill ten thousand, it's making the country better, a solidification of power. Look at Hitler. Stalin was worse."

"Well, thank god, Angelo hasn't killed, or had killed, that many. At least that we know of," David said shaking his head. "Maybe he'll get his own TV show, like "The Sopranos", except the real thing. Boost his ego even more?"

"Or run for Congress, or the Presidency. You never know who they'll elect these days. Just tell the great unwashed what they want to hear, and you've got their vote. They'll vote for anybody, no matter what his....or her, qualifications may be."

Mal said, "The mini-dictator personality is a very common personality type these days. It occurs around the world. The media, the internet, mass communication — all these sources of information bring these types to our doorstep daily. Look around, you'll see it everywhere. The problem is not recognizing them, it's what we can do about it when it becomes pervasive, becomes a threat to society, both locally and on the grand scale. We've got the diagnosis, but not the treatment, yet."

"Okay, there it is, Mal," Al Towns said with a grin. "There's your Nobel Prize. Right there for the asking. Get the answer. Solve all my problems."

"I'm on it," Mal said, "just as soon as you guys cure cancer. Piece of cake."

"Now that we've solved that problem, gentlemen, I've got to get to the office." John said as he stood, gathering his lunch tray. "Haven't been there much recently, thanks to our unpredictable friend,"

"You ought to put all your experiences in a book," Mal Salteese said, again displaying his Rocky Mountain teeth with his big, characteristic smile.

John, also smiling, "Someday, maybe, just maybe, I will.

With your picture on the cover."

With that the other three rose as one, and all four put their trays on the dirty-dish conveyor belt into the kitchen.

Chapter 97- A Sit Down Or A Showdown

"Angelo, my old and trusted friend. It's so nice I should hear from you. I'm returning your call", the voice on the other end of the phone was the most pleasant-sounding it had been all day, so far. "There must be sometin' I could do for you, my friend. Name it. Anythin', I'm good for it, Angelo."

Angelo knew the voice was lying. He knew it, and he knew that Carmine knew he knew it. It was part of the game age-old enemies played against each other.

"Yah, Carmine. Thanks for returning the call. You're a gentleman and a scholar." *Bullshit deserves more bullshit. You sure took your time calling me back, asshole.*

"So what's on that brilliant mind of yours that you should be callin' little guys like me?", Carmine asked.

"Carmine, you was at the sit-down Sal Ucciderita called for some of the families. When I was.....away......away on sick leave. You was nice enough to come. I guess your nephew, Tiny Gambini couldn't make it." *I have no idea why the fuck Sal included you, but he did. Now I got this problem. Even the score.*

"Yah. Your sub, Sal, handled hisself good. Had a question. Asked the question. Called the vote. Meeting over. He's a good boy. Keep yer eye on him, I would. One never knows. Right, Angelo?"

Angelo ignored the barb. "My waiter, Herbie, at Pasgucci's Italian, died. You heard, I suppose."

"Yah. I did. Too bad. They say he was a nice kid, too. A little short onna smarts, but a nice kid." *So what'd you call me fer? Not to talk about some dumbass waiter,* Carmine thought, *come on, out wit it, asshole.*

"There's been a lotta talk going around the city."

"Yah? What talk you speakin' of?" Carmine knew what talk Angelo meant, but he wasn't about to let on.

"They're saying that since that sit-down Sal had, when I was away.....and, by the way, I told Sal, he done good when I was away...... They're saying that our families are having a problem." *And the fact that your boy, Tiny Gambini hired to have me shot, that's a problem.* "No cooperation. I'm thinking a short sit-down, you and me. I got a nice bottle of Chianti. Puff on a Cuban, maybe. Then a photo op that we.....uh, as they say, 'leak', to the DA and the papers. Shows unification, cooperation, strength. You get my drift."

"Yah, sure, Angelo. That ain't a bad idea. I like the flavor of it. Good for public relations. Name the time and place."

They agreed on lunch at Pasgucci's Italian. Each ended the call thinking details, offense, defense, and a lot of "what-ifs."

"Juanito, my boy. Always my good boy," Angelo said. "I got a little something needs doing. Something only you with your class and talent can handle."

John Dominicci had heard this before, but it always made him feel good every time he heard it. This was from the Godfather, after-all.

"Yes sir. You're very kind. What can I do for you, Godfather?"

"You know who was responsible for my being away.....for my temporary illness."

"Yes, Godfather. We're talking about Tiny Gambini."

"The same." He nodded in silence.

"Yes, Godfather. I will take care of the problem."

Three days later a small item appeared near the bottom of page ten of *The City Tribune*: "Mobster slain in kitchen." The article went on to suggest, that according to a police spokesperson, it appeared to be a "professional hit, perhaps mob related."

"I called you, my closest and best advisors." Angelo, sitting in his throne, looked at the four men seated around the table. "We're having a sit-down with Carmine Sciucci and a few of his people. Only that ain't gonna happen. We need to have a little payback. I know you been wondering when it should happen by now. This is the time. One of Carmine's boys already had a little accident. It's time for the rest."

All four heads nodded, solemnly. Nodded with a small smile. Then, as one, all looked up at Angelo, waiting, totally focusing on him.

"Each of you will be assigned a target of responsibility. There will be three of them, with Carmine the fourth. John," he said to John Dominicci, "you will be with me, focusing on Carmine, himself. For you, Sal, Oogie, and Manny, I have a team of four very good, very discrete gentlemen, army ranger trained, coming on assignment. They work for a private organization. One will work with each of you to set up the plan, which will go as follows."

"The five of us will be riding in the big car. Sal, you drive. John, you ride shotgun. Me, Oogie, and Manny will be in back. Oogie, you get the jump seat. Carmine and his people will be coming from the East side in their car. One car per family. We agreed on that. We also agreed no one carries. Leave 'em home. We're going to Pasgucci's Italian. I picked it. But we're not actually going there. The snipers will have intercepted Carmine and his boys before they get there."

"Where they doin' that?", Sal asked, "Inna square there, two blocks before Pasgucci's?"

"Yah, the snipers will be in those four alleys that face on that intersection. It was their boss's suggestion. He took a look at it, and that's what he recommended. His boys move in, and take them out. Two shots in each head. Fire bomb the car with the bodies."

Angelo continued, "The sniper team arrives tomorrow. You guys go to the airport to meet and greet, and take 'em home to your place. Nice and quiet. Word gets out and the deal goes down."

"Billy's supposed to be comin' for supper tomorrow......," Manny said.

"Billy's not going anywhere near you or your place. You got that. This here meeting, this here plan never existed. You got that?" Angelo was staring at Oogie. Oogie stared at his crotch. "You got that?....... I asked you a question.....You got that?...... All of you got that?"

The heads nodded, again.

"Last thing we need is for this little caper to get out and start a range war of the families." He looked at each man in turn. Only John Dominicci looked him back in the eye. "They're all gonna figure it out eventually, but by then things will have calmed down. So keep a lid on it. End of discussion."

Chapter 98 - The Unexpected Encounter

Something bothered Angelo. A feeling in the back of his head. Something. He wasn't sure what it was. *Maybe it's me and my top people are all in the same car, going to a somewhat risky meeting. But if things all go as planned there's no risk. I gotta stop worrying. Like Yogi Berra said, "a deja-vu all over again,", or something like that. Leave it alone. Drive ya nuts.*

They were on Ash Street, a narrow, one-way road, unusually deserted for this time of day. Suddenly a City Police car showed up behind them, lights flashing, a brief whine of the siren.

That feeling grabbed Angelo again.

"I better pull over", Sal said even though there wasn't much room to pull over. Cars were parked on both sides, leaving only one-and-a-half lanes in the middle. Sal stopped just before the stop sign at the cross road.

The cop, in full uniform, hat pulled down over his shades, took his time to swagger, cop-style up to the window, which Sal had just lowered.

"License and registration, please."

"Officer, do you know who is in this car? What youse wanna stop him fer? Whatsa charge?"

"License and registration, please."

"Sal, give him the papers. We can straighten it out later. He may not be one of ours." Angelo said from the back seat.

Sal released his seat belt, and leaned forward to get his wallet from his rear pants pocket. John Dominicci was busy in the glove compartment, looking for the registration. Neither man saw the dump truck pull out from the side street and stop in the middle, blocking the intersection.

Angelo saw it all through the tinted windows. Saw the three men get out of the truck, each holding what looked like a hammer in one hand, and an Uzi in the other. *I shoulda listened to that feeling.* It was his last thought before the windows smashed in. It happened so fast not even John had time to get his hand out of the glove compartment and draw his gun. The last thing Angelo saw was the cop shooting Sal, then turning back toward his cop car.

The last thing he heard were loud explosions of gun fire inside the car, his car.

"Get 'em all? All five of 'em?"

"Yup. De Godfadder don't got no face no more. I made sure of that. Carmine'll want all de details. No back of the head no more, either."

"Got the udder two inna head, too . Gonna need prints to identify. Nuttin' else left."   The apparent leader looked at the third man. The third man looked back, "John Dominicci. That was John Dominicci. I done John Dominicci. Mr. Untouchable, an' I done him. Ain't no Mr. Pretty-boy left there, now. No head eidder."

"The cop got Sal, the driver. Pretty obvious."

Sal was a dead weight on the steering wheel horn, the continuous blare announcing the massacre to the faces half-peering, cautiously around apartment curtains on both sides of the street.

By now, the police car was backing down the one way, fast, to the intersection, where it swung a hard left, and sped away.

The curtain-peekers later attested, that three men got in the dump-truck, and were out of sight, "all within thirty seconds, sir. They was fast."

"So, Boss, how'd ja know, I mean that Ginnini was plannin' a trap?"

"So I called Pasgucci's Italian this morning and asked what time for Mr. Ginnini's reservation. Dey said he didn't have none. So, I says to myself, 'Carmine, if they don't got no reservation, they must be plannin' somethin' else', right?' So, what would I plan if I was him? It don't take no genius, ya know."

"Whatta we do now, boss? What you thinkin'?"

"Yer de new Sub-Boss. What you wanna do?"

"I wanna make nice to some of them what's left in their family. See if they lookin' for a new position."

"Dat's called cherry-pickin', my boy. I'm liking da way yer thinkin'. Yer gonna do good in yer new position."

Chapter 99 - Jeb's Loss

"Damn, damn, damn. That son-of-a-bitch. The nerve of the guy. Oh well, I guess he wasn't going to testify anyway." J Edwards Baird, the District Attorney, slammed down the phone.

"Who was that, honey? What's the matter, now", Molly called from the kitchen. She was putting wild flowers in a vase.

"That, my dear wife, was John Redman. You know, the police chief?"

"Bad news, huh?"

"I'll say." Jeb crossed over to the table next to his desk, piled with files and other paperwork. He sorted through them. Found what he was looking for, and pulled it out. After neatly stacking the rest of the papers, he opened the file and mumbled as he read as he moved toward the kitchen. He slapped the file down on the counter, and collapsed into a chair.

Molly came over, wiping her hands on her Earth Day apron, and looked at the name on the file. "Angelo Ginnini. Isn't he the mob boss you got to testify on tape?"

"Yup." Then through pursed lips, Jeb let out a long sigh,. "They've murdered him. Not that he would have testified willingly. He's had a change of heart since he made that tape in the hospital, and they'd probably prevent it from being admitted into the records anyway."

"So, good riddance to bad rubbish, no?"

"No. Pretty much a non-issue now with him dead, but we might have gotten some of the ugliness into the court minutes, and certainly into the papers. John said Angelo and three of his top guys got wiped out. The fifth guy in his car, that big guy, Sal Ucciderita, the so-called Under Boss, was apparently shot too, but he has disappeared. Gone into thin air. John Redman's got an APB out for him, but nada so far."

"Oh honey, that's too bad. I'm sorry for you. That was going to be a big break for you......to get these guys where it hurts them." She bent over and lightly kissed him on his forehead. He looked up at her with a smile.

"Thanks sweetheart. You always take the pain out of the evil

around us. I don't know what I'd do without you. You're the best."
Steepling his fingers under his chin and closing his eyes, he
silently chided himself: *all that work we put in on that bum, all
the concern, all the care — and for what?"* His phone rang. It was
John Pullman.

"Did you hear the news?", John asked.

"Maybe, but did you hear the news?" Jeb answered.

"Give me yours first." John said.

"Angelo's been assassinated, along with a couple of his upper
level henchmen.

"Great minds think alike. That's exactly what I was calling
you about. News travels fast. Bad news travels faster. Al Towns
called me."

"Sounds like a professional job by one of the other families."

"That's what Al said too. He said there was Angelo, John
Dominicci, the enforcer, Oogie Ucciderita and Mannie Parma.
They also shot Sal the Under-boss, but he's not among the
wreckage. He's missing.

"Uhhh", Jeb paused, "Oogie huh? Didn't know they got
Oogie, too"

"Who's this Oogie Ucciderita. He's new to me. Is he related
to Sal Ucciderita?

"Yes. He's Sal's little brother. He's a psychopath. Kills for the
fun of it, gets pleasure from killing. He's the guy that strangled
those three little old ladies in that knitting shop a couple of
months ago. Apparently they hadn't paid their protection money,
so he was sent in to collect the dough, and ended up killing them
instead. Word on the street was that he did it with his own hands.
Tied them each in a chair, and strangled them. One at a time. Slow
death. Actually, one of them died of a heart attack before he
strangled her, but he squeezed her neck anyway, according to the
M.E."

" Yah, I remember reading something about it in the papers.
Nice guy. Glad to have him gone from our community. Him and
that John Dominicci, who, I guess, murdered God-knows how
many," John said. "And, alas, Angelo, too."

"What a waste of your time and talents. No sooner do you get him over the last attack, than he gets wiped out. How's that make you feel? Suppose he hadn't been killed, but showed up in your ER again, looking for you. Would you bust your ass to save him a second time? Knowing who he is, what he's done? Or could you sort of try a little less hard.........you know? If you had it to do over?"

"Jeezis, Jeb. Of course, I'd do everything I could to save him." John said, astonished to even question the issue. "I took the Hippocratic Oath, and I completely believe in it. I'm a doctor, I'm not a judge of who lives and who dies. I do the best I can for every one I treat, no matter who they are."

"Yes, I know you do. I was thinking of it from my perspective. If I had another chance, I'd do my best to fry his ass. Send him away for the duration...............and, there, my good friend, therein lies the difference."

Chapter 100 - Not Again

"It's not really anyone's fault, Mr. Hubner. These things happen," John Pullman was speaking to a reddened face that was trying its best to get angry.

"The hell it's not. He operated on my hernia. I got the recurrence. It's his fault, pure and simple. No ifs ands or buts about it."

"Okay, I'm listening to you. I hear you."

"Yeah, that's good someone's listening to me. My wife won't."

"May I try to give you some objective information that you might find helpful? Let's see if we can work through this together, and get you back in good shape. What do you say?"

John's patience was wearing thin. It had been a long, stressful day, with a large number of patients. Neither he nor Annie B had had time for lunch, having munched a quick sandwich between patients, somewhere around one-thirty. It was all he could do to stay level-headed and objective with Mr. Hubner, who was enjoying being unreasonable and argumentative.

"The good news is that you have discovered your recurrence early, while it's still small, and should be relatively easy to repair for you," John said. "If you look at a thousand indirect inguinal hernia repairs, ten will recur. That's a one percent recurrence rate across the country. Well-published results."

"Yeah, you doctors all stick together." The flushed jowls shook as his head bobbed.

"I'm not protecting Dr. Arthur, Mr. Hubner. He's my competition." Thinking that over, Mr. Hubner quieted down and agreed to stick to his diet, lose some weight, try to get in shape at the gym, and return in three months to schedule the repair.

It had been a stressful day in the office. There were a number of patients who had been surgically challenging, others requiring extra time, some who never followed instructions, and some who had been emotionally taxing. There was no way to train for the stress of days like these, and John was exhausted. He would never admit it, not even to Annie B, but he was.

John went from the exam room out to Annie B's front office, flopped down in the chair, and let out a long sigh of exhaustion. Annie B replaced a chart in the filing cabinet, and looked back over at John, "He's the last one. It's been a long day. You look beat."

"Well, I'm not going to kid myself, I'm whupped. How about you? You as ready for a little down time at home? Or how about we go out to eat. No cooking, no dishes. A glass of Sauvignon Blanc or two for you and a couple of brown ales for me. Not sure who's on call tonight, but it's not me."

"I checked the schedule. It's Amy Salis on tonight, so rest easy. I'm giving you the night off," she said.

There were two phone calls to be returned, so John went back to his desk. He had just hung up after the second call, and was leaning back in his desk chair, hands behind his head, and eyes closed, when he heard the phone ring on Annie B's desk.

"Honey, it's the ER on line two." Annie B called to John.

"What do they want?" He knew what they wanted. They wanted him. He was tired and hoping that if he asked, they might just, magically, go away. No such luck

"They want you, sweetie. I'm afraid I can't help them."

John leaned back into his desk chair, and let if spring him forward to pick up the phone. He punched the flashing button, line two, "John Pullman."

"University Hospital Emergency calling Dr. Pullman", the cheery voice said. "Please hold for Dr. Ted Powers", double click, canned music.

Just what I need at this time of the day. Probably a typical Friday afternoon special. Oh well, Ted Powers is a good, sensible resident. He wouldn't call unless it was necessary.

Click, his thoughts were interrupted as Ted Powers came on line, "Dr. Pullman?"

"Hi Ted. Whatcha got?"

"This is Ted Powers, sir. A trauma case just came in. He's a big guy with what appears to be a gunshot wound of the abdomen. All his vitals are stable, sir. He walked in, and........"

"Ted, I'm not on the board tonight, but you're calling me

because...?"

"Yessir. Dr. Amy Salis is on tonight, but the patient has requested you specifically. Won't let anyone else touch him. Pretty demanding, sir."

A huge sigh. John hunched forward in his chair. "Okay. I'll be in. What's the patient's name."

"Mr. Ucciderita. Mr. Salvatore Ucciderita, sir."

You Call Me Roc

A John Pullman Medical Mystery Adventure

I am pleased to give you a brief look at the first volume of John Pullman's adventurous trials and tribulations in "You Call Me Roc". Below are chapters 1 (edited) and 2 for your exploration.

"Roc" took place in a different city and several years earlier than when Angelo was shot. Like "Angelo", "Roc" is pure fiction, but the model for Roc was a real drug dealer, and many of the events are based on actual events and people I encountered during my surgical practice in Connecticut.

Like "Angelo", you can get a copy of "Roc" through Amazon, or for an Autographed First Edition of either book from me personally, email me at: bblgbl@gmail.com

Happy reading!

Chapter 1 - Hospital ER, May 16, 1991

He was lean and surprisingly clean for a dealer. The nurses had him stripped naked, as usual. They had cut his clothes off with those big Kutz-all scissors while the residents were busy shoving tubes into every orifice of his body. Around 10 p.m. John Pullman turned into Room 4 with the paced urgency of so many Code Red calls from his hospital pager: Emergency Room -- Trauma.

A quick survey revealed that the situation was relatively under control. Not life threatening. No extreme urgency. He took in the two x-rays on the view box. Two of his residents and two ER nurses were at work with the practiced nimble fingers that come from so many repeats of the routines - quiet mumbles, requests, commands, and questions about the patient's vital signs.

"One hundred over sixty-five, pulse 120, no response to the IV fluids yet," said Liz Johns, the head evening ER nurse in a grey scrub suit covered with about six-and-a-half hours of other peoples' secretions.

"Yeah," said Rick McIver, a second-year resident, equally

tired and resigned. He was bent over the patient, his back to John Pullman. "How much has he had? Better bolus him. The IV wide open? The `crit back yet? Type and cross been sent, right? Dr. Pullman's gonna wanna get him to the OR. He might be losing a little blood, but not too bad."

John saw that the trauma protocol was being carried out. The NG (Naso-gastric) tube was in and on suction, the Foley catheter was draining blood-tinged urine, no clots. There was a large bore catheter in each ante-cubital vein, so he checked the chart: Malcolm Jones, 21, black male, unemployed, single, no home listed. Next of kin: Mother – Viola. Address – Father Anthony Project: Housing Development, Bldg. 6, Apt. 305D. Father – not available. GSWs (gunshot wounds) x3 in the abdomen, left groin and right thigh. Brought in by EMTs. IVs started at the scene. Initially hypotensive, tachycardia, but stabilized now. Patient awake and alert. Oriented to time and place. Moves all extremities.

Looking over at the patient, John saw he was obviously healthy, well-muscled. Probably pumped iron. His chocolate skin was clean and clear -- good nutrition, good hygiene, no needle tracks, not a user by the looks of it. Gold on the fingers, gold on the wrists, gold necklaces, heavy chains, gold in the ear lobe -- all being removed by one of the nurses and put in a large envelope, as the patient scrutinized every article, carefully. Another frigging pusher. Approaching the patient's side, he quietly said, "Malcolm Jones, I am Dr. Pullman, one of the attending surgeons here on staff. We're going to have to........"

"Roc! You call me Ready Roc!" the patient interrupted. "You got that, Honkey motherfuck! It's Roc!" The words seethed out of a row of clenched, perfect, white teeth separated by two gold upper central incisors. "R" etched on each one. Only the lips were drawn tight. The rest of the angry face showed no trace of the pain from the 16-gauge needle Rick McIver was shoving through his skin, scraping under the clavicle and into the subclavian vein. No trace of the pain from David Alan, chief surgical resident, palpating around the bullet wound in the left lower quadrant of his abdomen. No trace of the pain from the wound in his left groin, slowly oozing blood.

"OK, Roc," John responded in his subdued tone. "You and I gotta understand each other. It looks like you need an operation."

"You jist let me up, and outta here."

"It looks like you have two choices. Either you're gonna give us permission to operate on you and try to stop your bleeding and patch up the holes in your intestines, or you can try to leave here, but I don't think you'd make it to the door." The statement was met without a flinch.

John Pullman, a senior attending surgeon on the staff of University Hospital, had been trained by years of observation. He thought to himself as he looked over this newest patient: *alert black eyes, flashing on clear sclerae, round face unlined, clear brown complexion, bulging jaw muscles, and scalp shaved so close he makes Kojak look like Tiny Tim. Another hard guy -- tough, smart, and successful on the street. Too smart to use the stuff that he sells.* Scanning the naked body, he made mental notes: *breathing is OK, belly's slightly full, left groin not too bad, right medial thigh looks like a bullet wound.* All this took less than ten seconds, as David Alan came around the stretcher toward the x-ray view box to present his case to his mentor.

"Glad it's you tonight, sir." David said.

"Thank you, David," he replied. "And likewise, I'm glad it's you. Let's see what you've got here."

There were two x-rays hanging on the view-box. A single bright image was obviously a bullet low in the pelvis, and the lazy curve was the NG tube coming down from the esophagus into the stomach.

"Are the pulses ok all the way down?" the senior man asked David. Nothin' in (the leg) there but hurting muscle. He's lucky here. Wonder who kneed him? Looks like serious bucks, sir, serious bucks."

"Kneed him, David?" asked Pullman tiredly, almost sadly staring at the films. "You say, 'kneed him'?"

"Yeah. Yes, sir," replied David. "It's the new street lingo. Someone welches on a deal so you "knee" him. Shoot him in the knee. It's a grand at the knee and more for higher up the leg. A groin shot is supposedly worth about two grand, and a belly shot is maybe five to ten grand. Puts you out of commission for a while. Hurts a little, but you survive. No homicide and so the cops won't get into it too much. They can't. They haven't got enough time or people unless it's a homicide. That makes news. Otherwise it's a waste of the taxpayer's money."

"You're right on that," agreed Dr. Pullman.

"This whole cocaine thing over the past few years really sucks, if you'll pardon the expression, sir. It's like Dodge City out there. Every half pint squirt has a gun; most of them semi-automatics." They turned toward the patient.

"You're right, Davy. It's been really bad these past five years or so, and it seems to be getting worse." Both men paused pensively for a moment. "Well, Davy, what do you want to do with Jones here?" he inquired. "The OR got an open room toni...?"

"I tol' you, motherfuck, you call me Roc! Ready Roc!" Those piercing black eyes hadn't missed a trick. He knew the white bastards had him right now, but he didn't trust them any more than any other white honkey. He was pissed. Pissed at the Fat Man. Pissed at the fink who called the cops. Pissed at the fuckin' cop who stomped his balls cuz he "chose to remain silent," and pissed at being here in this place. Plus, he was hurtin'. *The only thing goin' for me right now,* he thought to himself, *is how I'm gonna get that fuckin' Fat Man when I get outta this place. Big whitey over there gonna fix me up, like they did before, last year. But I ain't takin' no shit!*

"O.K., Roc." John emphasized the Roc. "My error. Hang in there, buddy. We're going to fix you up," he said kindly, almost tenderly. The senior surgeon led his junior colleague around the head of the gurney, past the EKG monitor, to the corner.

"Anything in the past history?"

"Not that we know of. But this guy's not that cooperative,

Dr. Pullman. The usual, no-answer, clam-up type. He was here last year for a gun shot in the leg. The front desk is calling down for his old record now."

"Have we got any blood available, just in case?" John asked.

"Yeah, we type and crossed him for four units to the OR, and keep ahead four units." David replied. "He came in with a hematocrit of forty four and the electrolytes are in line. We sent off a tox-screen and an HIV."

The resident turned slightly, "Hey, Liz, the repeat labs back yet?" The two surgeons moved back to the patient's side again. Dr. Pullman pulled the stethoscope out of the left pocket of his clean, almost white lab coat, he hesitated a second, bending slightly over the patient. Their eyes met head on -- university wisdom versus ghetto street smarts.

"Breathe through your mouth for me please, Roc," Dr. Pullman asked, as he lowered his stethoscope. Roc's black eyes followed the surgeon's every movement. Through parted lips, his white teeth set off the two central golds, which John looked at again, inscribed with the letter "R." *Of course,* he thought, *Ready Roc.* Otherwise, Roc displayed no facial expression. None whatsoever.

John moved his hands down to the patient's groin, both sides, feeling first the right femoral pulse. Fairly strong and not too fast.

"Liz, what're his latest signs?" He looked over at the tall nurse in her six-and-one-half-hour scrub suit. *Bet she makes some guy one hell of a good wife,* he thought, *if she isn't too tired to cope when she gets home. Nice girl.* Not unlike his own daughter.

"I got 130 over 60, 90 pulse just now, sir. There's 60cc`s of bloody urine in the Foley bag, Dr. Pullman." Liz's tired voice was low, almost like Lauren Bacall answering Bogie. It would have been sultry in another time, another place. "What do you want me to hang for the next IV? We got Ringers lactate running now. More of the same?"

"Liz, you read my mind. You're the greatest thing since sliced bread!" Pullman's hands moved over to the left groin, just lateral to the small punctate bullet wound, finding the pulse. Blood and

Betadine stained his gloved fingers.

"Did you or Rick do a rectal?" John asked David.

"Yes, sir. It was negative, soft, brown stool, heme neg, sphincter tone and prostate normal. Checked it before we put the Foley in. I think we're ready to roll, sir."

"The OR ready for us?"

Rick McIver, hanging up the wall phone, turned to Dr. Pullman, and answered, "Yessir, Dr. Pullman. Marcie at the OR desk says we're going to Room 15. Anesthesia will meet us up in the OR. I gave 'em all the info."

The nurse at the wall desk quit writing, paper clipped the shuffle of papers while Liz Johns unfolded a clean, green sheet over the patient. The two residents rolled the gurney, one pushing, one pulling. Liz started to follow with the two IV poles dangling with several plastic bags and IV lines. John Pullman smiled at her. He had known her for many years. Turning and looking into her tired eyes, he said, "I can take those, Liz. You've got enough to do. I'm really sorry to leave you with such a mess."

"Thank you, Dr. Pullman." She thought, *That was so typical of him. Such a gentleman. So thoughtful. That's why everybody likes him so much. Wish he were MY husband!*

The entourage turned right out into the hall. Liz let out a long sigh and looked at the floor littered with bloodied gauze four-by-fours, tape, EKG strips, an empty IV bag, and a blotch of betadine slopped in those first few hectic moments. She glanced at the clock. Ten twenty seven.

"In and out in forty three minutes," she said to herself. "Not bad tonight, not bad.

Chapter 2 – Mr. Pella's Office

"Mr. Pella's office. This is Allison. How may I help you?" Her voice was youthful and cheery, almost singsong.

"Dis is Dr. Casio. I need to speak wid Mr. Pella. Izzydere?" By contrast, the voice was gruff and heavy.

"Certainly, Dr. Casio. One moment, please." Allison's

shoulder-long, straight, reddish blond hair swung forward ever so slightly over her peaches-and-cream perfect cheeks, as she pushed the hold button and then the intercom.

"Yes, Allison?"

"Mr. Pella, Dr. Casio's on line two, but he doesn't sound like his usual self." Allison knew more about the medical staff than their mothers did, and probably mothered them more than their mothers did too -- an extraordinarily capable young lady for her twenty-six years, and Frank Pella's most valuable asset, though he didn't know it. This sure didn't sound like Dr.Casio. This sounded like trouble. She was tempted to listen in, but knew she shouldn't. Not even to protect her boss.

Pella picked up the hold as he tilted his soft, fleshy body back, adding a slight, nervous swivel to his overstuffed desk chair. "Yeah, Mike, what can I do you out of?" His high voice, well oiled with professional camaraderie, added, "If it's the budget numbers for that new machine of yours, Allison's putting them in the computer right now. I promise you'll get a print-out at the meeting! You got my word on that, pal. So what else is new?"

Allison, in fact, didn't have the numbers. As usual, Pella hadn't done his homework, and as usual, he wasn't close to having them. But Pella was good at covering his tracks. One had to do that every once in a while in the financial department of a hospital with a two-hundred-million- dollar annual budget. "How ya hittin' the ball?"

"Pella, it's gonna be your balls, if you're late again. Ya know da Boss don't like no tardiness!" The voice was a full octave lower than when Allison had heard it, and had lost all hint of civility. The heavy spring in Pella's naugahyde executive desk chair bolted him upright. Wide-eyed, fleshy jowls flapping, he stared at the door to his office, almost expecting it to open.

"Mike? Is this Mike? This isn't Mike. Who's this?" The whining pitch in the staccato voice belied any authority. Pella's pasty-white skin broke into a cold sweat.

"Like I said, da Boss don't like no tardiness, you big tub-a-guts. He's expecting full payment on time, Mr. Pella, on time!"

About the Author

Born and raised in Fairfield, Connecticut, George B. Longstreth, MD earned his medical doctorate from the College of Physicians and Surgeons at Columbia University in 1965. Spending six years in New York, first in Spanish Harlem, then in Hell's Kitchen, he lived with many of the characters and events that he now uses in his novels. After a stint in the US Navy, followed by ten years in rural northwest Connecticut, George and his wife Betsy enjoyed an active surgical practice in Fairfield during the last quarter of the twentieth century, where many more characters and tales added to the fuel of fiction.

Betsy and George now live in active retirement in Kennebunkport, Maine, where they are kept busy by family, friends, hobbies, and a dog named Jane.

Made in the USA
Middletown, DE
11 February 2022

61008546R00205